A Foreseeable Risk

A Foreseeable Risk

a novel

Pierce Kelley

iUniverse, Inc.
New York   Bloomington

iUniverse books may be ordered through booksellers or by contacting:

iUniverse
1663 Liberty Drive
Bloomington, IN 47403
www.iuniverse.com
1-800-Authors (1-800-288-4677)

Because of the dynamic nature of the Internet, any Web addresses or links contained in this book may have changed since publication and may no longer be valid. The views expressed in this work are solely those of the author and do not necessarily reflect the views of the publisher, and the publisher hereby disclaims any responsibility for them.

ISBN: 978-1-4401-3600-9 (sc)
ISBN: 978-1-4401-3601-6 (ebook)
ISBN: 978-1-4502-2541-0 (dj)

Printed in the United States of America

iUniverse rev. date: 10/01/2010

To Matthew

"There are only two ways to live your life. One is as though nothing is a miracle. The other is as though everything is a miracle. He who can no longer pause to wonder and stand rapt in awe is as good as dead, his eyes are closed."

Albert Einstein, (1879-1955)

Acknowledgements

I thank those who have supported and encouraged me on this and other projects. I wish to specifically thank Sue Pundt, Reno and Fran Baldwin, Paul Christian Sullivan, Pat and Marlene Doherty, Doug Easton, David Chatowsky, Dennis and Gayle Geagan, and all others who have read drafts and offered their insights into this and other works.

I also acknowledge and thank Duffy Soto of the Hunter Printing Company in Lake City, Florida, for the graphic design work on the cover.

Last, but not least, I thank Matthew, whose story inspired me to write this book. He gave me the insight into his world to make this book as accurate and as 'real' as could be. Though this is a work of fiction, it is based on his life.

Preface

As Albert Einstein said, every day is a miracle. It is nothing short of a miracle that the planet we call Earth wobbles on its axis in a predictable orbit around a fiery star at exactly the right distance away from what is a relatively small sun in an ever-expanding universe of suns, so as to provide exactly the right temperatures and chemical combinations to sustain life. On any given day, though, life as we know it could cease to exist. A car accident, a medical abnormality, a toxic injection, a freak injury…a bee sting, could lead to an unexpected and untimely death, or a life-changing experience.

In this book, I address one of those "life-changing" experiences that could happen to any one of us at any time. As one of my friends recently told me after reading Asleep at the Wheel, it scared him. Another friend refuses to read any more of my books because they scare him, too. We all pray that nothing bad happens to us or anyone we know, but bad things happen to good people at times.

When people have physical ailments, they go to see doctors or other health care practitioners. When people have legal problems, they go to see lawyers. As a general rule, people don't go to see lawyers until there is a problem, not before. Hence, most of the time, lawyers meet people who are in crisis, some of which may have been caused by their own purposeful doing but many times it is due to a truly unfortunate and unavoidable occurrence or set of circumstances.

Through my many years of practicing law, I have seen many sad and unfortunate things. I still grieve over the plight of clients from decades ago, especially some sent to prisons, which are truly hell-holes on earth. To the extent that some problems can be avoided, it is my hope that by telling stories of what could happen if some unforeseen bad thing occurs, like being robbed at gunpoint as Haruki Tanaka was in *A Plenary Indulgence*, or getting in an unwanted fight at a bar, like Jake Norris did in *Fistfight at the L and M Saloon*, or hitting an unseen pedestrian on a dark road late at night as Dan Brennan did in *A Very Fine Line*, or falling asleep at the wheel of a car as Craig Forrest did in *Asleep at the Wheel*, readers might avoid some of the pitfalls along their road of life. I try to tell stories of what could happen to any of us at any time and then explain the legal ramifications of whatever it was that occurred.

In *A Foreseeable Risk*, I tell the story of Pete Collins, a likeable young man in the prime of his life, who experiences a "life-changing" event. What happens to Pete could have happened to me on any one of a thousand occasions, whether on the back of a horse high up in the mountains, on a raft in a river, while riding a motorcycle at high speeds or doing countless other dangerous things. What you are about to read may well frighten you. I hope it entertains you, too. It is loosely based on the true story of what happened to a friend of mine and it is much more about him and what he went through than it is about the law. I hope you enjoy it.

1

A Day on the River

"**LEFT SIDE, FORWARD! HARD!** Right side, back, back, back!" That's it! That's the way to do it!" Pete Collins, guide to the six fledgling paddlers on his fourteen foot Zodiac raft, hollered. The craft swung around in a circle on his command.

"Now, right side, forward! Go, go, go, go! Left side, back, back, back! Alright! Way to go team!" The raft made a circle in the opposite direction.

"Now, let's go backwards. Everybody backpaddle! Back, back, back, back! Alright, that's it! That's the way to do it! Are we ready? Everybody got the commands? Sometimes I might tell you not to paddle at all, otherwise it'll be forward or back, but when I say go hard I mean it. Got it? You're about to see some big water, so get ready. Are you ready?"

When the six paying customers shouted out that they were, Pete replied,

"Everybody dug in? Got a foot up in the crease? I don't want anybody falling out on this trip, and I know that you don't want to go swimming this time of year, trust me. That water is cold! If you feel yourself about to bounce out, grab on to the straps in the center of the raft. It's called our 'chickee' line. Don't ask me why because I don't know why, but if you do grab the line with one hand, be sure to hold on tight to your paddle with the other. You know what they say about being up a creek without a paddle. We don't want that to happen here."

Pete would guide the group down the Middle Fork of the Flathead River, through the southern part of Glacier National Park. Three crew members sat on each side of the raft, clutching their paddles. Pete stood in the back, high above the others, with his buttocks resting on top of the stern of the boat, so that he could have an unobstructed view of the river, an oversized paddle he occasionally used like a rudder in his hand. All had plastic helmets covering their heads and life preservers over the top of wet suits that went from their neck to their ankles. Most had the rubber booties on covering woolen socks.

All were novices on what promised to be an exciting afternoon in what many consider to be the most beautiful park in the continental United States. They were in the first of three rafts from the Great Northern Whitewater Rafting Company out of West Glacier, Montana. Pete was the lead guide. His girl friend, Abigail, was in the second raft, and the third raft was being guided by Dennis, another veteran guide. The three had just put the rafts in the flat water next to Devil's Creek Campground, one of the access points along the river where they could put in. Abigail and Dennis were getting their crews ready for the trip, just as Pete was doing.

It was a beautiful, sunny day in late September in Glacier, but the temperatures, even in the sun, had begun to drop from what they had been in June, July and August. It wouldn't be long before the first snowfall would change the activities from rafting, hiking and mountain-biking, to snow-skiing, snow-mobiling and other winter activities. The Great Northern would shut down entirely in less than two weeks.

"Now, if you should happen to fall out of the raft? What should you do?" Pete asked.

"Pray," one of the two older women in the group offered.

"Swim back to the raft," her husband guessed.

"Put your knees to your chest, point your feet downriver and lean backwards," the father of two teen-aged boys on the trip responded.

"That's right. Didn't you all watch that video before we left the office?" Pete asked. "This is important. Get your feet up as high as you can, preferably out of the water, and lean back. That way you can't get hung up on a rock, and look for a raft. If I can't get to you, one of the other rafts will pick you up. Depending upon where you are, I might throw a rope to you. If I do, you just hold on and let me pull you in. Got it? But if you get a good foot-hold in the raft and lean in when we go through a big rapid, you'll be fine. I don't want anybody falling out of this raft."

"How many times do people fall out? The mother of the two boys asked.

"It doesn't happen too often, but it does happen. So far this year, fewer rafters have fallen out of my boats than out of any of the other guides, right, Abigail?" He called out as Abigail's raft glided up beside his.

"It's true. Pete is in the lead so far, but the season isn't over yet. I'm right behind him."

"No offense, Abigail, but we hope you don't catch him today." The other woman on the raft said.

"I understand," Abigail said, laughing. "We don't like anybody falling out of rafts and you're in good hands today, Mrs. Crawford."

"That's right. Nobody's falling out of a raft today, especially mine, but just in case, remember to put your feet up, lean back and let the life preserver do its job. Okay? Any questions?" Pete asked.

When no one had a question, Pete asked Abigail and Dennis if they were ready, and when they responded in the affirmative, he said, "Let's go down river."

The Middle Fork of the Flathead River winds its way through the valleys between the mountains which surrounded them. Rescue Peak, Hemshot, Gunsight and Jackson Peak, among many others, stood majestically above them. The biggest of them all, Mount Cleveland, at 10,466 feet above sea level, was barely visible in the distance, at times. Most already had snow on their peaks.

The water level was low at this time of year, nothing like what it would be in the Spring when the melting snow filled the rivers to their capacity. This day figured to be a beautiful float trip for the seasoned trio of guides who were accustomed to seeing much, much bigger water. There were still some formidable rapids to navigate, but they had done it hundreds of times apiece over the years. They liked to make the customers feel a sense of adventure when going down a river, and they also continued to have a healthy respect for the power of the river, no matter what the level of water might be on a given day.

"Alright, the first rapid we're going to face is one we call the 'Tunnel.' It's a quarter of a mile long. As you can see, it starts right up here on the left side of the river where those two huge boulders sit and goes down river for over four hundred yards. That boulder on the left blocks the water in half of the river, pushing it to the middle of the river, so twice as much water is in half of the space, so there isn't as much room for the water, but the boulder on the other side does the same thing, so it creates a long chute, which is why we call it the 'Tunnel.'

"It looks like a tunnel, doesn't it? Now, I want to keep us in the rapid as long as we can, so I may tell you paddlers on either side of the raft to paddle hard so that we don't drift off to the left or to the right and get out of the rapid. We want to stay out of the eddys, too."

"Excuse me, Mr. Collins," one of the women asked meekly, but what is an eddy?"

"Good question, Mrs. Williams. An eddy is the place behind an obstruction, like this boulder up ahead, where the water actually goes back up river, not down river. If we're ever in trouble, an eddy can be our best friend. It's like a safe place in a river, but we don't want to 'eddy out' in this rapid. We want to stay in it all the way.

"Everybody ready? Let's paddle hard to get across to the other side of this river and as close to that boulder as we can. We might just give it a little kiss for luck. Everybody, paddle hard! Forward! Go! Go! Go! Go!

"Alright, that's good! Now, remember, hold your paddles down, but keep a good, strong grip on them. It's best to hold them outside the raft, or resting on the top of the raft. We don't want you bouncing up and down and swinging that paddle around. Somebody might get hurt. Here we go! Let's get wet!"

The raft brushed up against the boulder on the left, which was slightly closer to them than the other one, kissed it, and did a nose dive into the foaming white water. The spray soaked all of the occupants. The raft then bobbed up and down, side to side, like a rubber ball, through the turbulent waters before exiting the rapid a quarter mile down river and slowing down some as the white water disappeared.

Pete had given only a few commands during the minute or two it took to traverse the first of many such rapids.

"Alright! We made it through the first challenge. You can relax for a few minutes, catch your breath and get ready for the next one. Let's spin around and see how our companions on this trip did with 'Tunnel.' Left side, forward; right side, back."

The crew did as commanded and the raft spun around on a dime. They watched as Abigail and Dennis guided their rafts through the rapid. The rafts were spaced about 50 to 100 yards apart, and the other rafts were through the rapid and joined them in a matter of moments. The three rafts converged in the center of the river, in a calm stretch of the river, and Pete asked,

"No casualties? Everybody get wet?"

When everyone responded that they had, indeed, gotten soaked, Pete continued,

"Nobody stays dry in that rapid, no matter how good they are. Ready for some more?"

When everyone gave an enthusiastic response, he continued,

"Next up is 'Bonecrusher!'

The mere mention of the name brought exclamations of 'oooh!' and 'uh-oh, that sounds bad!' from several of the customers who were paying good money to put themselves in Harms' way.

"And it is!" Pete continued. This bad boy is going to rock your socks, so hold on tight. We won't have to paddle too much through this one, though. The rapid will carry us. What we don't want to do is get sideways in there, so if I holler out a command, hit it hard. I'll probably only need a good, strong stroke or two, but if I call out, I need it, okay?"

Everyone promised Pete they would do as he asked.

"Now, the main reason they call it 'Bonecrusher,' other than it'll crush your bones if you let it, is because there is no way to avoid crashing into that one big rock that sits in the middle of the river. Believe me when I tell you that we have tried this thing a hundred different ways, but the best way is to just hit that thing head on, bounce off, and go off to either side, whichever way it pushes us, and we will hit it hard and it will jar your bones! Are you ready?"

"Do we have a choice?" Mrs. Williams asked timidly.

"Nope. This is a place of no return. There's no getting off this ride just yet. Let's go! Paddle hard! Both sides! Follow us you two!"

At that, Pete's raft sprung forward and headed right for the huge rock in the middle of 'Bonecrusher.'

Just as he predicted, they plowed straight into the rock, bounced back and then shot down the left side of the rock, keeping a straight path as they did. The other two rafts followed far enough behind so that two rafts weren't in the rapid at the same time, or anywhere near close. A few minutes later, the three rafts came out of the whitewater into an area where the water was flat, though still moving quickly. Majestic mountains surrounded them on all sides, high above.

"If we try to take that rapid on either side, without hitting the boulder first, it throws us into the boulder anyway but puts us off on an angle and that's when boats flip or get sideways and swamp. I know it sounds silly, but it's the best way."

"What's next?"

"We've got a nice, easy one for you now…'Washboard.' It's a Class II and it's gonna give us a shaking, and we will probably get wet, but we'll do just fine."

"What was Bonecrusher?" Patrick, the 18 year old on the trip asked.

"That was a Class III rapid," Pete replied.

"How about the Tunnel?" his brother, Allan, who had just turned 16 and was barely old enough to make the trip, asked.

"That was a Class III also."

"Are there any bigger ones than them?" Patrick asked.

"The next one up after this is a Class IV, but let's get through this one and then I'll tell you all about it, okay? We're gonna take 'Washboard,' or it's gonna take us, depending upon how you look at it, frontways, sideways and backwards. It's gonna turn us around all kind of ways, and that's okay. Of all the rapids we do today, this one is the least likely to turn us over, so just enjoy the ride. I'll probably have to do more talking on this one than on any of the others, too, right, Abigail?"

Abigail and her crew had just sidled up against Pete's raft and heard what he had been saying.

"He talks all the time, doesn't he? She cracked, and everyone laughed. "He can't help himself. He even talks in his sleep."

"Whoa! More personal information than they need to know!" Pete chided. "Abigail's my girl friend," he told the group. "Okay, Abigail, for that, you go first. Show us the way."

Abigail laughed and positioned herself at the head of the three rafts, inching downstream towards the next rapid which lay a hundred yards ahead of them.

"Washboard is gonna clean us off. Anybody got any soap?" She asked. "It's a series of about six boulders, none as big as the two at 'Tunnel,' but they're spaced somewhat evenly across the river, kind of like a pinball machine, and they will knock us back and forth, spin us around a few times, and shake us up pretty good. So listen for your commands and stay in the boat."

"It's a nice rapid to swim if you do happen to fall out," Pete offered. "Just remember to keep your feet up out of the water and point them downstream."

"Nobody's goin' swimmin' out of this raft, Peter, but you and your crew can if you want," she responded, and then said, "Alright, rafters, let's show 'em the way."

At that, her crew began paddling and their raft leapt forward.

"We want to take this rapid from the right," she said. "But just as soon as we get past that first rock, we want to paddle hard to get over to the left, or else the river will throw us onto that next rock, and we don't want that. But once we get to the left, and get passed that next rock, we're going to want to paddle hard and get back over to the right. Now I'll steer us, but I need for you all just paddle hard when I tell you to so that this raft will get where I need for it to get. Everybody paddles forward, unless we get into trouble."

"Unless we get into trouble? Can you be a little more specific?" one of her crew asked.

"We might get turned around in there. In fact, I can just about guarantee that we will. The water is going in every direction, and that's why it's called 'Washboard.' That's okay, but we're going to want to get turned back around, and I might tell the left side to paddle back and the right side to go forward, or vice-versa. When I do, hit it hard. I'll probably only need four or five good strokes to get us back on track. You really don't need to paddle too much through a rapid. The water is plenty strong enough. We're just wanting to stay on course, but the water doesn't want to make it too easy for us. For now, nobody paddles. Here we go…"

Abigail positioned her raft so that it slowly drifted towards the huge rock on the right side of the river and once the bow hit the snarling waves that curled back towards it, the raft lurched up, and then dove violently down after breaking through the first barrier.

"Paddle hard! Everybody! Let's get to the other side of this river!"

Half the group was holding on to the strap with one hand and their paddle with the other. The raft only made it half way across. The nose of the raft pointed to the left and a powerful wave sent the stern of the raft down the river, ahead of the bow.

"Okay, left side, back! Right side, forward!"

The paddlers who were able to did as commanded and Abigail rose up and used her oar as a rudder, which, when combined with the movements of her crew, caused the bow to swing around so that it pointed back up river at Pete's raft."

"We're going to take this one backwards," she yelled.

The raft was pointed up river as it passed the second boulder. Once passed it, she then gave another powerful pull and, shouted out a command,

"Right side, forward! Left side back! With the aid of her crew, the nose swung around and completed the circle so that the bow was headed down river again, the way she wanted it to.

"Good job! Now, paddle hard! Let's get over to the right! We don't want to do that again unless we have to!"

All six crew members contributed this time and the raft made it to where Abigail wanted it to be. The raft was bouncing in all directions. Pete was in the second raft, following the course set by Abigail. His crew members kept a close eye on what was happening to Abigail's raft ahead of them. Pete smiled to himself as he watched Abigail fight to keep her raft under control. She was strong and able and he loved that about her. There was no real danger, but Abigail wasn't too pleased about the miscue.

"See there?" Pete said. "We don't want that happening to us. They didn't paddle hard enough and they missed the spot. Paddle hard when

I tell you to. Like I said before, we don't want any swimmers today. When a raft gets sideways in a rapid, that's one way it can tip and we all get wet. It's always better to go through backwards than it is sideways, but if we do this right, we can stay straight the whole way. Let's go!" he said as his raft entered the rapid.

Moments later, Abigail was shouting another command,

"Right side, forward! Left side, back!"

The raft spun to its left, with the bow pointed back upstream again.

"We're gonna take this one backwards, too! No worries!" Abigail said as she lurched behind her and put her oar as far out behind her as she could and gave a powerful pull, causing it to aid the rafters as their craft responded to the competing forces being placed upon it.

Their raft spun its way through 'Washboard' a few more times before exiting the whitewater and floating peacefully on a stretch of flat water several minutes later. The rafts re-assembled at the bottom of the rapid as shouts of "Booyah!", "Yeah!" and "Alright" echoed through the canyon.

"So tell us about this next one, the Class IV rapid," Allan, the youngest member of the group, asked.

"This one is called 'Jaws,'" Pete responded. "Everyone saw the movie, right? Well, this one is almost as scary."

"No way!" Patrick, the older brother, gasped. "I never go swimming in the Ocean anymore without thinking about that movie. It scares me to death!"

"This one here may not be as bad as a Great White, but it's pretty scary, I promise you that. It's what we call a 'keeper,' which means if you get stuck in its hydraulics, it wants to keep you there, and you don't want that. This is a rapid where you definitely want to stay in the boat."

"Can we sit inside and not paddle at all?" their mother asked.

"No, that's not permitted. Everybody participates on this raft. You'll do fine, but this one is the best on the river. It's like a combination of 'Tunnel' and 'Bonecrusher,' because it has three big boulders in it."

"That doesn't sound good," Mrs. Crawford murmured.

"It sounds great!" Patrick replied.

"We go in between the first two, just like in 'Tunnel,' but once we get through, there's another boulder right in the middle of the river, like in 'Bonecrusher.'"

"So what do we do?" Allan asked. "Do we crash into it, like we did in 'Bonecrusher?'"

"'Jaws has a slide in the center that we call the 'center slot' and we want to get right into it. We don't want to hit the rock behind it, like we did in 'Bonecrusher.' We want to ride the chute created by that 'slot' and let it take us through. It's big water, though, so don't be surprised if you can't see anything for a little while."

"Whoa! This is gonna be awesome!" Patrick exclaimed.

"There's some big water on both sides but we want to stay right in the middle. It's like a great big slide, Probably won't need to paddle too much as long as we hit it right. Hang on tight and enjoy the ride. Dennis, you take the lead on this one, okay?"

"Sure thing, Pete." Dennis said, as his team drifted to the lead position. All three rafts stayed in the middle of the river through 'Jaws' and followed the well-charted channel without any mishaps. 'Jaws' was much bigger water than either 'Tunnel," Washboard,' or 'Bonecrusher' and everybody was completely drenched when the three rafts made it safely to the bottom, where they re-assembled again.

"Alright, we've got a relatively flat stretch of river for the next half mile or so. This is a good time for you all to sit back and enjoy the scenery. You don't even have to paddle for the next ten minutes or so."

The three rafts were the only visible sign of civilization in the vast expanse of greenery around them as far as the eye could see. There were no sounds, other than from the rapid they had just traveled through as they floated serenely down river. Most of the trees were evergreens and few showed any signs of the changing season. The sun shined brightly above, but was off to the west, just out of sight, blocked from view by the towering ridge of mountain peaks to their right. There wasn't a cloud in the bright, blue sky overhead.

"This is incredible!" one of the boys exclaimed.

"This is so beautiful," the other continued.

Most uttered words such as 'wow,' 'unbelievable,' or 'spectacular.'

"So you like my office?" Pete asked. "I never get tired of this job."

For the next three hours, the group traversed the churning waters of rapids or admired the raw beauty of Glacier. Rapids such as the

'Narrows,' 'Repeater,' 'Staircase' and 'Goatlick' challenged the paddlers. It was a tired but happy group that arrived safely at the end. Reno Baldwin, the owner of the Great Northern Rafting Company, was standing by the side of the river, watching as the rafts glided to a stop at the take-out spot. A school bus which would carry the group back to the shop sat fifty feet behind him.

The back door of the bus was open and Reno told everyone to put their paddles and life preservers in the back of the bus.

"You can put your helmets back there, too, if you want, or you can take them off back at headquarters."

Pete and Dennis were busy hoisting the rafts on top of the bus where Abigail stood, securing them with bungee straps and ropes as they did. Within minutes, all were safely aboard the bus. Reno put it in "granny" gear and it noisily made its way up to the main road, Route 2, which would take them back to the starting point of the day's journey.

"Everybody have a good time?" Reno asked.

When all responded that they had, he said,

"There's some hot chocolate, cider and water for you, plus some cookies my wife made, back at the office, for those who are interested.

"And we had a photographer at 'Bonecrusher' taking pictures of you all as you went through. They should be ready for you to look at by the time we get back," he added.

"If you want to take a hot shower, there are towels at the desk. My wife, Fran, is there and she'll hand them out. Just leave the wet suits and booties in the bin outside the restrooms and we'll take care of them from there."

An hour later, after the din and chatter from all of the excited customers had died down, and after all the gear had been put away and stored where it belonged, and the three guides had showered, changed, and were ready to go home for the night, Reno said,

"Good job, you three. Now I've only got two rafts going out tomorrow afternoon and it's Pete's turn for a day off, so I'll see you, Abigail, and you, Dennis, tomorrow, right?"

When they responded affirmatively, he bid them a good night.

"Join us up at the Moosehead, Dennis?" Pete asked.

"Not tonight, Pete. Poker game at my house. Wanna play?"

"Not tonight. Maybe next time. Good luck."

As Dennis drove off, Pete and Abigail embraced and Pete said,

"So I'll see you up there after a while?"

"Yeah, I should be there in an hour or so. Gotta visit with my 'sis' for a while."

"Tell your sister I said hello."

"I will. See ya later."

✳   ✳   ✳   ✳   ✳   ✳   ✳

As soon as he walked into the Northern Lights Saloon, he heard a loud, but familiar, voice calling his name.

"Yo, Pete! Wazzup, bro'?"

"Nothin' much, Dave. How 'bout you?"

The two men shook hands and embraced.

"What's goin' on? I haven't seen you out on the town at all this summer. Where've you been, man?"

"I've been spending a lot of time with Abigail."

"That lady has got you hooked!"

"Yeah. We're goin' pretty strong."

"I haven't known you to be this serious about anyone in all the years I've known you."

"I haven't been."

"Man, don't tell me that it's the end of an era."

At 6'4" tall and a chiseled 190 pounds, with straight brown hair that he wore a little on the long side, and a friendly smile, Pete hadn't had much trouble finding girl friends in the four years he'd been in Glacier. He was young and handsome, but he hadn't been quite ready to settle down to a long-term relationship, until Abigail came along. He'd been with her all summer long and they had become inseparable.

"So what's goin' on tonight?"

"I'm about to sit down for dinner. Want to join me?"

"Sure," Dave said. The two men sat at the bar to order some dinner. "So is this somethin' serious or what?"

"This is as serious as I've ever been about someone, but who knows what will come of it. We're not livin' together yet, but we're talkin' about it, and we might as well be. We're with each other all the time. How about you, man? Who you seein' these days?"

"I've been flyin' solo lately."

"Where'd Anne go? You were with her most of the summer, weren't you?

"Just about."

"That's over?"

"For now. We just need to see other people for a while. Neither one of us wants to get too serious. We've both got another year of school. She's in Arizona and I'm up here and neither of us wants to have a long distance relationship goin' on during our last year in college."

"This place is great, isn't it? The most beautiful place in the country and people just like us doin' the things we love to do. Everybody's just lookin' to have a good time. I can't think of anyplace else I'd like to live, ever."

"I'm gonna hate to see it end."

"You're not gonna be back next year?"

"No tellin' what I'm gonna do after I graduate. That's a long way away from now. Whatchu doin' this year, man?"

"I'm headed back to school, too."

"I thought you were done. How much more do you have to go?"

"I've got two more years to go."

"Two more years?"

"I took some time off."

"When d'you do that?"

"I fished in Alaska one semester, spent a winter in Key West, workin' on one of those big party boats, and then I just took a little time off to work up here with Reno."

"Cool. What was Key West like?"

"Mostly, I baited lines for people who didn't know how to fish and then helped them bring in a fish if they happened to hook one, but it was fun. Plenty of girls in Key West, too, but they're different from the ones up here."

"How about Alaska?"

"That was completely different. No catering to the tourists up there. That was serious fishin'. It was no fun at all, just a matter of catchin' as much as we could as fast as we could. I was out on a boat for about a month at a time, just me and three other guys. That was hard work."

"What did you do?"

"I was the 'skiff man'."

"What's that?"

"I was the guy on a little boat with a big engine, pullin' a long net away from the big boat. The salmon come swimmin' along and get caught in the net. After I got the net out all the way, then I'd swing it around, back towards the big boat, and we load 'em in."

"Sounds easy."

"It's not, believe me, but knowin' where to fish is a big part of it. Getting' them in the net was the first step, then we had to get them in the boat, then unload them into the tender boat, and when we were finished with that, we'd get ready to do it again. I enjoyed it and the money was good. There were no women up there, though, even when we were in port. A few months of that was enough. I like it here a whole lot more."

"So what are you studying?"

I'm about to get an AA degree from Flathead in environmental science."

"Environmental science? What are you gonna do with that?"

"I'm gonna either be a ranger at one of the parks or maybe a firefighter. I'm not sure which just yet. I'd like to stay in this part of the country if I can."

"So you're at Flathead? I thought you were at Montana State."

"I was, for a while, but I left."

"Why d'you do that?"

"It wasn't my idea. I partied a little too much up in Bozeman first time around and my grades weren't too good."

"But that's where you're gonna go, right?"

"Yeah, if they'll let me back in after I get my AA degree."

"That's cool. So you'll be here for the Fall?"

"Yeah, what Fall there is. It'll be winter in a few weeks. Everything shuts down until skiing picks up the first part of November, but it's nothin' like summer. This is the best. So how about you? How much longer are you gonna be here?"

"If all goes well, I graduate in May. Your parents still helpin' you out?"

"Oh no, they stopped that after the first time I got kicked out."

"The first time? How many times have there been?"

"I was at Missoula before goin' to Bozeman."

"What happened there?"

"Same thing. I was havin' too much fun and then I got caught in the women's dorms one night. They were pretty strict about that stuff back then. I've heard it's loosened up some, but not in time to do me any good."

"You're too much, man! Say, what are you doing tomorrow?"

"No plans. Why?"

"Want to go for a trail ride?"

"Where?"

"I've got this friend who works at the Double-D Ranch and I'm goin' out for a ride tomorrow out near the Park. Rocky was supposed to go with me but something came up and he can't go. So do you wanna go or no?"

"Sure. Sounds like fun. How much will that cost us?"

"I'll tell you what. You take me down the river next week and I'll take care of the ride. How's that sound?"

"You're on."

"Meet me for breakfast at about 10:00 at the Two Sisters' Café and we'll leave from there."

"Cool. Whatchu drinkin'?"

"Silver Bullets."

"Yo, Richie! Two Coors Lights, please!"

While they turned to watch as Richie pulled two bottles from the cooler for them, a tall, blue-eyed, blonde walked up behind Pete and put her head on his shoulder, while wrapping her arms around his waist. Pete turned his head and she gave him a kiss on his cheek.

"Hey, Ab! How're you?"

"I'm better now."

"What are you drinkin'?"

"Corona."

"With a lime?"

"Of course! Is there another way?"

"Not as far as I'm concerned."

"How're you doin', Dave?" Abigail asked.

"Good, and you?"

"No complaints," she responded. "None at all," as she gave Pete another kiss.

When Richie brought the two men their beers, Pete ordered a Corona for Abigail. The band started playing an Eagles tune and the three turned to watch. Since the music was too loud to talk over, after he finished his dinner, Dave headed down to the other end of the bar, which stretched out over a hundred feet in a 'U' shape.

On one side of the Northern Lights Saloon were tables and chairs for people to sit and eat. On the other side was a stage where the four members of the band were playing, with a wooden dance floor in front. After they'd finished their beers, and when the band slowed it down, Pete and Abigail danced and stayed on the floor until the band took a break over an hour later. When it did, they went back to the bar for another round.

"So what're you going to do with your day off, Pedro?"

"Dave just asked me if I wanted to go on a trail ride with the Double-D and I said yes."

"Cool! I didn't know you liked to ride horses. Have you done it before?"

"A few times, but never up that way."

"So how'd that happen?"

"He knows a guy who works there and the guy who was supposed to go with him cancelled at the last minute."

"How much will that cost?"

"We're gonna do a little trade. I'll take him down the river and he'll take care of the ride."

"Reno's alright with that?"

"Yeah, but half of what he's supposed to pay comes out of my paycheck, though."

"Cool! If I can find someone to work for me, or if we're really slow, maybe Reno will let me go with you."

Since most of their co-workers were, like them, college kids, the slow-down of the business coincided with the time they had to be back in school. A skeleton crew could take care of business during the week but everyone who was available was still needed on weekends, until the first of October, when Reno Baldwin, the owner, shut it down for the winter. Abigail was a Grizzly and in her junior year at the University of

Montana. School had started the first week after Labor Day and they'd been attending classes for several weeks. Abigail had a schedule which allowed her to come to Glacier during the week and stay through the weekend.

"We're meetin' for breakfast in the morning. It gets dark so early these days that we've gotta be on the trail by 1:00 or we won't get a full ride in. Call me once you find out if you can go."

"I will."

"So what do you want to do tonight? Want to stay and listen to these guys do a second set or go someplace else? I heard that Kevin Costner's band, Mountain West, is playin' at Moose's tonight."

"On a Thursday?"

"He's formed this band and I guess they're practicing around here. I don't know. That's what I heard, though."

"I'd like to, but my sister's comin' over to spend the night. She needs a night out of the house so we're gonna order pizza and watch a movie, nothin' much, but I promised her I would."

"I'm disappointed."

"Yeah, me, too, but we just decided to get together this afternoon, after work. In fact, what time is it? She's supposed to come over around 10:00."

"It's 9:30. What are you up to tomorrow night?"

"That depends."

"On what?"

"On what you're up to."

"My plans are to meet up with you. So if we don't go ridin' together, wanna meet here again?"

"Sure, this place and Moose's are the only places left with music during the week, aren't they?"

"Yeah, I think so. Season's windin' down."

"Well, I gotta go. I've got to change up before I go over there. See you tomorrow."

"I'll walk you out to your car."

When they got to her car, they embraced and kissed. Ten minutes later, Abigail was spinning wheels and kickin' up rocks on the gravel road, headed towards her tee-pee in the woods, behind the rafting store, where Reno housed his summer employees. Some lived in a few of the old school buses that didn't run anymore. She was one of the lucky ones. She had one all to herself. Pete stayed and listened to another set of music, hangin' out with Dave and a few of his other buddies, and went home when the band shut down. Life was good.

2

A Trail Ride in Glacier

THE NEXT DAY, PETE awoke at 10:00 and hurried into town to meet Dave for breakfast at Two Sisters, thinking he was late. David, who had been a guide at the Great Northern a few years earlier, arrived half an hour after Pete he got there. He now worked as a bartender at one of the restaurants in town. A few minutes before noon, they left and rode together in Pete's black, 1987 Ford F 150 Pick-up truck to West Glacier. It was a beautiful day in Big Sky country, with temperatures in the low 60s and not a cloud in the sky. They arrived at the 'Double-D' right on time and their guide, Michael, was standing outside of the office, holding a cup of coffee.

As they stood there, another car pulled up and they introduced themselves to a father and his 18 year old daughter, who were from Miami and on vacation. The five were ambling towards the door to the office but turned and stopped as yet another vehicle pulled off the road and into the driveway. A young couple got out. Both David and Pete recognized them as they had been married a few days earlier on top of the mountain behind the rafting store. He was in the Navy, stationed at Norfolk, Virginia, and this was their honeymoon. They were obviously in love and stood very close together, holding hands.

Reno had a side business of hosting marriages. All he did was provide the site. Someone else handled all of the paperwork to make it legal. He also rented out rooms and had a 'Honeymoon Suite' in a lodge not far from the store, too.

Michael told them that everyone who was signed up for the ride had arrived so they could start getting ready to go. He said there would be a second guide on the trip, Christie, and as he spoke he pointed to a young woman who was leading a horse towards them. Pete kept looking for Abigail to pull up and said something to Michael about her wanting to come along. Michael told him he didn't have another horse ready to ride, so even if she did show up, she couldn't come with them.

The Double-D ranch was down valley several miles, south of Kalispell, but it had a small store in West Glacier, about a mile past the Great Northern, just across the road from the entrance to Glacier National Park, out of which it ran the trail rides. A large Chevrolet pick-up truck, with dual wheels in the back, was hooked to a big trailer off to the side of the store. There were hitchin' posts on the other side of the store and some make-shift stalls behind them, where the horses could get in out of the rain, if necessary.

There were seven horses tied up in front of the stalls. The horse Christie was leading made eight. All were saddled and ready to ride. Michael sized up the group and found out who had any riding experience so that he could put them on the horses that suited them the best. After telling everyone what horse they'd be on, he said,

"Before we get started, you need to go inside the office and see Miss Patty. She'll take your money and have you sign a form. Once you've taken care of that, come on back out here and we'll get goin'. There's stuff to eat in there if you're hungry, but we'll stop for some sandwiches and somethin' to drink in an hour or so if you can wait that long. And one more thing, do us a favor and leave your cell phones with Patty or in your cars. I'll have one for an emergency. Thank you."

They all walked into the office where an older woman, Patty, who they learned owned the place together with her husband, sat behind a counter. Everyone paid their money, signed the form, and came back out, standing next to their assigned horses. While Christie was taking care of the married couple, whose names were James and Caitlin. Michael took care of Pete and David, helping them mount up.

Pete was the biggest, so Michael put him on the biggest and

strongest horse. "He's a three year-old gelding who we cut early this spring. I've used him on trail rides all summer and he's comin' along real good. He's gonna be a real good trail horse. He should do just fine for you, Pete."

Pete said "Great. I'll let him know who's boss right from the get-go…he is."

"His name is Bucky. You shouldn't have any trouble at all with him."

"That's a bad name for a horse, isn't it?"

"Depends. I know lots of guys who want a horse with a little fire in the belly. They wouldn't ride a mare if you paid 'em, but he's named 'Bucky' because of the color of his hide."

"Buckskin. That is an unusual color, isn't it?"

"Not too unusual, but it isn't common, either."

"I'm not one of those guys whose looking for a horse with some 'get-up-and-go', Michael. Put me on a river and I'll take whatever it can give me, but I'm a fish out of water on one of these."

"You'll do fine. Trust me."

"If I don't, you better be ready to go swimmin' when you come down the river with me."

"I'm lookin' forward to that. It's gotta be next week, though, okay? Next weekend is my last weekend here and I'm sure I'll be workin' both Saturday and Sunday."

"That'll work. Whatever day suits you."

Michael, who Pete had met at Moose's a few weeks before, was riding Forrester, another young colt who was being trained for trail rides and was too 'green-broke' to be used with customers. Like Pete, Abigail and most of the others employed at the rafting companies, bars, outfitters and other businesses, this was a summer job for Michael, too. Christie, who was in her second year at Flathead Valley Community College and still lived with her family down valley, had her own horse, a ten year old gelding who she had ridden since she was a young girl.

David, who hadn't been riding too many times more than Pete, was on a big, sixteen-hand high fourteen year-old gelding called 'Gentle Ben', who had been used on trail rides for years. After they put the father-daughter twosome, whose names were Brian and Marjorie, on their horses, Michael and Christie began adjusting the stirrups for everyone as they sat in the saddle to get the lengths right. When they were done, he said,

"Everybody ready to go?" When everyone indicated that they were, he continued,

"Christie's gonna be our lead guide on this trip so we'll follow her, single file. The order we put you in is important. These horses have a pecking order and they don't like it when it gets messed up. If you don't believe me, just pass the horse in front of you and watch what happens, especially with Caitlin's horse, Princess. She hates it if any horse tries to get in front of her. Trust me on that. So Caitlin, you go right behind Christie and stay there. James will follow Caitlin, then Marjorie and Brian, and then David, Pete and I'll take up the rear, ridin' 'drag' as they say. Any questions?"

When no one had any questions, Christie moved the reins of her horse, Moonbeam, to the right, made a clicking sound and away she went. One by one, they formed a single file and followed behind. Michael was the last to leave the makeshift corral. They headed out through an open field and soon were in the woods.

"Be sure to keep within a few yards of each other. Don't let your horses stop and eat. We don't want to space out too much 'cause we want to be able to keep an eye on all of you."

The trail was narrow in most places and before long they weren't able to talk too much, because David didn't like turning around in his saddle while his horse was moving forward and Pete couldn't hear him unless he did.

"Keep your toes up. Don't bury those shoes in your stirrups. You might have to get off in a hurry," Michael hollered out.

Pete was wearing his New Balance running shoes, which he wore whenever he wasn't in the rubber booties he wore on the river. The two guides, Michael and Christie had riding boots on. David had on a pair of basketball shoes and the others were in hiking boots or walking shoes.

Within half an hour, the group was well into the woods, heading up at a 45 degree angle.

"Lean forward in your saddles. It makes it easier on the horse to carry you, especially you bigger folks," Michael called out.

A couple of the horses kept stopping to drop their heads and take a bite of the grass along the side of the trail, especially the horses the two girls, Marjorie and Caitlin, were riding.

"Keep those reins gathered up or those horses will do that every chance they get," Michael told them.

Christie turned her head every so often to make sure everyone was following along well, but as the lead guide, she couldn't see what was going on behind her most of the time. Michael could see everyone and everything and he was busy keeping an eye on things. He couldn't talk to Pete and David too much, except to get in some small talk about the weather or girls every now and then.

After an hour, they were high up the mountain and were able to look down on to and around at what was Glacier National Park. Everyone was 'ooohing' and 'aaahing' when the group came upon a particularly beautiful vista, which was every minute or so.

"We'll be stopping in a little while at a place where we can take some pictures and get something to eat. "

Every so often, the riders had to duck to get under limbs of the trees or hold a branch to make sure it didn't zap the rider behind. The main road through Glacier, Route 2, could be seen now and then through the trees, and it grew smaller and smaller as they continued their ascent.

"Damn! I'm glad this horse knows where it's goin'. I wouldn't want to fall off now!" David yelled out, as he looked down at the cars which seemed to be about as big as a pea, a thousand feet below.

"Just hold onto your reins. These horses have been here before, hundreds of times. They know where they're goin'."

Gentle Ben didn't like to be rushed and was continually falling behind Torque, Brian's horse. Bucky, on the other hand, was rarin' to go and kept ridin' up onto the backside of Gentle Ben.

"Give 'im a kick, David," Michael said. "Make him keep up. Let's go, Ben! Click, click, click, click! If you want a switch, I'll get one for you. Sometimes he needs to be coaxed a bit."

"Naah, that's alright," David said, as he gave him a nudge with the heels of his shoes. "I'll get him goin'."

A few times, when Bucky walked up on the backside of Gentle Ben, Bucky pinned his ears back and tried to go around, even when there was no room.

"Don't let him do that, Pete. Keep him behind Ben. Hold tight on those reins. Bucky would rather run up this mountain than walk it, I think. When he pins his ears back like that, rub one of his ears."

"When he pins his ears back like that it means he's pissed off about somethin'?"

"Yep. That's what it means," Michael responded.

"I think one of my old girl friends used to do that. When she was pissed, everyone knew it. Her ears would move," David chimed in.

"Horses have the brains of a three year old, and they have an attention span of a few seconds. If you rub his ears like that, he'll forget what he's mad about," Michael continued.

"I'll do it," Pete said, as he rubbed Bucky's ears a few times. "Man, it's beautiful up here. Are we close to the Road to the Sun?"

"It's over that way, about five miles to the north of where we are."

"Are we going to make it that far?"

"No, not on this ride, but we'll get close enough for you to see some of the same sights you'd see on it."

"There are so many beautiful views, it's hard to say that one is better than the rest, but no place is much prettier than right where we are."

"Yeah, that's true, but I'm lookin' forward to seein' the valley from the river. It's not that I ever get tired of this, but I'm sure it's beautiful lookin' up at the mountains, too."

"It's beautiful alright. You'll see."

"You enjoyin' this?"

"Oh, yeah. This is great. We couldn't have picked a better day, either."

"When it's cold or raining, it can be a real pain, but on a day like this, there's no place else I'd rather be."

"I can see why. I feel that way when I'm on the river, too, except I even like the rainy days, as long as I'm warm. The river's a little different when there's rain."

"You doin' alright on Bucky? He causin' you any problems?"

"Nothin' other than him gettin' right on Ben's ass. He's pretty frisky."

"Yeah, he's still a young colt, feelin' his oats. He doesn't know he's been cut. Nobody told him when they did it."

"Well, so far so good. Thanks for doin' this, Michael. Me and Pete appreciate it."

"No problem. This was a good day to do it. We only had four people on this ride, so the two of you were welcome. Normally we like to have at least six on a ride, and the most we'll take is eight with two guides. Any more than that and we'll break them up into two groups."

"I'll have to come back another time with Abigail. I'm sure she'd like this."

"Is the Abigail you're talkin' about Abigail Dressler?"

"Yeah, you know her?"

"Yeah. We go to school together. I have her in some of my classes. She's your girl friend?"

"Yeah. I've been with her for a couple of months now."

"I'll tell you what, have her bring one of her friends and we'll go for a ride, just the four of us, for free, but we gotta do it in the next week or so before the Double-D shuts down for the winter. Can you do that," Michael asked.

"I'll talk to her and let you know what she says. You got anyone in mind?"

"I've seen a few of her girl friends and any one of them will do."

"I'll get some names and let you know who's available."

"That'll be great. Thanks." Then he raised his voice and said,

"Okay, folks, we're gonna stop for some lunch up ahead. There are a few tables and some benches for you to sit on, plus a nice overlook where we can take some pictures of you, if you want, either on your horse or not, whichever you prefer. Just follow Christie and wait for one of us to hold your horse and help you dismount. Don't get off without one of us being there, though, okay?"

Ham and cheese sandwiches, potato chips and cookies, plus soft drinks and bottled water, which Michael had put in his saddle bags, were lunch. Brian and Marjorie, the father and daughter had a photo taken together of them on their horses, as did the newly-weds, James and Caitlin. Christie took the pictures while Michael, David and Pete talked about the Seahawks, the Broncos and girls. Michael, who wasn't a bad looking guy, although he looked more like the character Daniel Stern played in the movie City Slickers than he did Billy Crystal, was anxious to meet some of Abigail's friends. David, who was the shortest of the three, but the most muscular, became more interested in the idea the more Michael talked about it. Pete promised to set something up for them, if he could. While they were sitting there, finishing their lunch, an eagle soared overhead. Michael took a pair of binoculars from a pouch and passed it around so all could see. He thought he spied a grizzly on a distant mountain, but it had disappeared back into the woods by the time the others tried to find it. When lunch ended, the group saddled up and headed further up the mountain.

An hour later, as the afternoon sun slowly continued its descent to the west, the group approached what seemed to be the top of the mountain. Every time Pete thought they were at the top, they'd come around a corner and see more mountain ahead. Gentle Ben slowed his pace as the ascent became more vertical and Bucky, who was still full of energy, kept running up on the backside of Ben. The path was a well-worn one, but it wasn't more than a foot wide and a foot deep in spots. All Pete had to do was keep hold of the reins and lean forward. Bucky was doing all the work and didn't need to be told where to go. They were above the tree line and the side of the mountain dropped off precipitously to his right. From this vantage point, he had the whole valley in view.

When they reached a clearing at the top of the mountain, Michael said,

"We're gonna stop here to let the horses rest for a few minutes before we head back down. This is another photo-op, and we'd like to get a picture of the whole group. We're at the top of the Apgar Mountain and you'll have a great view of Lake McDonald down below, plus a vista of all the peaks, like Rainbow off to the left, and Red Eagle Mountain just to the right of it."

Christie chimed in, "If you want me to take a picture of you with your camera, just say so and I'll be glad to do it for you."

"Any photos we take, using our camera, will be developed and ready for you by tomorrow afternoon, or we could mail them to you, whichever works best for you," Michael said.

When they stopped, Brian and Marjorie had several more photos taken of them on their horses, as did James and Caitlin. They all dismounted and assembled for one group shot, with Lake McDonald in the background. Michael took the photograph while Christie held the reins of the horses, which were in the photo, too. When they were finished, Michael said,

"Alright, we're ready to head back down. On the way back, you'll need to lean back in your saddles and stay on your horse's rump as much as you can. They will appreciate that."

Pete turned to David and said, "Man, it don't get much better than this, does it?"

David agreed.

Moments later, as they re-entered the woods and temporarily lost sight of the sun, the wind picked up a bit and a hint of the cooler weather to come sent a shiver down their spines. Neither man was dressed too warmly as both had short-sleeved t-shirts on. They had plenty of time to get back down the mountain before the sun went down, though. They were enjoying the moment, thinking of what they would be doing later that night.

The Fall

PETE WAS LEANING BACK in the saddle, admiring the view, and enjoying the day. The sun shone through the trees like shafts of light around him. He thought of Abigail and wished that she was there with him. They reached the open spot where they had eaten lunch and stopped briefly, without getting off their horses. No more pictures, just a breather to admire the view and then, after a few minutes, they were back on their way, into the forest, with mammoth Firs and Tamarack trees surrounding them on all sides.

As they came to a slight curve in the path, Gentle Ben slowed to maneuver the turn and Bucky ran up on the back of Gentle Ben for what must have been the hundredth time, but this time Gentle Ben pinned his ears back, ducked his head down and kicked back with both of his hind feet. Since the two horses were so close together, and David was heavy on his back, Ben couldn't get his feet too far off the ground and his hooves hit Bucky just below his front knees, in the pastern area of his front legs.

Pete didn't see exactly what happened, but it must have hit Bucky in the wrong spot because it caused his left front leg to buckle. In an instant, Pete was being thrown to his left, onto the ground. The steep angle of the mountainside caused him to roll down the side of the mountain. Bucky was right behind him. In an instant, Michael was off his horse and grabbing for Bucky's reins but both horse and rider were in a full-scale descent and only the trees thirty feet below would stop them from falling further.

Within seconds, Pete hit smack in the middle of a six foot wide Fir tree. When he did, he bounced off of it and landed on his back on top of one of its roots. Bucky bounced off the same tree, scrambling to his feet as he did, but not after rolling over Pete, causing him to cry out in pain.

Michael watched in horror as he quickly unleashed the long rope he carried on the back of his saddle, and began unwinding it, preparing to go down to where Pete lay writhing in pain. David was already off his horse and side-stepping his way down as fast as he could to where Pete was, yelling his name as he went,

"Pete! Pete! Are you okay, man? Talk to me!"

Michael yelled down to him, "Don't move him, David! You could make things worse!"

"I know! I used to be a guide, too!"

Pete continued to cry out in pain.

David slid to a stop next to Pete and panted,

"How are you, man?"

"God, it hurts! I can't feel my legs! It was like a bolt of lightning went through me, right down to my toes, and now my ribs, my back, my stomach…everything hurts, man! But I can't feel my legs, Dave!"

Pete was praying that his worst fears weren't going to be realized.

"Stay still. We're gonna get help."

David hollered to Michael and told him to call for help. Michael told Christie to call the office and tell Patty that they had a rider down who was hurt bad. He tied one end of his rope to a tree, tied the other end to the rope Christie was carrying, and started to descend. He told everyone to dismount and hold their horses until he could figure out what needed to be done. Christie had tied her horse to a tree and had Gentle Ben's lead shank in one hand and her cell phone in the other, pushing numbers as best she could while finding a spot to tie up Ben.

Michael eased his way down the rope to where Pete was laying, moaning and groaning. David was by Pete's side, taking leaves and debris off of Pete's face and clothes, trying to make an initial assessment of the injury.

Bucky was standing a few feet away, picking up his left front foot every so often. It looked like he had been hurt in the fall, too. Michael gently grabbed hold of the reins which hung to the ground from the bridle and bit, trying not to spook him any more than he'd been spooked, led him to a sapling strong enough to hold him and tied him up. He then turned his attention to Pete. He got on the other side of Pete from where David sat hovering and joined David in conducting the basic first aid maneuvers of taking a pulse, feeling his forehead and looking for bleeding and broken bones.

"He's breathing okay, his airways are clear, he's conscious, no signs of broken bones or bleeding, but he may have some internal bleeding…"

"I'm sure some ribs are broken, but I can't feel my legs, guys. I can't get up."

"Lay still, Pete. We're calling for help," David said.

"I don't know what we can do other than to keep you as comfortable as we can until help gets here," Michael said as he took off his shirt and put it under Pete's head, to make him more comfortable and so that blood wouldn't rush to his head. Pete's legs were motionless and slightly twisted and contorted.

Pete didn't respond. His eyes were closed and he had one arm bent, covering his eyes, fearing the worst.

"Let's straighten out his legs and make him as comfortable as we can."

Together, he and David straightened them out.

"Let's get something to keep him warm. We may be here a while," Michael suggested.

"If he can't walk, we're gonna have to carry him down."

"There's no way we can carry him that far, man. We're gonna need help."

Pete continued to moan, occasionally crying out in pain. At one point he said, "I'm thirsty, man! Get me some water…please."

"If you've got internal bleeding, Pete, the worst thing we could do might be to give you water. I've got to have a doctor tell me what to do."

"Just a little, man, please. I won't swallow it. My mouth is dry."

"Let's give him a little water," Dave said. "I'll go get a jacket or whatever we've got to keep him warm."

"You stay here. I'll go get a saddle blanket and see what else I can find," Michael responded.

Michael pulled himself up the rope to toward where the others were huddled around, whispering to each other, staring intently to where Pete lay below.

"How is he? Christie asked in a hushed tone, hoping none of the others could hear her, when Michael made it back to the top.

"It's bad. He has no feeling in his legs and I'm sure he's got some broken bones and internal bleeding. Did you see that horse roll over the top of him? That horse weighs almost a thousand pounds!"

"What do you think we should do?" Christie asked.

"Did you get in touch with Patty?"

"Yes. She's waiting for us to tell her what to do. She doesn't know if she should send up some of the other guys or call 911."

"Tell her to call 911 and hurry. It's gonna get dark up here before too long and we've got to get Pete down off of this mountain as fast as we can."

Christie turned her back and walked a few feet away, speaking into the phone as she did.

"And tell her he can't walk," Michael said in a low, voice, trying not to let the others hear, but they did.

Michael then turned to the others and said, "Can any of you spare some clothes until you get back down to the store? We've got to make him as comfortable as we can and I don't have much with me."

Both Brian and James, who were wearing flannel shirts, with t-shirts underneath, gave Michael their shirts. Michael took the saddles off his horse and Ben, and threw the saddle blankets down in the direction of where David remained kneeling next to Pete. He stuffed his cell phone in his pocket, took all the food and water that was left in his bags and Christie's bags, plus the first aid kit, and started back down the rope. Before he did, though, he said to the others, who were grim with concern,

"I'm sorry about this, folks. This doesn't happen very often, but things like this do happen. There's nothing any of you can do now. Christie will lead you back down the mountain. Go slow and be careful."

A few seconds later, Christie said,

"She told me to bring all of our other customers back down and that she was sending Sandra and Wendy up to meet me as fast as they can get here. She says 911 will be calling you on your phone and to stay off it until they do."

He thought for a moment and then responded,

"Tell her to have them send a chopper. We'll have to put him on a stretcher and there's no way we can carry him down this mountain without makin' the situation worse. Tell them they can land on the bald spot on top of Apgar Mountain and we can carry him that far… and tell her to have Sandy and Wendy bring up some blankets, food and water. We might need them."

"Just a minute, Michael, I've got Patty on the line…yes, Miss Patty. Michael says to send a helicopter and tell them we're less than a mile from the top of Apgar Mountain, not far from where we have lunch and take our pictures. He says to send food, water and blankets, too."

Once Christie was off the phone with Patty, she began to get everyone back on their horses, one by one. Everyone offered to help but there were no doctors on this trip, only a sailor, a lawyer and two college girls. Michael went back down the rope, carrying all he could in one arm and holding onto the rope with the other.

"What about David? Isn't he's supposed to come with me, too," Christie yelled down to where the three men were huddled.

"I ain't goin' anywhere," David responded.

"He can stay with me, Christie." Michael said.

"But she said she wants all the customers back as soon as possible."

"Tell her that I need him up here with me."

"What about the other horses?"

"Leave 'em where they are for now. We can worry about them later. You need to get goin'."

After Michael put one of the saddle blankets under Pete's head and the other one over his chest, he scrambled back to the top to help Christie get everyone get back on their horse, and within a few minutes, Christie and the others were on their way back down the mountain. All were visibly shaken. When the sounds of the horses' hooves could no longer be heard, Michael went back to where Pete and David were and asked,

"Anything else you can think of to do, Dave?" Michael asked.

"I've had people fall out of the boat in dangerous rapids hundreds of times, and we had to get them back in before they drown or get caught in a hydraulic, and some have hit their head and had bruises, but no really serious incidents, thank God, nothing like this. I don't know what else to do," David responded.

"We've had our share of falls and broken arms or sore backs, but nothin' serious. We haven't had anything like this happen before, either."

Michael walked over to Bucky and unhitched the billet strap. He put the saddle down next to a tree and took the bit from Bucky's mouth, gently lifting the bridle and reins over his head, holding onto the lead shank attached to Bucky's halter. He threw the saddle blanket behind him and led Bucky to a different tree, further away, where he tied him up with enough slack so that he could graze quietly. He took the blanket, which was damp with sweat, and put it over Pete's legs.

Pete wasn't making as much noise and his eyes were closed.

"How's he doing?" Michael asked.

"I think he's gone into shock," David said in a barely audible response.

"Shouldn't we keep him awake or something?" Michael offered.

"I don't think so, not now. He's in really bad pain. I think we need to wait and see what the medics tell us to do. I'm not wakin' him up. I've been here with him and he's hurtin'….bad."

"Yeah, you're probably right, but I thought you weren't supposed to let a person in shock go to sleep."

"We should be hearing from 911 any minute. They'll tell us what to do."

The men knelt silently on either side of Pete, not knowing what to say or what else to do, awaiting a call.

4

The Wait

THE TWO MEN SAT next to Pete, waiting for the phone to ring. Michael grabbed the two flannel shirts lying on the ground next to him, put one on, handed the other to David and said,

"Here, you better put this on. It's going to get cold up here before too long."

David stood up and put on Brian's jacket, which was a little too small, but it provided some needed warmth.

"I'm going to start gatherin' fire wood, just in case we're here for a while," David offered.

"You can't start a fire up here, Dave. It's against the law."

"It is, but this is an emergency. If we get stuck up here, we're talking about a life-threatening situation. "

"Don't do that just yet. Let's see what happens."

David stayed next to Pete, while Michael fumbled nervously with his cell phone, waiting for it to ring. Pete remained quiet, except for some occasional moans, as he lapsed in and out of consciousness between them. The two men didn't really know each other all that well. After a minute or two, Michael asked,

"How long did you work as a guide, Dave?"

"Two years."

"How about Pete?"

"Five, I think. He was one of the more experienced guides when I got there. How about you?"

"This is my second summer of doin' this. What's the most serious thing that's happened at the Great Northern? Any serious injuries or deaths?"

"A few years back, before either me or Pete started workin' there, they had a few people get hurt real bad on one trip."

"Really? What happened?"

"It was the strangest thing I ever heard of. We had three boats goin' downriver on a beautiful day, no rain, no storms, no nothin'. It was at the end of the summer, like now. The river was low, so there wasn't any problem with that, and all of a sudden, a huge tree falls on the middle boat."

"You're kiddin'!"

"I'm not. Trees fall every so often, everyone knows that, but the odds of this tree falling and it falling exactly as the rafts are going by and exactly on one of the rafts is probably about a billion to one. I mean…talk about bad luck!"

"So what happened?"

"The tree hit the middle raft and two or three people were hurt badly and had to be hospitalized. The guides did everything they could but there was nothin' anyone could do. I mean the tree was huge. I saw pictures and it went from one side of the river almost all the way across to other. It wasn't one of the small branches that hit the raft, it was the middle of the tree. The guides had to get the other people in that raft out of the river and then do what they could until help arrived. A couple of the other people were hurt real bad, too. The guides did a great job. They had film crews and investigators, the State regulatory people and everyone lookin' into what happened and makin' sure that we did what we were supposed to do."

"Wow! That's pretty scary. That could happen out here any day. That could happen on a trail ride, too. I never even thought about something like that happening."

"Because of that, Reno makes all his guides take a safety course that lasts for over a month. It's like 200 hours or somethin' ridiculous like that. They all carry Wilderness First Responder certificates and are CPR certified, too, which is a separate course and it takes 16 hours to complete over two days of training. The river rescues are practiced, too, but mostly it's about bein' prepared and makin' sure that we were ready for any emergency. He goes through all kinds of things that could happen. It's really a great course. I learned a lot."

"Like what? What did you learn in that Wilderness course?"

"It's a course designed for outdoor trip leaders, like us. It lasts about 80 hours and takes 7 or 8 days. It taught us how to diagnose and treat outdoor emergencies.

"But nothin' that told you what to do in a situation like this, though, right?"

"I think we're doin' all we can. I think we're following the protocol for a serious internal bleeding injury. I'm not sure about what we should do with allowing Pete to drink water or keeping him awake. I think we need to keep him awake."

"We need to talk to a doctor."

"We should be hearing from one any time now."

"Maybe we should call somebody instead of waitin' for somebody to call us."

"They told me to stay off the phone."

"I don't think we should wait any longer," David said, "I'd like to call Reno and see what he says we should do. Let me have your cell phone. I didn't bring mine. If 911 calls, I'll get off."

Michael handed David his phone.

David called the Great Northern and got Reno on the phone.

"What's goin' on, Dave? Haven't seen you in a while. Everything okay?"

"No, Reno, it's not. It's Pete, he fell off his horse and he's hurt bad. I'm calling to ask if you know someone I can talk to about this or if you know what to do."

"Where are you? I'll be there as fast as I can."

"We're way up on top of Apgar. We were out on a trail ride with the Double-D. The only way to get here is by horse or helicopter."

"You're right. I can't get there fast enough. What are his signs?"

David proceeded to tell Reno what he knew and what he saw.

"I don't know what to tell you, but I'll tell you what. You should be hearing from those rescue boys pretty soon and they'll have doctors on call. They'll be sending a helicopter with them with a paramedic on board. I'll see if I can't get in touch with someone I know down at the hospital and see what I can find out. I'll call you back once I find out something."

"Thanks, Reno."

"Are you okay, Dave?"

"I'm fine. I didn't fall off or anything. I'm just all shook up about Pete. He's in a lot of pain and…"

"And what, Dave?"

"He says he can't feel his legs, Reno."

There was a long pause, and then Reno responded,

"Keep him as quiet and as comfortable as you can, Dave. Help will be there soon, I'm sure. We'll be praying for him."

"Reno, what about giving him water?"

"Better let the medics answer that one. I wouldn't until you talk to someone and get the okay."

"And letting him sleep?"

"I think you're supposed to make sure he stays awake. Ask them about that, too."

"Will do, Reno, and thanks."

"I'll be back in touch once I know more. Whose cell phone number is this, Dave?"

"It's Michael's. I don't know his last name. He's the guide."

"I'll call you just as soon as I find out something."

Abigail was in the shop, standing next to Reno and listening to his side of the conversation. She heard him say Dave's name and she knew Pete was with Dave. When Reno ended the call, she asked,

"Who's hurt? Is it Pete?"

"I'm afraid so, Abigail. He fell off his horse and is at the top of Apgar Mountain, waiting for rescue to arrive."

Abigail started to run out the door. "I gotta get there."

Reno grabbed her arm and said,

"Wait! Wait! Wait! There's nothing you can do. Help is on the way. I'd go there with you if there was anything either one of us could do. I gotta get in touch with a doctor who might know what to do in a situation like this."

"Reno, I can't just sit here! I'll be a nervous wreck! I've got to at least try to get there!"

"Wait until we see what's happening. Dave is right by his side and a helicopter will be on it's way to him. Maybe we can meet them at the hospital. You don't want to go flyin' up the mountain only to have to turn around and go back to the hospital. We can't panic. I care as much about Pete as you do. He's been with me for four years and he's like part of my family. Let me make a few phone calls and then we'll decide what to do. We'll go together, how's that?"

Abigail agreed and threw herself on a chair, watching, as Reno pulled out the phone book and looked up the number for the North Valley Hospital. He was able to get through to his friend, Henry Rutland, an internist on staff there. Henry said he'd try to get in touch with someone he knew at the Kalispell Regional Medical Center and ask him to keep a lookout for Pete, if and when he made it there.

While Reno was busy making phone calls, Abigail was becoming more and more impatient. She spotted Dennis down by the buses, cleaning them up. He had a four-wheeler and she went running out of the store to see about borrowing it. When he heard what was going on, he told her that four-wheelers weren't allowed in the Park, but she already knew that.

"They can arrest me if they want, but I'm going up there."

"Well, I guess they'll have to arrest the both of us. I'll go with you," he responded.

Abigail then told Reno,

"I gotta go. I can't sit here and wait like this."

Reno tried his best to talk her out of it, but when he saw that it was useless, he said,

"Well, if you're dead set on goin', you'd better take some supplies. If you're stuck up there all night, you're gonna freeze. Lemme get you some warm gear and some blankets. You should take some food, too. Soup and as much water as you can carry. You sure this thing can make it up that trail, Dennis?"

"Yeah, I'm sure. I've been up that way before. It's narrow in spots, but I made it through all right."

"Be careful, and call me when you get there."

When Reno had put as much as he could quickly gather on the vehicle, the two took off down the road. Although it was still an hour away from sunset, the sun had gone behind the mountains to the west and the temperature was dropping fast.

* * * * * * * * * *

The sun was no longer visible through the trees and both David and Michael knew that soon it would be completely dark. When that happened, a rescue would be even more difficult. Both realized that their circumstances were becoming grimmer by the minute.

When David hung up with Reno, Michael asked, "So what did you find out?"

"Reno is going to call a doctor friend of his and call us back. Where is that rescue chopper? We should have heard from them by now, don't you think?"

"I don't know. Sandra and Wendy are on their way up here, but they won't be much help, other than to maybe take our horses back."

"There won't be room in the chopper for us, Dave. We're going to have to ride back down, although we may end up walking 'em down in the dark. For now, we need to stay calm. People know we're here and people are doin' things to take care of the situation. We just don't know what it is they're doin', that's all."

"Damn! Somebody should be calling us. You sure they have your number right?"

"I know Patty does. I'll give her a call."

When he did, the line was busy. He kept trying and a minute or two later, he got through.

"What's goin' on down there, Patty?" Michael asked.

"We're doing everything we can, Michael, but these things take time. They're trying to figure out who should do what. The hospitals are talking to each other and to the Park Service. They're deciding what to do. It looks like they're going to use the Park Service helicopter to get him out from where he is and have a Medi-Vac helicopter waiting. The trouble is that the Park Service doesn't have a para-medic available right now and I guess they're thinking that the Medi-Vac helicopter is too big to get where it needs to get."

"We haven't heard from anyone yet!" Michael yelled.

"They know about you and they're working on it, I can tell you that much."

"Tell me who to call. We need help now!"

"Just sit tight. They're trying to get a para-medic from the hospital to the Park Service so they can get a para-medic to Pete as fast as they can. They want Pete evaluated as soon as possible just as much as you do, trust me. Anything change up there? Is he any better?"

"He's unconscious right now. I think he's in shock."

"Call me back when you can."

As Michael was ending the call, Pete regained consciousness and said,

"Guys, you gotta give me some water. My mouth is as dry as a bone and I'm hurtin' so bad…do you have anything I can take?"

Michael said, "Pete, we think you probably have internal bleeding and that giving you water might make things worse. I'll give you just a little but don't swallow it, okay?"

"Son of a bitch, Michael! I might be dyin' here! Give me some freakin' water, would ya?"

"Okay, Pete. Here you go, man." Michael handed him a 12 ounce plastic bottle of water. "I hope it doesn't make it any worse."

"You got anything for the pain?"

"I got some Tylenol in this kit."

"Gimme what you got."

Michael took out four pills and handed them to Pete.

"Gimme the whole bottle, man! I hurt so bad." Pete let out another loud and tortuous scream and then swallowed several pills.

Moments later, Michael's phone rang. It was Patty.

"Okay, here's the deal. The helicopter from the Park Service is coming to get Pete. The pilot is going to bring a para-medic with him. The Medi-Vac helicopter will be ready, once an assessment is made, to get him if that's necessary."

"I guess that makes sense. How long do you think it will be before the helicopter gets here?"

"I was told that they would be in the air any minute. The Park Service was waiting on the para-medic, last I heard. Someone should have been in touch with you by now, but they've been making all the arrangements between themselves and the hospitals."

"Patty, do they know where we are or should I get on top and light a fire?"

"They should be calling you soon, so ask them, but they told me that the Park Service pilot knew these woods better than we do. I'd say you should be ready to get up there and build a fire if they need help finding you."

"Should I ride up there?"

"You think you can make it faster if you walk or run?"

"It's a mile or more and it's straight uphill."

"Then I'd ride if I was you. There's no way I could run faster than I could ride. Two people are on their way up to you on a four-wheeler. They've got blankets and some supplies. They should be there before too long, Michael."

"It'll take them at least half an hour to get here and besides, I'm not sure they can even make it this far."

"The driver says he's done it before, Michael."

"I can't wait that long, Patty."

"That's up to you, Michael."

"Damn! I guess I'd better just wait until I hear from the helicopter pilot and then decide. I'll be ready to do whatever he tells me."

"Is he doin' any better?"

"He's awake, but he's in pain bad."

"Help is on the way."

"Thanks, Patty. You sure you gave those people the right number?"

"Yes, I'm sure. They should be callin' any minute."

"I got a call right now. I better go."

It was Reno. Michael handed the phone to Dave.

"Abby and Dennis are on their way up there. They left ten minutes ago. They should be there before too long if that four-wheeler can make it through."

"Thanks for whatever you did, Reno."

"I'm just prayin' that Pete's gonna be okay."

As they were talking, the phone began buzzing. Another call was on the line.

"I gotta go, Reno. This may be the people in the helicopter on the other line."

"Call me back when you have a chance, Dave."

"I will."

He gave the phone back to Michael, who picked up the other call. It was the helicopter pilot.

The Rescue

5

"**I**S THIS MICHAEL BYNEN from the Double-D Ranch?"

"Yes. Who's this?"

"Paul Lynskey. I'm flyin' the Rescue Chopper out of the Park. I'm told you've got a rider down somewhere near the top of Apgar Mountain. Is that right?"

"That's right."

"Exactly where are you?"

"I'm sitting in the woods about a mile from the top of the mountain where we stop and turn around. Do you know where that is?"

"I've got a pretty good idea. There's a bald spot up there, right? That's where you all stop to take pictures and things?"

"That's right."

"I'll be there in less than ten minutes. I've got a medic with me. He'd like to talk to you, but before I hand this over to him, can you light a flare for me? It'd help out a lot."

""It'll take me ten minutes to get back up to the top of the mountain."

"I'm at the park headquarters in West Glacier and I'm leaving now."

"I'm leaving now, too."

"If I'm not there already, light it when you get there. I have a pretty good idea of where you are. Here's the medic."

Michael handed the phone to Dave and said,

"Here, you talk to him. I gotta get up to the top of the mountain and light a fire." He grabbed the flare pack and started running.

Dave picked up the phone and said,

"Hello. This is Dave Nickel."

"Dave, My name's Eric. I'm a para-medic. What's the condition of the patient?"

"He's in a lot of pain and he can't feel his legs."

"I understand a horse fell on him. Is that right?"

"Yes sir."

"Is he conscious?"

"He goes in and out. I think he's in shock."

"Is his head elevated?"

"Yes sir."

"Is he communicative?"

"Yes sir, except he's in pain and can't talk too long."

"Can he talk?"

"He can right now."

"I'd like to talk to him, but before I do, tell me…does he have any broken bones or is there any bleeding?"

"Nothing that we can see."

"What's his name?"

"Pete Collins."

"Put him on."

Dave handed the phone to Pete, who was writhing in pain, with his eyes closed.

"Hello."

"Pete, this is Eric and I'm on my way to where you are right now. Are you going to be okay until I get there?"

"I don't know, man…I…"

"You hang in there. We're bringing the cavalry and we're going to do everything we can to help you, okay? Let me speak to Dave again."

Pete handed the phone back to Dave.

"Keep him awake and as quiet as possible until I get there."

"Can he drink water?"

"No."

"We gave him some Tylenol. Is there anything else we should do?"

"I've got pain killers and sedatives and all the medicines we need to keep him quiet until we can get him to a hospital and see what's wrong with him. I'm going to stay on the line with you until I get there."

"What do you think?"

"It could be any number of things. Keep him still until I can get there. We're flying as fast as we can. Let's not talk too much about that right now. I just want to keep an open line in case anything happens."

"How far away are you from where we will land?"

"You're going to land on the West face of Apgar about as high as you can go. Those helicopters can't make it all the way to the top, you know. We're going to meet you about a mile down the trail from the top, but we're gonna have to hike down to get him and hike back up once we do."

"Can we get any closer to him than that?"

"I don't think so. There's a flat spot for you to land there and that's about the only place I know of where you could land, and then we're gonna have to walk down."

"Pretty steep in through there, is it?"

"Yeah."

"Are we going to have any trouble getting him out of there?"

"He's off the trail by about fifty feet and it won't be easy, but Michael and I can help and between the three of us, we should be able to manage it, but Pete's a pretty big guy, so we'll have our hands full, plus it bein' dark and all, it won't be easy."

"I'll hit the ground running with our equipment."

"I guess you'll have to put him on a stretcher and carry him, won't you?"

"I'll have to wait and see him to assess the situation, but yes, we'll probably want to secure him to a board and carry him back. We don't want him falling again or getting hurt any more than he already is.

"He's in a whole lot of pain, Eric."

"I'll be there as fast as this pilot can get me there."

" Another guy, whose name is Michael, will be at the top when you get there. He was the guide on this trip. He'll lead you down to where we are."

Pete became more alert and started asking a few questions. Dave told him what he knew and then said,

"Abby and Dennis are on their way up here, too."

"Abby? How'd she find out about this?"

"I called Reno and she overheard the conversation."

"God! I don't want her to see me like this. I hope I'm gonna be alright! I don't want to be a cripple!"

"Take it easy, man. Help is on the way. They're gonna do everything they can. Everything's gonna turn out okay. I'm sure of it. Just lie still until they get here."

Michael ran as fast as he could and reached the top before the helicopter had arrived. He immediately lit the flare he had been carrying in his right hand like a relay racer carrying a baton. The flare immediately began to emit a bright light and orange smoke. He shielded his eyes and stood back. On top of the mountain, there was usually a fairly strong wind and this day was no exception. It was dusk but there was still some pink in the sky over the top of the mountains to the west.

He heard the sound of the chopper before he saw it. His vision was obscured by all the smoke from the flare. Within a few minutes, the chopper was hovering overhead. Michael sought shelter behind a tree as the turbulence created by the spinning blades almost knocked him over. Once the helicopter was on the ground, a side door burst open and a man jumped out and ran towards Michael, carrying an eight foot long backboard with him in one hand and a bag in the other. When he had cleared the spinning blades, he looked back and gave a thumbs-up sign to the pilot, who kept the engine running. The two men shook hands, and Michael took the splint from the man, who hollered,

"Let's go!"

"Follow me!" Michael yelled in response, and began running down the trail.

Eric ran behind him, carrying his medical supply kit. Every so often, Michael turned to make sure he wasn't going too fast. Eric was right behind him. They had to slow down as they left the open area on top and got into the forest. Either of them could easily have slipped or tripped and sprained an ankle, or worse. They had to make certain that in their haste to get to Pete they made sure to take care of themselves.

It was nearly completely dark in the woods, but there was just enough light for them to see the path, barely. Five minutes later, Michael slowed to a stop and said,

"There he is!"

David was standing beside Pete's motionless body, waving his arms overhead. Eric used the rope to shimmy down to where Pete was. He immediately began pulling items from his bag, preparing to perform some tests. The three horses stood tethered nearby, eating what grass and vegetation they could find, as if nothing had happened.

Pete had lapsed into a shock-induced state of unconsciousness again. Eric put on a stethoscope and performed a few tests to get a read on Pete's breathing and blood pressure. He stuck his finger in Pete's mouth, to feel the tongue and lifted up the eyelids to see the pupils, manipulated his legs and tested some joints. After several minutes, he pulled a syringe from his bag, together with a vial of some sort, and inserted a needle in Pete's exposed right arm.

Michael and Dave assembled the stretcher and lay it down on the other side of Eric, anticipating that he would have them place Pete on the stretcher. They also partially inflated a few air pillows which would fit around Pete's neck and other parts of his body.

Moments later, Eric said,

"Let's get him on the board. Gently! Gently!"

In a matter of seconds, the men log-rolled Pete's body onto the board. They adjusted his position on the board and began tightening straps. They finished inflating the tube around Pete's neck and some others around his head and his upper torso. They tied several more straps around his body to hold him securely to the board. In less than a few minutes, the two men were standing, each at one end of the stretcher, which looked like the top of a casket with holes along the edges, holding it up with both hands, ready to go.

"Let's get moving. I know these woods better than you guys do. I'll lead the way and do my best to light the way for us." Michael said. "We've got to get Pete to a hospital as fast as we can."

Without another word, all three men sprung into action. They moved slowly at first as they struggled to get back up to the trail, trying not to shake Pete any more than necessary, but they were going up at a 45 degree angle and it was a steep incline. Pete was fastened in tightly or he might have fallen off. Eric was on the down-side, holding on, trying to keep the stretcher as level as possible. David had the front end.

Once they were on the trail, they began walking as fast as they could back up the mountain to where the helicopter and its pilot sat waiting, its' engine still running and its' blades still spinning. Michael did his best to shine a light on the path ahead for David and Eric, but it was slow going.

When they got to the top, with the help of the pilot, the men lifted the stretcher into the back of the small helicopter. There was barely enough room for the stretcher to fit. Once the stretcher was in place and secured, Eric jumped in the passenger seat. Dave and Michael backed off, saying,

"Thanks, guys!"

Once they were far enough away, Paul gave the thumb's up sign and lifted the machine thirty feet straight up. In an instant, the helicopter was flying off. Not long after that, the flashing lights were specks in the night sky.

6

Emergency Medical Care

DAVID AND MICHAEL STOOD side by side on the top of the mountain, not saying a word, as they watched the helicopter fly into what was now a pitch-black sky. When the flashing red lights of the helicopter became specks in the sky, and after they could no longer hear the sound of the helicopter, they turned and started walking back down the mountain. Michael called the Double-D and let Patty know what was going on. When he was finished, David called Reno and gave him the same information.

When they got back to the accident site, they could hear the sounds of the four-wheeler carrying Abby and Dennis coming towards them. They both grabbed hold of the halter of two of the three horses still tethered to trees and shone flashlights in the direction of the oncoming vehicle to let them know where they were. Dennis immediately slowed his vehicle down and came to a stop, twenty feet away. He turned off the motor and, carrying a battery-operated lantern, he and Abby walked to where the two men were standing.

David told them that Pete was on the helicopter and probably at the hospital by now.

Abby immediately said,

"I've got to get to the hospital."

"I'm going, too," David said somberly.

"We've got to get ourselves and these horses off of this mountain first," Michael replied. "We're going to have to walk them down. I think it'll be too dangerous to ride them back down."

"These horses see better in the dark than we do. They know where they're going," David said. "We can ride, can't we?"

"Hey, after what just happened to Pete, I'm not taking any chances. We're walking them down," Eric replied.

"Either of you want anything to eat or drink? Need any blankets or clothes?" Dennis asked.

"Got anything hot?" Michael asked. "I've got a chill."

"Yeah. Reno gave us a thermos of coffee. Want some?"

"Yeah, please," Michael replied.

"Me, too." David said.

Dennis located the thermos, gave each man a cup and, as he was pouring, said,

"I don't have any cream or sugar so this is the best I can do for you."

"That's the way Reno drinks his coffee…straight black," David offered.

"We passed two girls on horses a mile or so back down the trail. They should be here any minute," Dennis continued.

"That's Wendy and Sandra. Patty told me that they were coming. She had given them some supplies for us, but it doesn't look like we'll need them now."

Abigail was fretting nervously to the side, obviously anxious to get moving. Dennis noticed it and said,

"Once they get here, we'll head back down. I have room to take some things back, if you want," he offered.

"I'll walk one of the horses down," David said in response. "There's not much I can do now that he's at the hospital. I just hope he's gonna be alright."

No one spoke in response. Everyone knew what he meant.

They heard the sound of the horses' hooves and some snorting as the horses approached. Minutes later, Wendy and Sandra arrived, only to learn that there was nothing more to be done.

"I thought one of you was going to stay with Christie and the rest of the group," Michael asked.

"They were doing fine and we didn't think it was a good idea for

Wendy to ride by herself up here, so I came along with her," Sandra replied.

After an exchange of good wishes and a collective prayer for Pete, Dennis and Abby went to get on the four-wheeler and get back down the mountain.

"You want us to stay with you and lead the way? Dennis offered.

"No, we'll be fine. You go on ahead," Michael responded, but then he thought of something else and said, "Hey, Dennis! Before you go, do you have an extra flashlight or two? David and I are gonna need one."

Before Dennis could answer, Michael asked the two girls, "How about either of you two? You got any extra flashlights?"

"No, we've only got one each," Sandra replied.

Dennis gave a flashlight to David which he could wear on his head so that he could keep his hands free. When it was decided that there was nothing more they could do to help, Dennis started up the motor and he and Abigail went noisily down the trail, leaving the other four in the silence of the cold and dark night. Michael tied Bucky's lead shank to the horn of his horse's saddle and they began to walk down the mountain.

"The horses are gonna get spooked by the flashlights so we're gonna have to walk slow," Sandra said, as she and the other three led the horses in the dark back down the path towards the Double-D stables.

*   *   *   *   *   *   *

Dennis couldn't go fast enough for Abby. She prayed to herself, saying,

"Please God, make him be alright! Please God, make him be alright! Please God, make him be alright!"....over and over and over....

They arrived back at the Double-Ds office in twenty minutes. Patty was waiting for them, as were her husband, Tom, and Reno. They were relieved to know that Pete was getting the help he needed and that there were no further mishaps during the rescue efforts, so far. The temperatures had fallen to the high thirties. The warm clothing Reno had convinced Abigail to take with her had come in handy, but she was cold upon arrival. Patty had a fire going and all gathered around it to get warm and hear the details. Abby wasn't there but for a few minutes before she was were ready to take off for the hospital. Reno stopped her as she was headed towards the door and said,

"Where you going?"

"North Valley."

"Wait, wait, wait! He's not there.'

"Where is he then?"

"Kalispell Regional, but you're not going to get to see him, Abby..."

"I can try."

"He'll be surrounded by doctors and nurses and they may well put him under to perform surgery, Abby."

"But we don't know how bad it is yet, do we?"

"No, we don't. That's true, but..."

"Then I can try."

"Abby, I got a call from my friend, Henry Rutland. He had spoken to a neurosurgeon and..."

"So what did he say?" Abby asked.

Reno lowered his voice and said,

""Well, he couldn't be sure. He said they were going to have to do more tests in Seattle with some very sophisticated machines, machines that aren't available at Kalispell, and he said it would be best not to jump to any conclusions."

"What does he think it is?" Abigail persisted.

"He told me that it would be best to wait and see what the experts say once they have a chance to take a look at him before jumping to any conclusions."

"But what did he think it was, Reno?" Abigail continued.

Reno looked her straight in the eye and said,

"Abby, they're afraid it's a spinal cord injury, but Henry told me that the spinal cord is a very resilient thing. It can be shocked and then the shock can wear off. He said all we can do right now is pray."

Abigail started to cry. Patty, who was standing next to Reno, put her arms around her to comfort her.

"There's nothing you can do at the hospital, Abby," Reno said. "You might as well stay here with the rest of us for a while until we hear something. When it's time, we'll all go see him. Right now, all we can do is pray, like the doctor said. Henry said he'd heard of cases where people had made miraculous recoveries and maybe Pete would. He told me that he'd give me a call as soon as he found out anything."

Abigail slumped into a nearby chair, covered her eyes, and continued to weep.

Dennis said, "Abigail, I have to go. I was supposed to be someplace an hour ago. If you want a ride back to the store, I'll take you but I've got to go now. I'm sorry."

"Go ahead and go, Dennis. Reno's right. There's nothing I can do up there now. Thanks for what you did."

"You're welcome, Abigail. Pete is my friend, too."

After Dennis left, Patty said to Tom, her husband, that they'd better start getting the horses loaded up and ready to take them back to the ranch. She wanted to get as much done as they could before Michael, Wendy and Sandra got back with the other horses. She wasn't sure if there would be any trail rides the next day, but if she decided to cancel them, she'd have to let people know. She, like everyone else, was pretty shaken up over what had happened.

Reno knelt down next to Abby and said,

"You don't have to come to work tomorrow, unless you want to, but I can understand if you don't."

Abigail stared at the fire burning in the woodstove in the corner and didn't respond.

"You're welcome to stay here as long for as long as we're here. It's gonna take us a while to get everything loaded up and ready to go," Patty said as she turned to head out the door.

Tom walked over to where Abigail was sitting and said,

"I'm real sorry about this, Abigail. I hope everything turns out alright."

She turned, and with tears in her eye, managed to mutter "Thanks."

When it was only Reno and Abigail left sitting by the fire, an awkward silence filled the room. Reno said,

"I'm going to wait until Dave gets back. When he does, you're all welcome to come back to my place. Fran made a big pot of beef stew and there's plenty for all of us, if you'd like."

"Thanks, Reno, but I don't feel much like eating right now," Abigail replied, continuing to stare at the fire.

"Well, you have to eat, and I expect you're cold after being out there as long as you were, but you do whatever you think is best. You're welcome, though, and you know that."

They sat in silence for another twenty minutes or so until they heard some commotion outside. Michael, David, Wendy and Sandra had made it back. David came into the room and silently exchanged greetings with the two. In a hushed tone, he said,

"I'd better be goin'. My dogs have been inside all day and there's no tellin' what they might do to my apartment if I don't get there pretty soon. Abby, are you gonna be alright?"

"Yeah. I'll be alright. I guess there's nothing else we can do until we hear from the doctors. Can give me a ride back to the shop, Reno?"

"Of course."

"I'll need a ride in to town, Reno, if you don't mind," Dave said. "I rode out here with Pete and I don't have the keys to his truck, unless you have them, Abby."

"No, I don't," she responded.

"You ready to go, Abby?"

Abby stood and said, "Let's go."

The three rode in silence to the restaurant where Dave and Pete had eaten breakfast that morning. After David got in his car and drove off, Abby and Reno went back to the Great Northern. When they arrived, Abby followed Reno inside to get her purse and some other belongings. Reno said,

"You sure you don't want to have some of that stew, Abby? I think it would do you some good."

"Maybe I will. To be honest, I don't know whether to sit or stand, come or go. I'm in a daze right now. I just can't believe this happened."

"Don't give up hope, Abby. We fear the worst, but let's hope for the best."

"I'll ring Fran and let her know we're comin'."

Reno lived in a two-story log cabin, half a mile from the store. They drove in separate cars to his home. Fran, a short, slender woman with graying blonde hair, several years younger than Reno, was at the doorway to greet them. She knew what had happened to Pete and had a grim look of concern on her otherwise amiable face. She gave Abby a hug and told her how sorry she was about the news and that she'd been praying steadily ever since she heard it.

The table was set, next to a roaring fire, and they walked straight to the table and sat down. The three held hands and said prayers in silence for a long time. Reno then squeezed the hands of his wife and Abigail and said, "Amen."

The warm food put some life back into Abby's sullen countenance, and she had three of Fran's hot biscuits before she touched the stew. No one said much. They all hoped to hear some good news about Pete from Reno's friend, Dr. Rutland.

7
The Diagnosis

WHEN THE HELICOPTER ARRIVED at the Kalispell Regional Medical Center, Pete was immediately taken into the hospital. The plan was for him to be taken by Medi-Vac helicopter to the closest regional trauma center, once the diagnosis was confirmed. The closest Medi-Vac helicopter was in Spokane and it had already been summoned. It was much larger and had medical equipment and supplies on board. It flew much faster, too, at speeds of almost two hundred miles an hour.

The Park Service helicopters had to be small enough to get into tight spaces on the mountain and it had done its job. The neurosurgeon, Dr. Gillis, and others at the hospital had made all of the arrangements and before the Park Service helicopter touched down, the decision to fly Pete to Seattle, which had a regional trauma center and all of the facilities to care for such a patient, had been made. The Medi-Vac helicopter would have Pete at the hospital in Seattle in little over an hour. Clearly, Kalispell could serve only as a triage center at best. The medic on board could do much of what needed to be done in-flight. Some tests couldn't wait, however, and those were to be performed before he left.

X-rays could be taken to determine if the spinal column was damaged. Ribs may have been cracked or other bones broken, but they were not a priority. A cat-scan to determine the extent of internal bleeding, which could be life-threatening, was vital and of immediate concern, and an MRI was needed to view the spinal cord. Those tests had to be conducted before Pete could be sent to Seattle.

As soon as the two orderlies took Pete into the hospital, they transferred him onto one of the hospital gurneys, and a team of nurses took over. The first thing they did was cut the clothes off of Pete and clean him, as well as they could. He was in a state of semi-conscious drowsiness from the pain-killers given him by Eric. Though he was, at times, awake, in a clinical sense, he was dazed and drifted in and out of consciousness.

Although the plan was for Pete to be at Kalispell Regional for only a short time, they would do all that they could to assess the situation. If there was any internal bleeding, that would have to be attended to immediately and that would delay Pete's departure. The results of the tests would be sent to the staff in Seattle so that they would be ready to go to work when he arrived.

The staff internist stood by, awaiting the results. Dr. Gillis conferred with him briefly, to discuss his assessment of the situation. The internist and Dr. Gillis agreed that provided surgery wasn't necessary to repair a ruptured artery, the spleen, or other internal organ, Pete would be on his way to Seattle as soon as the tests results were read and analyzed.

The tests took nearly an hour to complete. No rupture of a major organ was found. There was no need for immediate surgery. The MRI confirmed Dr. Gillis' suspicions. The spinal cord had been damaged at T-12. Pete was going to Seattle. Once the Medi-Vac unit arrived, Pete was put on board and the aircraft was back in the air and on its way to Seattle.

Pete was left strapped on the gurney, covered with blankets, to keep him as still as possible on the hour long flight. A large and growing medical bill went with him.

After Pete was on his way, Dr. Gillis went back to his office. He had been up since 6:00 and in the office since 7:00 that morning. He was due back the next morning at the same time. He was tired and ready to go home. His job was finished. He had done all he could. Pete was now in the good hands of others. Before he left to go home, he called Dr. Rutland and gave him the news. Dr. Rutland then called Reno.

Reno, his wife and Abigail were just finishing their dinner when the phone rang. Reno immediately jumped up and hurried into the kitchen to get it.

"Henry! Thanks for calling."

"Hi Reno. I wish I had some good news for you, but I don't. I called to let you know where they've taken your young friend."

"Thanks, Henry. I appreciate that, and please be sure to thank your friend, Dr. Gillis, for me. It sounds like he went above and beyond the call of duty on this one."

"He did. He stayed at the hospital and was there when the young man arrived, but he was sorry that he couldn't do more to help."

"I'm sure he did all he could."

"He did, and he said the young man, whose name is Pete, right?"

"That's right."

"He said that Pete is on his way to the trauma center in Seattle as we speak."

"Seattle, huh? That's not too far."

"Jim told me that as soon as Pete got there, they ran a few tests, confirmed the diagnosis, and sent him on his way. It was a good thing Jim was there. If he hadn't have been there, it might have delayed things a bit, but Jim felt it was best to get him where he needed to be as fast as possible, especially because Seattle had a bed open. He told me that the other closest trauma center is in Denver but they were full up. He did what he could and made the decision not to keep him any longer."

"When things quiet down, I'll call him myself to thank him. So he's already on his way is he?"

"Yes, he is. From what I can gather, they basically just took him out of one helicopter, cleaned him up a little, ran the tests, put him on the Medi-Vac helicopter and sent him on his way. He wasn't there long."

"I just hope that it isn't as bad as we fear it is."

"Reno, I'd like to give you some reason for optimism, and you know I would, but I'm a medical doctor, and although I don't treat spinal cord injuries, I have dealt with a few during my career. I know that if the spinal cord is injured, as Dr. Gillis thinks it might be, there isn't much anyone around here can do to treat that. If anything can be done, the doctors in Seattle can do it."

"Mmmm. Dr. Gillis thinks it's pretty serious, does he?"

"I'm afraid so."

"Mmmm."

"You're my friend and I know that this young man is close to you, but I've got to be as straight with you as I can. I think that you would expect that from me."

"That's true, and I thank you for that, Henry."

"But they're doing miraculous things these days. There are drugs that, if given within the first twenty four hours, can help prevent paralysis from being permanent, from what I'm told."

"Really?"

"Sometimes if the cause of the compression on the spinal cord is removed, the problem can go completely away in a few weeks time."

"All we can do is hope for the best."

"I'll call back once I get more information, but it probably won't be until morning. I'm at home now and I'll be going to sleep shortly."

"Thanks, Henry. I appreciate that."

"When I find out anything more, I'll call you."

"Thanks, again, Henry."

"You're welcome, Reno. I'll talk to you in the morning."

When he hung up and returned to the table, both Abigail and Fran, who had only heard his part of the conversation, wanted to know what the doctor had said.

Reno, who was an older man, in his mid-sixties, usually spoke softly and always considered his words very carefully. He was a deeply religious man and genuinely cared for those who worked for him. His small frame, which couldn't have been more than about 5'7" in his prime, without an ounce of fat on it, shook visibly before he spoke. His balding head, with gray hair and glasses gave him the look of a kindly, fatherly figure. With moisture in his eyes, Reno cleared his throat and said,

"They're taking Pete to a hospital in Seattle. He should be there any time now. Henry's going to call me with more details tomorrow. He really didn't know any more than the last time we spoke."

Reno couldn't bring himself to tell Abby the whole story. She was already devastated by what news she had.

"What did Dr. Gillis think the problem was?" Abigail asked.

"He said it was a spinal cord injury and that Pete needed to be taken to a hospital which specializes in those things."

Again, Reno didn't want to share any more information than was absolutely necessary.

"But I heard you say that we can hope for the best..." Abigail persisted.

"That's right. We won't know for sure until the specialists see him in Seattle. They've got a special unit there, I'm told. They have the most modern equipment and things, you know."

"Is he conscious?" She continued.

"Henry didn't say."

"Please let me know when you hear anything, will you, no matter how bad it is?"

"I will, Abigail. I promise. He did say that a lot of times these things can clear up in twenty four hours, so there's hope that everything's going to be alright."

Abigail straightened in her chair, took a deep breath, and said,

"I'm better now. Thank you so much, Mrs. Baldwin, for dinner. I'm ready to go home now."

"Call me Fran, please, Abigail. Do you have someone living with you? A roommate or guest?" Mrs. Baldwin asked.

"No. Pete was the closest thing to a roommate I've had all summer."

"Are you sure you'll be alright"

"I'll be fine, thanks, Fran."

"Have you and Pete been together long?" Fran asked.

"We've been together the whole summer."

"You're welcome to stay here, if you'd like. We have a spare bedroom now that our son, Brooks, is away so much. It's no trouble at all."

"Thank you, but I'll be alright."

"Remember, you don't have to come in tomorrow if you're not up to it, Abigail." Reno interjected.

"I know. We'll see how I feel in the morning. I don't think I'll want to sit around an empty room and think about it. I'll probably come in."

"It's up to you. Just let me know what you decide once you do."

As Abby turned to leave, Mrs. Baldwin, said,

"Come here, girl. I've got to give you a big hug."

At that, she put both arms around Abigail, who was at least six inches taller than she was, gave her a bear hug, and said,

"Before you leave, I have to tell you a little story. It won't take long. When Brooks was about the age of you and Pete, he went off on one of his kayaking expeditions to the headwaters of the America River with a few of his buddies. It's a 70 mile stretch through the Royal Gorge without too many access points. He'd done things like that so many times before that we didn't think much of it, but when his buddies came back and he didn't, we became real concerned. They had search parties out looking for him for days. They had run into some bad weather and Brooks had an accident in which he wrecked his kayak.

"We later learned that his kayak got wedged between two rocks as he was going over a drop, and the force of the water broke the kayak in half, forcing him to swim for it. He had to swim through what they call a 'worm hole,' which is an under water cave.

"The others were too far down river and, well, they got disconnected. Brooks had no choice but to climb out, but the walls of the canyon he was in were almost vertical and it was at least 4000 feet to the top. There was no way he could have swam the whole river. The others continued down river but they didn't get off the river for two days, so it was that long before anyone even knew he was in trouble and went looking for him. Well, needless to say, once I found out what was going on, I was a nervous wreck. I made Reno take me down there to the closest Ranger station and I had to know every tidbit of information as it came in, and there wasn't much.

"The daytime temperatures ran about 100 degrees, but at night it dropped to near freezing. He lost his water bottle a couple of hundred feet from the top when a large piece of rock broke loose and sent him sliding back down the side of the mountain. He wasn't hurt too badly by the fall, but he didn't have any water after that.

"Once he finally made it up to the top of the canyon, he still had a hike of over twenty miles, without water. There were a number of deep ravines he had to walk through, some of which were several thousand feet deep. There weren't any other humans anywhere around.

"They had just about given him up for dead when he got picked up by a hunter in a pick-up truck who happened to find him out there.

I cried for joy for three days straight. Don't think the worst. Say your prayers and hope for the best."

"Thank you. I will. How long was he gone?'

"He was out in the woods, under those conditions, without food or water, for almost four days."

"Wow. That's a long time."

"He said he almost gave up several times. It wasn't just the lack of food and water that was the problem, but the terrain was grueling and the weather was bad. It rained a couple of those days. The cold nights made him think he was gonna freeze to death and during the day he thought he'd die of thirst. He said he thought he was as good as dead more than a few times."

"That must have been awful for you, and for him."

"For all three of us, it was. Have you ever met Brooks?"

"Not yet, but I've heard lots of stories. I can't believe he goes down those sixty foot falls like he does."

"I stopped watching a long time ago. I can't believe it either."

"Thank you, again, Mrs. Baldwin. Good night, Reno."

"Good night, Abby. Keep the faith," Reno said as he closed the door, with tears in his eyes.

* * * * * * * * * *

Upon arrival in Seattle, Pete was immediately taken to the spinal cord unit, where a crew of medical personnel took over. They wheeled him into an operating room, where a team of masked men and women stood waiting. Several people, all in hospital garb, sat in seats above the floor of the operating room, where a team of eight, including Dr. Carl W. Johnson, the head doctor at the facility, stood ready to assess the situation. If any surgery was to be performed, an orthopedic surgeon, a Dr. Depperman, would most likely be the one to do that.

Dr. Johnson immediately took the MRI films and other test results, which had accompanied Pete on the flight, and put them in a machine by his side, which was then illuminated on a big screen overhead.

Dr. Johnson would debride the wound and visually assess the condition of the damaged spinal cord. Depending upon the severity of the injury to the spinal column, it might be necessary to put rods in to stabilize the spine, but that would come later on. This first examination was more of an exploratory procedure, and it was critical that Pete's condition be evaluated immediately upon arrival.

Dr. Depperman, the orthopedic surgeon, who would be the one to insert the rods and address the anatomical issues at the appropriate time, wanted to visually examine the wound. Depending upon the severity of the 'crush' wound, immediate surgery to remove any bone fragments impinging on the spinal cord might be necessary. Dr. Johnson would deal with the injury to the spinal cord itself and all neurological problems.

Although it was late in the evening, the seriousness of the injury warranted the attention it was being given. It wasn't every day that a new spinal cord patient came to the staff. They much preferred to see the patient as soon after the trauma as possible. In Pete's case, the incident had occurred less than four hours before. They would do whatever was necessary.

After a short period of time spent looking at the films and discussing the situation with his colleagues, Dr. Johnson immediately went to work. Pete was gingerly rolled from being on his back to being on his stomach. The top of his surgical gown was removed. Injections were given and the site was prepped. A reddish substance was swathed across Pete's bare back. Dr. Johnson ordered one of the attendants to hand him a scalpel and he made an incision, all of which was captured on the screen overhead, for viewers to observe, and a video tape was being made, for use in the treatment to follow, as well as for instructional purposes.

Once the skin was folded back and the area of T-12 was exposed, Dr. Johnson cleaned the area and located the site of the injury. He probed it, while looking at it microscopically, to see what could be done. He remarked to one of his colleagues, "It's one thing to see the films. It's quite another to actually see the spinal cord."

He had new laser technology to employ, as well as improved microscopic fibers to allow him to visualize things that doctors had not been able to see in years past. X-rays revealed multiple broken ribs, a fractured sternum and, most importantly, a fracture of the T-12 vertebra, which was the likely cause of the damage to and compression on the spinal cord.

Dr. Johnson spoke slowly and softly, but his words were on a loud speaker for all to hear.

"We are about to perform a hemilaminectomy to alleviate pressure on the spinal cord. The cord has sustained a blunt trauma to it at T-12. We will remove the bony fragments that are impinging on the cord and inject polyethelene glycol, or PEG, as it is sometimes referred to, directly into the site of the injury in an attempt to restore nerve impulse conduction. It is a hydrophilic polymer that has been shown to provide dramatic results when given soon enough after the incident. However, tests have also shown that the longer the delay in administering this drug the less effective it is. PEG has been shown to seal the cell membranes of injured nerve fibers and prevent further injury. It can also promote healing, but it does not work in all cases. We can only hope that it will work for this young man."

After less than an hour, Drs. Johnson and Depperman removed their masks and allowed others to repair the wounds made by their scalpels. Before he left the operating room, Dr. Johnson said to those remaining spectators,

"Unfortunately, as you can see, the injury to T-12 is profound. The disc has been severely damaged and is beyond repair. We will begin an aggressive course of treatment which will include an oscillating electric field stimulus. It has been shown that an applied electric field in which the polarity is reversed every fifteen minutes can improve the results dramatically. We will also provide all of the more traditional methods of treatment as well. The first thing we need to do is reduce the swelling. If the chord continues to swell, it will become too large for the sheath through which it passes and that will cause more problems."

After the team had completed their assigned tasks, Pete was wheeled from the operating table to a post-surgical room, where he was observed and his vital signs were monitored until he was cleared for placement in yet another room.

Pete continued to sleep, if you could call it that, for almost two days. The accident occurred late on a Thursday afternoon and he didn't wake up until early Saturday afternoon. When he did, he found himself in a groggy and dazed stupor. His father and mother were in the room with him when he opened his eyes. Despite his weakened condition, he knew he had been badly hurt and feared that he was permanently paralyzed, but he desperately hoped that he was going to be able to get better. He didn't know where he was or what had happened to him since he fell into shock at the top of Apgar Mountain in Glacier National Park.

Pete's head was firmly secured to his bed and he couldn't lift it. There were no mirrors on the walls, so he couldn't see anything except what was in his immediate line of vision, which was the floor below, but he heard the sound of his parents' voices, which he immediately recognized.

"Mom! Dad! What are you doin' here?" he mumbled. He couldn't see that his head had been shaved bald and he couldn't feel the large wounds in his temples where surgical devices had been screwed in to keep his head from moving involuntarily during surgery.

His mother, Florence, had told herself over and over not to cry, but as soon as Pete spoke, she started to cry and went over to him, put her head as close to his as she could and kissed his forehead.

"We're so happy you're still alive, Peter! We've been so worried about you these last few days, ever since we got the news," she blubbered through her tears."

"We're with you all the way on this, son, whatever it takes," his father, Anthony, chimed in.

"Where am I?" Pete asked weakly.

"Seattle," his father replied.

"How did I get here? The last I remember is that tiny helicopter on the mountain."

"A Medi-Vac helicopter brought you from Kalispell to here after that. You've been through a lot, son."

Pete was flat on his stomach, strapped down and couldn't move anything, not even his arms, even if he wanted to. He was conscious of there being a mechanical apparatus of some sort surrounding him.

"My ribs hurt and so does my chest and my back, but I can't feel my legs."

"You just lay still, Peter. We'll get one of the nurses and let them know you're awake," his mother said.

She stood, wiped the tears from her eyes, and hurriedly walked towards the door, looking for someone to summon.

Thinking that his worst fears might have been realized, he asked,

"How bad is it, Dad?"

His father wasn't sure how to respond. He wasn't sure how Pete would react.

"I think we need to talk to a doctor and have him explain it to you and to us, son."

"Dad, tell me, please."

"I'd rather that you hear it from your doctor, Peter. He can answer all of your questions, I'm sure."

"Come on, Dad! How bad is it?"

His mother had returned and was back by his side. She held his hand. His father was standing next to him on the other side of the bed, resting his hand on Pete's shoulder.

"We've been told that your spinal cord has been badly damaged, son."

Pete knew what that meant. He was able to move his hands and his fingers. He couldn't move his toes. "There's been a mistake," he thought to himself, "This didn't happen to me." I'm not hurt as bad as they think. I'm going to get better. I'm going to be back on my feet in no time."

"How long am I going to be here?" he asked.

"We don't know. That's why you're here, son. This is one of the best facilities in the world for treating people who have spinal cord injuries."

"How long am I going to be like this?"

"Peter, we don't want to say the wrong things. We don't want to give you wrong information, good or bad. Let's wait for your doctor to come see you, please?" Florence pleaded. She began to tear up again.

Pete knew that he would get better, he just knew it. Things like this happened to other people, not him. He wasn't as bad as they were thinking. He was sure of it.

"Okay, Mom. I'll ask him."

Out of the corners of his eyes, Pete was able to see a few of the flowers and cards which filled the room.

"Where did these come from?"

"Your brothers and sisters have sent most of them, Reno Baldwin and his wife sent one, plus a girl named Abigail sent that one over there. Who's she, Peter?"

"She's my girl friend. I've been with her all summer. We work together, too."

"She's called a couple of times, too, since we've been here. Several other people have called, too. I wrote down the names and numbers and all."

"When did you get here?"

We got the news late Thursday night and flew out the next morning. We got here yesterday afternoon and came straight to the hospital. We've been here for about a day."

"You've been watching me sleep all that time?"

"They wouldn't let us stay with you overnight, so we went to our motel last night and got here first thing this morning, as soon as they'd let us in."

"Thanks, Mom, Dad." Pete said, causing his father, a tall, distinguished-looking man in his late sixties, with a slim, athletic build and a healthy head of white hair, to bristle with emotion and pat Pete on the shoulder several times, while his wife smiled through tears.

"Your father has to be back at work on Monday, but I'll be with you for as long as it takes, Peter."

"I don't know where I'll go if…"

"You're going to come home with us." Florence assured him.

Pete had been out of the house and had been on his own for five years. The thought of going back and living with his parents, though he loved them, was not in his plans.

"I'm gonna get better. I know I will."

"Amen to that," Pete's father replied. "We're saying our prayers morning, noon and night, and so is your whole family. They'd all be here except for their jobs and kids and the rest, you know that."

"Yeah, I'm sure they would. They all know?"

"You betcha. They all know and they're all saying prayers for you," Florence responded.

"How'd you find out about it?"

"Your boss, Reno," Anthony said.

"Yeah, I guess Dave told him."

"He sent that basket over there. He's called a couple of times, too," Florence said.

"Who, Dave? Or Reno?"

"Well, Reno and his wife called and they sent that plant over there, and Dave called, but he didn't send any flowers," she responded.

"You talked to them?

"Your Dad did. I didn't."

At that, Pete's eyes sunk back in his head and, as he began to drift out of consciousness, he managed to say,

"I'm sorry. I can't talk anymore. I can hardly keep my eyes open… wake me up when the doctor comes, okay? I'm goin' back to sleep. Thanks for being here. I love you."

"You go back to sleep, Peter. We'll be right here when you wake up again. We love you."

Anthony and Florence sat down in the two chairs they had occupied for the last day and went back to reading a book. Not long after Pete fell back asleep, Dr. Johnson walked in the room.

Anthony and Florence were whispering to him about not waking up Pete, and he said not to worry about that. He had enough sedatives in him that he wouldn't hear a thing, even if they screamed. Sleep was the best thing for him for the time being.

"Does he have to be in that cage you've got him in, Dr. Johnson?" Florence asked.

"As a matter of fact, he does. That's what is called a Roto-Rest bed. As you have seen, it can be tilted any which way, even upside down."

"Does it keep moving like that all the time?" she asked as the bed rocked back and forth in a rhythmic fashion.

"Yes, it does. That will help prevent Decubitis ulcers."

"What are they?" she continued.

"They are the most common complications of a spinal cord injury. They're pressure sores that occur almost exclusively over boney prominences. The skin over the heels, the sacrum and hips are the most common sites of skin breakdown."

"Why is that?" Anthony asked.

"Well, there are a number of explanations and reasons for it. One reason is that the peripheral blood flow is compromised, which causes a reduction in oxygen as well as nutrition for the area."

"What can be done to prevent that?" both Anthony and Florence asked at the same time.

"First, let me say that before Pete is discharged, you and he will receive extensive training on what to do and what not to do. While he's with us, the main thing we do is what this bed allows us to do, which is take the pressure off various parts of the body for a while. It's a common problem and it's a particularly difficult one to avoid for patients with spinal cord injuries. We'll do our best, though."

"And what about those things hooked up to his arms?" Florence asked.

"We're feeding him intravenously for now. He's also getting some pretty strong pain-killers. I'm afraid that he'd be in severe pain, not to mention the possibility of shock, when he comes to."

"What are you giving him?" Anthony inquired.

"Morphine is the main drug, but there are others, Demerol, Percocet. Are you aware of any allergies he may have?"

"None that we know of. He's always been a healthy child." Anthony responded.

"We have to make sure he doesn't have an allergic reaction."

"How much longer do you think you'll need to keep him like this?" Florence asked.

"We're hoping to see some dramatic improvement within the first two days. If that doesn't happen, we'll have to be more patient, but we'll change our plan of treatment accordingly. We are going to perform a surgical procedure once he his body has stabilized from the initial shock."

"What for?" Anthony asked.

"The bones around the T-12 disc have been shattered. We're going to insert some rods in his back to stabilize his spine as soon as possible."

"When do you think that might be?" he continued.

"Within the next few weeks, unless some dramatic change takes place. I'm hoping for that change any day now. He suffered a very serious injury. He'll be fortunate to be able to regain the use of most of his body."

Although there was nothing but bad news coming at them from all directions, Anthony heard some good news, or reasons to be optimistic in what Dr. Johnson had just said.

"I know that Pete will have a number of questions for you. We didn't want to tell him too much because we're not sure what to say." Anthony offered.

"By tomorrow morning, we should be ready to re-assess the situation. I'd like to see him in a more cognitive condition before having that conversation, and it is not an easy thing to do. It's the least favorite part of my job. I sincerely hope to have some good news to share with him and with you by then."

"Is there anything else you can tell us now?" Florence asked.

"I'd rather wait until tomorrow and we can discuss it with your son at the same time. I'm still hoping to see some improvement, but he sustained a substantial blunt trauma to his spinal column and his spinal cord when that horse fell on him. We're doing all we can. Sometimes prayer is as valuable as anything we do."

"If that's the case, we're doing all we can, too," Florence responded.

"I'm sure you are. My prayers are with you. If you'll excuse me, I have several other patients to see and I have a surgery scheduled in an hour."

"Of course. We understand. Thank you for your time, Doctor." Anthony said.

"I'll stop the morphine drip when I think the pain in his upper body will be tolerable and, unfortunately, I'm afraid he won't feel much of anything in his legs. You should begin to see him become more alert and responsive, but he's going to need all the love and compassion he can get. Coping with his changed condition is not going to be an easy thing for him to accept, as I'm sure you expect as well. From what I've been told, he was quite the outdoorsman, and very adventurous."

"That's true, Doctor. He was." Anthony whispered, barely able to talk, as the gravity of the situation overwhelmed him.

The doctor's lips pursed as he said,

"Let's hope for the best and that he'll be back at it before too long. You've got to give these things time. The spinal cord was injured and it is now swollen. It will take some time for the swelling to go down. Your son could return to normal at any time during the next month. He will still have the orthopedic injury to deal with, but the paralysis could go away. We can only pray for that to occur at this point, however, as there is nothing more I can do to make that happen right now."

"We are sure that everything that can be done is being done," Florence responded.

"He'll need all the encouragement you can give him," Dr. Johnson added.

"He'll get all we can give, Doctor," Anthony chimed in, "and then some."

With that, the doctor scribbled some notes on the chart hanging from the end of the bed and left. Pete was in a private room and the doctor closed the door behind him, to give the family more privacy.

Not long after the doctor left, Michael's cell phone began to ring. He turned it off. He would return the call later. For now, he needed quiet time to reflect on what he and his wife had just heard.

8

A Distorted View of the World

LATER THAT AFTERNOON, AS Florence sat looking out the window, listening to her husband breathe deeply and occasionally snore, watching her son intently for all signs of movement, there was a knock on the door. A young woman with a clipboard, dressed in a stylish business suit, asked if she could speak to her for a few minutes. Florence stood up and was about to ask if she could come back later, when Anthony woke up suddenly, rubbed his eyes, got to his feet and walked over to where the two women were standing.

"What can we do for you," he asked.

"I'm in the business office and I need to get some information from you. May I come in?"

"Would you rather us go to your office?" Florence offered.

"No this will be fine. I'll get someone to bring in a chair for me and I'll be fine, sitting right here with you."

When she exited the room, Anthony and Florence exchanged worried looks. They had wondered about the cost of the treatment their son was receiving and how those costs would be paid. They knew that they wouldn't be able to pay for it. When she returned, a young man carrying a folding chair followed her in and opened it up for her. Anthony and Florence pushed their chairs next to hers and sat down. Once she was seated, she said,

"First, let me begin by introducing myself. My name is Mary. I've been here for almost a year now, ever since I graduated from Puget Sound University. Ever heard of it?"

"I can't say that we have," Anthony responded. "We're from the East coast." Florence had a blank look on her face and shrugged her shoulders, suggesting that she hadn't heard of it either.

"It's not too far from here and the campus looks out over Puget Sound. It's beautiful."

"It sounds very nice."

"It is. This is my first job since college and I just love it. I like to help people. I know that sounds kind of funny, since I'm in the business department and I'm here to collect money, but when things like this happen to people like your son, I love to be able to help, and let me just say that everyone here is just so sorry about what happened to your son. We are all praying for a miraculous recovery."

"Thank you," Florence said. "So are we."

"I've ridden horses since I was a little girl. God knows something like that could happen to me or any of my friends."

"It's a risk everyone takes when they ride a horse," Anthony offered. "Peter hadn't ridden too many horses in his life, that I know of, but he certainly had participated in a number of dangerous activities."

"We see so many people who have been injured in tragic accidents. It can be something like diving into a lake or a river, sky-diving or a freak thing like a car accident or falling out of bed. You can't be too careful, but young people like to do exciting things and they never stop to think that something like that could happen to them. I didn't, until I came to work here. It makes me so sad, but I'm glad to help any way I can and that's why I'm here. I need to talk to you about the cost of your son's medical treatment, both now and in the future."

Anthony looked sheepishly at her and said,

"I'm retired from the military and we live on what we get from social security and my military pension. We can't afford to pay for any of this, I'm afraid."

"Oh, that's understandable. There aren't many people in the country who could afford this. You'd have to be a multi-millionaire, I think. There are some people who could pay for it without insurance, but those are the people who usually have the most insurance and they have all kinds of insurance...health insurance, travel insurance, car insurance, catastrophic insurance and every kind of insurance that's available, with big limits, too, so they are always covered to the hilt. I never know until I ask, but don't you worry about that, we'll just have to do what we can. Let's start with the basics."

Mary proceeded to get all of the details about Pete, such as his date of birth, social security number, home address, where he had lived for the last five years, family members, medical history and everything else requested on the standard form she had on her clipboard. Then she asked,

"So your son has pretty much been on his own since he graduated from high school, is that right?"

"We helped him with his college expenses when he first went away, but when he was asked to leave during the very first semester, we told him that until he became more serious about his studies and until he was ready to apply himself, that we weren't going to help him any more, financially that is," Anthony told her.

"So he's been pretty much taking care of himself for the last several years, right?"

"That's right. He's worked as a fisherman in Alaska and in the Florida Keys, and as a river boat guide, or whatever it is you call it, in Montana for several years, at least during the summer months. He's been making more than we have, ever since Anthony retired from the Navy." Florence responded.

"Then we need to submit an application for social security benefits right away, I'd say."

"Peter might be eligible for social security benefits?" Florence asked, thinking of social security retirement benefits, like what she and Anthony received.

"He will be eligible for what is called Supplemental Security Income, or SSI. Are you familiar with it?"

"I've heard of it, but I don't know much about it." Anthony replied.

"It's designed to help the aged, the blind and the disabled in our society."

"And it's not based upon how much money you paid in?" Florence asked.

"No, it isn't."

"And it pays for all of the medical bills for eligible people?" Anthony said.

"Well, actually, Medicare does that, at a discounted rate, but SSI gives people a small amount of money on a monthly basis so that eligible recipients have something to live on."

"We're on Medicare, aren't we, Michael?"

"Yes. Once I turned 65, I became eligible for Medicare, but that won't help us for this, will it?"

"No, if your son isn't a dependent child, then he wouldn't be eligible under your account, but he would be eligible for benefits under SSI."

"So he's eligible for Medicare and SSI because of his injury?"

"Although the doctors are still hoping for a miraculous recovery, if your son has a permanent spinal cord injury, and it's serious enough to prevent him from working, he would be considered a disabled person and then he would be eligible for SSI. Based upon what we know so far, I think we should submit an application for him now. What do you think?"

"If we do that, and he's found to be eligible, would it pay for all of his medical expenses up to this point?"

"Yes, it would, or most of them, at least, but not if you wait too long. It may not pay expenses that are more than thirty days old, but I'm not sure of that myself. I know that the sooner you apply the better and I'm suggesting that it would best to apply now."

"Can you help us with that?"

"Of course. I have all the papers and we can do that today. But Mr. Collins, you said you are retired military, correct? If so, you should still have Champus insurance, yes?"

"That's right, I do."

"We could try to see if they would cover it. One of the first questions will be whether or not he's a dependent child."

"We haven't declared him to be a dependent on our tax returns for several years now, as Florence told you. He made more money than we did the last couple of years. I don't think that would work, but whatever you suggest. We'd like to see these medical bills paid. It's just that we can't pay them for Peter," Anthony said, apologetically.

"We can also help you submit an application for Medicaid," Mary offered.

"I'm confused," Florence said. "Can you explain to us the difference between Medicare and Medicaid?"

"Sure. Most people are confused by that. Both are programs funded by the Federal government, but the Medicaid program is run by the States. So you would apply to the State of Washington, or Montana, or wherever he's been living, for Medicaid and to the Federal government for Medicare."

"Is Peter eligible for both?"

"Well, technically, I think he is. Medicare is primarily intended for older Americans, but it also provides benefits for disabled persons, too. Medicaid is for low income people of all ages who don't have the money or insurance to pay for health care. It provides benefits to people who are blind or disabled, too. Since your son won't have any income, other than SSI, he should be eligible for Medicaid, too."

"Will he be eligible for Medicaid here in the State of Washington even though he never lived here before?" Anthony asked.

"I'm not sure about that, but it's worth a try." Mary responded.

"Would he have to go back to Montana, since that's where he's been living most of the time lately? He's travelled around so much it's hard to keep up with him sometimes."

"I'm just not sure, but we'll find out."

"He hasn't lived in any one place for more than a few months at a time for several years now, but Montana is where he's been for most of the last several years, ever since he went away to college," Anthony said. "And what about the bills from up in Montana?"

"Those would have to be paid by the State of Montana under its Medicaid program or the Federal government under the Medicare program."

"Do they pay all the bills?"

"Medicare pays most of the bills, at a reduced rate, but it doesn't pay for all kinds of medical expenses. Sometimes hospitals and doctors write some expenses that aren't covered off. We can worry about that later. For now, we just want to get your son as much help as we can, agreed?"

"Of course. He needs all the help he can get and we're just not able to get it for him, but who could? A millionaire? Anymore it would have to be a multi-millionaire." Anthony said ruefully.

"Let me have your insurance cards and I'll make a copy, just in case there might be some coverage available to your son through you, though I doubt it," Mary asked.

Anthony pulled his wallet from his back pocket, took out his Medicare card and his insurance cards, and handed them to her.

"I think I have all that I need for now. I'll try to get back to you later today, but if I can't, we can talk more tomorrow."

"Thank you so much for your help," Florence said.

"You're welcome. As I said, I like being able to help people and I love my job. I just hope that your son is going to get all better and he won't need any of this, but that part is up to the doctors and to God, right?"

"It's out of our control. All we can do it pray," Florence responded.

"If you need anything else, and we're not here, you can reach us at the Best Western motel, just down the road here. If we're not there, you can leave a message for us," Anthony said.

"Or you can call us on our cell phone. It's 904-424-6824," Florence offered.

"Thank you so much. You've been very helpful. I'll say a prayer for your son, and for you, too. I know how hard this must be for the two of you as well."

"This isn't something any parent wants to go through," Florence responded.

"It is one of our worst nightmares," Anthony said, "among the many that we and all parents have about their children. It's always something, whether it's their health, a job, a relationship, getting in a car accident or arrested...the list goes on and on."

"And the two of you have how many children?"

"Nine," Florence replied.

"Nine children! Wow, how did you do it? I can't wait to have a baby, but I'm not married yet, so I'll just have to, but I don't see me having more than two. I don't know how you did it."

"One at a time. No twins. And we loved having each and every one of them, but Peter was always the one getting hurt and getting into trouble. He just had this wild spirit about him, always wanting to do the most dangerous thing, whether it was going the fastest on his bicycle or jumping off the highest bridge or whatever. More than any of the others, he loved being outside."

A tear came to Florence's eyes as she continued,

"He loved it when he was in Alaska or being a guide in Montana… the bigger the river the better…" she began sobbing. Anthony put his arm around her and said,

"We'll get through this, dear. Let's keep the faith. We'll find a way."

"I'd better be going now," Mary said softly and she backed towards the door. "I'll be back in touch soon. Thank you again."

When she was gone, they stood for a few minutes with Anthony having both arms around his wife and her with her head on his chest. He was much taller than she. Pete continued to be in a drug-induced sleep, unaware of all that was going on around him.

"Maybe now would be a good time to go back to the motel, freshen up a bit and get some lunch. What do you say?" Anthony asked.

"I think that's a good idea. I look a mess. I'll feel better after I shower and change."

When she regained her composure, she mustered a laugh and said,

"I guess a bubbly personality is a good one to have for the job she has, isn't it?"

"She has that and then some, and to think, she's not but a year or two younger than our Peter."

"Everybody has a different path to follow. Our son's path came to a dead end."

"Don't say that, Florence. Keep the faith. His path took a turn, that's all. Thank God he's still alive."

"You're right, Michael. I know it, but I can't bring myself to thank God just yet. I'm still hoping for a miracle, then I'll really thank him."

Florence was a few years younger than Michael. She had turned 65 earlier in the year, but since she had been a stay-at-home mother most of her life, and the wife of a Navy man to boot, she hadn't paid much into the Social Security system and wasn't eligible to receive any retirement benefits. Their combined income didn't change when she reached the age of 65. Chasing after her children for all those years had kept her in good shape, though, and she had been going to the gym on a regular basis to ride the exercycle, do the stairsteps and a few other machines ever since her youngest child, Katie, who was two years younger than Peter, had gone away to college two years after him. They had been 'empty nesters' for the last three years and they had been enjoying it.

At 5'7", her frame carried 130 pounds nicely. A weekly trip to a hairdresser kept the auburn color she was born with and hid the white hair that would have taken over many years before. She had the soft white skin of the Irish and she was 100% that. Her maiden name was Donoghue and her mother's maiden name was O'Connor.

She was an ardent Catholic and she prayed fervently for all of her children on a daily basis, but this was dire need now. She doubled, or tripled, her daily offerings of prayer, but she was also a realist, much more so than her husband. She knew what was in store for her son, and for her. She would have to find a place to stay for a while and it couldn't be the hotel where they were staying. They couldn't afford that. She would ask Mary about it next chance.

Neither the miracle drugs nor the prayers for a miracle worked to bring about the dramatic change that had been hoped for, but Dr. Johnson told them that he was guardedly optimistic that their son would not lose the functioning of his upper body, and he continued to hold out hope that he would regain the use of his lower body. The realization that their son would be a paraplegic and need their care hit them like an anvil. They knew that they should be thinking more about how Peter would take it and less about themselves, but they couldn't help but think about how it would affect their lives, too. It would be difficult for everyone.

Anthony flew back to Jacksonville that Sunday. Pete had been kept heavily sedated and he hadn't had a chance to really talk to him about what had happened and what was going to happen. Florence would have to do that. He wished he could have stayed, and he planned to return as soon as possible, but there were scheduled appointments, the dogs, the house and a multitude of loose ends for him to take care of. They had left as soon as they received word of the injury and hadn't planned this trip at all. Florence found a small cottage, not far from the hospital, where she could stay for as long as need be. The hospital had many such places available. The Collins' weren't the first family to face a crisis such as this.

Once Pete was fully conscious and relatively stable, and not before, the surgery to insert the two titanium rods in Pete's back would be performed by Dr. Depperman, the orthopedic surgeon, with Dr. Johnson by his side, in the operating theatre where Dr. Johnson performed most of his surgeries. Without any doubt, he was one of the premier neurosurgeons in the country and, since this was a teaching hospital, most of his surgeries were used for instructional purposes also. This particular surgery required the services of Dr. Depperman, but it was not uncommon for both surgeons to perform operations together and they did so on a regular basis.

On Wednesday of the following week, Florence was among the many who watched the surgery performed on her son. She felt as if she had an inkling of what Mary must have felt in Calvary, as depicted in Michelangelo's sculpting, La Pieta.

The next day, when Pete awoke, he was out of the private room he had been in and was now in a room with three other men, all of whom had complete and permanent spinal cord injuries that would render them quadriplegics for the rest of their lives. He was lying on his front side, seeing only the floor below. His mother was sitting by his side, holding his hand while reading a book. When she saw him stir, she spoke and he responded.

"Mom?"

"Yes son."

"Where am I now?"

"You're in the spinal cord unit with three other men. You won't have a private room anymore, Peter."

"I can't move anything now."

Pete was securely attached to his bed, facing the floor. He was told that he would rarely be on his back for a while as doctors and nurses would need to inspect the wound on a regular basis. His doctors didn't want him moving anything other than his eyeballs, if possible, for a while.

"What's this I have around my chest?"

"That's what they call a clam shell. It protects you, Peter. You're going to be wearing that for a while, so you're going to have to get used to it, son."

"Shit!" Pete was still groggy but not so groggy that he didn't understand what his mother had said. He just couldn't accept it as being true. He still prayed for the miracle. He thought about having to go to the bathroom and what he would do if he did, and he was told that a catheter had been inserted during the operation. Little did he know that he would have that catheter for years to come.

The liquids from his bladder were draining into the catheter as Pete lay there, unable to move, unable to do what had been the most natural act of any acts he had performed countless times every day of his life. When the attendants left, he said,

"Mom, I can't even go to the bathroom by myself." He started to cry, something he hadn't done in a long, long time.

His mother saw the tears and said,

"We'll make it through this, son. Thank God you're alive. We'll take it one day at a time, that's all we can do," she whispered.

Pete didn't respond. He didn't say anything at all for quite some time. His mother sat quietly by his side, intuitively understanding what thoughts were going through Pete's head. No sounds were coming from any of the other three beds in the room. Moments later, Pete was asleep again and silence filled the room.

Two weeks after surgery, as the two sat quietly with Florence reading her Bible and Pete laying there with his eyes closed, the silence was broken when a middle-aged woman, in the traditional white lab coat with white tennis shoes walked over to the other side of Pete's bed. Her name tag read 'Joy', something neither Pete nor Florence was feeling.

"Good morning. My name is Joy and I am a physical therapist. My job is to help get you sitting up as quickly as possible."

"Where will you take him?" Florence asked.

"We're going to do that right here. There's no need for us to move him at all just yet, other than to turn him over."

No sooner had she spoken when an assistant walked in and, after flipping the Roto-bed, turning it right side up, began attaching a device to the end of the hospital bed which was nothing more than a pole which stuck up several feet above the bed with a cord coming from it, and a bar at the end of the cord.

"Mr. Collins, your job will be to try to sit up. You can grab hold of this bar and try to pull yourself up. Do you think you do that for me?"

Pete thought to himself that it was a silly request and that he would have no trouble doing it. He was tired of being flat on his stomach and wanted very much to sit up, but he couldn't because of all the straps and braces over his body. The therapist and her aide put the clam shell back on him, tied the various straps, and handed him what looked like the end of a tow rope he'd used while water skiing so many times in the past.

Joy positioned herself at the other end of the bed, behind Pete, and waited while Pete took hold of the bar, preparing to lift himself up. The 'clam shell' kept his back completely rigid, like the cast that he had worn when his ankle had been broken playing baseball his junior year in high school, or the arm he had broken while roller-blading the year before that. He was able only to move his neck a few inches. He had no stomach muscles. He had to pull with his arms as hard as he could. He strained.

"God damn! This is hard!"

"Peter, watch your language," his mother scolded him. She couldn't help herself. She never let her children curse and this was no exception.

"That's it, Mr. Collins. You're doing fine. Keep it up. Keep pulling," Joy said as she gently supported the area behind his neck to help him rise up. When he could move no more, he let out a breath, collapsing back onto the pillow.

"Damn! That was a lot harder than I thought it would be!"

"You did just fine, Mr. Collins. We'll do this every day until you can pull yourself up without any difficulty at all."

Pete hadn't been in anything but a prone position for days and days, although he wasn't cognizant of exactly how long it had been. His body knew, and much like a sailor who comes off a ship onto dry land after being at sea for a while, Pete's sense of equilibrium had been disturbed. He felt dizzy and weak. He wanted to be able to sit upright, but he couldn't do it.

"The next thing we're going to do is to start working on transferring you from your bed to a wheelchair."

"I'm not sure I'm ready for that," Pete offered.

"You don't have to do much of anything just yet, but you will soon enough," Joy said.

At that, an assistant rolled a gurney up next to Pete's bed, placed a board in between the bed and the gurney, and began pulling on the side of the bed sheet, bringing Pete's body onto the gurney as he did so. Once Pete was centered properly, and fastened in, while lying on his back, he began to raise the back of the gurney ever so slightly to move Pete's head up. In a matter of seconds, Pete began to feel light headed and they lowered him back down.

"That's enough for today. We'll be back later today and try again," Joy said.

"What happened there? I got real dizzy when you did that."

"Pete, you know that arteries take blood from your heart and pump it out to the various parts of your body, right?"

"Yeah, I know that much."

"And veins bring the blood back to the heart, right?"

"Yeah."

"Well, the muscles in your legs are what push the blood back to your heart, but they aren't working like they used to, so blood isn't flowing back to your heart like it is supposed to. Your heart is still pumping good and strong but the circulation of blood through your body isn't what it used to be. It's going to take a while for your body to adjust to that."

"So what's going to happen?"

"In a week or two, you'll be able to transfer yourself from your bed to a wheelchair and your body will adjust, so that's what we're trying to accomplish, to get you to the point where you can sit up in a wheelchair and then we can start to work on other things," Joy said.

Pete thought to himself that it was going to take a while before he would be able to do those things, the way his body felt, and said,

"I can't do any more right now."

"That's enough for now. I'll be back to see you again tomorrow. You did just fine, Mr. Collins. See you tomorrow."

With that, she, together with her assistant, turned Pete over so that he was on his stomach again, un-did the straps to the clam-shell and prepared to leave.

"Say, can you do something about this thing around my chest? It's hard to breathe. I think I could sit up a lot easier if this wasn't so tight around my chest like it is."

"You can talk to your doctor, or one of the other nurses about that, Mr. Collins. I can't help you with that. It's supposed to be tight, to prevent any movement. I'm afraid you're going to have to get used to that. You won't want to do anything without that on you for a while, I'm afraid. You'll be okay with it off while you're in your bed, but whenever you start moving around, you want that on you."

"How long am I going to be in this thing?"

"For as long as it takes. When you're body is ready, we'll take it off, I'm sure."

Pete thought to himself how weak and pathetic he'd become. Less than a few weeks earlier, he would have climbed any mountain, swam in any sea and jumped from the highest of heights with the best. He had been fearless. Now, he was exhausted after trying to sit up for less than a minute. He lapsed into a drug induced sleep.

When he awoke, a nurse was standing next to him, examining his arm. Several minutes later, a doctor came into the room, examined him and wrote something on a clip board he was holding. Moments later, a tube running into his arm was taken out, but the receptacle for the tube was left in his arm. After the doctor had left, he asked the nurse what that was about.

"You're allergic to morphine. The doctor changed the script to add demerol and take you off the morphine, that's all."

"That's all? Isn't that something serious?"

"It could be, but you're in a hospital and it's our job to notice such things. At the first sign of trouble, we made the change. You're fine, Mr. Collins."

Pete couldn't turn his head to read her name tag, but she had a pleasant voice, so he asked for her name.

"I'm Amy. I'm your day-time nurse. You've got me from 7 to 3. After that, it's Anne from 3 to 11 and then the late night shift, which is from 11 to 3, and you've got Kristen. Now you be careful with her! That girl is a wild child, you hear!

It made Pete chuckle to hear her talk, even though there was absolutely nothing he could do to get in any trouble with anyone.

"Thanks for the warning," he replied.

"I've got to check on your buddies in here, but I'll be keeping an eye on you, Mr. Collins. Don't you worry about that. I'll be watching you."

"Pete. Please call me Pete. Okay, Amy?"

"We're not supposed to be too friendly with our patients, but I guess I can do that…when nobody's watching. Now don't you go tellin' nobody when I do, you hear?"

"I hear. Say, before you leave, tell me who else is in here with me. What are their names?" Pete whispered.

Amy leaned down and put her mouth next to his ear and whispered back, "You've got Greg over in the corner to your left, which is the southeast corner of the room. Jeffrey is occupying the southwest corner of the room. Ernesto is in the northeast corner of the room and you have sole possession of the northwest corner."

"How are they doin'? I'm not hearin' much out of any of them."

"They're feeling about like you're feeling, Pete. I think you will all feel better when you can introduce yourselves to each other."

"I hope that day comes real soon."

"So do they, Pete. So do they. I've got to go now, but I'm pleased to make your acquaintance."

"Say, one last thing. Is my mother still here?"

"No, she left just before you woke up. She asked me to tell you that she'd be back in an hour. She had to go to the store to get something. I think she finished her book and went to get another one. She sits right beside you all day long and reads. You're a lucky man to have a mother like that."

"Yeah, I am, although I'm not feelin' too lucky these days."

"Count your blessings, young man. Your buddies in here weren't quite as lucky as you were," she whispered as she put her hand on his shoulder and tapped him lightly a few times. He didn't say anything in response and thought to himself what that must be like. He didn't think it could get any worse, but maybe he was lucky it wasn't worse.

Later, when his mother returned, they spoke for hours until it was time for her to go. They let her stay in the hospital, by his side, from 8 in the morning until 8 at night, but they made her leave after that. The hospital grew quiet then, with the only sound being that of nurses' rubber-soled shoes squeaking down the halls, or the slow, steady rolling of the wheels of carts.

9
Roommates

IN THE WEE HOURS of the morning, when any sound, no matter if it was at the far end of the hall, seemed to resonate, as Pete lay quietly in his bed unable to sleep, he thought to see if anyone else was awake, too. He whispered,

"Greg, can you hear me?"

There was no response.

"How about you, Jeffrey? You awake?"

Again, no response.

"Ernesto! You there, man?"

He heard a soft, barely audible reply,

"Si, soy aqui. I am here," he said in broken English.

"Hola, amigo. Me llamo Pedro."

"Hola, Pedro."

"Yo no hablo espanol muy bien, amigo, pero espero que tu vas bien."

"Gracias, Pedro, y usted tambien."

At that, another soft voice was heard,

"What the hell did you just say to him?"

"I told him I don't speak Spanish too well but I hope he's doin' alright," Pete responded. "Who are you, Jeffrey or Greg?"

"Jeffrey here. How you doin', Pedro," he said with a strong Southern drawl.

"You from Georgia, Jeffrey?"

"Lucky guess."

"Call me Pete. I'm from Florida by way of Glacier, or the other way around."

"You ain't a 'Gator, are ya?"

"Hell if I ain't."

"Damn! If that don't beat all. Here I am laid up in the State of Washington, as far away from Florida as I can be, can't move and just when I think things couldn't get much worse, they do. Now I'm stuck with a damn 'Gator!"

"Just don't start barkin' at me, Jeffrey. I can't take it right now, man."

"I hear ya, brother. How'd it happen?"

"Fell off a horse and it landed on me. You?"

"Motorcycle."

"How 'bout you, Ernesto. Comprende'?"

"No hablo ingles, amigos."

"He fell off a truck and landed wrong. He was standin' on the back of a pick-up truck comin' back from a day in the fields, pickin' vegetables from what I heard. Supposedly 'bout ten of 'em were standin' on the bumper when it hit a bump."

"How about Greg?"

"I'm here, but I don't feel like talkin' right now. Maybe tomorrow." came a soft, barely audible reply.

"Yeah, me neither, but we'll talk later. I'm not goin' anyplace for a long time from what they tell me. G'night, guys. Buenos noches, Ernesto."

Nobody responded, but Pete knew he wasn't alone. There were others in the same boat he was. Tomorrow he'd try to sit up long enough to see what his new friends looked like. He didn't know it, but all three of them were quadriplegics, or quads. Their injuries were at the level of their cervical spines and they faced challenges far more difficult than those which awaited Pete.

* * * * * * * * * *

The next day arrived in much the same fashion as the days before. If his eyes were open, he knew he was awake. The 'clam shell' around his chest which restricted any movement in his upper body, other than his arms, was taken off at night and while he was in his bed, but put back on during the day or whenever he was to be rolled over, which was not too often or for too long. It extended from the base of his skull to the area of his hips. Pete had no ability to move his legs and his head was locked into a fixed position, not allowing him to turn it to his left or his right. He could see only straight below and as far as his peripheral vision would allow him to.

He was eating regular meals, though since he wasn't sitting up yet, it wasn't easy. He had been fed intravenously for the first few days and when there were sounds and signs that his bowels were functioning again, they had allowed him to begin to eat solid foods. The catheter that was inserted in him during surgery remained in place and allowed his bladder to function at somewhat regular intervals. His body continued to be plied with pain killers and antibiotics.

He was still in a state of denial and remained optimistic that a miracle would still occur, despite whatever the odds were against him. His brain and his thought processes had not been otherwise damaged in the accident and the resulting consequences. He continually ran through how to deal with his changed circumstances and what options he had. He wasn't bored, even though he had little to do. His mind raced continuously, thinking that it was a bad dream and he would wake up and be alright. It was more like a bell sounding in his head, like a fire-drill, that wouldn't go off. It was more like being in a constant state of panic. But for the continuous presence of his mother, and her constant assurances that things would get better, morbidity could have taken root.

Not long after the day shift had arrived, Joy, the rehabilitation therapist, appeared at his side, ready to begin the daily exercise regimen.

"Good morning, Mr. Collins, and how are you today?" She asked cheerily.

"I'm not sure how you expect me to respond."

"Let's go with 'Fine, thanks,' that always works for me."

When Pete didn't say anything, she continued,

"Are you ready to break the record you set yesterday?"

"What is the record?" he asked gloomily.

"I have it officially recorded as 7 seconds."

Pete thought to himself that he would do everything he could to get from where he was to whatever the next step would be and he mustered a response of "I'll do my best."

"That's all I can ask of you," she said as an assistant again inserted the apparatus which was Pete's exercise bar. The 'clam shell' was put back on Pete after the Rolo-bed was turned off.

When all was ready, again Pete struggled to pull himself to an upright position. What had previously been an unconscious, almost reflex type action, had become a monumental chore.

"Damn, I can't believe how hard this is!" he exclaimed through gritted teeth. He pulled himself upright and then had to hold tight to keep himself there as the weight of his torso would have otherwise caused him to fall back to a supine position. It was like lifting weights used to be, except now he was the weight.

After he had tried, and failed, Joy and her assistant moved the gurney next to Pete's bed and placed the transfer board between the two. Again they pulled on the bed sheet and moved Pete onto the gurney. Again they raised the back of the gurney to bring Pete's head up.

Once he was up to a 45 degree position, he was able to look around and see the assistant standing in front of him, at the foot of his bed, another man lying in a bed with tubes and wires and an assortment of contraptions in front of him. He was able to move his eyes to his left and see a second man lying in a bed, and out of the corner of his eye he saw the third bed. All three men, whose faces he couldn't see, had large, circular objects around their heads. He was held in that position until he began to get dizzy again and they immediately lowered him back down.

"Very good, Mr. Collins. Tell us when you start to feel light-headed and we'll lower you down. We don't want any abrupt movements and we would prefer that you not lose consciousness."

"You would prefer that I not lose consciousness? What do you mean by that?"

"We expect that you'll pass out a few times when we do this. It's normal. We try to avoid it, but it happens. We went over this yesterday, Mr. Collins."

"I wasn't paying attention. Now I am. So did I set a new record?"

"You did."

"What was it?"

"I've got you down for 14 seconds on pulling yourself up and you sat up for about six."

"When do you start counting?"

"From the moment you lift off to the moment you set back down."

"I wasn't upright for very long. I know that."

"You did just fine. You'll be sitting up before you know it. We've got to strengthen those arm muscles some. You're doing it all with your arms. You may get a visit from another physical therapist today."

"Another physical therapist? I thought that's what you are. Why do I need two?"

"I'm a physical therapist, too, and we all work together. We have different responsibilities regarding the care we give to our patients. I'm going to help you get yourself out of your bed and into a wheelchair. She's going to help you strengthen your body and help you to be as healthy as you can. She works more with your general strengthening. I work more with your mobility and transfers."

"At this rate, I'll be out of here sometime next century."

"The protocol is for you to be out of here in six months, you know that, don't you?"

"Six months!"

"Yes. Dr. Johnson hasn't explained that to you yet?"

"No, he hasn't. I'm going to be out of here before then. I promise you."

"You're going to make progress every day, and when you're ready, you're ready. Not a moment too soon. We aren't going to rush things. You're body is still in a very fragile condition. That shell you are wearing is protecting you from further injury. We have to be very careful. That's why we have James here with us, in case anything should go wrong."

"James?"

"That's our assistant here."

"Good morning, James."

"Good morning, Mr. Collins," he replied. It was the first time Pete had heard him speak.

"We'll be back to see you tomorrow, Mr. Collins. That's all for today. I've got to see some other patients."

"Are you working with Greg, Jeffrey and Ernesto, too?"

"No, I'm not. Another physical therapist is working with them," she said as she departed somewhat hastily.

Pete's mother was in the room, in her chair by the window, watching it all happen.

"You're making progress, Peter. That's a good thing."

"What did I get to? Fourteen seconds?"

"One day at a time, Peter."

"So now I sit and wait twenty four hours until I do that again? This is bullshit. I'm goin' crazy inside my brain. I can't take this too long. This is no way to live, Mom."

"Count your blessings, son. Let's say a rosary together."

"No, Mom. I won't. I'm not ready to talk to God right now."

"Then I'll say one for you."

"Do it later, okay, Mom? Not now, please."

"What would you like to talk about? Want me to read the sports page to you or anything?"

"No, I don't want to know how the damn Seahawks are doin', but thanks, Mom. I'm sorry, I'm just not dealing with this too well right now."

"I'll leave you alone for now. When you feel like it, we'll talk. How's that?"

"Thanks, Mom. I'd like that."

Later that morning, another woman came up to Pete's bed and introduced herself. Pete had his eyes closed and was half-awake, thinking of where he'd be if he weren't where he was.

"Good morning, Mr. Collins. My name is Chelsea Pisano, and I'm here to talk to you about how you're doing with things."

Pete opened his eyes and turned them to his left to see who it was that was speaking to him. He saw a woman in her late thirties, with large, thick, black-rimmed glasses and brown hair pulled straight back and tied in a bow behind her head, though all he could see was the yellow from the bow. She was thin and dressed in white garb, but more like that of a doctor than a nurse, so he asked,

"And what are you? A nurse? A doctor? A specialist?

She had caught him at a bad time.

"Actually, I'm a psychologist. My job is to check on patients to see how their coping with things, but I don't stick needles into people or draw blood or anything like that. I'm just here to talk to you, that's all," she said, in a professional manner.

"So what do you want to talk about, Miss…Pisano, is it? What should I call you?"

"Mrs. Pisano will be fine. Just tell me how things are going. You're going to be here for a while and I'll be checking up on you every so often. I just like to meet my patients as soon as I can after they arrive and establish a rapport as quickly as I can."

"Well, then, Mrs. Pisano, thank you for coming to see me. Things are just peachy-keen here in the spinal cord unit. Me and my buddies are doin' just fine."

"Peter!" his mother said, softly but firmly. "She's here to help. Be nice."

"I know this is very difficult for you, Mr. Collins, and…"

"With all due respect, ma'am, you have no idea of what I'm goin' through. You may think you do, and you may have talked to a hundred guys like me, but until you lie here in this damn coffin, not bein' able to…"

"Peter! That's enough!" his mother scolded, coming to his side and holding his hand.

"Maybe this isn't a good time, Mrs. Pisano," she offered.

"I'll come back later, Mr. Collins."

"Right! I may not be here, though. I was thinking of going out for a few beers later with my buddies here. Maybe you could join us…"

Mrs. Pisano turned and walked away without saying another word.

"Now, what was that all about, Peter?"

"She just caught me at the wrong time, Mom. I'm sorry. I can't pretend that this is something other than what it is. You can sugar-coat it all you want, but I'm in hell."

Not long after Mrs. Pisano left, a nurse came to Pete's bed and put a tube in his arm. Unbeknownst to Pete or his mother, she had included an anti-depressant medication in the cocktails that were being fed to him.

Late that afternoon, not long before it was time for Florence to leave, Dr. Johnson came into the room. Pete couldn't see him, but his mother did, and she stood to greet him as soon as he walked through the door.

"Good afternoon, Dr. Johnson. How nice to see you."

"Good afternoon, Mrs. Collins. How's your boy doing?"

"He's not having a good day today, but the nurses say he's doing as well as can be. I think he needs some cheering up."

"I wish I had a pill for that and I'd give a few to all of my patients, but I don't. I'm here to talk to Peter for a few minutes. You're welcome to listen in if you'd like."

"I would."

At that, Dr. Johnson turned his attention to Pete and said,

"And how are you doing today, Pete?"

"I've been better, Doc."

"I'm sure you have, and you're going to get better every day. Keep that in mind. It's been several days since we put those rods in your back and I came by to check on you," he said as he took the clip-board which hung from a bed post and examined it. He then stuck his face directly next to Pete's, less than a foot away, and began talking;

"From what I can see, things are going pretty well."

"How can you tell, Doc?"

"Fluid levels, plus the various films, nurse's notes, things like that."

"How long am I going to have to lay on my stomach, Doc?"

"It's going to be a while longer, Pete. I can't say for sure just how long, but not until the wound has healed completely and you can put extended pressure on the site."

"Am I going to have to wear this shell for very long? I itch so bad when I'm inside this thing I wish I could scratch for about a week, I think."

"I'm sure it's uncomfortable, Pete. I've never had a patient who said it wasn't, but let me explain what we did to you. I put two long titanium rods into your back to stabilize it. I took bone from your hips and grafted it near the site of the injury."

"You put some new bones in my back?"

"Bone shavings, actually, and mixed them with some things to make a pasty kind of substance, and put that alongside the bones in your back."

"Really? What's that supposed to do?"

"Think of your back as a garden. We planted something back there and it's got to grow. If we dig up that soil or disturb the root system we're trying to develop, that could prevent it from happening. If it does, I'll have to go in and try to do it again, and you don't want that."

"How long is it going to take for this thing to grow?"

"About six months."

"Six months! Are you kidding? I've got to sit here like this for six months! Just shoot me now! I can't do that, Doc!"

"Yes you can, and you will, but please don't misunderstand what I've said. If that plant doesn't take root, I have to operate on you again, and that means taking out the old seeds, which means the bones I took from your hip, and putting down new seeds, or new bones, and then we'd have to wait another six months to see if it takes. Do you understand me?"

"Yes sir. I do," Pete responded. Dr. Johnson had succeeded in getting his complete attention. He asked, "How often is this successful, or how often does it fail?"

"It works most of the time, but I've had patients who had to undergo that surgery as many as three times. For some, it never takes, so you say your prayers and let's hope that this works. I don't want to have to operate on you again, okay?"

"What do I have to do?"

"Just follow the instructions your nurses give you and pray. There's not much else you can do. It's up to a higher power than me. I've done all I can, based on the most modern technology and knowledge available to us on the planet, but now we just have to wait and see."

"And that means we wait for six months? I'll have to be in this thing all that time?"

"No, you won't."

"Thank God!"

"Not while you're in bed and lying down, but whenever you sit up and move around, you'll have this on, at least for the next six months and maybe longer."

"So it can come off while I'm sitting up?"

"That's right, but not for a while."

"Damn! How long will that be?"

"I don't know right now, but I won't take it off until I'm sure that it wouldn't hurt you to do so. Let me explain it to you like this…your backbone, if you will, which is comprised of a series of vertebrae with discs in between them, was broken, basically, and we're trying to put it back together. It's like splicing a board together after it's been broken in half. Ever do construction work, or carpentry?"

"No, I was always out on the water, fishing or rafting, things like that."

"Well picture a four foot long two by four board cut in half. What carpenters will sometimes do is take another two by four, say a foot or so long, and put it on either side of where the break occurred. They put nails in both sides of the broken board and through the smaller piece, which they call a splice. That's what we're doing with your back. I've put some bone along side where the break occurred and we're splicing it back together, and don't forget the rods that Dr. Depperman put in there, too. Does that make sense?"

"I get the picture."

"But if that splice doesn't hold, what happens?"

"The boards fall apart."

"That's right, and that's exactly what we don't want to have happen to you."

"Amen to that."

"Alright. I'm not good at small talk, Pete. I see too many sad, unfortunate situations and I get new ones every day. Maybe that's why I didn't become a gynecologist or family physician, I don't have good bedside manners, or at least that's what my wife tells me," he said with a laugh.

"I'm only kidding, Pete, but I tell it like it is. I think you want that. I'll leave it to others to put the icing on the cake, so to speak, but I'm the one who has to deal with the here and now."

"So when do you think I can get this off me, even for a little while at a time, when I'm sitting up?"

"It's going to be several weeks, maybe as long as two months. You don't want to hurry this, Pete. You can hurry other parts of the healing process, but not this part. We've got to let that bone meld into and connect with the remaining bones in your back. That's not something that can be rushed. The conditions for growing have to be perfect. Inside that cocoon of yours, the conditions are as perfect as we can make them. We're watering it every day and doing everything we can to help it grow…growth hormones and the rest. You've got to trust me to do my job well and I've got to count on you to be the best patient you can be. If not, it won't work. Understood?"

"I understand, Doc."

"Good. I'm sorry I can't stay long to chat. I'm late for dinner as it is, but my wife is used to that by now, and I wanted to talk to you before I left today. You take good care of yourself, Pete, and hope for the best."

"I guess it could be worse, couldn't it, Doc?" Pete said, to which the Doctor responded by looking him straight in the eye, eyeball to eyeball, and said,

"You'd better believe that, son. God bless you."

With that, he stepped back from the bed, placed the clip-board back onto its peg on the bedpost, and turned to leave, and as he did he turned to say,

"And Pete, take it easy on my staff. They're just doing the job I've asked them to do, okay? I don't want to see you on any of these psycho-tropic drugs for any longer than necessary. They can cause more trouble than they're worth. Good night, Mrs. Collins."

When he had left the room, Florence returned to Pete's side, held his hand and said,

"He's one of the best in the world, you know."

"I hope so, Mom. I need all the help I can get right now."

"It's time for me to go. I'll see you in the morning."

She leaned over and kissed him on the back of his head, as she did repeatedly throughout the day. She then gathered her belongings and left, to return to her solitary confinement at the cottage. Since it was now early November, the days were growing shorter, but there was still enough daylight for her to be able to stop and rest in the park next to the hospital before retiring for the night in her cottage. She would later call her husband and the rest of her children to say hello and report the events of the day.

That night, in the wee hours of the morning, as Pete lay awake, unable to sleep, he heard a voice,

"I liked what you said to that damn psycho lady today, Collins."

"Who's that? Is that you, Jeffrey?"

"No, it's me, Greg."

"Greg, how are you doin', man?"

"Not as good as you."

Pete could barely hear him. His voice seemed so soft and youthful.

"Really? What happened to you?"

"I dove off of this little cliff into a big lake, to impress my girl friend and all my friends, and hit a rock or something below the surface."

"How long ago did that happen?"

"I've been here a month."

"Damn, man! I'm sorry to hear it. How old are you, if you don't mind my askin'?"

"Eighteen. I had just graduated high school and was about to go off to college…I guess I got a little too wild too soon."

Pete didn't know what to say. He knew that there was nothing anyone could say to him to make him feel better, so he didn't try. He just said,

"I fell off a horse and the horse landed on me. It was a beautiful day and a great ride, but in a split second it was over and so was my life as I knew it."

"I know what you mean, man."

"Where are your folks, Greg?"

"Wyoming."

"They can't be here with you?"

"I'm the oldest. I've got two brothers and a sister younger than me. They both work and they gotta take care of them. They've been here a couple of times. It's a long drive and it's too expensive for them to fly. They said they'd be back over Thanksgiving if they could."

The kid sounded like he didn't have a friend in the world. It gave Pete a jolt. He had his mother at his side and the support of his entire family. He'd had an opportunity to travel, go to Alaska, feel the thunder of rivers in the springtime, as the melting snow flooded them with millions and millions of gallons of water, to know what it felt like to make love to a woman, and to know what it was like to be in love. He thought of Abigail and how much he missed being with her, laying by her side, making love to her, and then he thought of Greg, who'd probably never known any of that and never would. It brought a tear to his eye. Then Greg said,

"Yeah, what you said to her is what I want to tell her, but I can't. I just answer her questions. I hate it when she comes around."

"Take it easy over there, kid," Jeffrey chimed in. "We're gonna be ridin' motorcycles in no time. I told you about them bikes that have a side car that'll hold you just right. You're gonna be ridin' down a road through the mountains, beautiful prairies, flowers comin' up…all that. You just wait and see."

"How you doin', Jeffrey?" Pete asked.

"I wish I could say 'better than you are, you damn 'Gator, but I can't. I heard what Doc Johnson told you. He had a conversation about like that with me a while back, 'cept I don't have no garden growin' in my back like you do."

"I'm havin' a hard time thinkin' of myself as bein' lucky, Jeffrey, but talkin' to the two of you sure makes me think that way…and then there's Ernesto. He doesn't even have anyone to talk to. Ernesto! Como estas, amigo?"

"Bien, gracias," came the reply. "Y tu?"

"Bien, gracias, amigo. Ernesto, por favor, digame en espanol y yo hablo ingles con usted, si?"

"Si. Yo me gusto, pero no ahora."

"Si, no ahora."

"Now what did you say?" Jeffrey asked.

"I just told him that I'd try to teach him to speak English and he could try to teach me some Spanish, that's all."

"It sounds to me like you do pretty good with that stuff. I don't know much more than 'si' and 'cerveza', plus 'cuantos dinero', and 'mama, sita',too, though that don't do me much good in here."

"Mama sita…yeah, I know that one, too, and cuantos dinero… I know all those…but then I just hand them the money and they give me change."

"Maybe you could learn a little Spanish, Jeffrey."

"I doubt it."

"We'll see. Say, tell me, what's that thing you guys have around your heads?"

"You saw that?" Jeffrey asked.

"I sat up for about ten seconds and got a look. I wasn't sure what I saw."

There was a pause, then Jeffrey spoke,

"That there is what they call a 'halo', though there ain't nothin' angelic about it. They've got to keep our heads straight, not lettin' 'em move a little bit, so they put three bolts in your skull so that…"

"Four," Greg injected.

"You got four in your head, Greg?"

"Yeah."

"They put three or four bolts in your head so your head and your shoulders turn together and they secure that thing as tightly as they can without killin' ya, right guys?"

"That's right," Greg responded. Ernesto didn't say anything, because he couldn't understand what was being said, but he made a sound of some kind, like he did.

"And we wear those fuckin' things all day long and all night long, too."

"Mmmm. Sounds painful," Pete offered.

"It is," Jeffrey responded.

"I wear a clam shell that keeps the weight of my head off of my neck."

"Yeah, you got a broken back and we've got broken necks." Jeff said in a deep, gruff voice.

Nobody spoke for several minutes. Pete pondered the fact that his three roommates had it much worse than he did. He thought of what Jeffrey had said to Greg about goin' riding on a motorcycle. That was a nice thing to do, even if it wasn't true. Then he thought to himself that was something he could do, too.

"Hey, Jeffrey."

"Don't be callin' me Jeffrey no more, alright? That's what my mom used to call me when she was really pissed at me. Call me Jeff. Whaddya want."

"You got a side car for me, too?"

"Hell, yeah. I got lots of friends out there who'll be more than willin' to take all of us for a ride."

"Count me in."

"Yeah, you hold that thought, man. You're alright, even if you are a damn 'Gator."

"You, too, man."

"That's the only thing that keeps me alive, man. I'da pulled these damn plugs off of me a long time ago if it weren't for that. That's the only thing that keeps me alive…the hope of riding again, even if it is in a sidecar."

Nobody spoke any more that night, each with their own thoughts. Pete drifted back to sleep, to be awakened by the changing of the guard and the day shift.

10

A New Best Friend

THE NEW DAY ARRIVED with a start for Pete as the sounds of several orderlies bustling about the room, talking somewhat louder than usual awoke him. He couldn't see what was happening, but he could hear that things were being moved. Gurneys were constantly being moved around all during the day, but not at this hour, at least not on any of the other days since he'd arrived. He lay awake, unable to go back to sleep. After a while, the day shift came on and Amy was chirping at him.

"And how are you this morning, Pete?"

"I'm still here."

"And thank God for that. We have another day to live on this earth."

"What's good about it?"

She leaned over and whispered,

"Better than a dirt sandwich, isn't it?"

"Say, you're not supposed to talk to patients like that, are you?"

"Well is it?"

"Right now, any sandwich would be good, I think, especially if I could have a beer with it. Do you know if they let patients drink beer in this hospital?"

"Not that I know of, and you're not getting out of here until you can sit up, that much is for sure."

"Damn! Who'd have thought that sitting up would be the biggest challenge in my life…"

She leaned over again and said,

"Remember what I told you about your roommates."

"Say, Amy, what was that noise all about this morning? What was that all about?"

"You lost one of your roommates."

"Which one?"

"Mr. Morales."

"You mean Ernesto?"

"Yes."

"What happened to him?"

"Now you didn't hear this from me, but he wasn't legally in the United States so when he became stable enough to be moved, he was transported back to where he came from."

"Where was that? Mexico?"

"I've already said too much. I've got to be on my way, Mr. Collins, but I pray that you have as nice a day as you possibly can under the circumstances."

Amy was the nicest nurse he had. All through the day, various nurses and doctors would pass by his bed, read the chart and move on, without saying a word. Amy was the friendliest of them all. Although his disposition and mood didn't match his words, he managed to muster an "I'll do my best" in response.

"That's better! I'll be by to check on you later. I've got my rounds to do for now," and off she went.

There was no telling what fate awaited Ernesto in Mexico or Guatemala, San Salvador or who knows where he came from, Pete thought to himself. He figured that they were in one of the best facilities in the United States where they were, and probably one of the best in the world. No matter where Ernesto was going, it would have to be worse than where he'd been.

An hour later, Joy arrived with James and the apparatus. He managed to raise himself up and hold himself up for over thirty seconds. Although it didn't seem like much, Pete felt that he had made progress and Joy praised him for his efforts. She told him that he would be rewarded for his accomplishment. He was able to sit in the chair for a full minute. It depressed him to think that he would have to wait another twenty four hours before trying again, but later that morning, Joy returned with the two orderlies, who transferred him onto the gurney, but didn't raise it up.

"What's up?" He asked.

"We're taking you for a ride. Just lie still."

"That's all I can do."

"Well, don't blink then."

"What are you doing?"

"We're taking you for a ride, like I said."

With that, once Pete was firmly secured to the gurney, with Joy by his side, a hand on his arm as the two orderlies carefully pushed the gurney out of the room and into the hallway.

"Where am I going?"

"Dr. Johnson wants to get you into a wheelchair as quickly as possible. He'd like to see you sitting up even if you aren't able to bring yourself to a sitting position by yourself just yet. We're going down to get you fitted for a chair that will best accommodate you."

"You can't do that here?"

"We're going to make a stop along the way. He also wants to see some films of your back."

"Can I come along? Florence asked.

"Afraid not, Mrs. Collins."

"How long will you be gone?"

"About an hour."

"I'll go run some errands then. See you in an hour, Sweetie."

"Mom! Please!"

Pete didn't have to do much along the way as he was shuffled from one room to another. Joy was no longer at his side, but James stayed with him.

Pete was surprised how uncomfortable he felt inside the long tube into which he was pushed for the MRI, or magnetic resonance imaging test. The top of the chamber was only inches from his nose. It made him feel claustrophobic, and being unable to move made it worse. The test lasted over half an hour. He felt a sense of relief when it was over.

"Where to now, James?"

"Back to see Miss Joy," he said. "You're gonna get to meet your new best friend."

"Who's that?"

"It's not a who, it's an it."

"A wheelchair?"

"That's right."

"My new best friend?"

"This will be your lifeline to the world from now on. It will be like your right arm."

Pete hadn't fully accepted the fact that he would be in a wheelchair for the rest of his life. The thought sent shivers through him. He had been an adventurer, an idealist, one who would take any chance, run any risk, chase any dream, accept any challenge, but now the harsh realities of his life were falling down upon him like the weight of a cascading waterfall, pushing him to the bottom of a rapid. Now, sitting up for more than a minute was his biggest challenge. Sitting in a wheelchair for the rest of his life wasn't on the radar screen.

He just lay there while Joy and others measured his torso, measured the length of his legs, his outer leg, his inner leg, the width of his hips, weighed him and took all kinds of measurements. At one point, Joy asked Pete what color seat he'd like for his chair.

"What color? Black, what else?"

"To match your mood, I'm guessing?"

"You got that right."

"We'll do our best to change that, Mr. Collins, but for now black it will be. This is only a temporary chair. You'll go through a few before you leave here, but when you do, you'll have a permanent chair that will be a constant companion for you, wherever you go."

The thought of being physically able to leave the hospital hadn't entered his mind, though the thought of getting away never left his mind. He knew that there was no way he could do anything or go anywhere in the condition he was now in. Dr. Johnson had told him it would take six months for the bones in his back to meld together, if all went well. He figured he was going to be in the hospital for at least six months.

"I guess that's going to be about six months from now, right?"

"Not if I do my job well. I hope to have you in your chair and mobile long before that."

"Really?"

"Really."

"Like when? How soon?" Pete felt a ray of optimism shoot into his brain, one of the first in a while.

"I'm not going to give you any timetable, as it depends entirely on you, but the sooner we can get you into a wheelchair and the sooner you learn how to use one, the sooner it will be. How's that?"

"I'll do the best I can."

"That's all we can ask. That's all you can do."

When all the tests were taken and all the measurements made, he was wheeled back into his room, transferred back into his bed, and left alone. He was surprised at how tired he was, even though he hadn't done anything at all. He fell asleep.

He awoke to the sounds of people bustling about his bed and a new voice.

"Mr. Collins? Are you awake?"

"I am now."

"I'm Nancy. I'm a physical therapist and I'm here to help you."

"No offense, Nancy, but I've got a physical therapist. In fact, I've got two, I think."

"We all work together and we do different things. My job is to help with your muscle strength and your general physical condition."

"Great. What are you gonna do for me? Wanna go for a run?"

"No, no running today."

"Swim? Let's go swimming."

"Actually, I see no reason why you won't be able to go swimming after a while, but not today."

"So what are we going to do, Nancy?"

"We're going to work on your arms. You've got to have strength in your hands, your fingers, your forearm, your biceps and triceps…we can work on all those right now."

"I've never been one to have any problem with that before. Why do I need to do that now?"

"Because we can't allow those muscles to atrophy. The better shape you are in, the sooner you're going to get out of here, and I know that's what you want, right?"

"Nancy, how old are you?"

"I'm 26. Why do you ask?"

"I'm 23. I played football in high school, wrestled, lifted weights for years…I don't need to work on any of that right now."

"Of course you do! You've got to keep yourself in the best shape you can, no matter what problems you've got and I know you've got a lot to deal with right now."

"Nancy, I'm not ready for that right now."

"Mr. Collins, we work as a team on every case…the doctors, the nurses, the orderlies, the rehab specialists, the psychologists and others. I'm just part of the team. My job is to help you with your muscles and your functioning level."

"I appreciate that. I really do, but I'm not ready for it right now, Nancy."

"Well I can't make you do anything that you don't want to do, Mr. Collins, but…"

"Thank you, Nancy. I appreciate that, and I'll do whatever you ask of me if it means getting out of here any sooner, but I'm just not ready to do calisthenics or lift weights."

"But…"

"You can check with me later, like next week or something, but I'm not ready for that."

"Alright, Mr. Collins, but I will be back to see you again."

"Thank you, Nancy."

Nancy left, not happy that she was unable to coax Pete into compliance with her requests. Before he drifted too far down the path of despair, after she had left the room, his mother began a new conversation. About the only thing Pete wanted to hear was all about his brothers and sisters and their families. She would share with him all the news she had gathered the night before. She thought to herself that he must be bored with nothing to do all day, staring at the floor below. She wondered what she could do to make the situation better. She'd talk to Anthony about it later.

That night, when the room was completely dark, with only a few night lights and emergency lights providing illumination to the room, it was Jeffrey who broke the ice,

"Too bad about Ernesto, huh, Pedro?"

"Yeah…"

"I'll tell you what, homeboy, before I got hurt, I'da said send him back with a shoe planted firmly up his ass, but I don't feel that way no more."

"Makes you see things a little different, don't it?"

"Yeah, and the same thing on that stem cell research shit."

"I don't know much about it. I wasn't all that good in science."

"Well, the science is there, homeboy, and they are your best chance of walkin' again, I'm guessin'. I know it's my best chance and the best chance ole Greg has, too. You with us, compadre?"

"I'm here," Greg replied meekly.

"But it's all political now. The damn religious right, or the Evangelical right, as they call themselves, says that the doctors are playin' God 'cause they're clonin' sheep today and the next thing you know, they'll be clonin' humans, so they say."

"I'm not down with you on that one, Jeffrey. I have to go along with them on that one. I think they're doin' stuff with that without having any real good idea of what might happen. They could fuck up a whole lot of people and say it's all in the name of science…I don't agree with that shit."

"You don't agree with that shit? Are you crazy? That's not only our best chance of ever walkin' again…it's our only chance. Now don't get me wrong, like I said, before I got hurt, I saw things differently, but now, it's you and me and Greg over there that all them politicians are talkin' about. Come get me boys! I'll be your guinea pig right now! And you lay there another month or two and you will be, too, homeboy."

"I don't know about that, man, I really don't."

"Don't be lettin' religion get in the way of what you're thinkin', Pedro. I hear your mother over there sayin' her prayers and all, and you're lucky to have her, don't get me wrong, but that kind of thinkin' ain't doin' me no good. You get my drift?"

"I hear ya, but I feel pretty strongly about that…"

"Oh, bullshit, man! You're a fuckin' cripple! You wanna stay crippled your whole life? Maybe you ain't hearin' me or maybe you ain't been crippled long enough to accept the fact that you're gonna be laid up for the rest of your life, man! You, and me and Greg gotta be the ones in favor of that research. If we're not, who will be?"

"Shit, man! Don't get yourself worked up over it! You're liable to fall outa bed."

"I know, but it really is our only chance, man. I don't wanna be this way the rest of my life…"

"How about you, Greg? What do you think?" Pete asked.

"If I gotta be the way I am for the rest of my life, I want to die right now. That's what I think."

There was a long pause in the conversation as both of the other two men considered what Greg had said. Both had undoubtedly had the same thought on many occasions. Then Jeff said, in a low, gravely voice,

"I ain't there yet, Greg, but I hear ya, man. I feel your pain."

There was another long silence, which Pete broke by asking,

"Where do you guys go during the day? Where do they take you?"

"We go swimming." Jeff responded.

"Really?"

"No, not really. They won't let us get near the water. We'd be like flounders, right, Greg? No, we just sit there and try to make things move."

"That's the best part of my day." Greg offered. "It's the only good part of my day."

"Make things move? What are you talking about?"

"Pedro, it's like this…when you're a quad, like me and Greg, you can't move your fingers or your toes nor much of anything else…"

"Not even a little bit?"

"Can you move your toes?"

"No."

"Well, we can't move our fingers or our toes…not even a little bit."

"So how do you make things move?" Pete asked.

"We've still got a little electrical activity in our triceps…"

"In your triceps? You mean in your upper arm, behind your biceps?"

"That's right, our triceps."

"So what do you do?"

"They teach us to use those electrical stimulations from our brains to the triceps to make things move."

"Really?"

"Yeah, really."

"Wow! I had no idea…"

"Neither did we, Pedro. We're learnin' this shit as we go along, right, Greg?"

"Yeah," came a soft reply.

"And you make things move?"

"They put these straps on our arms and on our hands and we've got these pads to make things go. They're teaching us to sit in a wheelchair and make it go, to feed ourselves and to do as much as we can by ourselves."

"Sounds hard, real hard."

"Oh, it's a barrel of laughs, ain't it, Greg?"

There was no response.

"You can thank God that horse didn't break a bone in your neck, Pedro. Your life could be a lot harder," Jeff said in a low whisper.

After allowing that thought to sink into his brain for a few seconds, Pete asked,

"How long you guys been here?

"Greg got here just a few days before you did. I've been here a few days more than that."

"Are you in chairs yet?"

"That's what we're workin' on. We're gonna get stuffed in a big ole chair and make things move with our minds and whatever other parts of our body that still works, if we can. Right, Greg?"

"That's what they tell us."

"Kinda like that pinball wizard the Who sang about…'he's a pinball wizard…deaf, dumb, blind kid…sure plays a mean pinball…' How's that song go? You know, Pedro?"

"No, man. That was before my time. I've heard the song but I don't know the lyrics. How old are you, man?"

"Fifty five and still alive…barely."

"Fifty five! Got a wife and kids and all that?"

"Used to. Don't no more. Let's not go there, man, at least not tonight. Point is, I don't see things the way I used to no more. I wish Ernesto was still here, God bless him. I never did say a word to the man 'cause he didn't speak no English, and I never even laid eyes on him while he was here, but what they did to him, that ain't right."

"I hear ya, man. I guess we'll get a new roommate here before too long."

"Maybe it'll be a woman," Jeff said.

"Naah. You think they'd put a woman in here with us?"

"Why not? What difference would it make?"

"Whew! Let's not go there either, okay, at least not tonight. I don't want to think about that," Pete responded.

"That's enough thinkin' for me for one night. I try not to think any more than I have to…tires me out." Jeff added.

"Yeah, I'm goin' back to sleep, too. G'night, guys."

Pete lay awake, thinking about what Jeff had said. He was going to have to re-think a lot of things. Everything looked different from a horizontal position. He also thought a lot about what Greg had said, too.

11

Trying Too Hard

A FEW DAYS LATER, THE morning came and, much like each of the ones before it, Pete set another record. He was now up to two minutes. Later that morning, Joy came back with two assistants, James and another man who he couldn't see.

"Any rewards for me today, Joy?" Pete asked.

"You're going for another ride."

"Like I did a few days ago?"

"Today is going to be a little different. Ready?"

"No, actually this isn't a convenient time for me. My mother and I were just about to go out and play a game of tennis. Right, Mom?"

"Pete! Be nice."

"Yeah, I'm ready. What else am I doin'?"

"Okay. James, if you will?"

"Who you got helpin' you today, James, my man?"

"Jason is my assistant today, Pete."

"James and Jason. I can remember that easy enough. Let's go guys."

They transferred him to a gurney and out of the room and down the hall they went. This time, no stops for tests and they went straight to the room where he was fitted for a chair.

"So this is my new best friend?"

"For now," Joy responded. "Think of this as if it were a bicycle with training wheels. After a while, we'll take off some things but for now, this is it."

Pete's body was still in a frail and fragile condition, and he was handled delicately. It took the men several minutes to position him in a horizontal position on it. Once he was stabilized and strapped in, Joy said,

"Ready?"

"For what?"

"You'll see. Here we go."

With James on one side and Jason on the other, both having firm grips on the chair, they raised the back of the chair so as to put him in a 45 degree position.

"How does that feel, Pete?"

"Strange, like I never sat up before in my life."

"Want to go up further?"

"No, that's enough for now. Let me just stay like this for a while."

Pete felt dizzy as he sat there. He was uncomfortable, but it was good to see things again from a near vertical position.

"How does it feel? Joy asked.

"Different."

"I mean the width of it, check out the arm rests. Anything seem out of place?" she continued.

"With this damn cast on my body, I can't feel anything, but the arms seem okay. I'll know better when I'm sitting straight up."

"We're trying to fit you to the wheelchair that is going to be built just for you. We want you to tell us what you think, so you can have some input in this."

"What do I know? I don't know one wheelchair from another."

"But does it seem to fit you alright, Pete?"

"I guess."

After a few minutes, he said,

"Put me down. That's enough."

The two men lowered Pete back down. Joy then said,

"That's enough for today. We'll do this every day until you become more comfortable in the chair, Pete. James and Jason will take you back to your room now. I've got to see another patient."

Later that day, Dr. Johnson paid a visit. He startled Pete when he stuck his face right up next to Pete's and began talking. No one else did that, not even his Mom, though she'd lean in to give him a kiss many times a day. Dr. Johnson kept his face there the whole time he talked to Pete.

"Good afternoon, Mr. Collins. How are you doing?"

"You tell me, Doctor. How am I doing?"

"It's way too early to tell, but things are positioned properly and I think you're making progress. I want to see you in a wheelchair as soon as possible. I want you to be able to take care of yourself and out of here as quickly as we can get you there and I'm sure you want that too. Am I right?"

The thought of taking care of himself wasn't something Pete could see happening for a while. He responded by saying,

"I'd like to be able to eat by myself, bathe myself, go to the bathroom by myself…when can I do those things?"

"All in due time, young man. All in due time. In fact, that is what you will be doing very soon, and you are just about ready to begin doing that. Generally speaking, I deal with acute care issues, and by that I mean when patients first arrive. I leave it to others to take care of the rehabilitative process, but you will remain my patient until you are out of the woods, so to speak, because of the transplanted bone matter is concerned. I'll be keeping a close eye on that."

"When can I get out of this shell completely?"

"Ever break a bone, Mr. Collins? Like an arm or a leg?"

"Yeah, I broke both back in school."

"Remember that cast they put on you?"

"Yeah."

"Remember how badly you wanted that thing off and how you would stick screwdrivers and wire coat hangers in there to scratch the area you couldn't touch?"

"Yeah."

"This is a lot like that, except you're not going to be able to scratch anything and the shell doesn't go completely away until you are fully healed, and that's going to be a while."

"This is killin' me."

"I'm sure it is. I can give you something to look forward to, though."

"What's that?"

"After a while, and not for a while, I will allow your nurses to keep it off for longer and longer periods at a time. It will stay on you for at least six months, but you can look forward to being able to have it on you less and less in a few weeks."

"A few weeks…"

"Yes, a few weeks, and Mr. Collins…"

"Yes."

"I see where you aren't cooperating with some of my physical therapists."

"I'm not ready for that, Doc."

"But I think you are."

"I'm not. I'm not ready."

"And you're not cooperating with my counselor, either."

"She caught me on a bad day. She hasn't been back since. I guess I scared her off."

"Someone else will be by to see you tomorrow to get you ready for the outside world. I want you to cooperate with him and with all of my staff members. We're a team and we're trying to help you."

"I'll do the best I can, Doctor Johnson."

"That's all we can ask, and the next time I see you, I hope you're able to sit up. It hurts my back to lean over like this," he said as he stepped back, straightened and turned to leave.

"You do the best you can, Mr. Collins, and so will we."

"Thanks, Doctor Johnson."

He was gone as abruptly as he had arrived.

That night, when all was quiet, once again the three men in the room conversed.

"So tell me about this motorcycle chair you've got for us, Jeff."

"It's just what I said. It's a motorcycle with a side car, like the German officers used to have in World War II. You know what I mean?"

"I know what you mean, and it can be fitted so me and Greg can sit in one?"

"And me, too. Hell, yeah! Why not?"

"I don't know. You got friends that'll do that for you?"

"Yeah. Once you wear the colors, you're family…thicker than family."

"So you wore the colors, eh? Which ones?"

There was a pause, and then Jeff said,

"I don't like to talk about this much in here…some people get the wrong idea, but I was what you call an angel from Hell."

"A Hell's Angel?" Pete asked, somewhat incredulously.

"That's right. San Bernadino."

"Wasn't that one of the oldest and biggest or something? I read something about that once."

"That's right."

"So that's how you got hurt? Riding with your gang?"

"I don't like the word 'gang' there, Pedro. We call ourselves brothers."

"So what happened?"

"We were out ridin' one day, about a hundred of us, and we were doin' the Hell's Canyon Run up near Joseph, Oregon, ever hear of it?"

"Can't say as I have, but that was a long way from San Bernandino. What were you guys doin' up there?"

"That's a pretty well-known ride. It goes from Baker, Oregon to Joseph and then back to Baker. It was supposed to last for a couple of weeks. They call that area the Alps of Oregon. It's named after Chief Joseph. Ever heard of him?"

"Can't say as I have."

"Well, anyway, we're ridin' along one day, in the middle of the day, when some fuckin' trucker comes up behind us. I was the last rider, maybe 50 feet or so behind the rider in front of me. So this asshole pulls up behind me, gets right on my rear wheel and leans on his horn."

"Damn! That must have scared you."

"I saw him comin' in my mirrors, so I knew he was there, but it pissed me off, so I shot him a bird."

"What did he do then?"

"He pushes down on the accelerator and goes to pass, but he clips my rear wheel as he does, sendin' me flyin'."

"Damn!"

"My buddies didn't even know I was missin' for half an hour."

"Did they ever catch the guy?"

"Hell no."

"So you just lay there for half an hour before somebody came to get you?"

"No, another car came along a few minutes later, called the cops and rescue came and got me."

"So what did you do? I mean, what could you do to find the guy?"

"Not a damn thing. Cops went lookin' for the hit-and-run driver, but they never found him, so I couldn't sue nobody. Lost everything I had. I think about that mother-fucker every day."

"Damn!"

"You can say that again."

"How you doin' over there, Greg. Hangin' in there?"

"I'm here," he responded. "Tell me about that sidecar again, Jeff. You sure they're gonna take me, too?"

"I told you they would and they will, my man. My brother is their brother. They're gonna take care of the both of us, Pedro, too, if he wants to come with us. He's not like us, Jeffrey. Hell, he might even be able to ride his own motorcycle, right, Pedro?"

"I don't know about that. I'm trying to sit up for more than two minutes right now."

"Yeah, well, me and Greg over there, we can't do that. Can we, Greg?"

There was no response.

"But they've got hand pedals for you, Pedro. You can drive a car and maybe even a truck for all I know. Maybe you'll take us for a ride, Pedro. How about it?"

"If I can, I will," Pete responded, "but that seems like forever away from somethin' that might actually happen."

"Gotta have a dream, Pedro. Gotta have somethin' to hold onto. Can't let go. Right, Greg?"

"If you say so."

"So you were a Hell's Angel, Jeff."

"I AM a Hell's Angel, Pedro, and proud of it."

"Stay strong, man. Stay strong."

"Amen!"

"You, too, Greg…Greg?"

There was no response.

"G'night guys." Pete lay there in silence, pondering the life that Jeff must have led, before the injury.

* * * * * * * * * *

The next day, Pete awoke with a purpose. He was going to stay up as long as he could. He was ready to get off his back and into a chair. He wanted out of that hospital as soon as possible. Joy and James arrived at their usual time and were surprised by the change in attitude they saw.

"Let's do this thing! I'm ready for you today!"

"Now, don't over do it, Mr. Collins. One step at a time…and baby steps at that. We are not in a hurry."

"I am."

"Well then," she said, after James and another assistant had set up the apparatus and were in their positions, "go for it."

Pete grabbed hold of the bar and pulled himself up, straining as he did. His arms began to quiver, but he grimaced and held on tighter. He wanted off the bed and into a chair, where he could sit up. He gritted his teeth…and then everything went black.

When he woke up, or came to, a doctor was at his side, as were two nurses. He could hear Joy's voice in the background.

"What happened," he asked.

"You blacked out, Mr. Collins."

"How'd that happen?"

"Mr. Collins," he responded, "My name is Dr. Annis, Ned Annis. I just happened to be making my rounds and was the first one to get here when you lost consciousness. There's no problem. You are fine, or as fine as you were before you blacked out. What's going on here is that your circulatory system has changed due to the loss of functioning you now have in your lower extremities. It's going to take your body a while to adjust to the changed circumstances, that's all."

"So this might happen again?"

He put a hand on Pete's forearm and said,

"Yes, it might, and from what I've been told it probably will when you push yourself too far. Be patient with yourself and let your body tell you what you can and can't do. Alright?"

"I'll try."

"Don't push it. These things take time."

"I hear you."

"I've got to get back to what I was doing, but you take good care of yourself, Mr. Collins. Everything is fine." He scribbled something on the chart and left.

When Dr. Annis was gone, Joy stepped back over next to the bed and said,

"You really were determined today, weren't you?"

"How far did I go before I blacked out?"

"You made it to almost a minute, and you were nearly vertical. You made real progress today."

"A new record. So when will I see you again?"

"Tomorrow, but we will pick up the pace and start doing more activities as you are able to do them."

"Great. I'm up for it."

"The pain wasn't too bad?"

"It isn't the pain so much as this damn clam shell. I couldn't quite get vertical with this on me. I was almost there, until I blacked out."

"You'll just have to get used to it, Mr. Collins. You're going to have that on for a long time and you know it. Just go as far as you can and don't try to go too far or you'll pass out like you did today. I've got to go. See you later."

Pete and his mother talked about what was going on and how slow the progress was. Pete's brain was moving fast and his body couldn't keep up. All he could do was lay there and wait for someone, anyone, to come and work with him. After lunch, a stimulus arrived.

12
Re-learning Old Habits

PETE WAS LAYING FACE down on his bed, eyes half-closed, late one afternoon, when his semi-slumber was interrupted by a loud, deep voice,

"Mr. Collins?"

"Yeah," Pete said, as he looked into the mirror on the floor and saw a tall, thin man with long, brown hair and a goatee, standing next to his bed.

"Good afternoon, my name is John Cunningham and I'm a therapist. I'm here to help you."

"John, it's nice to meet you, but I've already got a therapist. In fact, I've got several, don't I?"

"You've got several physical therapists working with you. I'm an occupational therapist."

"So what's the difference?"

"We work together, but I'm going to help you learn basic life skills. I'm going to teach you how to do things. I'll teach you how to take care of yourself when you get out of here."

"So what are you talking about? Job skills?"

"No, you'd think that I'd be teaching you an occupation and how to get a job, but that's not right. I'm talking about things like bathing yourself, cooking and feeding yourself, cleaning up after yourself, dressing yourself…things like that. All the things you'll have to do for yourself on the outside. We don't teach job skills in here. Maybe we should, but we don't. We're trying to get you ready so that you can get out of here as quickly as possible."

"Okay. I'm up for that."

"A vocational rehabilitation specialist has you take tests to determine your aptitude and find out your strengths and weaknesses, and it's possible that you'll see a vocational rehabilitation specialist before you leave, but I'm not sure of that and I don't do that. I am all about teaching you the things you need to know how to do to get out of here. Understood?"

"Yeah, I can understand that."

"Great, but just out of curiosity, what interests you, Pete? What would you like to do once you get yourself in position to leave the hospital and re-enter the outside world?"

"Actually, I've always wanted to be a professional athlete, Mr. Cunningham. Do you think I can still do that?" Pete asked mockingly.

Mr. Cunningham, who was an older gentleman, with a large, round bald spot on the top of his head and a toothy grin, laughed and said,

"I wish you could. I really do, but I don't think that's likely to happen. So tell me, what do you think you might want to do, once you get out of here? Have you thought about that?"

"To be honest, Dr. Cunningham, I never saw myself doing anything but being outside, being in nature, whether it was fishing, guiding raft trips, being a forest ranger. That's all I ever wanted to do. I haven't thought about what I'll do if I can't do that."

Pete's voice quivered a bit and trailed off as he spoke.

Mr. Cunningham took Pete's left hand, put it in between his two hands and said,

"I can only imagine what this must be like for you, Pete…and can I call you Pete?"

"John, can I call you John?"

"Absolutely."

"John, I'm 23 years old. Nobody's ever called me anything but Pete my whole life, so please, call me Pete. When you say Mr. Collins I'm thinkin' that my Dad walked in the room."

"Good. I'm glad we've got that straight. Pete, I'm here to help if I can, but I'm not a doctor and I can't make you better, physically, that is. I have a degree and a lot of training and experience, and I can teach you a whole bunch of practical things, things you can and will use everyday. They call me an occupational therapist. I'm not sure why. I help people learn to do things that will enable them to find an occupation, but when you're in here my job is basically to help you re-learn all those things you knew how to do and took for granted since you were a kid. Now you're going to have to learn how to do those things, given your present physical condition, so that you can take care of yourself and get out and get yourself a job, later on, understood?"

"Understood, but I'm still planning on making a complete recovery, John."

"And I hope you do. If you do, none of what I'm going to teach you will matter, but if you don't, you will need to know everything I'm going to teach you, understood?"

"Understood, but what kind of job am I going to be able to get if I don't get better, John? If I don't get better, what the hell am I going to do?"

"You'd be surprised at the things you can do, maybe not now, but after a while, with some training, and I'll say this to you, no matter what you decide to do, you're going to have to know how to use a computer. Will you agree with me on that? In this day and age? You gotta know computers no matter what you do. Am I right?"

Mr. Cunningham had a New York accent and gestured with his hands when he spoke. He extended his arms in front of him, with his palms up, as he asked the question. He had a quizzical look on his face, as if to suggest that the answer was obvious and everyone knew that to be true.

"I've never been much with computers, John," Pete responded. "Not even computer games."

"Pete, if you don't know computers, I'd say you should learn!"

"John, I don't know anything about computers and I don't know that I can do that."

"Pete, you can learn. Kids all over the country know how to use computers, even little kids. What makes you think that you can't?"

Florence was paying close attention to what Mr. Cunningham was saying. She didn't know much about computers, either. She listened as Pete responded,

"I guess I could try."

"Well, the hospital won't provide you with one, so whatever you do you'll have to do it on your own, but that would be my suggestion. If you got a computer, at least you'll have things to work on and do while you're lying there. Am I right?"

"You think I can do that like I am now?"

"Sure you can! Get a laptop or a flat screen computer and put it on the floor or above your head so you can watch some things and learn how computers work. You can do that right now."

"Yeah, I guess I could. I could watch television, movies…things like that. Think they'd let me?"

"Like I said before, I can't help you with that. You'll have to ask someone else about that, but I don't see why not. That's what I'd do if I were you, I think. That's my advice to you, Pete Collins, but that's not what I'm here for. You and I are going to work on things like going to the bathroom, shaving, taking a shower, changing clothes, putting on shoes and socks…the basics."

Pete hadn't thought too much about how he was going to be able to do those kinds of things. Everybody had been doing all of those things for him. He thought for a moment and offered,

"John, I'm still planning on making a full recovery and walking again. I really am. It's gonna get better. I know it is."

"And we all hope that you do, Pete. We do. We all hope that none of this will be necessary, and our goal is to get you out of here and on your own as quickly as possible, so we're gonna teach you these things just in case it doesn't go the way we want it to, okay? Can you work with me on this?"

"Yeah, John. I'll work with you. When do we start?"

"We won't start doing things until you are able to dress yourself. You are going to have to learn to do that all by yourself, and once you do, then we'll work on learning how to transfer yourself from the bed to the wheelchair. When you can do that, we're ready to go to work, and from what I've been told, you'll be there very soon, which is why I came to see you today."

"Great. I'm all for getting out of here as soon as I can. I'll do whatever it takes. Dr. Johnson says I'll be here for six months but I'm planning on leaving a little earlier than that."

"I'm even going to teach you how to cook for yourself, Peter, in case you don't know much about that. I didn't when I was your age. Plus you're going to learn about hygiene and taking care of your urinary system, too, Pete."

"Yeah? Nobody has talked to me about that. So far, all I know is that a nurse comes and takes this catheter away every so often and puts a new one on me."

"You won't have nurses around once you're out of here, Pete."

"I know."

"And this isn't a job for your mother, either."

"I know that, too."

"I'll help you with it the first time or two, but then you're on your own. That is one of the least favorite parts of my job."

"I'll do the best I can to get myself out of here as fast as possible."

"You'll do fine, Pete, I'm sure. Most of these are things you've known how to do since you were a kid. Like I said, you're just going to be re-learning these things, that's all."

At that, Mr. Cunningham stood, shook Pete's hand and said,

"Nice to meet you, Pete. I look forward to working with you."

"You heard about me and the psychiatrist and the other lady, yes?"

"It's in your chart. We weren't sure how you'd respond, but I'm glad to know that you'll work with me. I'll be back to see you tomorrow."

With that, Mr. Cunningham turned and walked hurriedly out the door in a matter of seconds.

Florence, who had sat quietly ten feet away, listening intently to the conversation, thought to herself that Mr. Cunningham was probably right. A computer might be a good thing for Pete to learn about. At least he could watch movies or play video games, listen to music or whatever else he wanted to do while he was lying there. She was delighted to hear Pete show some interest in learning about computers, and that he would cooperate with the therapist. She didn't like it when he got testy with the people who were there to help him, but she couldn't even begin to imagine what it was like for him to be going through what he was, knowing the way he was and how he had been since he was a baby. When she said so to Pete he responded by saying,

"Mom, I don't know that I'll be able to learn too much, but right now I'd watch a video on learning how to speak Swahili or Japanese. I could use having something to do other than just lie here like this. Yes, I agree to give it a try."

"I'll talk to your father about it, Peter, and we'll see what we can do. You've always been a bright boy, you just weren't ever interested in books and schoolwork, that's all. You always wanted to be outside playing, even as a baby."

"Do you think they'd let me watch videos or television?"

"I don't know. You can ask, but if they let you, they'd have to let everybody, don't you think?"

"Probably, but what's wrong with that?"

"I don't know, but aren't hospitals supposed to be quiet places, so people can do their work and all?"

"Maybe they'll let me at night, when no one's around?"

"We can ask, Peter, but don't get your hopes up just yet. I have to discuss this with your father first."

"I won't, but we can ask, right? And you don't want to go out and buy one if they won't let me use it, do you?"

Florence agreed that it would be wise to make sure that the hospital would allow him to have a computer before too many plans were made.

That night, and during most of the next day, Pete asked all of the nurses and everyone who came near his bed for the next few hours about him watching movies or listening to music if his parents got him a computer. He hadn't received his first SSI check yet and had no money of his own, so he had to rely on his parents for financial support. It was up to them. Florence talked to Anthony about it and he said that he'd see what he could do. They were on a limited budget and he needed to know how much those things would cost.

Later that day, the psychologist returned and asked Pete if he was willing to talk to her. He told her that he wasn't in the mood and asked if they could do it another day. She didn't push it and left. As she did, Joy entered the room, together with James. Pete was taken to the room where the wheelchairs were located. He was put in a different chair and elevated to an angle slightly higher than the 45 degree angle he had been on the day before. It required no effort on his part, but after a few minutes, he asked to be lowered, as he had the day before.

"Was I able to sit up longer today?"

"A little. Be patient. It will come. Trust me," Joy responded.

When he got no firm answer about when he could get a computer and start watching movies and playing video games, Pete was disappointed. He was in a foul mood and began asking why he couldn't have music, at least, especially if he used earphones. He couldn't help himself. He was just so frustrated with his situation that he couldn't control his emotions.

That night, no one spoke. Maybe everyone was sleeping or maybe no one wanted to talk. Pete didn't.

The next day, Pete continued to make improvement, both on the apparatus when he pulled himself up, but also when he pushed and pulled himself across the platform that connected his bed to the wheelchair so that he could just about get into the chair and then get back out of it again, but not quite. That was the 'transfer' board. Joy told him that he was about ready to spend more time with Mr. Cunningham and learn some 'life' skills.

Later in the day, his mother came to the side of his bed, handed him a laptop computer, and said,

"Your father talked to some people and made all the arrangements. He hopes you like it."

"Thanks, Mom, for all you did to make this happen."

"It really was your father, not me. Thank him next time you talk to him."

"I will."

"But Pete, he told me to be sure to take it home with me at night."

"Why? Do you think someone might steal it in here?"

"There are signs up all over the place about not leaving valuables out in the open. Your father told me that I am to take it with me when I leave. That's what I'm going to do."

"Okay, but I don't think that is necessary."

"You know how your father is, Peter. He spent a lot of money on this. Do as he asks, please?"

"Okay, we will.

As they were talking, Mr. Cunningham appeared.

"Glad to see you got that computer, Pete. The more you can learn about it the better prepared you will be for the outside world. No doubt about it. More and more people are working from their homes nowadays and that might be something that could be perfect for you. Am I right? You can do that."

"Thanks for the suggestion, John. Now that I've got it I'll start playing with it right away and see what I can do. Who knows, maybe I can learn how to use this thing."

"So I'm told that you're just about ready for me. Now, keep in mind we're going to have to go slow and…"

"That's all I hear anymore…go slow…go slow."

"You'll see. You're going to have to be patient with yourself. What used to take you five seconds might take you an hour now, or more. Just do the best you can. That's all you can do. We'll start tomorrow. The first thing we're going to do is teach you how to dress yourself."

"While I'm still laid up like this?"

"Yes."

"Whatever you say, John."

"I'll see you tomorrow. Have fun with your computer."

When Mr. Cunningham had left the room, Pete and his mother turned the power on and started to play with their new toy.

"Well, we're going to have to teach ourselves how to use this thing, but we can do this, right, Peter?"

"It's gotta be better than just laying here, Mom."

"I would think so," Florence responded.

"So let's see what this tells us," she continued as she handed Pete a disc and some reading materials. "It says this is an informative disc about the MacIntosh computer system and that you should view the tutorial immediately upon turning on the computer. You can watch this as many times as you want, and that's one thing you've got plenty of, right?"

"I've got a lot of time on my hands. That's true."

"Here are some headphones, Peter. You shouldn't be a bother to anyone if you keep them on."

"But what about you, Mom? We're doing this together, right?"

"I can listen while you're sleeping, or when I take it home at night, but this is for you. We want you to learn this."

"Can you get me some music videos or somethin'?"

"I'll see what I can do. You tell me what you want and I'll see about getting it, okay?"

After making sure that the system worked, while Pete was busily engaged in learning about it, Florence said,

"I'll go ahead and leave a little early today. Maybe I can find a store and get a music disc or a movie or something. What would you like? Maybe I'll get just one or two for now."

"See if you can find some Pearl Jam or Aerosmith, but don't buy anything. Just find out how much it costs. I hear people can download the music for free no sweat. Besides, it'll take me a few days to figure this out. Thanks anyways, Mom."

After his mother had left, Pete started reading the User's Manual. At first, it was like learning Latin or Greek, but after reading it over and over, some of it began to sink in.

When Dr. Johnson came around again, Pete asked about being able to listen to music or a watch a movie. He was told that since he was not in a private room that he couldn't do it without headsets on or else other people would want the same thing. He could do it if he was in a private room, because the door to his room could be closed and no one would be bothered. Since he was a recipient of Medicaid, he was in a room with other patients, receiving what was permitted by the government. He couldn't bother the other patients or the staff. He could use earphones and listen to or watch whatever he wanted to, though, and he could watch videos or play music all he wanted, during the day, but not at night. Dr. Johnson said, though, that he would start to get busier and busier as he became more able to do things.

The days began to become more routine, though Pete continued to see noticeable improvement. Every day began the same way. The nurses and the doctors and the specialists came at a specified time. Food was delivered at a specified time. Lights were turned out at a specified time. Visitors were permitted to visit at specified times, but they made an exception for Florence. She was allowed into the hospital at 8:00 and she could stay until 8:00 at night, beyond the normal visiting hours, because of the situation. The hospital was run in an organized fashion and it didn't vary much from day to day, and it didn't vary the rules much, either.

For Pete, his regimen changed as much as his physical condition would allow and as it improved. Gradually, he went from doing one exercise per day on the apparatus on his bed to ten exercise sessions per day. It was a slow and painful process. He blacked out a few more times, but it didn't seem to bother anyone too much when he did. He was assured, again and again, that it was normal. It was just the blood pressure in his system making adjustments. After a few weeks, and as he spent more time in a vertical position, his circulation improved and the blackouts didn't happen nearly as much.

As far as the wheelchair was concerned, he was becoming more and more comfortable in it. Just as with the exercises in bed, once he demonstrated that he could sit up in his bed or in his chair, his activity level increased. Learning how to get into and out of the wheelchair took some time, and it was a major accomplishment when Pete learned how to put the transfer board up by himself and then transfer himself to his wheelchair. Once he learned that, he was on his way to spending more time with his occupational therapist and learning how to take care of himself.

Pete couldn't shower yet, because of the stitches in his back, but John told him that was a relatively easy thing to do. Provided the bathroom was handicap accessible, he could use a special chair, not his everyday chair, and wheel himself into the bathroom, take a shower and do all the things he needed to do without assistance from anyone else. The chair was high enough so that it sat up over the toilet and had an opening in the bottom of it. It was awkward at first, but Pete caught on fairly quickly. The bathroom sink was high enough so that Pete could wheel the chair up under it, wash his face, brush his teeth and shave.

Changing clothes was a major challenge. John tried to show him how to do it while in a wheelchair, but Pete had trouble doing that. It was much easier for him to put on clothes while on his bed or on the floor, when he was able to do that.

Putting on pants, socks and underwear required him to lift up his backside, but since he couldn't stand and he only had two hands, it involved several steps. That was difficult for him and he wasn't ready to make any violent movements, and lifting up his body to get his clothes on required him to move his torso quite a bit. He didn't want to hurt himself. Pete wasn't sure if the pain was lessening or if he was just getting used to it.

After a while, Pete could put on clothes by lifting up one side of his body and pulling a sock, underwear or shorts up as far as he could on that side, then shifting his weight to the other side and doing the same thing. After four or five, or more, shifts, he could get one item on at a time. Something as simple as putting on a pair of shorts was a lengthy and tedious process. He learned to put the socks on first.

Joy and the other physical therapists had started putting Pete on a mat about a month and a half after surgery. At first, they wanted Pete to learn to roll over. Since he had no help from his lower body, it wasn't as easy as it sounded, especially with the clam shell on. Gradually, he learned how to do that. He would throw one arm across his body and torque over at the same time. It took a while, but he learned it. He learned how to 'scoot' like a seal across the mat, too, and just moving around felt good to him.

Eventually, they wanted him to be able to get into and out of his wheelchair from a position on the floor, just as he had to learn to get into and out of the bed by himself. Both actions took some time to learn. To get into a chair from the floor, he had to position the chair next to him and lock it so it wouldn't move. He would then lift himself up with both hands on the floor, like doing a push-up, but throw his head down while pushing his butt high enough in the air to get it on the chair. Then he would push himself backwards and into the chair in one quick motion. It required arm strength and Pete had plenty of that.

By two months after the surgery, Pete was able to sit up for an hour. He would then have to lie down for forty five minutes after doing so, but he was improving. By then, he was exercising or working on his 'life skills' most of every day. He didn't have nearly as much time lying on the bed. He was spending more and more time in his wheelchair.

Pete no longer thought about waking up and being what he was before he fell off the horse. He thought about making progress and getting a little better every day. He still hoped for the miracle, but he didn't have the time to sit around and wait for it to happen. He was better off than his buddies, Greg and Jeff, were, but Pete was feeling as if he was hitting a wall. Dr. Johnson assured him that wasn't the case.

"You're going to continue to get better and better until you reach the point where you can sit or lay down just like anyone else, whenever you want, and get into your wheelchair and out of it like it was nothing."

"When is that going to be?"

"I can't say, but don't rush it. Remember, what's most important is that bone in your back healing. If it doesn't, you're going to be seeing me again for another surgery, and I know you don't want that. Each surgery will degrade your entire system, make the bones weaker and lengthen the healing time. We want it to work the first time. We want it to work this time, Pete."

"So when will I be able to take this shell off? Will I ever be able to take it off?"

"Yes, you will. As to when, that depends. If it heals right and I'm satisfied that the bone was calcified, or hardened to the point that it would take another major trauma, to break it, then I'm going to take it off, but not until then, and I still say that you should expect to have this on for at least six months. Don't try to rush this part of it, Pete."

"So I'm going to have to keep this another three months?"

"Yes, you are, but I do have some good news for you."

"What's that?"

"Based upon the films I've seen, everything is looking good so far. Now, you could suffer a severe setback at any time, and we don't want that, agreed?

"Agreed."

"And you understand that what we're really looking to see happen here is for the bone to firm up and become a solid part of your spine."

"Isn't that what the rods are doing?"

"No, the rods are there to hold everything in place, but the bones and the paste are what must graft together and that takes time. There is no way to hurry that, Pete. From what I'm seeing, though, you don't have all that much free time on your hands, though, do you?"

"No, I'm pretty active these days. Between the wheelchair and the mat and the exercises, I stay busy."

"My nurses will keep a close eye on you, but as long as you're careful, you should be fine. You are making good progress."

"Will the pain go away?"

"You mean the pain in your back when you sit up?"

"Yes."

"Yes, it will. As the bones harden and the muscles around them strengthen, you will feel less and less pain, but you're going to feel pain, or discomfort, for quite some time, maybe for a year or so, maybe a little less, but not much."

"So when do you see me getting out of here?"

"Basically, when we think you're able to take care of yourself and are comfortable in your wheelchair, but the most important thing is that you are healed as much as we can heal you. Once I see that you can do all the exercises and things on your own, I'll be ready to discharge you, not before, but I'll need to see the MRIs of your back on a regular basis to make sure the graft takes. You don't need to be in the hospital while that is taking place."

"What about this wheelchair I'm being fitted for? How does that figure in?"

"When you leave here, you'll have your very own wheelchair, made for you, Pete Collins, and no one else, but it takes a while for them to build that for you. Once it is here, you'll be that much closer to leaving us."

"So you wouldn't discharge me until I get that chair?"

"That's right."

"And you wouldn't loan me one until it arrived?"

"Nope. We don't do that."

"How long does it take, usually?"

"Sometimes as long as three or four months."

"Three or four months! I want to be out of here way before then."

"Pete, when you're ready, I'll discharge you, but the chair has to be here, as well as all of the other things we talked about. You should take advantage of all that we have available to you here. Once you leave us, depending upon where you go, you probably won't be able to have access to things as easily as you do here. I think you're ready for another source of assistance."

"What's that?"

"Vocational rehabilitation. Mr. Cunningham is helping you to acquire the physical skills you will need to be able to go out and get a job whereas the vocational therapist is the one who really is out there to help you actually find jobs that you can do. Those are two different things. I suggest you work with him. I think you'll find him to be a very interesting person."

"How so?"

"You'll see. I'll come back by to see you next week."

Pete was somewhat puzzled by Dr. Johnson's cryptic remark, but he didn't give it too much thought. He was becoming quite proficient on the computer and began teaching his mother how to do things. Within a week or so after getting the computer, he began teaching himself how to type. He began using the two finger 'hunt and peck' method.

"It's important for you to learn it and learn it right, Peter. You can't be a two finger typist. I don't care how fast you can go, someone using eight fingers will go faster. Take your time and learn it the right way. Trust me."

Somewhat reluctantly, Pete began doing as instructed. Florence liked the e-mails best of all.

"And it's free? We don't have to pay anything for this?"

"Mom, you talk like you're from a different planet. This has been around for over ten years."

"You didn't ever use e-mails, Peter Matthew Collins, so don't you be so high and mighty with me, young man," she said jokingly.

"But I knew about it. You have to pay for the internet connection, though, and that's about Fifty dollars a month or so, I think."

"I told your father that we have to get that at home. He doesn't think we need it. Once he knows that how much our phone bill will go down if we get it, he'll do it."

Together, they sent e-mails to and from their family all during the day.

Late in the afternoon, when Mr. Cunningham came to visit, he told Pete,

"It seems as if you have a pretty good understanding of how these things work. There's a market out there for people with knowledge of computers. No matter what you do, though, it will help you. With some training, maybe you could become a computer programmer. They make a whole lot more money than data entry clerks, who are people who type information into the computer. It's the difference between giving the orders and taking the orders, creating the format or following the format. Keep that in mind, Pete, and experiment with all those icons. See if you can figure out all the things they can do. I can't. I've been doing that for years and I'm not even close to knowing all there is to know about them. Have fun with it."

* * * * * * * * * * * * * *

The next day, as he was sitting up in his bed, composing a message to his sister in Boston, Belinda, about her new baby, he felt the presence of someone behind him. He then heard a man ask,

"Peter Collins?"

"That's me. What can I do for you?"

"I don't want to interrupt and I can come back if this is a bad time, but I need to talk to you for a while."

"Who are you?"

"My name is George Frias and I am a vocational rehabilitation specialist."

Pete took a mirror and held it up at an angle so that he could view the man who was speaking to him. He saw a man in his mid-thirties, with glasses, long, dark, curly hair, a scruffy beard, wearing a coat and tie, sitting in a wheelchair.

"Good morning, Mr. Frias. What can I do for you?"

"Actually, the question is what can I do for you? That's why I'm here."

"You tell me."

"I'm going to help you figure out what you can do with the rest of your life, if you're going to be in a wheelchair."

"Excuse me for asking, but how long you been in a chair?"

"Ever since I can remember."

"Why's that?"

"I was born with spina bifida."

"I've heard of it, but I really don't know what that is. What is it?"

"It's a disease of the spine. Some people are born without a fully developed spinal column. I was one of the lucky ones."

"I've never met anyone who had it before you."

"It's actually not that uncommon. From what I've read, it happens about one in every one thousand births."

"I'm sorry, but what did you say your name was?"

"F-R-I-A-S. Think of it as "Free" and "As." George Frias, but call me George, please."

"You know, before I got hurt, I don't remember ever seeing all that many people in wheelchairs. Now, I'm hearing more and more about it happening to all kinds of people. How did you get that disease, George, if you don't mind me asking?"

"From what I know, it happened before my mother even knew she was pregnant. It was a genetic thing, not something she did wrong or I did wrong, or something my father, whoever he is, did wrong."

"So what made you decide to do what you do, George?"

"I chose this job, Pete. It was something I thought about for a long time and by the time I was in high school, I knew what I wanted to do with my life and that was to help others with this problem. Actually, I'm one of the lucky ones. A large number of children with Spina Bifida died. Others were completely paralyzed. They were able to perform surgery on me and get me to where I am now."

"How long you been doin' this?"

"I've only been here at the hospital for the last four years. I spent the first twelve years working for insurance companies."

"What did you do for them?"

"Basically, it was my job to act as an expert witness for them and go to court to show that a person who had been hurt in an accident, or as a result of a mistake by a doctor, or whatever, was still capable of doing all kinds of things. They wanted the judge or the jury to see me and to say, 'Look at him. Look what he can do. If he can do it, this poor guy over there could do it, too.'"

"Did you like doing that?"

"I was like a monkey on the end of a leash. I'd wheel myself into the courtroom, put my chair right in front of the judge and jury, and then talk about all the jobs that were out there that this particular plaintiff or worker's compensation claimant could do. The attorneys for the insurance companies would then argue that the person wasn't entitled to a dime, that he or she was just a person who felt sorry for himself or herself and was looking for a hand-out."

"To be honest, I don't have a problem with that. If a guy can work, he should. The government shouldn't be givin' money to people who can work but don't want to. Nobody would work if that was the case. Same thing for insurance companies. They're in business to make money. They're not charitable organizations."

"You can say that again, my friend. They are not charitable organizations, and they will lie, cheat, steal and take advantage of people who are weak, desperate and without hope, especially when they are hurting so bad that they can't afford to fight the powerful insurance companies. A lot of those people were really hurt, Pete, and they deserved the money and the benefits they were asking for but, because of me and my testimony, they didn't get it. I feel really badly about that."

"Doesn't sound like such a good job when you put it like that, George."

"Basically, I reached the point where I hated what I was doing and I hated myself for doing it. I took a huge cut in pay to do what I'm now doing, but I feel good about what I do and who I am. So here I am and I want to help you, Pete."

"So George, is Frias a Mexican name?"

"I am from Mexico, that's right."

"Well, if you don't mind, I'll call you Jorge. Are you okay with that?"

"If that's what you want, Pete, that's fine with me, but if you do, I'll call you Pedro, how's that?"

"Jorge, tell me what I can do to help you help me."

"From what I've been told, you'll be out of here before you know it and then you'll want to talk to someone like me, someone who can help you find a job."

"I'm getting there. It's not easy, but they tell me I'm just about there."

"Dr. Johnson asked me to come see you. It's a little early for me to be getting involved with patients, since I don't generally see people until they are ready to be released from the hospital and are to the point where they are employable, so this is unusual for me to be meeting you so soon, but you're such a young man, and you have so much life ahead of you, Dr. Johnson wanted me to make sure that you get going in the right direction as soon as possible."

"That was nice of him."

"He said something about you not cooperating with his psychologist?"

"Yeah, I didn't hear what she had to say...still don't."

"And one of his physical therapists?"

"Yeah, she wanted me to start lifting weights to keep my arms strong. I told her I would when I was ready. I cooperated in every way possible when it came to things like getting me into a chair and all of the rest. I'll start lifting weights when I'm ready. I've lifted weights since I was in junior high school. I'll lift weights again, I'm sure, I just wasn't ready then, that's all there was to that, really."

"That may be part of the reason why he was concerned about you."

"I can understand that."

"I'm going to leave a DVD with you and ask that you take a look at it when you have a chance. It's a promotional, informative type video, and I'm hoping that it will just open your eyes to the possibilities that are out there for you. I'm sure that there are times when you want to give up and see it all come to an end, and I'm sure that there are plenty of those times ahead of you, too, but you're not dead and you have a lifetime ahead of you. It's just not going to be the same life that you had before you fell off that horse."

"You've read my chart, I see."

"I read everything I could about you, Pete, or I should say, Pedro, before I came to see you."

"You did?"

"Yes, I did, and you can still lead that kind of life, if that's what you want. There may be a thousand things you can't do because of your injury, Pedro, but there are still ten thousand things you can do."

"You may be right. I hadn't thought of it that way."

"You won't be riding horses, and you probably won't be guiding any trips on rafts, but there are opportunities out there that will surprise you."

"Right now, I wonder if I'll ever be able to go fishing or get back in the woods again."

"From what I know, there is no reason in the world you won't be able to do that in a few weeks, Pedro. You're one of the luckier ones. There are plenty of people like us who won't ever be able to do those things."

George put his hands around Pete's left hand and said,

Count your blessings, Pedro, and try not to think about all the negative things going on in your life. I've got to go now. I'll be back in a week or so to check in on you."

"Hey, man. Good to meet you, George. I'll watch the video and think about what you said."

"Hasta la vista, Pedro, vaya con Dios."

"Y tu tambien, Jorge."

After Mr. Frias had left the room, Pete said to his mother,

"That was pretty impressive, wasn't it? A guy in a chair comes to talk to me about vocational rehabilitation? I can't very well tell him I can't do it, can I? He's been in a chair his whole life. He never had a chance to ride a horse or go down a river and feel the spray of a huge rapid come barreling across his face. Damn! Seein' him makes me feel like I shouldn't be feelin' so bad about myself."

Florence felt a surge of emotions run through her. She was happy to hear her son talk like that. She added,

"Like he said, Peter, count your blessings."

"Well, I'm not there yet, Mom, but it makes me think about things a little differently, I'll say that much."

"One step at a time, Peter."

"No, Mom. I don't think I'll ever be able to take any steps, ever again, but I know what you mean."

"I'm sorry, Peter. You're right. That was an unfortunate choice of words. I'll never use that expression again, I promise."

"It's okay, Mom. I know you didn't mean anything by it. I was makin' a little joke, that's all. I've gotta find humor here and there and wherever I can."

Pete stuck the disk in his computer and began to watch.

13

A Bucket of Cold Water

THAT NIGHT, WHEN ALL was quiet, and no one was talking, Pete called out,

"Hey, Jeffrey! What's goin' on, man?"

"Everyday's a struggle to survive, you damn 'Gator, you. It's just that some days are harder than others. This is one of them kind of days."

"Why's that, you ole redneck?"

"I don't want to talk about it, Pete. I can't right now."

"How 'bout you, Greg? How you doin', man?"

There was no response. After a while, Pete asked.

"Hey, Jeff, what's up with Greg? Is he alright?"

There had been other roommates since Ernesto, but most had come and gone within a matter of days or at most a week or two, but the three of them had been there together for several months.

"He ain't here no more," Jeff responded. His voice was shaking as he did, as if he was crying.

"Did they move him out?"

"Yeah, you could say that," Jeff replied, in a low, trembling voice.

"They didn't kick him out or send him home, did they? Those damn insurance companies…or was it the government?"

"No, they didn't kick him out, Pete. They carried him out," Jeff replied, barely able to speak.

"They carried him out...you mean..."

"Yeah, that's what I mean, Pete. His little ole heart just couldn't take it no more..." and then he started to cry, unable to hold back his emotions.

"I can't talk no more, Pete."

Pete didn't say anything else that night. He thought of Jorge, and he thought of Greg, and Ernesto, and of his circumstances, and then he fell asleep as he did.

* * * * * * * * * *

Every week, usually on a Wednesday, the physical therapists, occupational therapists, case managers, sociologists, psychologists and a variety of physicians specially trained in treating patients with spinal cord injuries would meet to discuss each patient in the spinal cord unit. Dr. Johnson, as head of the entire program, for which Seattle was nationally famous, would attend as often as time would permit. Emergencies often arose without warning and were never on his schedule. Aides and students were allowed to attend the meetings as well, since it was a teaching hospital. Patients knew of the meetings but were never allowed to attend.

Other than his refusal to lift weights or talk to the psychologist, it seemed as if every week someone was offering a glowing report of progress Pete was making. His attitude was good, although his continued refusal to talk to her baffled the psychologist, Mrs. Pisano. The physical therapists gave up asking him to lift weights or do other types of exercises, because he was doing so well on other tasks, such as getting in and out of his bed and wheelchair. Pete was a good patient, if not an excellent one, and was making improvement. The ones who showed no improvement were the problem patients.

If a patient wasn't progressing, the hospital staff made a concerted effort to provide that patient with more attention and to make as much progress as possible. After time, when the decision was reached that the patient had reached MMI, or maximum medical improvement, the patient was moved out of the hospital and into some post-rehab facility, since there was little more the staff at the hospital could do for the person. There were too many people who needed their help waiting for an open bed. Although the protocol for patients with injuries like the one Pete had was a six month hospital stay, Pete told himself that he would do everything he could to get an early release.

A week after Greg died, Jeffrey was moved out, without any warning or fanfare. Before he left, Pete was able to get an address for him, but he wasn't able to say good-bye. One of these days, they'd be moving him out, Pete thought to himself. He hoped that day would be coming soon.

Later that week, Dr. Johnson paid a visit to Pete, who was sitting up in his bed, busily typing away on his keyboard, as he approached.

"Good afternoon, Doc! And how are you today?" Pete chirped.

"I'm good, thank you, Pete, and I couldn't be more pleased with the progress you are making. We are using you as an example of what can be accomplished with the right frame of mind, despite your reluctance to cooperate with us on a few things that we don't need to discuss. You're doing terrific and, as I said, I couldn't be happier for you."

"So when do I get out of here?"

"Pete, as you know and as I have told you on many occasions, I plan to keep you here until I am completely satisfied that your back is healthy and resilient and can take a punch, if you will, and, in any event, you're not leaving until your wheelchair comes in."

"And when is that gonna be again?"

"I have no control over when your chair arrives. Who did you order from? Was it from Quickie?"

"Yes, I think that's who we finally agreed on."

"They're all pretty much the same, I think, as far as how long it takes to make a chair. The difference comes in the amount of demand for their product. Quickie is one of the better ones as far as quality is concerned and they're in higher demand because of that. It takes longer for them to deliver one than some of the others."

"So does it look like I might get out a little early or should I plan on being here for six months then?"

"Pete, I don't want to see you leave us too soon. We could lose all the gains and all the successes you have achieved if we hurry the healing process one little bit. I've told you about the bone graft and the healing process. I don't want to have to repeat the surgery I performed on you last fall. I've told you that you should expect to be here for six months and nothing has changed to make me change my opinion on that. Are you expecting to get out any sooner?"

"I was hoping so," Pete said dejectedly. "I just want to get out of here as soon as I can."

"I understand that, Pete, but you've got to be patient. I know it is hard to do at times, especially when Spring gets here and it's so beautiful outside, but you cannot, and I repeat, you CAN NOT hurry that healing process one little bit, understood?"

"I understand," Pete said gloomily, "so when is that going to be?"

"You arrived at the end of September of last year. It's been four months now. When that chair arrives, I'll take a good look at you and then decide what to do. But even if I release you early, you're going to wear that clam shell for the full six months, and then some, understood?"

"Understood."

"When I think it's safe, I'll let you go, but before I let you go, I want to personally watch and see you fall out of your chair and put yourself back in it, all by yourself, with no help whatsoever from anyone else, and get yourself in and out of bed. How does that sound?"

Pete wasn't quite there yet. He was close, but that was still a challenge for him. He spent most of his time working on those two tasks every day.

"I can get myself out of my bed and into the chair without any help."

"You can?"

"Well, almost, but I'm close. Maybe tomorrow I'll do it."

"It sounded like an impossible task a few weeks ago, didn't it?"

"It did. I admit it. It did."

"Well, you're going to continue to be surprised at the level of functioning you're capable of, Pete, but you're not ready for that just yet. Be patient and keep up the good work. Trust me, if all goes well, you'll be out of here before you know it. How does that sound?"

"It sounds good to me. Would it speed them up if I called them?"

"Who, Quickie?"

"Yeah."

"It can't hurt but I'm sure they're working on yours and a whole bunch of others. That's how they make their money. They'll get it to you as fast as they can, but you can call them if you want."

"Then I will."

"Pete, you told me that you broke a bone once. I think it was in your leg, yes?"

"It was my ankle. I was playin' a baseball game and a guy tried to jump over me to avoid my tag. My back foot was planted in the dirt and he bent my body back over my ankle. The spikes held my foot in place and something had to give. Plus I broke my forearm skateboarding one time, too."

"Well, do you remember how tender your ankle was for a while and how you couldn't put weight on it at all for a long while after you got out of the cast?"

"I remember."

"It's the same thing here. First of all, you had to stay in a cast for a long time, right?"

"That's right."

"And then when you got out of the cast you were on crutches for a long time, right?

"That's right, and I walked with a limp for a while, too."

"And then it was a long time, even after the injury had healed, before you forgot about the injury altogether, right?"

"Yeah, that's right."

"It's the same thing with this, because as far as your spinal column is concerned, the bony parts, not the spinal cord, are going to get almost as strong as that healed ankle of yours."

"Really?"

"Really. It's going to take another accident, maybe not as strong as the trauma you experienced when that horse fell on you, but it will take a powerful force to break those bones again, once they heal."

"No kidding! Right now that's hard for me to imagine."

"Trust me, it's true, but we have to let the bones heal first, and they seem to be doing just fine, but the healing process is going to take another two months."

"And there is nothing I can do to hurry it up?"

"No, there isn't. The only question in my mind is whether you have to be in this hospital while that healing process takes place. That would be the only reason I let you go early, and you've done well with your physical skills and learning how to use your wheelchair, but you're not ready to leave us yet and you know it, don't you?"

"I'm just tired of being cooped up in a hospital, not that I don't like the staff or that I don't appreciate all that you have done and continue to do for me, but…"

"That's understandable, especially for someone like you, but that doesn't change anything as far as I'm concerned."

"I understand," Pete responded.

"I'm told you have an aptitude for that computer you bought."

"I'm enjoying it. I've learned how to type and I watch movies, play video games, play solitaire and do lots of other things on the computer. I taught myself how to play cribbage. I do everything everyone asks of me. I keep waiting for the miracle to happen, Doc, and it's hard for me to just lay here like I do, most of the time."

"You can get bored with so much time on your hands. That's understandable. I'll see if I can't help you out a little with that, too."

"What does that mean?"

"You'll see."

"I don't like it when you leave me hanging like that, Doc."

"Have I failed you yet?"

"No, you haven't."

"Trust me."

With that, Doctor Johnson departed, leaving Pete and his mother, Florence, to ponder what was in store for him next. Pete thought about where he was and what he had become. He and George, the vocational rehabilitation expert, had become the best of friends, as were Joy, Amy, Mary, John and the others who were treating him on a daily or weekly basis. He had made it through the holidays without too much difficulty.

Many of his friends from the past had sent him cards and best wishes, but he wasn't able to bring himself to send cards, not even to Reno, Dave or Abigail. It had been a long while since he had talked to any of them. They had called, sent flowers and letters, but Pete had kept them all at a distance. He didn't want anyone seeing him as he was. He wanted them to remember him as he had been.

Even when his mother flew back to Fernandina Beach to be with his father for a week, he had handled it well. He was being provided with a strong support system at the hospital, and he appreciated it and them. Although he couldn't wait to get out of the hospital, life outside the hospital was becoming a more difficult concept to visualize. What would he do? Who would he be? Who would still be his friend?

The expense of Florence staying in Washington with Pete was putting a heavy toll on his parents' finances. They were using up their life-savings and the pot was dwindling. Although his mother never mentioned it, Pete knew of the sacrifices his family was making for him. He was lucky to have them and he knew it. Most likely, he wouldn't be leaving the hospital much sooner than the scheduled six months and there was nothing he could do about it.

14

One Road Ends and Another Begins.

PETE HAD NO IDEA what Dr. Johnson had in mind for him. He found out the next day. He was lying on his stomach, watching and listening to a music video Amy had brought him, with his earphones on, looking straight down, eyes closed, when he felt a finger tapping on his right shoulder. He opened his eyes, took off the earphones, positioned his mirror so he could see who it was, and saw a beautiful young woman with long brown hair and light brown eyes standing next to him.

"Hello," he said. "Who are you?"

"My name is Rebecca and I'm here to help you put more fun in your life."

It caused Pete to laugh out loud, too much. His body started to shake some as he did. Rebecca noticed it and said,

"Don't get too excited there, Mr. Collins. I'm a leisure specialist. I'm here to teach you a new way to have fun."

"I'm sorry. I couldn't help it. I took one look at you and it brought back some memories."

"I could tell."

"But that was a life-time ago. I'm sorry."

"That's quite alright. I'll take that as a compliment."

"It made me laugh. That was the best laugh I've had in a long, long time."

"I'm glad I was able to do that for you."

"That made my day. I hope I didn't tear some stitches or break any bones."

"Me, too. Okay, Mr. Collins, let's get to work," she said, with a smile. "I'm here on business. I get paid to do this."

"Okay, if you insist. What can I do for you?"

"No, it's what I can do for you. Dr. Johnson asked me, well, actually he told me to come see you and find out what kinds of things you'd like to do for fun."

"Right now, the most fun thing I do is listen to music. When you came up, I had that Eddie Vedder CD in there, 'Into the Wild.' I understand it's a pretty good movie, too."

"About some kid who went up to Alaska and died?"

"Well, I haven't seen the movie, so I don't know, but as I understand it, the kid just wanted to get away from it all and I can relate to that. I especially like that song called 'Society.' It goes 'I hope society, won't miss me'…somethin' like that."

"So how would you like to learn how to play a guitar and sing that song?"

"I'm not a singer and I've never played a musical instrument in my life."

"So now's a good time to learn, don't you think?"

"I don't know that I can do that. I mean, I can't do it now, can I?"

"When you're able to sit up in your chair, and I'm told you can do that now, you can. It's all about having some fun and Dr. Johnson wants to see you put some fun in your life. It can be a guitar or any one of a thousand other things, but if you want, give the guitar a try. It can't hurt and it might be fun. You'll never know until you try. Trust me."

"That's what Dr. Johnson says to me all the time."

"Okay, trust him. He's the one who sent me."

"So what is it you do?"

"I'm called a recreational therapist and my job is to help people find fun things to do with their time. Sometimes it's not as easy to do as you might think, and other times patients aren't receptive to my suggestions, but I do the best I can to put a little fun in their life. All of our patients are dealing with something and everyone needs to have a hobby or something that takes their minds off of their problems for a while, Mr. Collins, including you."

"Amen to that, so what do I have to do to help you do your job?"

"All you've got to do is say yes, or even a maybe will do for now."

"Okay, I'll give it a try."

"Great! I didn't bring anything with me today, since I didn't know what you would say. There are so many things you could be interested in."

"Like what? What other options do I have to choose from?"

"Like card games, bridge, canasta, poker, solitaire…you name it; or chess, checkers, mahjong; stamp-collecting; coin collecting; art and painting; the stock market can be fun for some people; reading books; going to school; sewing, knitting…I could go on and on."

"You know, you're right. I'm glad you mentioned all those things. I've changed my mind. The one thing I've always wanted to do is to learn how to knit."

"Peter!" his mother said. "Be nice. This woman is here to help you!"

"I'm kidding, Mom! She knows that!"

"There's nothing wrong with knitting, Mr. Collins, although I have to admit not too many men seem to choose that activity. I'll be back tomorrow with an instructional CD. I'm thinking that a musical instrument is a good place to start. I think you made a good choice. Nice meeting you, and good luck. I might take me a few days. I'll get back to see you as soon as I can."

"Hey, before you leave, I just want to say thanks."

"For what?"

"For giving me the best laugh I've had since I fell."

As she was leaving, Rebecca turned her head and said, "You're welcome."

After Rebecca was out of earshot, Florence said,

"She was pretty, wasn't she, Mom?"

"She is a very pretty woman," Florence responded.

"I'm afraid that's as close as I'm going to get to a pretty woman any more."

"Pete, you're still a handsome young man, and you can be fairly clever at times."

"At times? What does that mean?"

"There are times that you make me laugh, too, and that was one of them. I enjoyed hearing you laugh. It made me feel good to hear it, and she is no more beautiful than that girl in Montana."

"Abigail? You saw a picture of her?"

"She put that photograph of you and her next to a river in the Christmas card she sent you."

"Oh, that's right. Yeah, she's a beautiful girl." He paused and said, in a low voice. "I loved her."

"You should write her, Peter. She calls and writes and you ignore her."

"I'm not ready for that, Mom."

"Okay, Peter. That's up to you."

That night, Florence mentioned the visit from Rebecca to Anthony and others in the family. The next day, a guitar was on its way to Pete from his sister, Judy, who played guitar and had an extra one sitting around the house.

A few days later, the guitar arrived. Judy sent a couple of instructional books and an instructional video along with it. Pete was in his bed, lying on his stomach, when it came. He immediately asked to be put in his chair so he could play it. An assistant helped him get in his chair and he began playing with it. Although he was improving, he was a long way from any semblance of independence. He was entirely dependent upon the schedule of others, and couldn't envision the day when he wouldn't be. It still seemed far off.

Pete inserted the DVD into his computer and began with Lesson Number One: An Introduction to the Guitar. From that day forward, at every opportunity, when he was able to sit in his chair, without having tests to take or being required to perform some function at the request of one of the staff, he was strumming on his guitar, trying to learn how to play. When Rebecca returned, she was pleasantly surprised to see that he had already begun to learn how to play. She promised to visit regularly and see how he was progressing.

Although she was engaged to be married that summer, she playfully engaged in flirtatious conversations with Pete, and he enjoyed them, knowing that was as far as things would ever get. Occasionally, though, he would experience sensations and feelings and it made him wonder if he had lost his ability to have sex or not. He would ask Dr. Johnson first chance.

Dr. Johnson told him that having sex, or achieving an orgasm, was much like any other bodily function and that although the system had been damaged, semen could still be produced, much like how other fluids and bile were excreted from his system. He couldn't predict how that would be for Pete, though, and was unable to give him a clear response. Pete had more immediate concerns and still looked forward to the day when he could go to the bathroom by himself. Having sex was another matter altogether that would have to wait. He was relieved to know that there was a chance his penis could still function.

Dr. Johnson told him that day was coming when he could shower. Pete hadn't been able to shower because of the stitches and the condition of the wound, so others had to bathe him as best they could, without getting his back wet.

As the days turned into weeks, Pete continued to improve. He was becoming more and more proficient with the computer. He was learning to play the guitar and was now able to sit up for hours at a time, but he would have to lie down for an hour or two if he stayed up too long. He wondered when that would change.

With John's help, Pete had learned to clothe himself, get in and out of bed by himself, get into and out of his chair without assistance, and to cook some, among many other things. He was regaining some dignity in his life. He was not as dependent upon someone else for all of his basic needs.

Early one morning, five months and one week after he arrived at the Seattle Medical Facility, he was taken to the room where MRIs were performed. He knew it well. He never lost the feelings of claustrophobia he experienced when he was pushed into the cylinder and forced to lie still for an hour, with barely an inch or two separating him from the inner walls of the chamber. Later that day, Dr. Johnson came to see him.

"Pete, I've got good news for you."

"What's that?"

"I have decided that we can release you as soon as your chair gets here. I'm still going to want another MRI in a month to see if the bones and paste we took from your hip and put in your spinal column have melded together with the bones in your back and make sure that you are ready to start putting it to the test."

"Whew! That is great news! So what are my limitations? What can't I do?"

"Remember when you broke that ankle you told me about?"

"Sure."

"The same rules apply. You remember how you were so timid and afraid to put any weight on it, even when your doctor told you to?"

"Yeah."

"Same thing here. You do what you think your body will allow you to do. You're going to be tested and you're going to be afraid that you're going to break something when you do things, and that's normal. Listen to your body. Don't do anything stupid, but don't be afraid to try something new. I'll need for you to establish with an orthopedic specialist once you get to wherever it is you're going and have him or her call me."

"When do you think that chair is going to get here?"

"I had one of my assistants to call about it today. I can't tell you exactly when it will be here, but I'm told that it should be here no later than at the end of next week and maybe sooner. My nurses tell me that you've become very good at getting into and out of your bed by yourself, and that you can fall out of the chair and get back in by yourself, too. My staff tells me that they think you're ready to get back into the world outside of these hospital walls. I've given it some thought and I'm in agreement. We are ready to turn you loose. I'm confident that you're going to make it on your own."

"Any different instructions on this clam-shell from what you told me last time?"

"No, you must keep that on when you're not in bed for at least another three months. I expect that you are going to want to keep that on even after that, as hard to believe as that might be, Pete. Although you see it as a cage, it protects you."

Then Dr. Johnson took Pete's left hand and put it between his two hands, looked him in the eye and said, "And don't think that I'm not available to speak to you at any time. If things start happening and you feel like you need to talk to me, just call. I'll talk to you any time, day or night. I consider you part of my family. I try to stay close to every single patient I have ever treated and that goes double for you. It's been a pleasure to meet you, young man, and I hope you won't become a stranger."

"I'm going to see you again before I leave, aren't I?"

"Absolutely. My best guess is that you'll probably be here for another week. The chair hasn't been shipped yet. We'll know when it is. I expect that we'll be saying our good-byes about the middle of next week."

"How long before I can sit up all day if I want to?"

"That's hard to say. It could take several months, and maybe even longer. Again, listen to your body. Let it tell you what you can and can't do. I can't. It varies from patient to patient. You're going back to Florida with your mother, aren't you?"

He looked over at Florence, who was shaking her head up and down.

"Yes, I am."

"I understand you're learning to play the guitar."

"Thanks to you and Rebecca."

"And I'm told that you've learned quite a bit about computers, too."

"I don't know about that, but I've learned a lot. I didn't know much of anything about them and now I know a little. I have learned how to type, slowly, but I can type now and I've learned a whole lot about the internet. Thanks for that, too."

He shook Pete's hand firmly and said,

"I thank you, son, for being so brave and for having such a good attitude despite your injury. Now, you didn't start out that way, mind you, but you finished strong. I'm confident that you are going to do just fine out there. I want to hear all about it. There is little I enjoy more than getting a letter from a former patient who is doing well, and I get quite a few of them. I want to hear from you, Pete."

"You will, Doc. I promise."

"Good luck, young man."

Pete thought he saw a little moisture in Doc Johnson's eyes as he turned to go. He thought to himself that this man really did care about him. He'd miss him, but he was ready to get in his wheelchair and get on down the road.

He was still seeing John and Joy three times a week, as well as Jorge every now and then, but they had already done their jobs. Pete was ready to go. They had done all they could do. Everyone had done all that they could to help him get better.

At the weekly staff meeting, Dr. Johnson announced his decision that it was time to move Pete out. They had all grown accustomed to the coming and goings of patients, so much so that they tried hard not to become too emotionally attached to patients. They had failed in that regard with Pete.

Traveling on an airplane from Seattle to Jacksonville would be difficult. In all the times he flew before, he couldn't remember seeing many handicapped people on a plane with him. He didn't know if they could make special accommodations for him or not. The hospital had a person on staff whose job it was to assist with all of the details surrounding a patient's exit from the hospital so that it would be a smooth one. Her name was Jeneene.

Part of her job was to make sure that the accommodations in the home would be suitable, too. She helped people get the equipment they would need and educated the parents or other care-givers about what would need to be done. In Pete's case, she spent a lot of time with Florence. She told them about a private service Florence or Pete had never heard about before.

"There's a group of pilots called the Air Angels who might be able to help. Ever hear of them?"

"No, I can't say that I have, Jeneene. Who are they?" Florence asked.

"They're pilots who fly special needs people all over the country. They've been doing it for years, mostly on corporate jets, and mostly for cancer victims who need medical treatment and can't afford to fly from place to place to get it. Last I heard they had flown over 25,000 flights. I know one of the pilots. I can ask."

"And they have specially fitted planes and all?"

"That's what I understand, though I don't have any personal knowledge of it, but that's what I've been told."

"And how much do they charge?"

"They don't charge anything. Everything is free, but it's not for everyone. Like I said, as far as I know, it's mostly for cancer patients, but I can ask, if you'd like for me to.

"Please. It can't hurt to ask. Going through an airport and getting on a plane is going to be a challenge."

"Everything is going to be different, Pete, but you're ready to face those challenges, and you can do it. We know you can and you have to believe that you can," Jeneene assured him.

"Have you ever been on a plane with someone in a wheelchair? Someone like me?" Pete asked. "I can't remember a time when I was. What will they do? Put me in a seat and strap me in? Secure my chair to the floor? I've just never seen it done, that's all."

"Let me call my friend and I'll see what I can do. The airlines make arrangements for special needs passengers, but since this will be your first flight, maybe they'll be willing to help. It can't hurt to ask."

"Thanks, Jeneene."

A few days later, she returned and told them that a private plane would be taking them back to Fernandina Beach when they were ready to leave, although there might be a delay of a day or two, depending upon when the plane was needed for more pressing corporate matters.

"The flight I had out here took over ten hours," Florence said, "and that was with a change in Dallas. We couldn't get here any faster."

"There are no direct flights from Seattle to Jacksonville, so every flight is going to involve at least one connection," Jeneene offered. "I've checked with every airline that services this area."

"I can't sit up for more than two hours at a time. How could I do that, unless there's a place on board for me to lay down?" Pete asked.

"I don't know," Jeneene responded. "We can ask Dr. Johnson. Maybe he can medicate you or something, but unless something goes wrong, you won't have to worry about that. You can lie down on this plane if you need to. I asked and they told me so."

"Thank God," Florence said. "I don't know what we'd do if we had to fly a commercial airlines."

The only thing remaining was the chair. All of the discharge papers were ready to be signed, his personal belongings were gathered up and Pete and his mother waited anxiously for the arrival of the chair. On the Friday of that week, they were told that the chair was to be delivered that day. They were able to track the location of the driver on the FedEx website as he wound his way through Seattle making deliveries. Finally, late in the morning, the chair arrived. Once it was taken out of its crate and Pete was able to sit in it, the time had come to leave.

As he was heading out the door, under his own power, with his mother and Jeneene traipsing behind, Dr. Johnson stopped him in the hall and asked him to go into his office for a minute. When he did, all of the staff members who had treated him from the day shift were there to say their good-byes. A card had been signed by the 3 to 11 shift and by the night shift.

Pete wasn't expecting it and he didn't know what to say, and when he tried to speak, he couldn't. While he was fighting back the tears, trying to speak, everyone came up to him, one by one, put their arms around him, gave him a kiss and wished him well. The last person to come up to him was Dr. Johnson, who said,

"And so you won't forget about us too soon, we've all chipped in and bought you a present."

At that, James handed him a beautiful color photograph of the hospital, with Mt. Rainier in the background. It was in a 16" by 20" mahogany frame and had been signed on the back by all of the staff who had treated or cared for Pete while he was there.

"We've got to get back to work now, Pete, old boy, but know that you have a home here. We thought this would be the best way to make sure you remembered us. We hope you like it. You are loved. Good luck."

A teary-eyed Pete bid adieu to his friends and wheeled himself down the hall and out the front doors of the hospital, with his mother and Jeneene by his side, as a large, white van pulled up in front of them. It had a picture of a wheelchair and the words 'Para-Transit,' indicating that it transported paralyzed people, on the side. It was an unseasonably warm, spring-like day in mid-March, and it felt good to get fresh air in his lungs, but the sight of the words on the van had a sobering effect on him. He knew that he was a disabled person in a fast-paced society who wouldn't be treated like he had been for the last six months inside the nurturing arms of the Seattle Medical Center. Things were going to be different. He wasn't sure that he was ready for all that awaited him. He was sure that he didn't want to be in the hospital anymore, no matter how good they were to him.

The driver lowered a three by three foot metal platform and Pete pushed himself onto it. When he was securely in place, he waved good-bye to Jeneene until she and the hospital were no longer in sight.

15

Starting Over

THE FLIGHT HOME WAS hard on Pete. Even though the plane was one of the fastest non-military planes on the planet, a Gulfstream V edition, considered the "Queen of the Airways" in aviation circles, it was still a long and tedious flight. The plane made the journey without stopping and traveled at speeds approaching 500 miles per hour. Pete was able to lie down on a comfortable bed or sit up if he wanted to, which helped enormously, but the flight still took almost six hours from take-off in Seattle to touch-down at the Jacksonville airport, a distance of over 2500 hundred miles, and it put a heavy strain on Pete and his body, especially with the clam shell on him the whole time. He was tired and sore when they exited the plane.

Anthony was there to greet them as they came off of the plane, out at a private hanger, not at the main terminal. He had a large, white Econoline van with two Captain's chairs in the front and a bench seat in the back. Two doors on the passenger's side were open. Warm greetings were exchanged. Anthony hadn't seen his son in almost five months and he hadn't seen his wife in almost three.

"I don't know how we're going to do this, but this was the best I could do," Anthony said as he wondered out loud how he was going to get Pete from his chair and into the van.

"I think we can do this, Dad, but I'll need a little help," Pete said as he wheeled himself over to the van. "Hold me steady."

Anthony held on to the back of the wheelchair as Pete leaned forward and grabbed hold of a bar near the top of the open door and lifted himself up.

"Now, push me into the van, Dad."

Once Pete's butt was inside the van, he lowered himself down and scooted himself to the bench seat in the back and found another bar to use to hoist himself onto it. Anthony put the wheelchair in the van and Pete pulled it next to him, secured it and said,

"I'm fine. Let's go."

"Nicely done, Peter. I thought I'd have to lift you up and put you in. I wasn't so sure I could have done it, but you did that most of that all by yourself."

"That's the one thing they worked on most, Dad, getting out of bed and into my chair. That and getting out of my chair and onto the ground and then getting back in my chair again. They spent more time on those two things than anything else, I think."

"Well, I'm glad to see you were able to do that. My back has been bothering me lately and I was afraid I might hurt it trying to get you in this thing."

"I'm not as heavy as I once was, Dad. I'm down to 130 pounds now, I think."

"That's still too much for me. I'm glad you were able to do it by yourself."

Once they were settled and headed home, Florence said,

"This is nice. When did you get it?"

"I've had it for a month."

"You didn't tell me about it!"

"I wanted it to be a surprise."

"Well, you surprised us," she responded.

"It's really nice," Pete added. "What year is it?"

"2007. I got it used. You'd have been proud of me, Peter. I found it on the internet."

"All by yourself, huh, Dad? I am proud of you."

"It's because of you and Florence with all that e-mail stuff you've been learning. Your mother said we had to have it, so I went out and got it. You've got a few more surprises in store for you when you get home."

"Like what, Dad?" Pete asked.

"You'll see."

When they arrived home, both Pete and Florence were surprised to find that some changes had been made to the house. Jeneene had helped with the arrangements to have accommodations made in their home, which was standard procedure, and it involved things like putting in ramps and bars to make it a handicapped friendly environment. A few doors had to be widened. A special bed, much like the bed he was on in the hospital, was in his room and the bathroom had a special toilet.

A new vanity was in his bathroom that was high enough to allow him to wheel his chair up underneath it and there weren't any cabinets below the sink. He noticed that there was an insulated cover over the line supplying the hot water, so he couldn't or wouldn't get burned. He could get into the shower easily, too. The tub had been removed and the area for him to shower in was enlarged so that he could wheel his chair straight into it.

"You did all this, Dad?"

"Well, I didn't do it, the young woman from the hospital made all the arrangements."

"But you paid for it," Florence asked.

"Some of it, but a lot of that was taken care of through one of the programs Peter is eligible for."

"This is great, Dad. Thanks."

"Thank that woman from the hospital. Ginan, is that her name?"

"It's Jeneene, and I will, but not now. I've got to lie down. I need to take this clam shell off of me. My back is killing me."

It was late in the afternoon by the time they arrived in Florida, and getting dark by the time they got home. With the three hour time change involved with traveling east, it was now almost 7:00. Pete slept until early the next morning. He awoke, by habit, at the usual time of 7:00, and was glad to realize that nobody was there to poke him or prod him. He lay in his bed for a while, feeling as if it was a luxury to be able to do so.

At 8:00, he got into his chair and went into the kitchen. His parents had finished their breakfast and were drinking coffee, reading the morning paper. They had missed being together for the many months Florence had been in Seattle with Pete and were happy to be back together.

"What are you going to do today, Peter? His mother asked.

"The first thing I'm going to do is go outside and get some fresh air. I've been in a hospital for almost six months. After that, I don't know. Get on the computer, play my guitar…nothing too much, just take my time getting used to being out of a hospital and being back home. How about you two?"

"We're going to go into town, maybe do a little shopping. Your father tells me there's a nice new restaurant down just off of Eighth Avenue, next to O'Day's. We're going to have lunch there. You'll be alright while we're gone, won't you?" Florence asked.

"Sure," Pete responded.

"I thought we'd just walk up and down Main Street there. it has changed a little since your mother's been gone. It's a lot different from when you were last here, Peter. There are several new businesses and restaurants in town. All the curbs are cut so that you can get around pretty good, too. I didn't notice such things before, but I keep a lookout everyplace I go now," Anthony continued.

"I'll be fine. You two go and enjoy yourselves."

"Peter, out the back porch, I put in a concrete path that lets you get out to the tree in the back. If it's not too buggy, you can sit out there and play your music as long as you'd like. Your mother tells me you're learning and getting better every day."

Pete looked out into the back yard and saw the path. The house was a large, one-story, concrete block structure, with the red stucco tiles, which gave it a look of Spanish or Hispanic architecture. Fernandina Beach was one of the oldest cities in the state, not far behind St. Augustine. It was named after King Ferdinand of Spain when it was colonized back in the 1600s. It still had the look and feel of a Spanish community. Most of the streets and all of the churches had Spanish names.

Their house sat on a quarter of an acre lot, not far from the downtown area, which wasn't much more than one street that was five or six blocks long, with businesses on some of the side streets, too. Anthony and Florence were going to ride their bikes to town, which wasn't a mile away. The back yard had an eight foot high privacy fence surrounding it, with a magnificent Spanish Oak tree that was supposedly well over a hundred years old in the middle. It provided shade for the entire back yard.

When Anthony and Florence had left, Pete fixed himself a bowl of cereal and wheeled himself out into the back yard and into a ten foot by ten foot gazebo. He heard birds sing and felt the light breeze. Although it was almost April, the temperatures were a little cool. He had been in a temperature-controlled atmosphere for months and it was much cooler than he was used to. He went back inside and got himself a light jacket which he put on. He put a blanket over his legs. He was alone, under a tree. He took a deep breath and let out a long sigh. He felt good.

By noon, he was back in bed, where he lay for almost two hours, allowing his body to continue to adjust to his changed circumstances. His parents arrived back home shortly after 2:00 and he got out of bed and went to greet them. They were enjoying being together again. By mid-afternoon, he began what would become daily rituals, which consisted of playing guitar and working on the computer.

Although he wasn't really looking for a job just yet, because he knew that until he could stay awake and in his chair for a full day, he wouldn't be able to get one, but he would scan the classified ads every now and then. He looked first for things that would allow him to work from home, and there were some things out there that looked interesting, but he wasn't ready for that yet either. He exchanged e-mails with his family and kept himself busy. He didn't stray from home. It was going to take a while to adjust to life as a disabled member of society.

Good news came a month after he was home. At Dr. Johnson's direction, he went to a local medical facility where he was given another MRI. Dr. Johnson himself called a few days later to tell him that it looked like the meld had taken. Pete should follow with an orthopedic specialist, but unless something traumatic were to occur, he could begin wearing the clam-shell less and less.

Gradually, over the next few months, Pete was able to stay in his chair for longer and longer periods of time. He had his good days and his bad days. Unless it was raining, and if the mosquitoes or other flying pests, like deer flies and horse flies, weren't too bad, Pete would be outside, playing guitar, reading the paper, a book or a magazine or else he was on the internet with his lap top.

His parents had moved to Fernandina when his father retired, which was after their last child graduated from high school. Because Pete had left home two years before that while his parents were still living in Rhode Island, he didn't have any friends in the area. All of his friends were back up north, where he had gone to school. He wasn't ready to go looking any of them up yet, either. He was still very much like an injured bear that had retreated into a cave high up in the mountains, licking his wounds.

It wasn't that he was feeling sorry for himself, Pete told his parents and himself, he just wasn't ready. He was able to sit up most of every day, but not a full day from 8:00 to 5:00, which most employers would require for full-time work. He looked for part-time work, too, but hadn't been able to find anything which suited him. He was doing what Dr. Johnson had told him to do and he was letting his body tell him when he was ready. He just wasn't ready yet.

Playing his guitar provided him with the greatest sense of release, that and just sitting under the tree, especially early in the morning , when the fresh smells of a new day enveloped him, and when the song birds sang to him, alone, with no noises from the cars and the bustling world outside. Fernandina wasn't too big, so there wasn't much of a bustle, but passing cars would break the spell, temporarily.

Late afternoons were good, too, after the sun had gone down, when a coolness would descend upon him. He couldn't see the sun set any further than the houses and trees around him would permit, but that was enough. That was a beautiful time of day, too.

His best days were the days on which he could convince or cajole his father or mother to take him down to the beach to watch the sun rise. Florence was a little uncomfortable about driving the van with Pete in it. She was afraid that something would happen and she couldn't lift him up or do anything to help. She preferred that Anthony would take him, and he did, most of the time.

Looking out on the Atlantic Ocean from shore, there was nothing to impede his view of the sun as it mystically and magically made its daily appearance on the horizon. Pete liked getting there as early as possible, as early as he could get either his mother or his father to awake, while it was still dark, but not too early. The best days were when they got to the parking lot of the beach just when a hint of the coming sun became perceptible. He would wheel himself up to the paved sidewalk and down to a stretch of the beach that had no bushes blocking his view of the water. He couldn't get any closer to the water than that, because he couldn't propel his chair through the sand, but that was close enough.

Although he felt funny doing it, he liked having a blanket around him, with a stocking cap on his head to keep him warm, even in the summer. It surprised him how cool the mornings could be, even on what would become the hottest of days. Whichever parent brought him, and sometimes it would be both, would stay in the van most of the time, but sometimes they would bring a chair and sit next to him. When they did, though, they rarely spoke to one another. Pete enjoyed the quiet almost as much as the beauty of his surroundings.

He would always bring a full thermos of coffee with him, every day, and he would slowly sip on it, timing himself so as to finish his coffee just when he was ready to leave. His parents thought he would go into a trance, as if hypnotized, as he watched the sky turn from black to varying shades of gray, before turning pink. He liked seeing how the little dot of orange first appeared on the horizon and then grew. He played little games in his mind to figure out exactly where it would appear. It was interesting to see how it migrated from place to place. It was never the same, never exactly the same, that is.

One of his favorite games to play was to time how long it took for the sun to make it into the sky from the moment when he first could see the dot on the horizon to the moment when the full circle of the sun. There was a brief period of time when he could view the sun, in its majestic orange coat, and he enjoyed those moments. This and the setting sun were the only times he could look straight into the sun without being blinded by it. He stared at it, transfixed, every day he could, never tiring of it.

When the shades of orange became bright yellow, it was time to leave. He enjoyed watching the sun turn the sky from pink to blue, and he enjoyed watching the rays from the sun come over the water straight to him, but once the sun was fully in the sky, it seemed to move more quickly, as if it was in a hurry to make its way around the planet. He enjoyed the stormy days, too, but the rain caused him to stay in one of the several picnic areas, which had roofs overhead and kept him dry.

While in school, he had liked reading about the ancient gods of Greek and Roman literature. He liked to think of the rising sun as being a huge ball of fire pulled by Apollo in his chariot on his daily trek across the sky. Apollo, son of Zeus, with his curly, golden locks, always watchful for a beautiful maiden to seduce, was the father of Orpheus, the semi-divine goddess of music.

Pete prayed to Apollo to bestow blessings upon him, fully aware of the heresy of his thoughts. No other god in Greek or Roman mythology was as honored. No other god was called by the same name in both Greek and Latin. They were called Zeus, Poseidon, Hades, Ares, Athena, Aphrodite and Hermes by the Greeks, and Jupiter, Neptune, Pluto, Mars, Minerva, Venus and Mercury by the Romans. All had different names given them by the Greeks from those given them by the Romans. Only Apollo had the same name to both the Greeks and the Romans.

Pete thought to himself that he had once been god-like. He had once owned the universe. He was once capable of truly heroic feats, but that was then. This was now. He had been more like Icarus, the son of Daedalus, who had flown too close to the sun, causing the feathers on his wings to melt, which caused him to crash to earth and die. Pete had crashed to earth, but he wasn't dead yet. Each day, after watching the sun rise, he returned to his cave, happy to have had an opportunity to commune with nature, content to allow his body to continue the healing process.

For months, Pete was content to play his guitar and be absorbed by the complexities of the computer, although he had his moments when, for no apparent reason, he would feel a rage inside of him about his condition and he'd have to take his guitar and put it down or else he'd damage it, which happened several times. When it did, his father would tell him,

"Peter, this is the last time. I can't afford to be paying money to fix your guitar any more. I really can't. I know you get frustrated at times, but you're just going to have to control yourself better. Can you do that? Please?"

And Pete would always reply,

"Yes, Dad. I'm sorry. I don't know what comes over me. I don't want it to happen, but when it does I try to put the guitar down as fast as I can so that it won't happen. I'll try not to let it happen again."

By the fifth time it happened, both realized that it was going to happen again. Maybe it was a good thing, Florence said. Maybe he was beginning to get back some of the fire that had always been a part his very soul. She would always be the one to go out and find another guitar for him. They were both happy that he didn't do the same thing with his computers. They couldn't afford to buy new guitars and they soon learned of the various places that fixed guitars and of pawn shops in the area where used guitars could be purchased cheap.

Maybe he was getting better. Maybe his soul was healing. Maybe his soul was adjusting to his changed circumstances. Only time would tell. It was now mid May and his thoughts turned to Glacier. It was rafting season back in Montana. He fell asleep thinking of the many good days he had spent in rafts, canoes and kayaks on rivers in Montana, Idaho and other places, and the people he spent those days with.

16
A Secret is Revealed

THE FOLLOWING SPRING, AFTER the accident, while Pete was healing, Abigail was back to work at the Great Northern. She loved being on the water and she couldn't find a better place to work or better people to work for. Reno was happy to have her back. He even offered to let her stay in his house if she wanted, but she preferred her own tee-pee in the woods, the same one as the year before. The same one she and Pete had shared together on many occasions.

About half of the group from the year before, including Dennis, returned as well, which was normal. During the height of the season, Reno had ten buses going back and forth to the river from his store with rafters. On a good day, he might put well over a hundred rafts on the river. He had to have a guide in each raft and most guides would do two runs in a day. Fortunately for him, there were twenty some locals who were willing to come out and work whenever he needed help, so he didn't have to find all of his employees a place to stay and some were part-time employees.

Abby and the returning guides helped Reno train all the new guides. Each year there would be at least twenty or more new guides hired and there were always more than enough applicants, not all of whom would make the cut. Ever since that accident when the tree fell on a raft, Reno took great pains to make sure his guides could handle a crisis. After the injury to Pete, he made sure that his guides received extra training on how to handle a spinal cord injury, too.

In early spring, the middle fork in the Flathead River would be filled with the runoff of melting snow coming off the mountains. The river would rise far above flood stage in Glacier, but Reno could still safely put rafts on the river because the mountain walls easily contained the waters of the raging river and actually made the river safer in some ways. As Reno explained it, objects in the river, such as boulders, and the hydraulics created by those obstacles, was what could kill a person, not the swiftness of the current. A hydraulic is water spinning in a circular motion which keeps a swimmer in it, like a washing machine. A 'killer' hydraulic is one that doesn't spit the swimmer out.

The way to get out of a 'killer' rapid like that, he explained, was to swim down to the bottom of the rapid and then let the current push you out the bottom, and down the river. Most people wouldn't do that. Their natural instincts were to get to the top, so that they could breathe.

When the waters of the river rose thirty, forty and at times as much as a hundred feet above normal, there would be no obstructions in the river to create the 'killer' hydraulics. The waters, though huge, would carry a swimmer downstream and, eventually, to safe ground. A rafter had to be able to swim, and everyone, even the guides, had to keep a life preserver on at all times, but there was less of a chance of death or serious injury at higher levels than there was at lower levels when the monstrous boulders in the river created the snarling rapids that excite the white-water enthusiasts but occasionally kill people.

Nearly half of the guides were women. Abigail was one of the best of the bunch, men and women included. Normally, three or four rafts would go downstream at a time and there would be one lead guide for the group. Abigail was always the lead guide in whatever group she was in.

Most of the rafts could hold as many as eight rafters, but that included the guide. Six paying customers in a raft was a good number, and four was acceptable. The guide would be in the back with an extra large paddle to direct the path of the raft, while the rafters used normal size paddles to provide power when needed to propel the raft from one side of the river to the other to get into or away from a rapid. The guides basically steered the raft down the river, choosing the course to take.

As Reno explained, the raft would make its way down the river, with or without the guides and rafters. As long as the raft held its air and didn't get punctured, it was going to stay on top of the water and float like a rubber ball down the river. It was the guides' job to keep it away from trouble.

The guides kept a running score of how many rafters became swimmers. The bottom ten guides with the most number of swimmers at the end of the season had to pay extra for the season-ending bash, not to mention having their name put on the wall of shame as winners of the Polaris award, in recognition of the submarine from the Jules Verne movie, Twenty Thousand Leagues under the Sea. They took it seriously and tried very hard not to lose anyone on their trips. Some customers liked to swim rapids and they'd jump out, or fall out, on purpose. Guides were always wrangling with each other about whether or not it should count when someone supposedly jumped out of the raft due to no fault of the guide.

The Native-Americans of the region included the Flathead, Crow, Blackfeet, Shoshone and at least eight other tribes. The area around Glacier was their home before the arrival of the 'white man' sometime in the mid 1800s and it was still their home. Many reservations exist in Montana, Idaho and the Dakotas. As rough and rugged as it was during the winter, with snowfalls of hundreds of feet, it was beautiful and serene in the summer.

There was no place on earth Abby had seen that she would rather be. She was the happiest when there, despite the catastrophe of the year before. She was glad to be back and everyone was glad to have her back. She was always a big hit with the rafters, too, especially a crew of 'macho' college-age boys. She knew what she was doing on the river. When she wasn't guiding a raft down the river, she was often in a kayak. On days off, it was nothing for the guides to pack up a few boats and drive hours to other rivers in Montana or Idaho, such as the Snake, the Salmon or the Selway and run those rivers. It was in her blood.

While there were many suitors, Abby hadn't let anyone get too close since the injury to Pete. She knew that she would have to move on, but she wasn't emotionally ready to do that just yet. She wasn't sure why Pete wasn't letting her in to share what he was going through, but she thought it was because of the pain he was in.

On one level, it would help her to move on if she could get him out of her mind. On another level, it remained a wound that had not healed. She still cared deeply for Pete but she didn't know how to get through to him or if she should continue to try. She didn't know what it would be like for her to see him in a wheelchair. She wasn't' sure that she could handle it. Her heart was heavy, far too heavy for a young, beautiful girl.

Every so often, though, and at least once or twice a week, she'd go out with her fellow guides to the Moose, have dinner and a few beers. After dinner, while everyone else stayed to dance or party, she'd leave and go back to her tee-pee. Coincidentally, like Pete, she was learning to play a guitar, too, and spent hours at night in front of a fire, strumming on it. Even during the summer, temperatures would regularly drop into the forties, but even when the temperatures were in the low sixties, she liked having a fire. It made her feel better. It warmed her soul.

Her sister still lived in Kalispell and came to visit often. Other than that, Abigail had few visitors, but she was content. There was an emptiness inside her, caused by what had happened to Pete, and that would take time to heal.

One night, as Abby was having dinner at the Moose with Dennis and six other guides from the Great Northern, Dave came in. As soon as he saw them, he immediately sat down with them, as if he was still one of the guides. Not long after, Sandra walked in. When Abigail saw her, she did a double-take, trying to place her. She saw so many people at school at the University of Montana, and as a guide, that she didn't immediately recognize her from that fateful night of almost a year ago. Sandra gave her the same kind of look. She asked Dave if he recognized her. He turned around and immediately said,

"I do. That's one of the girls from the Double-D. She came up to help with the horses that night."

Just as they were figuring out where they knew her from, Sandra walked over to where they were sitting and said hello. Dave pulled up a chair from the next table and asked her to join them and she did.

Dennis had ordered two large plates of Nachos and extra chips, and three pitchers of beer, all of which arrived just as she sat down. They exchanged small talk about their jobs, school and other things and, after a while, when Dave and the others were engaged in an animated discussion about the Mariners and their need for better pitching, she turned to Abby and asked,

"So how is Pete?"

"He's paralyzed from the waist down and in a wheelchair."

"That's what I heard. Have you seen him or heard from him?"

"No. Reno told me that he's down in Florida with his parents. As far as I know, he hasn't communicated with me or anyone else other than Reno since the accident."

"It's just such a shame. That never should have happened."

Abigail's ears perked up, and she asked,

"Why's that?"

"Michael never should have put those two horses together the way he did. Everyone knew that Bucky and Ben didn't get along."

"Why'd he do it then?"

"They were the two biggest horses we had and he wanted to put the two biggest guys on them. Pete and Dave wanted to ride together and Michael rode right behind them. I guess he felt like he could handle the situation."

"Is he back this year?"

"No, not after what happened with Pete. He wanted to come back, but Tom and Patty wouldn't let him."

"He seemed like a nice guy. Did they have other problems with him?"

"About a month before that thing with Pete happened, there had been a similar incident."

"Another guy got hurt like Pete did?"

"No, the guy didn't get hurt at all. He fell off, but he just got up and climbed back on. Nobody ever found out about it, but I was there when it happened, so I saw it. He made me promise not to tell Tom and Patty and I didn't, until after this all happened and then I told them about it."

"Geez! Do you think he forgot or what?"

"He knew. I guess he just didn't think it would happen again. I mean, those horses went out on the same trail rides all the time, and they both were good trail horses, you just couldn't put them together like he did, that's all."

"So why'd he do it?"

"Maybe he was thinking that he could change the way they acted and make them get along, but you can't. That's just the way horses are. They don't change much. Christie told me that she said something about it to him that day and he told her he'd be careful, or something like that."

"Damn! I wish you hadn't told me that. Now I feel worse about it for some reason."

"He was a nice guy, he just made a mistake. He felt terrible about it, but that didn't make it any better for your friend."

"Let's not talk about it anymore. It makes me sad when I think about it."

"Okay. Don't tell Tom and Patty that I told you though, okay? They don't want us talking about it."

"I won't. Thanks for telling me and for what you did to help out that night."

"You're welcome. If you're talking to Pete, tell him that I asked about him."

"I will, if he'll ever talk to me."

"He will, when he's ready, I'm sure."

"I hope so. I think that he's just so hurt inside that he doesn't want people to see him the way he is now. I think he's afraid people, including me, will reject him when they see him in a wheelchair."

"I can't imagine what that would be like. It scares me to think about it, too. Every time I get on a horse I think about it."

"I think about it when I go down a river, but let's not talk about it. It makes me want to cry."

"Okay. I've got to get goin' anyway. I was supposed to meet some friends here and I see them over in the corner. They're probably wondering where I am. Good to see you again. I'd offer to take you out on a ride but I don't know if you'd want to go after what happened to Pete."

"I've ridden horses since I was a kid. I'd love to go out with you sometime, and if you ever want to go down river, just call and I'll take you down any time you want, whether I'm working or not."

"I will. Maybe in a few weeks when it calms down a little."

"Just give me a call and we'll do it."

After she had left, Abby mentioned to Dave what Sandra had told her. Dave was planning to go to law school when he graduated and his uncle was a personal injury lawyer in Bozeman. He didn't say anything about it to anyone, but he thought to himself that he'd mention it to his uncle.

Dave thought that there was probably nothing that could be done about it, even though it seemed to him, based on what Abigail told him and from what he'd seen and heard on the night it happened, that the outfitter had made a mistake. To him, it made it worse that they didn't tell anyone about it. Dave knew that Pete's parents weren't wealthy and he didn't know how they were paying for things. It wouldn't hurt to ask.

* * * * * * * * * * * * * *

That weekend, Dave called his uncle, Bob Nickel, and told him about what Sandra had told Abby. He had already told his whole family about what had happened to Pete the previous summer and they had all talked about it many times. His uncle told him that while he would like nothing more than to be able to help his friend, in most cases, whether it was white-water rafting, sky-diving, scuba-diving or any other such thing, the proprietors require patrons to sign a release.

He said that the releases generally prevented anyone from making a claim when an injury occurred, because the customer 'waived' or 'released' any claim that he or she might have against the proprietor. Everyone knew that riding horses could be dangerous, so that if anyone chose to ride a horse, knowing the potential danger, the person accepted the risk of doing so. Bob said he would have to see the release before he could say whether or not Pete had a case. He told Dave to get a copy of the release Pete signed and he'd take a look at it.

Dave wanted to get a copy of Double-D's release but he didn't want to make it too obvious why. While he was at work the next day, one of the guides was having a beer at the bar where he tended and happened to mention that she was going to go riding at the Double-D. She was a new guide and, although she had heard something about what had happened to Pete, she didn't know Pete. She had been riding most of her life and wasn't at all afraid to get up on a horse's back. Dave casually mentioned to her that she would have to sign a release before she went out on the ride and he asked her not to throw it away, that he'd like to see it and compare it to what the Great Northern had patrons sign. She didn't think much of it and told him that she'd be happy to do that for him.

The day after that, the girl, whose name was Robin, brought the release she had signed back to Dave. Later that night he read it.

> *Release*
> *'I, Robin Imhoff, in consideration of my being allowed to rent a horse from the Double-D Ranch, do hereby release and discharge the Double-D Ranch, its owners, employees, agents and all others associated with the operation of the Double-D Ranch, including its trail guides and anyone who provides any assistance to me who is in any way connected to the Double-D Ranch, from any and all claims or demands which I may have or which may arise as a result of my trail ride for any and all personal injuries sustained by me during the trail ride. I also agree that I am responsible for any harm that I cause to the horse and for any damage I cause to any of the equipment provided to me by the Double-D Ranch for the trail ride, such as to the saddle, bridle or other equipment. '*

"Boy, that looks pretty clear to me," he thought to himself. "I think we waived any claim we had against them when we signed this." Although he didn't see the point, he faxed it to his Uncle with a note. "Here's a copy of the release my friend signed. What do you think?"

The next week, just as he was about to sit down for dinner, his Uncle gave him a call.

"Dave, how are things going up there in God's country?"

"Couldn't be better, Uncle Bob. How about you?"

"Can't complain. There's more work than I can handle but that's a better problem to have than not having enough work to do, right?"

"If you say so, Uncle Bob, as long as your clients pay their bills, right?"

"That's right, Dave. Collecting your fee is half the battle. Get it up front if you can."

"But you don't do that in what you do, do you?"

"Well, not if it's a personal injury matter, but if it's a contract dispute, or a divorce, or criminal defense, then I try to get my fee up front, or at least a substantial retainer."

"You do all those kinds of things, do you?"

"Oh yeah. When you're a solo practitioner in a small town, you take whatever walks through the door and you're thankful for it."

"I didn't realize that."

"You sure you want to leave the sun and the water and all those beautiful girls and put on a suit and tie and work in an office?"

"I start law school in a year, if I get accepted, that is. I'm looking forward to it."

"Well, you know you have a job waiting for you whenever you want."

"Thanks, Uncle Bob. So what did you think of that release? I don't guess we have much of a chance, do we?"

"I'm not so sure about that, Dave. I think that there's a good argument that the document you and your friend signed doesn't release the Double-D for the negligence of the trail guide, if there was any."

"They shouldn't have put us together on those two horses like they did, Uncle Bob."

"So they put Pete on the wrong horse?"

Dave explained what he had heard and about the prior incident.

"It wasn't that he put him on the wrong horse, he just shouldn't have put that horse behind the horse I was riding."

"Darn, Dave. You could just as easily have been the one on the horse Pete was riding that day, couldn't you?"

"That's right."

"I didn't realize it was that close."

"It could've been me just as easy as it was Pete."

"Scary, isn't it?"

"You bet. I think about it every day. He was my best friend up here."

"Well, I'll tell you what. You put me in touch with Pete and I'm willing to give it a try."

"Really? But the thing says we released any and all claims we might have?"

"But it doesn't mention the word 'negligence' and that's the key. I think we have a good argument and I'm willing to take a shot at it."

"And it won't cost Pete anything?"

"No, I won't charge him anything."

"Not even the costs?"

"I'll advance the costs. I'll get them back if we win."

"I'll get in touch with him and see what he says."

"Where is he now?"

"In Florida. Where would the lawsuit be filed, Uncle Bob? Here or there?"

"It would have to be here, Dave. This is where the Double-D has its principal place of business and this is where the incident occurred."

"I'll let him know."

"Dave, so you'll know, and you can tell him this if you want, with the severity of the injury for a young man like he is, the damages would be enormous. If we win this, it could pay for all of his medical expenses in the past and in the future, plus a whole lot more. There would be a big fee in it for me, too. It could be me thanking you when it's all over."

"But maybe not, right? I don't want to get Pete's hopes up and then have him be disappointed again."

"I can't guarantee anything, Dave, other than that I'll do the best I can. I don't make any money unless he makes some money, but I wouldn't waste my time on this if I didn't think we had a chance to win."

"I'll let you know what he says."

"And Dave, have him call me directly. I shouldn't be calling him. He should call me first."

"I'll tell him."

"And Dave, one more thing. Enjoy yourself. These are the best years of your life. Before too long you'll be working long, hard hours, just like I am, maybe with me, and wishing you could go rafting or fishing or whatever else you are doing up there."

"I'll do my best. Where are you, Uncle Bob? Are you at home?"

"No, that's what I mean. I'm still at the office. This is my last call of the day. I wanted to talk to you before the day ended and now I can go home."

"What does Aunt Kathleen think of that?"

"She likes it when I bring home a paycheck."

"I hope you can bring home a paycheck on this case, Uncle Bob. I'd like to see something good happen for Pete's sake."

"Take care, nephew, and say hello to your mother and father for me when you talk to them next, okay?"

"I will. Bye, Uncle Bob."

17

To Sue or not to Sue

THE NEXT DAY, DAVE got Pete's number from Reno and called him that night. It was late afternoon in Florida and Pete had just finished his dinner. He answered the phone and was surprised by the call. They spent most of the time catching up on what had been almost a year since they had seen each other. At the end of the conversation, Dave told Pete about what Sandra had told Abigail.

When Pete received the news, he didn't think too much of it at first. It didn't make him feel any better and he would still be paralyzed for the rest of his life. An apology or an explanation would do nothing to cure that problem. He thanked Dave for the information and told him he'd think about it. He wrote down Mr. Nickel's number. When he got off the phone, he told his parents and said,

"When I signed that release I gave my word I wouldn't sue them. How can I now sue them?"

"Because you didn't say that you would release them even if they did something wrong. You just said that you understood that riding horses was dangerous, not that you wouldn't blame them if they put you on the wrong horse or did something else to cause you to get hurt, Peter," his father responded.

"But Michael wasn't a bad guy. He didn't do it on purpose. He was doin' us a favor, Dad. I didn't even pay any money to go on that ride. How can I sue him and blame him for what happened?"

"Peter, I admire the ethical position you're taking, but…"

"How can I say I won't sue them and then sue them, Dad?"

"Peter, I'm not a lawyer. Mr. Nickel, who is your friend's uncle, says that you can still sue them. He thinks you have a good case and he's willing to…"

"Dad, what if we lose? Who's going to pay? Dave's uncle or us?"

"Peter, he's not going to charge you any money. He's not going to make a dime unless he wins your case, not even for the costs."

"Are you sure of that?"

"That's the way it usually works, I think, but you can ask him and make sure. Peter, I don't know this man, and maybe he's doing this because you're a friend of his nephew's. I don't know. Do you trust your friend?"

"Yeah. He was about my best friend up there. He's a good guy."

"So do you trust Dave to believe that if he says his uncle isn't going to charge you any money, not even for costs, that he's telling the truth?"

"I guess I'll go that far."

"So will you let him look into it further or not?"

"You still didn't answer my question about how I can say one thing and then do another. How can I do that, Dad?"

"Peter, I admit that from what you told me it sounds like you agreed to accept the risks involved with riding a horse, and falling off is certainly a risk that you could foresee happening, but you didn't agree that you wouldn't make a claim against them if they did something wrong, son. At least, that's what I understand the lawyer to be saying, and that's why you can still file suit."

"I don't want to sue Michael! He was a nice guy, like me, just doin' his job, Dad! Would I want someone suing me if I tipped over a raft in a big rapid? It's the same thing."

"Peter, you're not suing Michael, and you're not suing the Double-D Ranch, either, son. You're suing their insurance company. They have insurance to cover this sort of thing. Your friend, Michael and the Double-D Ranch won't pay a penny!"

"Are you sure of that, Dad?"

"I tell you what…I'll bet dinner at whatever restaurant you want to go to on it. In fact, you can even make sure that the Double-D and Michael don't pay any money."

"How's that?"

"Your lawyer will find out about the insurance and when he does he'll be able to tell you exactly how much money the insurance company has insured the Double-D Ranch for, and you can agree not to take a penny more from them than what insurance money there is. Would that make you feel better?"

"Dad, you don't understand…"

"What don't I understand, Peter? Let me ask you a question, did you do anything wrong, like gallop up the side of the mountain, or go off the trail, or do anything silly to cause that horse to fall?"

"No."

"So why did that horse fall, Peter? What do you think?"

"Dad, it happened so fast…we were just coming down the mountain, walking slow…I was leaning back in the saddle, like they told me, and my horse ran up behind Dave's horse and Dave's horse pinned his ears back and must've kicked my horse or something, I don't know how it happened. I really didn't see it, but I saw Dave's horse raise up its rear-end and that's when my horse fell."

"Well, from what we've been told, Michael shouldn't have put your horse behind Dave's horse. Supposedly something like this happened once before, right?"

"That's what Dave told me."

"Peter, I can't make you sign anything or do anything you don't want to do, but for what it's worth, I don't think that you are breaking your word by allowing this lawyer to see if he can get some money for you from the insurance company for the Double-D Ranch. I really don't."

Pete didn't say anything for a short while, and then his father added,

"And son, I really hate to say this, but you could use the money, you know."

"I know, Dad. I hate bein' a burden on you and Mom, I really do. When I'm able to, I'll get out of here and get my own place. I'm just not ready yet, Dad."

"I understand, son, and you're welcome here as long as you like.

You know that. This is your home and we love you, that's not what I mean...I mean for you. We're not going to be around forever and you're going to need all the money you can get, son."

"I'm gonna get a job, Dad, when I'm ready."

"And I'm not trying to rush you, son. You've been through a lot. I'm just saying that if you have a chance to get some money for what happened to you that you'd be foolish not to try to get it."

"I hate what I read in the papers about lawyers and lawsuits, Dad. Everybody sues everybody over everything and it's all about money."

"But Peter, if the lawsuits are good ones, based on the truth, not upon lies or tricks, what's wrong with that? That's what courts of law are for, to find the truth and make the other side pay for the injury and damage it caused. I don't see anything wrong with that. Now, if it was your fault and you were just trying to blame it on them, then that's a different story, but that's not what we're talking about here."

"I don't know..."

"You don't have to decide today, son. Just think about it, but please, think about this, too...how much money do you think a case like yours is worth? A million dollars? Two million dollars? How much?"

"I have no idea, Dad."

"How much money would you pay to get your legs back?"

"Are you kidding? I'd pay all the money in the world to be able to walk again."

"Or saying it a little differently, how much money would you take to give away your legs?"

"I wouldn't take all the money in the world, Dad."

"That's what a jury has to do, decide how much it's worth to lose your legs...that's a lot of money, isn't it?"

"I guess it could be."

"You know it could be, but there are no guarantees that you'll get anything, but I can guarantee you that you won't get anything if you don't try, son."

"I don't know..."

"And think about what you could do with that kind of money, son...or where you would ever have the chance to get that kind of money. Not unless you win the lottery, or something like that, will you ever have a chance to get that kind of money, son."

"Maybe I'll become a financial wizard, you don't know."

"I hope you do, but you've got to have money to make money and you don't have any money to invest right now, do you, son?"

"No, I don't."

"And don't forget that you only have so long to make a decision. They have a statute of limitations for bringing a lawsuit like yours. I don't know what it is in Montana but I know that it's four years in Florida."

"How do you know that, Dad?"

"Oh, about thirty years ago, before you were even born, your mother and I were involved in a car accident. We were hit from behind by a young man from the University of Florida who was driving way too fast. We could've been killed. The impact pushed us into a tree and our car missed one of those big electrical transformers by about a foot. If we had hit that, I don't think either one of us would be here now, son."

"So were you hurt?"

"We were both hurt. Your mother was stiff and sore for a month or two. She had to go to see a doctor, a physical therapist and a massage therapist several times a week for a couple of months. She was pregnant with your older brother, John, at the time, so we were very concerned about that."

"And what about you?"

"I hurt my low back and my neck. The neck got better but I had a herniated disc in my lower back, at the L4-L5. My doctor wanted me to undergo surgery and fuse the vertebrae together, but I didn't want to go through with it."

"So what did you do?"

"I just kept doing my exercises, strengthening the back muscles, and I had to be very careful with the things I did. No more lifting 300 pounds on my bench presses, things like that."

"Yeah, you wish!"

"Okay, maybe it was 250 pounds."

"Dad?"

"Okay, maybe it was 200 pounds."

"Dad?"

"No, I promise you son, I could do 200 pounds at one time, now not when I was forty and had three children, I grant you that, but you know what I mean."

"Did you have to see a lawyer?"

"Yes, and that's what I'm telling you. The insurance company for this young man tried to blame the accident on me since I had made a U-turn in front of him. At first they wouldn't agree to pay me anything except medical expenses. I was in pain and I was afraid that I would need surgery and that I might end up…"

"Paralyzed? Go ahead, say it, Dad."

"Yes, son. Paralyzed."

"So was it your fault or not?"

"No, it wasn't my fault. The young man admitted to the police officer that he was doing well over 70 in a 45 mile an hour zone. I had fully completed my turn when he hit me. I saw him as I started my turn and he was way down the road. I didn't think there was any danger at all. He must have been doing at least 80 miles an hour when he hit me right square in the middle of the back end of my vehicle. He admitted he was at fault, but when his parents got there, that's when he changed his tune and said some things that weren't true, trying to blame it on me."

"So you had to get a lawyer?"

"Yes, I had to get a lawyer and he had to file suit for me."

"And you won?"

"Well, actually we ended up settling the case, and I got the policy limits of $100,000. The lawyer took 40% of it, but I never would have gotten anything if I hadn't gone to see her."

"So you've been through this, huh?"

"Yes, I have, but nothing like what you're going through, son."

"I never knew that."

"We don't talk about it much. I'd just as soon forget about the whole thing, but now with this news from your friend, Dave, it reminded me of that."

"Okay, Dad. Thanks for your advice. I'll think about it."

"That's all I can ask, and if you have any questions, write them down. If I can't answer them, we can maybe ask someone around here or we can ask your friend's uncle. What's his name?"

"Robert Nickel. Robert Henry Nickel."

The next morning, after Pete had a chance to think about it some more, and to sleep on it, he told his parents that he'd agree to let Mr. Nickel look into it for him. He called Mr. Nickel who said that he'd prepare the necessary paperwork, which would include a retainer agreement and some medical release forms, and have it sent to him by overnight mail with a return envelope so that it could be signed and returned to him.

18

Back to work

After signing the retainer agreement and other forms, Pete didn't hear anything from Mr. Nickel for quite a while and didn't think much about the lawsuit. In the months following the decision to allow Mr. Nickel to look into the matter, and possibly file a lawsuit, Pete thought about other things and decided it was time to move on with his life. He went from being inert to being in action.

One brisk Fall morning in late October, eight months after he had come home from the hospital, Pete decided it was time to get a job and face the world. He had been in his cave long enough. He had gone through stages of denial, anger, remorse and depression. He was ready for acceptance. He was ready to accept who he was and what he was and deal with it. He wheeled himself into the kitchen, fixed himself a bowl of cereal, picked up the newspaper and turned to the classified ads. His parents, who had finished their breakfast and were drinking their last cups of coffee, looked at each other, but didn't say anything. Then Pete said,

"There's an ad for a data entry clerk at Walgreen's. That sounds like something I can do."

Anthony and Florence exchanged looks of wonder and then Anthony replied,

"It probably involves just entering numbers, like items bought and sold, items to be purchased, inventory, maybe even money, like what came in, what went out. Maybe even loss due to theft or breakage. Who knows, maybe keeping track of what employees do, like payroll, benefits, days they take off, things like that. I think that is definitely something you could do, Peter. It could be interesting."

"I think I'm going to apply."

"Really?" his mother asked. "I think that's a great idea. I know you'll be good at it."

"I don't want anything too challenging at first, nothing that requires me to interact with the public or with any other people."

"That's a good idea," Anthony offered. "Start slow and see how it goes."

"I think you'll have a really good chance to get that job. Don't they have to give special consideration to people with disabilities?"

"I don't want that, Mom. I want the job because I'm the best qualified person, and I'm gonna tell them that. I don't want any special considerations."

"Okay, Peter. You tell them that. I'm sure that you're going to be the best qualified applicant. Your computer skills are excellent and if there is any math involved, you excel at that, too." His father said.

"Yeah. As long as it doesn't require standing for prolonged periods of time and running around in circles, I'll be great." Pete responded facetiously.

"Well, that's a good point, Peter." His mother responded. "This job may not be the right job for you. Maybe it's not exactly what you're looking for, but it's worth looking into, don't you think? You never know until you ask, but you're right, don't get your hopes up too much, because all you know about the job so far is what they put in the paper. You've got to ask questions."

"So how do you apply? Does it say?" His father asked.

"It just gives a number to call."

"So you're going to call?" His mother asked.

"I'm going to call."

"Now?"

"When I'm finished with my breakfast."

His mother beamed, walked over behind him, leaned her head over his right shoulder and planted a big kiss on his cheek.

"Don't get all excited, Mom. I didn't get the job or anything yet."

"I know, but I'm happy that you're going to apply. I'm going to say some prayers and hope you get it, if that's what you want. Don't take the job if you can see that it isn't right for you. You have to interview them just like they are interviewing you. Am I right, Anthony?"

"That's right, dear. Before you go on an interview, be sure to think of all the questions you would want to know the answers to and write them down. Actually, I think people who ask intelligent questions about what the job is going to involve show that they are serious about the position and that they've given the matter a lot of thought. I think prospective employers are impressed by that sort of thing. If you want to talk about it before you go, we can do that."

"I can do this by myself, Dad. I've had jobs before. I've gone on interviews before."

"I know, son. I didn't mean anything by it, just that if you want some help say so."

"I will. That's a good idea. I'll think of questions to ask them."

When Pete had finished his breakfast, he wheeled himself back to his room, showered and then made the call. He was told that he could complete the application on line or come in to the store and fill out the application. Since the position involved entering data in a computer, Pete thought it made more sense to complete it on line and demonstrate some computer skills.

There was no place on the application form for him to indicate that he had a disability except for one question which asked if he had any special needs. He reasoned that for a data entry position, he didn't have needs any different than any other applicant so he checked 'no.' An hour after he did so, he received a call from the store and was asked to come in for an interview later that day.

Since Pete wasn't able to drive yet, he had to rely upon either his parents or a van service operated by the county, which picked up people like Pete and took them places, to get wherever he was going. The problem was that there weren't very many of those vans, three to be exact, and they came when they were available and sometimes that took hours. Anthony had plans to go to fishing off a pier and Florence was going to go to the gym and then do some shopping. Both offered to take Pete to the interview.

When they arrived at the designated address, Pete was surprised to see that it wasn't a regular Walgreen's store like the hundreds of them all across Florida. Walgreen's was one of the largest chains in the state. A sign out front indicated that it was their corporate office. It was a newer one-story building with plenty of parking spaces in the front, with ramps and rails leading to the building. Anthony opened the sliding doors to the van and Peter unhooked his chair, maneuvered himself out of the van and into his chair on the ground.

"I got it from here, Dad."

"You want me to go with you?"

"No thanks. I'll do this myself."

Anthony fidgeted nervously, cleaned out the van, three times, balanced his check book, and called Florence twice while waiting for Pete to come out. When Pete emerged from the building, Anthony asked,

"So how'd it go?"

"I start tomorrow."

"Great! How did that happen?"

"Well, when I went in, I handed the girl at the reception desk a copy of what I had submitted on line. She then called personnel and another woman, the assistant director of personnel, came to see me a couple of minutes later. She was very nice. She took me back to her office and we spoke for about half an hour. She had me do a couple of tests on their computer system, and then she took me on a tour of the place."

"How was that?"

"I didn't see anybody else in a chair, so I think I may be their only physically handicapped employee, I don't know. Maybe I helped them fill a quota or something."

"Well, how was the place? What will your work place be like?"

"All the data entry clerks are in a big room, but everyone has their own little cubicle. She showed me where I'll sit and it'll be fine."

"So, do you have a private office with a door and a desk and all that?"

"No. I'll have a cubicle with some privacy, but the clerks share space. Say, can we talk about this in the van? I'm ready to get out of here."

"Sorry, Peter. I just wanted to hear all about it," Anthony said, as

Pete got himself back inside the van. When Anthony had closed the doors and was behind the wheel, he continued,

"So tell me about it. Did you meet any of your soon-to-be fellow employees?"

"She introduced me to a few people. They seemed nice."

"And no problem getting in and out or anything?"

"I didn't see any."

"Did you check out the bathrooms?"

"I'm sure they're fine. Dad, can we go now?"

"Oh, okay," Anthony said as he put the van in reverse and began exiting the parking lot.

"So what are your hours?"

"I have to punch a time clock and I work seven and a half hours a day from 8:00 in the morning until 4:00 in the afternoon, with half an hour for lunch."

"Really? Do you think you can do that?"

"I think so. We'll see."

"Did you tell her you might not be able to sit that long?"

"No, I was trying to get the job, Dad. If I told her that, I might not have gotten the job."

"So what is it you'll be doing?"

"Basically, they give me a whole bunch of forms and my job is to input them into the computer, so I'll be filling out forms all day long."

"I think you'll do just fine, son. All you can do is try."

The two rode quietly for the rest of the way home, both deep in their own thoughts. When they got home, and as Pete was about to tell his mother what had happened, Anthony went into the garage to get some fishing tackle out.

"So tell me all about it," his mother bubbled.

"I think this is a job I can do, Mom."

"Can you take breaks and come home for lunch, if you want?"

"I think we get a ten minute break in the morning and one in the afternoon. I get a half hour for lunch, so I won't have time to come home."

"It would be good if you could lay down during the day and take some the pressure off your spine and backside, Peter. You might have trouble working an eight hour day, Peter. You've been on a pretty flexible schedule for a while."

"I'll be alright."

"Will they give you training?"

"They call it orientation, and yes, I'll be given an orientation packet tomorrow and I'll be shown videos most of the morning."

"And did you meet any of the people you'll be working with?"

"Yes. I met a guy named Randy, an older black guy, I should say African-American, who is my immediate supervisor, and he'll check my work. Then there's a supervisor over our entire unit, and she keeps an eye on all of us."

"How many of you are there?"

"Sixteen. Think of it as two big rectangles, or squares, actually, with four cubicles on each side and eight employees in each square."

"How big is your office?"

"It's ten by twelve, something like that."

"That's pretty big."

"Yeah. It gives me plenty of room to move around. My desk is at the back so I can just wheel myself in and my back is to the door, so I shouldn't have any distractions."

"Any windows?"

"No, just the see-through plexi-glass on the outside walls and partition walls made of some kind of fake wood."

"So the walls don't go to the ceiling?"

"No. They're eight foot high."

" Well, it sounds great, Peter. What do you think?"

"We'll see. It's a job."

"And they pay you how much?"

"I start at $7.50 per hour."

"And you get good benefits, too, right?"

"I'll be on probation for ninety days. They said the benefits don't kick in until I complete my probationary period."

"I am so happy for you, Peter!" She exclaimed.

"Don't get all excited, Mom. It's just a job."

"I am excited, Peter, and I hope you like this job," she replied.

As they were talking, Anthony walked back into the room. At a break in the conversation, he asked Pete if he wanted to go fishing, something they hadn't done since Pete had come home. Before the accident, Pete used to love to fish, and he was very good at it, so good that he earned a living doing it for a while. He had learned a lot in Alaska and in the Keys, and he had become a good fly-fisherman in the rivers of Montana. He hadn't been fishing in well over a year. He agreed to go and the two headed back out the door.

"Bring home dinner for us," Florence said as they did.

"So where are we going?" Pete asked.

"I was planning to go to the County Park and fish off the pier."

"You gonna stop and get some bait or what?"

"No. I figured we could just use a few lures I've been having some luck with."

"You can always use some shrimp. We should stop and get some frozen shrimp for bait, if we can't get any live ones. We've got to at least do that."

Anthony agreed and they picked up some frozen shrimp at a bait shop not far from the pier.

"You bring along an extra pole for me?" Pete asked.

"Of course I did. You think I'd bring you along just to watch me have all the fun?"

The two men spent the next couple of hours fishing. There were a few other people on the pier, but they had the place to themselves most of the time. Pete kept prodding his father on where to cast and how to handle the bait. At one point, Anthony offered,

"Let's not forget who taught you how to fish, young man."

"I remember, but that was a long time ago."

"We'll see who catches dinner," Anthony responded. Using the lures as bait, they managed to catch a few croakers, a small whiting, one under-sized red-fish and a few stingrays. Just as they were getting ready to take in their lines, Anthony caught one legal trout.

"I'll cook it in a pan with a little butter in it over a charcoal grille. There's enough for the three of us."

"I'm bringing my own bait next time," Pete teased.

"Oh, it was the equipment?" his father responded.

That night, they shared the trout and celebrated the development of the day. Pete was going back to work.

The next day, Pete was up early and at work by eight. Again,

Anthony took him. Florence had packed him a lunch. When Anthony picked him up that afternoon, he asked about going fishing again, but Pete was beat and went right to sleep, without any dinner. He slept through until the next morning. Fortunately for him, since he started work on a Thursday, and he only had to work two days before he had the weekend off. He needed it to recuperate. He didn't realize how stressful an eight hour day of work could be on his body and his mind. He wasn't used to having all that weight compressing his spinal column for that length of time.

That weekend, Pete didn't do too much, other than lay around and rest. He did go out with his Dad to Sports Authority and buy himself a better fishing pole and a tackle box. Pete came home bedraggled and tired every day for the first few weeks, but he kept getting up and kept showing up. It was late Fall and the clocks had changed, so the sun went down at about 6:30. There was still enough sunshine left in the day for them to get an hour of fishing in. Pete said that after a day cooped up inside an office, he needed to be out in the fresh air.

Some days, they went to the beach and Pete would watch as his parents swam and enjoyed the sunset. Other days, they would go to a local park and take the nature walk, which Pete was able to handle without assistance. Even when it rained, they'd find someplace to go.

"That's more like the Peter we know, isn't it?" Anthony said to his wife. She agreed.

His employers seemed to be quite pleased with his performance. At the end of every week, he received an evaluation from his supervisor, Randy, who had given him high marks every time, so far. When Pete received his first paycheck, he took his parents out to dinner at a small diner near their favorite fishing spot, called O'Steens, which had ten tables and served fresh fish with all the fixings, without any fanfare. He was clearly proud of himself.

It wasn't too long after he had brought home a few paychecks that he began to think about getting a vehicle of his own. He'd get it rigged so that he could do everything with his hands and then have enough room so that he could maneuver himself into and out of his chair, get on the lift and get in and out of the vehicle.

Anthony told him that if he took over the payments on the van he had bought, he could have it. It had an automatic transmission, with the shift lever on the steering wheel. They could have brake levers installed and a lever to operate the gas pedal put on the steering wheel, too. If they took out the passenger seat and the Captain's chair altogether, it would be wide open and Pete could drive himself. He could keep the wheelchair right next to him as he drove and secure it so that it wouldn't move when he got into or out of the driver's seat. Anthony said that he thought it would cost a couple of thousand dollars to make the changes but he had heard there was a mechanic shop not far from where Pete worked that could do it.

Pete was interested and made a few inquiries. The first shock was that the cost to make the repairs was about as much as what his father had paid for the van.

"I'm going to have to save up a little money before I can do this, Dad," Pete told his father. "This is way more expensive than I thought. Plus, if we decide to do this, it will take them a couple of months to do the work."

"I didn't realize it was that involved," his father offered. "I'll help you out with the money, but…"

"No, I'd rather pay for it myself, Dad, but thanks."

"Do you think you can finance the repair work, Peter, or does it all have to be paid up front?"

"I'll find out, Dad, once we find out how much it is. Also, I'm going to have to learn how to drive. I can't just have all that work done and get in and drive. I should do that first."

"I'm sure there are people out there who can teach you that, Peter. Call a few of those Driver's Training programs and ask."

Pete followed his father's suggestion and found a Driving School which offered a program for handicapped drivers. After making arrangements to have the changes made to the van, Pete signed up for the course. His instructor was a retired occupational therapist. It was a twenty hour course that involved eight hours of classroom instruction and twelve hours of driving.

Pete began the course that Saturday and completed the course over the next four consecutive Saturday mornings. His instructor showed him how to operate the levers and gave him some suggestions about what to consider when he had the changes made to the van. There were multiple lift options available that Pete had no knowledge of before taking the course. He chose one that had a mechanical lift as opposed to a ramp. With the ramp, it extended so far out from the van that it made the incline too steep. Pete felt that it would be much too difficult to find enough space to use a ramp, especially in most parking lots, plus they were heavier and more unwieldy and it was hard for him to move it himself.

Most afternoons, except when it rained or it was too windy, Pete and his dad went fishing. They found a few places to go other than the county park, but the long pier out into the ocean was the best place. Anthony talked about getting a boat with a big fishing chair on the back for Pete to sit in and they started looking around for a good used one.

Every night, as he had for much of the last year, Pete played his guitar. He liked the music of the sixties and the seventies, Eagles, Jackson Browne, Bruce Springsteen, Bob Seger and others. Lynyrd Skynyrd and Stevie Ray Vaughn were his favorites, but he also liked some of the country stuff with Garth Brooks, Johnny Cash, Kris Kristofferson and Charlie Daniels, too. After he learned the chords, he started singing songs. He played and sang by himself, though his parents could hear him and liked what they heard, for the most part.

After ninety days, he was told that he had successfully completed his probationary period and was given a raise. He was now making $8.00 an hour. He also became eligible for all the benefits. A month after that, he felt that he could afford to have the van modified. The repair shop agreed to take half down and financed the rest over time. Work on making the repairs was begun, but it would take a while to complete. Slowly but surely, Pete began to find the smile he had lost in the accident.

However, a few weeks after becoming a full-time salaried employee, he experienced a setback. He first noticed it after work one day when he saw an abrasion in the area of his right buttocks. He couldn't feel any pain and it wasn't bleeding, but it was an open wound. He tried putting on a 4 x 4 inch Band-Aid, which covered it up, but the wound seemed to get worse, not better, after a couple of days.

He went to see his doctor after work one day. He prayed that it wasn't a decubitis ulcer. He had heard about them. If it was, he'd been told it could take months to heal and he would surely lose his job. The skin was decomposing and looked nasty.

The doctor told him it looked more like a cut of some kind and asked if Pete had cut himself or hurt himself lately. Pete remembered having bruised his right buttock a few days earlier when he had landed awkwardly on his exercise mat one morning. He hadn't given it much thought. The doctor said he had to stay off it and let it heal. He gave him some ointments and medications and told Pete it would probably take two weeks. The doctor said,

"Pete, you can put anything you want on that wound, except you. Any weight on that spot, or heat for that matter, and it won't heal. You're going to have to lay down and stay down. That's all there is to it."

Pete didn't want to miss any work for fear of losing his job, but his supervisors were understanding when he told them about the problem and gave them a letter of explanation from his doctor. Unfortunately, there was nothing Pete could do but lay on his front, with the wound exposed, and wait for it to heal.

Every morning, he would wake up, look at the wound, and call in sick. He didn't begin to notice any improvement for almost a week. It took two full weeks to heal. The doctor said that things like that were not abnormal with an injury like Pete had. He confirmed that if it had been a decubitis ulcer Pete would have been out of work for at least two months.

In fact, he told Pete, decubitis ulcers were not only common, they were expected. He said it was important to keep the area dry, not to allow moisture to accumulate, and to try not to stay in the same position too long. Given the nature of Pete's work, that would be hard to do, since he couldn't get up, move around and change positions. He told Pete that when he went back to work he should use pillows, try to keep the pressure off the areas of contact, and take more breaks during the day to change positions or move around some. He said they were sometimes called 'pressure sores' and sitting in one position for too long could cause them. Pete was lucky, this was just a bruise.

Again, Pete's employer, and it was primarily Randy going to bat for him, was understanding. They agreed to allow him to make some adjustments to his working conditions. They agreed to give him more breaks during the day. It would extend the length of his work day, but if it would help, they were willing to make those accommodations.

Pete could start at 8:00 and work to 9:30, take a half hour break from 9:30 to 10:00, then work another hour and a half, take another half hour off and so forth through the day to get him to seven and a half hours of work per day, which was required. Pete didn't like that suggestion, but it was a necessary thing to do. This was the first time that he had come close to experiencing a decubitis ulcer and it scared him. He remembered hearing about other patients having them in the Seattle Trauma Center when there. It made him realize how fragile he still was.

He was able to take his sick leave during his time off, so he still drew a paycheck, but he used up all of his sick leave in doing so. Any more absences and they would either come from vacation days or be days for which he wasn't paid. It made him feel uncertain about his job.

It was repetitious work, but Pete was good with numbers and very agile on the computer. He had become one of the most productive workers in a short time. Walgreen's was all about high numbers with no mistakes. Pete was exceeding their expectations in that regard, but he wasn't any good to them if he wasn't at work. He asked them about working from home, but that wasn't an option. Walgreen's wasn't going to allow their sensitive internal documents and procedures to be compromised, or potentially compromised, for Pete or anyone else.

The time off allowed him to think about and do other things. A vehicle of his own became his primary focus. The idea of getting his Dad's van was clearly the best idea, so after going over the numbers as carefully as they could, they agreed to go forward with the deal. Anthony began looking for a new vehicle for himself. There was the insurance to figure, and that was much higher than either of them expected, plus the tags and transfer fees, not to mention the cost of a new vehicle for Anthony. He had never owned a van before purchasing the one for Peter, and he and Florence liked it.

They decided to get one that they could go camping in, since both of them liked doing that, so Pete started looking on the internet for them. He found several off of Craig's list which he thought his parents would like the best.

He also investigated the insurance issue to figure out if it would be better for him to have his own policy or stay on his parents' policy. He was a 'high risk' driver and the rates were high no matter which way they did it. He found out all he could about deductibles, uninsured motorist coverage, bodily injury coverage, property damage, collision, PIP, stacked insurance versus non-stacked, catastrophic coverage and other things. He was surprised how much difference there was in the rates between companies. He considered having the minimum coverage required by the state of Florida, which was that he have PIP, or personal injury protection, and PD, which meant property damage. He'd have to decide before he could have the vehicle put in his name, which is what he wanted to do. Adding a vehicle and Pete as a driver to his parents' policy would have more than doubled their premium, which was already high, and Anthony and Florence were reluctant to do that.

By that Friday, Pete had figured it all out. His parents agreed with what he had found for them, and chose another 2007 Econoline Conversion Van, with fewer miles and more of the trimmings, which was being offered by a dealership in Delray Beach, not too far south from where they were. They liked being able to purchase the warranties and having the ability to take it to their local Ford dealer for repairs, plus they could finance it, whereas with a private owner it had to be cash up front. Pete told them they could save over a thousand dollars by going to their bank and getting a loan, but they preferred doing it the conventional way. They wouldn't have to add Pete as a driver until the work on the van was complete, and since it wasn't operable, they took the van he was buying from them off of their policy, which didn't change their insurance payment much at all.

That weekend, Pete went with them to buy the vehicle from Wallace Ford off of Linton Boulevard and I-95 in Delray Beach. He rode back with his mother in the new van. Three weeks later, the work on what was to be Pete's van was complete. Pete took out a policy of insurance, with the lowest rates he could find, and a formal sale of the van was completed at a Department of Motor Vehicles office not far from their home.

That weekend, Pete practiced sitting in the driver's seat and getting used to the mechanical levers which had been installed. On Monday, he drove himself to work, allowing an extra half hour to do so, in case he had any problems. Anthony was up with him and followed him to work that day, just in case. He wouldn't miss getting up in the mornings to get Pete to work on time.

The feelings Pete had experienced due to being out of work and fearing a decubitis ulcer were replaced by feelings of freedom and more self-confidence in being able to drive himself to work. His co-employees noticed the change and were supportive. He was re-gaining his independence, slowly, but there were still times when he had to pull off the road while driving home and turn off the vehicle for a while because he was crying and shaking so hard from the stress of it all, too.

19
The Lawsuit

FIVE MONTHS TO THE day after he had signed the retainer agreement and allowed Mr. Nickel to look into his claim against the Double-D Ranch, Pete received a phone call about his case. He was at work at the time and didn't get to return the call until after he got off, but with the two hour time differential, it was no problem as it was still the middle of the afternoon in Montana.

"How are things goin', Pete?" Mr. Nickel asked.

"Alright. How about with you?"

"I'm busy enough. I don't want to be any busier, I can tell you that."

"Is Dave planning to work with you when he graduates from law school?"

"I'm not sure what he's going to do. Last time I talked to him he was more worried about making it through law school than he was about where he was going to work when he gets out."

"Naah. Dave's a smart guy. He'll make it through just fine, don't you think?"

"Actually, Pete, I think the hardest part of law school isn't the academic side of it. It's the emotional side of it. They make you read and read and read, and then when you think you're done, they make you read some more. Some people just get tired of it and say they'd rather do something else."

"Is that what Dave is doing? Thinking about something besides law?"

"No, he'll stick it out, and he's doing very well with his grades. I was just kidding about that. But he's thinking he'd like to be a trial lawyer, so my advice to him was to go to work for the District Attorney's Office, or the Public Defender. He'll get a whole bunch of trial work, and more jury trials there in three years than he'd get in ten years with me."

"So he's going to be a prosecutor, maybe? Prosecute people for drivin' drunk and smokin' dope, things like that?"

"Among other things, but he might decide that he'd rather be a Public Defender and defend. He hasn't decided yet."

"I think he'd be better at defending people than prosecuting them."

"When was the last time you talked to him, Pete?"

"I haven't spoken to him since you and I last talked."

"That's been a while."

"Please tell him I said hello next time you talk to him."

"I will, but why don't you just call him up yourself and tell him?"

"You're right. I will."

"Pete, I called to tell you that you'll be receiving some papers in the mail in a few days and I didn't want you to be surprised."

"What are they?"

"They're copies of the suit papers."

"So you had to file suit, did you?"

"Yes. They're taking the position that when you signed that release you waived your right to make a claim."

"That wasn't a surprise, was it?"

"No, it wasn't, but I was disappointed. I thought they might make an offer and try to settle this case because of the severity of your injuries."

"And they didn't do that?"

"No, they didn't. They just denied the claim and denied that they owe you any money."

"So what happens next?"

"I'm sure the first thing they'll do is file a motion to dismiss your complaint. They will argue that, as a matter of law, you can't sue them."

"So then it would be up to the judge to decide?"

"Yes, that's right."

"So we should know something pretty soon whether or not I have a case, yes?"

"I expect that this judge will rule on it within a month or two."

"Well, I'll keep my fingers crossed, but as I told you right from the beginning, I didn't think I could sue them in the first place. You're the one who said you think we might have a chance."

"I still do, Pete, and even if we lose before the local judge, I intend to appeal it to our Supreme Court."

"Regardless of how it turns out, I thank you for what you're doing for me, Mr. Nickel. Did you find out anything interesting since I talked to you last?"

"I got a copy of their insurance policy. They had a million dollars in coverage, Pete, just as I suspected."

"Anything else?"

"Not really. I obtained all of your medical records, your school records, your work records and letters from a couple of your fellow employees. Also, I made a formal demand upon them for the policy limit. You should have received a copy of that. Did you?"

"I did. That's been a couple of months ago, but I don't remember seeing any letters in there. Who'd you get letters from?"

"When Reno Baldwin sent me a copy of your employment records he included a nice letter with them in which he said that you were a good employee and a fine young man. Then I got letters from Dave and a young woman named Abigail about what happened that day and what she had heard."

"Did Abigail tell you all the things I told you the other girl had supposedly said?"

"Yes, she did. I talked to that girl and tried to get a letter from her, but she wouldn't put anything in writing. She didn't deny saying it, but she just wouldn't give me a formal statement. She'll tell the truth when the time comes, I'm sure. Her name is Sandra Graber."

"What about the guy who was the trail guide, Michael?"

"He wouldn't talk to me at all. I had a helluva time finding him. He's a senior at Swarthmore College."

"Where's that?"

"Just outside of Philadelphia, I think. I'm not sure. Smart kid."

"He was a nice guy, too. I feel bad about suing him."

"I've named him as a defendant, but the Double-D is responsible for his actions. It's a legal technicality. I don't expect to get a penny from him, just like I told you. We'll get our money from the insurance company, if we can get any money at all, that is."

"Well, I'm sure you're doin' the best you can."

"I am, but like I said, I just wanted to let you know that I'm working for you and that you should expect to get some things in the mail from me, that's all."

"Well, thanks for the call, Mr. Nickel."

"You're welcome, Pete. Say, before I let you go, anything new I should know about?"

"I've got a job now."

"Really? I didn't know that. You've got to tell me these things. That's something I should have put in our demand letter."

"It wouldn't have made any difference, would it?"

"No, but I still need to know. So what are you doing?"

Pete proceeded to tell him about his job, what he did, how much he made and all the rest. When he was finished, they said their good-byes and Pete started playing his guitar.

Ever since he had his own vehicle, Pete and his Dad didn't fish together as often. Anthony had bought a boat and he went out with Florence most every day. She began showing a lot more interest in fishing with him now that he had a boat.

Pete told his parents of his conversation with Mr. Nickel when they returned from fishing that day.

"Well, son, if nothing comes of it, you won't be too disappointed, right? I don't want you to get your hopes up too much." Anthony offered, when told of the conversation with Mr. Nickel.

"I won't. I thanked him for all that he's doing for me."

"I'm glad you did it. If nothing comes of it, at least you tried. I'm proud of you for that."

"You talked me into it, Dad."

"I thought it was worth a shot, and I still do. It hasn't cost you anything. Let's hope for the best. So how's your music coming? When are we going to have a concert?"

"Maybe when Judy comes down. She'll be here at Christmas, won't she?"

"Last I heard she and her son, Jonah, were coming down."

"That's strange, isn't it? You and Mom have nine kids and only one of them learns how to play music?"

"It's just the two of you. We encouraged you all to play, but Judy was the only one to have an interest, until you started playing."

"I'm still learning, but I'm enjoying it."

"There are a thousand things for kids to do, so we just let you all decide what it is you wanted to do. We didn't push any of you into anything."

"I guess I was always the one who wanted to go fishin' or out on a boat or things like that, wasn't I?"

"Since you were old enough to walk," Anthony said.

"Before that," Florence chimed in. "Remember when we'd take him to the pool? He thought he WAS a fish. You had to go get him, Anthony, or he wouldn't come up for air! You were dangerous, Peter! You were always the wildest of the bunch. You weren't afraid of anything."

"That was before I lost my legs. Now I'm afraid to be more than an arm's length away from my chair."

"You're becoming more independent every day, Peter. In fact, your mother and I were thinking that you are capable of taking care of yourself without us around. We're thinking of taking a week off and heading up to North Carolina at the end of the month. Do you think you'll be alright alone if we did?"

"Yeah, I'm sure I will be. If I need any help, I can always call one of the neighbors."

"Are you making friends at work, Peter? His mother asked.

"Yeah. A couple of the guys go out for a beer after work on Fridays. They've asked me to go along a few times."

"You should go," his father said.

"I will, one of these days."

"It's been so long since you've had any alcohol, you should be careful if you do," his mother warned. "There's no telling how it will affect you."

"That's true. I don't weigh near as much as I did and it'll go through me that much faster. Maybe I'd better start practicing up some."

"You're a big boy. You can take care of yourself. You'll do what's best."

"Yeah, I won't be takin' chances like I used to. I don't think I'm ten feet tall and bullet proof anymore."

"But you're getting better every day."

It was true. Pete was getting better every day, and he was becoming more confident in his abilities to get around and go places without someone to open doors and be there in case he fell. He was surprised that one or two of the young women at work were showing some interest in him. He didn't tell his parents about that, but he thought that no one would be interested in him because of his condition. He wasn't sure if it was them feeling sorry for him and being nice or something else. It had been a long time since he had been with a woman, but he was having feelings he hadn't experienced in a while.

One night, just before going to bed, Pete decided to give Dave a call and see what his old buddies were doing.

"Dave, it's me. How you doin', man?"

"Pete! Good to hear from you, bro'! I'm good, how about you?"

"I'm better. I think I'm ready to return to the human race."

"Good to hear, man. So what are you up to?"

"I've got a job. I've got a van. I've been playin' music. I go fishin' every so often. Things aren't like they used to be, but I'm better than I was."

"You've been through a lot, man. Good to hear. So where are you workin'?

Pete told him all about that and about fishing with his Dad, and then he asked,

"So how's Abigail? Ever see her?"

"She's good. I see her every now and then around campus. I didn't go back to work with Reno last summer."

"No? What did you do?"

"I was an intern in a law firm."

"Yeah? What kind of work?"

"Basically, I carried this guy's bags wherever he went and I'd go pick up lunch whenever he wanted me to."

"No way."

"Really, that's what I did. I mean, they had me doing legal research, filing things in court, serving subpoenas every now and then, things like that, but I was a 'gopher'."

"So what kind of lawyer was he?"

"Criminal defense. He's a friend of my Uncle's and I think he gave me the job more because of him than anything else. It's hard to get a summer job around here. Most students go to Seattle or Portland or wherever they can find a job."

"So your Uncle says that's what you might do when you get out, be a criminal lawyer."

"Yeah, he says if I want to be a trial lawyer that's what I should do. I don't want to be a lawyer who just stays in the office and prepares deeds, wills and contracts. I liked my trial practice course and I think that's what I'm gonna do. We'll see. First I've got to graduate and then I've got to get a job."

"But you're gettin' there."

"Yeah, I made it through my first year."

"Damn! You were about to start your senior year when I had my accident and now you're in law school…it seems like a long time since that happened."

"It was. It's been over two years now. A lot has happened."

Pete thought to himself about all that had taken place in the last two years. In many ways, he felt as if he had lost two years of his life, but then he snapped out of that and asked,

"So do you see any of the other guys?"

"Not really. I don't get up to Glacier much any more, just on a weekend every now and then, and when I do, everybody is working and busy, so I feel like I'm kind of in the way. It's not the same. There aren't too many of the people there from when you were there."

"Does Abigail still work there?"

"Yeah, she does, but she's in her senior year now, so this may be her last year up there. Most people seem to move on after college."

"What's she going to do when she graduates?"

"I don't know. You should call her, man. I know she'd like to hear from you."

"I doubt it."

"No, really. Everytime I see her she asks about you. She says you won't talk to her."

"I wasn't feelin' too good about myself for a long time there, Dave. I didn't feel much like talkin' to anyone for a while."

"I can understand that, my friend, but it's good to hear that you're feelin' better."

"I am."

"Give her a call, man. It can't hurt."

"Yeah it can. I loved her."

"She loved you, too, man."

"That was then…"

"You do what you want, Pete, but I'm tellin' you what I think. I think she'd like to hear from you."

"We'll see. Maybe I will."

"In case you decide to call, her number is 404-965-5728. Got it?"

"Yeah, I wrote it down. I don't know…"

"Hey, I gotta go. I've got class in fifteen minutes. Good hearin' from you, man. How's that lawsuit coming along anyway?"

"Your uncle filed suit a few days ago. He sent me a copy of what he filed but I haven't seen it yet."

"Good luck with that, man. I hope you win."

"If I do, I have you to thank for that, Dave."

"And Abigail. She's the one who talked to that Sandra girl."

"That's true."

"Call her, man. I gotta go. Stay in touch."

Pete didn't sleep too well that night. He kept tossing and turning, thinking of Abigail and wondering what to do. His mind was distracted over the next few days and it was good for him to go to work and not think too much about the emotional turbulence he was going through. When the package from Mr. Nickel arrived, he read each and every word in the documents Mr. Nickel had filed on his behalf. It felt funny to look at them and see his name, Peter Collins vs. The Double-D Ranch, Inc. and Michael J. Bynen. That weekend, he called Reno.

"Pete! How are you, young man!"

"I'm doing better, Reno."

"It's been a while. What are you up to?"

"I'm working as a data entry clerk for a large chain of pharmaceutical stores."

"How long have you been doing that?"

"About four months now. How are things with you and Mrs. Baldwin?"

"Fran and I are fine. She asks about you now and again. She'll be glad to hear the news."

"I'm driving a van and getting around on my own pretty good now, too."

"That's great, Pete! I'm glad to hear it. Any chance you'll make it out this way any time soon?"

"Oh, I don't know about that. It's a long way and I'm not ready for that long a trip just yet. I'm doin' good to get to and from work."

"Well, you know you have a place to come to any time you're ready."

"I spoke to Dave the other day and he says you've got a new crew of guides."

"That's true. We always get a big turnover from year to year, as you will remember from your days with us. Abigail and a few others are still with me. Not now, of course, but she's told me that she will be. Have you spoken to her lately?"

"No, but I've been meaning to call."

"I think she'd like to hear from you, Pete."

"Maybe I'll give her a call."

"Anything I can do for you, Pete?"

"No, not really. I just called to say hello and to thank you for all the cards and letters of support you sent me. I appreciated them."

"You're welcome, Pete. You're still in our daily prayers and I meant what I said about you having a home here."

"Thanks, Reno."

"You take care of yourself and stay in touch, okay?"

"I will, Reno."

"And get out here when you can."

"I will."

"Thanks for calling. Good talking to you."

The Return of Abigail

20

T HE WEEK CAME FOR Anthony and Florence to go off camping in their van to North Carolina. They were both excited about the trip, and Pete was happy for them. He assured them that he'd be fine. Florence put enough food in the refrigerator to last a month, and gave him the number of a man who would go to a grocery store, buy things and then deliver. He did it for a number of shut-ins who Florence knew, but Pete told her that wouldn't be necessary. He could shop for himself if he ran out of food.

As they drove off, Pete felt pangs of being alone, since he was without his support group, but he quickly put those thoughts out of his mind. His parents left on a Friday morning, as Pete was getting ready to go to work, so that they could get a jump on the weekend traffic, get to the park before most of the other campers arrived and get a good camping spot. They decided to go to a place called Tsali, which was very close to the Nantahala Outdoor Center, where they could hike, go white-water rafting, mountain-bike, fish or anything else, like shop for antiques. They had read about it in a magazine and checked it out on the internet. They planned to stay for a few days and then go visit their oldest daughter, Judy, who lived in nearby Asheville. In fact, Judy said she'd come see them in Tsali if the weather was good.

That Friday, after work, Pete decided to go out with some of the people from his office to have a beer. He followed them to a bar on the water called O'Day's. It faced north and overlooked the St. Anne's River, one of many inlets off of the Atlantic Ocean, which was less than a mile away to the east. Fishing boats and shrimping trawlers were tied to the docks nearby. It was an Irish bar and there was live music starting at 5:00. The group always went to the same place and they always arrived by 4:30 so that they'd get the best table.

Since they were regulars, the bartender, a tall, dark-haired man in his thirties named Mark, greeted them. He knew them all by name, except for Pete, of course, but Pete was welcomed. This was the first time he'd been in a bar since the night before the accident. He felt out of place and as if all eyes were on him.

Mark cleared a path for Pete and put him in a corner spot where he'd be out of the way of the waitresses and the path of other customers, but be close to the musicians. Most everyone ordered the house specialty, pints of Guinness. Pete ordered a Coors light. This would be his first beer since the accident.

It was a nice, sunny afternoon, and the sun was nearing the end of its journey across the sky. Pete was in the shade, under an umbrella. There was a slight off-shore breeze and, after a few minutes, he began to feel more comfortable in his surroundings when the commotion of getting his wheelchair up a ramp, around chairs and to where he was put wore off.

The musicians, a man and a woman, were busy setting up less than ten feet away. The woman was tuning a guitar and the man had both a regular six-string guitar and a four-string bass. Both were testing the microphones and adjusting the speakers and other equipment.

Pete noticed that the woman had a Taylor guitar, which was what he hoped to get some day. He knew that it cost several thousand dollars, which was a whole lot more than he could afford, especially after he'd broken so many others. He asked her about it and they talked for several minutes about guitars.

Her name was Sue and she was from a small town on the west coast of Ireland named Glencolumbkille. She had a thick brogue, as did her companion, Brendan, who was busy moving the speakers and the stools they would sit on so that they were exactly where he wanted them to be. He jumped into the conversation as he walked around and by her.

She asked Pete what songs he liked to play and he told her. Little did he know that part of their act was to pass a microphone around every now and then and get the crowd to join in. They opened with The Irish Rover, a popular tune with a lively beat to set the mood. It had a chorus that had people clapping their hands rhythmically, while singing "no, nay, never!" …clap, clap, clap, clap…"no, nay, never, no more"…clap, clap…"will I play the wild rover"…clap…"no never, no more…"

They continued with the "What do you say to a drunken sailor" song and then with "Finnegan's Wake". After that, they slowed it down a bit with "My wild Irish rose" and "Not reason I left Mullingar". Pete was enjoying himself and the music. The others were talking amongst themselves as best they could with the music so close, and they had to scream to be heard at that, but they all turned when Sue brought the microphone over to Pete and said,

"Our friend Pete here is going to help us out on this one. It's a country-western song, sung by Johnny Cash, who's part Irish we're told. It's called 'I walk the line.' Please join in if you'd like."

Pete wasn't expecting that, and he was taken aback a bit as he'd never sung outside his room before, let alone in front of people, but the crowd and his companions started to clap and he couldn't say no at that point. Both Sue and Brendan starting strumming their guitars and singing with him. The next thing he knew, he was singing…

"…because your mine, I walk the line…"

Before he knew it, the song was over and everyone was clapping again. He was embarrassed and felt a flush come to his face, but he smiled and waved, and they went on to the next song, "Four Green Fields". After they'd sung for over an hour or so, they took a break. When they did, Pete decided to leave. He'd finished his beer and was feeling a little buzz. He was worried about how he'd be able to drive after not having a drink in almost two years, and he was ready to go.

He put down a five dollar bill, dropped a dollar in the tip jar and said good-bye to his friends and to Sue and Brendan, who told him that they were there every Friday for the next few months and to bring his guitar next time he came. They also told him that they played at another Irish bar on Saturday evenings and Sunday afternoons and gave him a card. Mark, the bartender, said good-bye, remembering his name, as Pete wheeled himself out of the bar and into the parking lot.

He made it back to his house without any problems at all, though he could feel the effects of a single beer, which surprised him. He felt good, though. He had enjoyed himself. He found himself singing "I walk the line" over and over in his mind. After he got settled in the house, he pulled out his guitar and played for a while. He thought to himself that it would be fun to go back there again. He wouldn't bring his guitar with him just yet, but he'd be ready to sing next time. Maybe they'd let him sing a Bob Seger song, "Turn the page", which was one of his favorites.

Later that night, he called Abigail. She was just getting back to her apartment after a late afternoon class and a work-out at they gym.

"Abigail, it's Pete."

"Pete! I'd better sit down before I fall down. How are you? It's good to hear from you."

"I'm better, and how are you?"

"I'm fine. I'm in my last year here and getting ready to make a decision about what I'm going to do with the rest of my life. I guess I can't be a river guide forever."

"Yeah, I spoke to Reno and he told me you were one of the few that were still guiding for him from when I was there."

"Yeah, there are a few of us left, and I'll be back there this summer. It's not the same, but I haven't found anything else I'd rather be doing or anyplace else I'd rather be than on a raft in Glacier."

"Yeah, I think about those days all the time. Those were days, weren't they?"

"Yeah they were, and they still are. It doesn't change. It's always beautiful here. Where are you now? Last I heard you were in Florida with your parents. Are you still there?"

"Yeah, I am, although they're not here right now. They went camping in North Carolina for a week."

"That's cool. They sound like really nice people."

"Yeah my Mom told me that you'd called a few times…"

"I spoke to your Dad once, too. I was hoping you'd call me back…"

"I know…I just couldn't do it…"

"So what made you call now, Pete?"

"I'm doin' better, Abby. I'm feelin' better about myself. I finally got up the courage to call, I guess."

"So tell me about it. How are you doin'?"

"I'm in a chair and unless they come up with some miracle to repair a spinal cord, I'll be in one for the rest of my life, but I've got a van and a job and I'm learning to play the guitar and I'm just feelin' better about things."

"I am so glad to hear it, Pete! You've been in my prayers every day since the accident."

"It's been over a year now, but it seems like it was a lifetime ago. In some ways, though, it feels like yesterday. I still see all of the people and all the things that happened so clearly in my mind. I'll bet you haven't changed a bit."

"I probably do look pretty much like I did when I last saw you. I may have put on a pound or two, but I'm the same, although what happened to you changed my life, too, Pete. I loved you."

Pete had to hold back tears when he heard her say that, but he managed to reply,

"And I loved you, too, Ab."

There was an awkward moment of silence, while each let those words sink into their thoughts, then Abigail said,

"I've thought about you and what you must be going through every day, Pete."

"Yeah, I heard that you came up the mountain that night…"

"And I would have gone to Seattle to see you, but you didn't call and I wasn't sure that you wanted to see me."

"I didn't want you to see me like that, Ab."

"It must have been really rough for you…"

"It was hard not bein' able to do anything for myself, and just layin' in bed, not bein' able to…well, do anything, and it took me a long time to get used to bein' in a chair, but the hardest part was accepting the fact that I'd never be able to walk, run, do the things… we used to do…"

Pete was fighting back tears, and Abigail could hear it in his voice.

"But you're better now."

"Yeah, I am," he sniffled. "Sorry, I've got this cold…"

"So tell me about your job?"

"I work for a big company called Walgreen's. I enter data all day long."

"So you've learned how to use the computer since I saw you?"

"Yeah, I didn't spend too much time at a desk before the accident," Pete said with a forced laugh, "Did I?"

"Not the Pete Collins I knew, and people are doing all sorts of things with computers now from their homes, but I'm sure you know all about that."

"Not really. I just sort of found this job out of the classified ads one day and next thing I know I've been here over four months."

"Sounds like you're enjoying it, though, yes?"

"It was good to get me out of the house, Ab, and I work with other people, so it made me be more sociable. We went out for a drink after work today, and I sang a song at a bar, and it made me feel good... good enough to call you."

"I'm glad you did. I've been hoping you'd call for a long time now, Pete."

"I'm sorry I didn't, Ab. I just couldn't bring myself to do it. I've thought about you a lot, though, and it helped me get through what I've been through..." Pete's voice quivered as he spoke.

Abigail sensed Pete's mood and asked,

"And you sang a song at a bar? What was that like?"

Pete brightened a bit and said,

"I was just sitting there, listening to these two Irish singers when this woman puts a microphone in my hand and tells the crowd that I was gonna sing Walk the Line by Johnny Cash, and they started playin' it on their guitars, so I sang."

"How'd that happen? Did you know them?"

"No, but I was sittin' right next to where they were playin' and I talked to them a little before they started up and I told them that was one of my favorite songs. I had no idea that they would make me sing it like they did."

"That must have been fun, and you're playing a guitar?"

"Yeah, bein' laid up like I was, I had a lot of time to sit around and feel sorry for myself. To kill the time I read a lot about computers and guitars. After a while, I guess I got better."

"And you're singing, too?"

"I'm no singer, yet, and I never would've done it if she hadn't put that microphone in my face like she did, but when she handed it to me and told everyone that I was about to sing, I didn't have a choice."

"Sounds like you had fun. You always did like music. Last time we were together we listened to music at the Moosehead…"

"I remember."

"And you've got a vehicle?"

"Yeah, it's a converted van so that I can get in and out with a mechanical ramp."

"So you've got a job, a van and you're playing the guitar. It sounds good, Pete, and how's everything else?"

"I don't have any friends around here. It's just me and my folks. I'm starting to meet people, but it gets lonely. I miss the old days…"

"Well you should get in your van and get out here then. You've got friends out here. You know that. People are asking about you all the time."

"Naah. No they're not."

"Yeah, they are. I swear. Whenever I see anyone who knew you from the Great Northern or wherever, they ask about you. They do."

"Yeah?"

"Yeah. People liked you, Pete, and they remember you."

Pete sighed and said,

"Yeah, and I remember them, too."

"Everybody liked you, Pete. They still do."

"Yeah, there were a lot of nice people out there. I miss it."

"Pete, I really am glad to hear from you, and I'd love to talk to you all night, but I'm supposed to be someplace in fifteen minutes and I haven't showered or anything. Can you call me back another time?"

"Sure I can."

"Will you?"

"I will, Abby, I promise."

"And you won't wait another year or two before you do?"

"I won't. I promise."

"I'll look forward to it, and Pete…"

"Yes."

"I still love you."

"Thanks, Ab. I still love you, too."

Abigail hung up and when he heard the dial tone, Pete disconnected the line but held the phone in his hand for a long time, staring blankly at it.

Twenty One: Dock o' the Bay

THAT SUNDAY, AS PETE lay around the house with wild thoughts running through his brain of Glacier, Alaska, rafting, fishing and Abigail, among other things, with nothing to do and no one to talk to, he decided to go to the restaurant where Sue and Brendan would be playing. He remembered the name, which wasn't hard to do as it came from one of his favorite songs, 'Dock o' the Bay' by Otis Redding. He looked up the address and drove downtown after lunch. He arrived well before they were supposed to start. Since they had mentioned it, he brought along his guitar. If it was a slow afternoon, if nothing else he could practice.

Pete thought that the music was to start at 2:00, but the sign outside indicated that it wouldn't begin until 3. The restaurant was on the water, not far from O'Day's, and it had a large wooden deck, with slips at the end for boats to tie up to. The area where Sue and Brendan would be playing was in the far corner of the deck, closest to the water. The stage was in the shape of a triangle and had a twenty foot long hypotenuse. It faced the large area where the customers would sit. There were umbrellas over each of the thirty tables, of which only a few were occupied.

Pete wheeled himself over to a table next to the stage and within a minute a scantily dressed, pretty, young, blonde waitress sat down to take his order. He knew he couldn't drink too many beers, two at most over the whole afternoon, so he ordered water. He told her he was there to listen to the music and would have something to eat and drink later.

It was a beautiful, sunny day, not too hot and not too cold. The weatherman had predicted lows in the sixties with highs approaching eighty. It was a typical day for late October in North Florida. Pete was enjoying sitting out in the sun in the middle of the afternoon as it was something he rarely did. He could take the cold much better than the heat and his doctors had told him to stay out of Florida's hot, summer sun as much as possible as those were the conditions most likely to bring on the decubitis ulcers.

The other customers in the back patio area were on the far side of the deck, a good thirty or forty feet away, so he opened up his guitar case, pulled out his guitar and started to tune up. He positioned himself so that he was looking out over the water with his back to the restaurant. He played some songs by Clapton, Jackson Browne, Van Morrison, Otis and a few others, humming the tune and occasionally softly whispering the words to himself. Next thing he knew, an hour had passed. When he looked around, he saw Sue and Brendan coming towards him.

Sue was an attractive woman in her mid-forties with long, wavy, auburn hair. In the sun, it seemed to have more red in it than he remembered from the night he first met her. She was tall and thin and had the soft, white skin of the Irish. He thought to himself that she couldn't stay in the sun too long in the sun, either. Brendan was an older man, much taller than Sue, with white hair and a white mustache. He looked to be an athlete and was easily carrying all three of the guitar cases under his arms. Sue had their music bags and all the miscellaneous items that went with them wherever they went.

"Top o' the mornin' to ya, Sue!" Pete exclaimed.

"We're well past that, aren't we?" Brendan responded. "And the rest of the day to you, Pete. That's right, isn't it? Pete?"

"That's right, and hello to you to Brendan," he said as Brendan, who was walking a good thirty feet ahead of Sue, put down the guitars and began to take them out of their cases.

"Fine day, isn't it?"

"That it is."

"Grand, simply grand," Sue offered as she stepped onto the stage.

"So you've come to play with us, have you?" Brendan asked.

"No, I came to watch the two of you play. I brought my guitar along to practice a bit while I waited for you to get here."

"You can't get here too early for our sessions, not if you want to get a good seat, that is," Brendan said facetiously, as he looked out over the empty tables all around him.

"They'll start arriving soon enough," Sue responded. "They always do. We usually get a pretty good crowd if the weather's good and today it's marvelous, isn't it?"

"That it is," Pete replied.

"I'll be back in a few minutes," Brendan said. "I've got to lug the PA system from the car."

As he turned to leave, Sue asked "So tell me, Pete, what other songs do you like to play? The other night it was Johnny Cash. What will it be today?"

"I guess I'd say Dock o' the Bay."

"Well that's the one we do here as our first and last numbers just about every day we play here, so you can join in on that one, for sure, but what else? What others do you play?"

"I guess that would be 'Turn the Page' by Bob Seger."

"You'll have to teach us that one, Pete. I'm afraid we don't know it," Sue said.

"How about Jackson Browne or Eric Clapton? Do you know any of their songs?" Pete asked.

"Sure we do," she responded. "'Running on Empty' or 'Before you accuse me' and a few more, actually, especially Clapton. He's quite popular back home."

"Either one is good," Pete said. "I know both of them."

"Well, we'll do those two for ya today. How's that? Sue said. "And just play along and sing with us. You won't be miked up or anything, but it'll give you a chance to play. How does that sound?"

"That'd be grand, Sue, simply grand." Pete responded.

"Spoken like a true Irishman," Brendan piped up, as he returned with a large rectangular box into which he began plugging the microphones and guitar cables. "But you've not a drop of Irish blood in ya, do ya?"

"That's not true, Brendan. My mother's maiden name is Donoghue."

"Donoghue is it?"

"And I've got eight brothers and sisters."

"Well then, you're an Irish Catholic, sure enough, and what's your last name?"

"Collins."

"Collins! Well, that's as fine an Irish name as there is. Have you heard of Michael Collins?" Sue asked.

"That's my grandfather's name."

"You're jokin' with me!" she responded.

"I swear, it's true, but I don't know anything about a Collins from Ireland before."

"That's the name of one of the very finest of Irish patriots. There's a book out called Michael Collins: The Man who Made Ireland. Have you not heard of it?" she asked.

Pete thought to himself as he listened to her talk that it was as if she was singing to him. He didn't know much about his Irish heritage and he really had never heard of the Michael Collins she was talking about. He thought she was kidding him.

"Now it's you who's jokin' with me, aren't ya?"

"No, I'm not! I swear to ya, it's true!" Sue replied. "He was involved with the Easter Revolution of 1916 and he's the one who organized and led the fight to Ireland breakin' away from England. Unfortunately, the best he could do was the Treaty of 1922 that ended up with six of our counties in the North stayin' with England. Half the country was against the treaty and half was in favor of it. They fought with each other after England made them a Free State. Part of the treaty required the Irish to swear allegiance to the King of England and some refused to do it. Michael Collins was killed by one of his countrymen who was against the treaty. Peter Collins is it? Well, it's a pleasure to meet you, indeed, Peter," she said as she came over and gave him a hearty handshake, as did Brendan, who said,

"It's always a pleasure to meet a fellow Irishman."

"I've never been there and I don't know as much as I should, obviously."

"Well, there's plenty of time to learn. You're a young pup, you are." Sue chimed in.

"Compared to us you are, for sure." Brendan added.

"Speak for yourself there, Brendan. I'm not near as old as you!"

"Not to change the subject, dear, but would you mind givin' me a hand with our sound system?"

"It'll be my pleasure, love."

"Anything I can do to help, just let me know," Pete offered.

"We've done this a few times over the years, Pete, but we'll let you know if we do. Thanks for askin'." Brendan responded.

That afternoon, Pete sang 'Walk the Line' again, and he sang along on all of the tunes he knew, and he played along, strumming the chords, like a rhythm guitarist would, to all the songs, even those he didn't know. It didn't matter when he got them wrong because no one could hear him anyway. At 6:00, after they sang Dock o' the Bay for the third and last time, and as they were packing up their equipment, Sue said,

"That was fun, wasn't it, Pete? Did you enjoy yourself?"

"I did. Thanks for letting me join you."

"It was a pleasure for us as well, wasn't it, Brendan?"

"Aye, it was. You're welcome to join us most anytime you'd like."

"Really?"

"Indeed! For now, the only steady jobs we've got are here on Sunday afternoons and at O'Day's on Fridays," Sue responded. "We've got a few others but they're more hit and miss, nothing regular. Our next 'gig' is on Friday and you're welcome to play along. I'm sure they wouldn't mind."

"I'll see you on Friday then."

"That'll be grand, Pete. We'll see you then." Sue responded.

As he drove home that night, Pete thought to himself that this had been one of the best days he'd had since the accident and it brought a smile to his face.

* * * * * * * * * *

The week at work passed quickly. Pete's mother and father were still off on their camping trip and wouldn't return until the following Monday at the earliest. His mother had called every day to check in on him. She asked if he'd mind if they stayed a little longer. They were enjoying themselves so much at Tsali and the Nantahala Outdoor Center that they hadn't made it to Judy's house yet and were feeling a bit guilty about it. He assured them that he was fine. When he told them about him singing at the Dock o' the Bay, they were ecstatic. They said they couldn't wait to join him there.

Most of his fellow employees, including many who hadn't spoken to him much before, came up to him during the week and said something about him singing the week before. Everybody seemed to make a big deal of it. He told them about him being at the Dock o' the Bay and that he was going to bring his guitar on Friday. Several more said they would join him there.

That Friday, he and about a dozen of the people he worked with went to O'Day's. Mark, the bartender, remembered Pete's name and began clearing a path as soon as he saw him wheeling himself into the bar. Pete had his guitar in his lap but Mark took it and carried it in one hand as he picked up chairs with the other and moved them about.

Again, he was positioned right next to the stage, which was much smaller than the one at Dock o' the Bay. It was rectangular shaped and less than 15 feet wide and six feet deep. There was enough room for the two large speakers on either end, space for Sue and Brendan to sit on two stools, or stand if they preferred. The microphones and PA system were in place and all they had to do was plug in, which made it much easier for them than at 'Dock of the Bay' where they had to bring all their own equipment. The stage sat a foot off the floor so they were just high enough over the seated patrons to be seen.

Sue and Brendan had been playing for an hour when they arrived. It had rained earlier in the day so they had moved the music inside. The bar area may have had a maximum seating capacity of 50 and that was with four people at each of the ten tables squeezed together into the room, which may have been 50 feet long and 30 feet wide. Another dozen or so people could sit at the bar, which ran for most of the length of the room. There may have been ten people scattered about the room when Pete's group arrived, so the crowd doubled in size when they did.

Between moving chairs to accommodate Pete, and the noise and commotion as all of the others took their seats, Sue and Brendan stopped playing and waited for the group to get settled. As they were waiting, they took the opportunity to introduce their newly found band member to the rest of the audience. Although Pete really didn't want the spotlight on him, and he was still quite unused to any attention, he felt pangs of excitement as he heard Sue say,

"Pete Collins and his friends have joined us today. Welcome, Pete and all of the rest of you. I see you've brought your guitar and you're goin' to sing with us again, I hope." She added, "Last week, Pete sang for us and told us it was the first time he'd ever sung in front of an audience before. Now look at him. He's ready to join the band!

"Brendan and I play at another restaurant here in town, not too far away, which we won't mention by name but you can find on our website, on Sunday afternoons from 3 to 6 and you are all invited to join us there as well. When you're settled in, Pete, join right in."

Brendan spoke up and said, "The next song we're going to sing for you this afternoon is 'The Wild Colonial Boy'. You're welcome to sing along if you know the words and if you don't, you can just clap your hands."

Pete was busily getting his guitar out of its case while listening to the music. He had heard this song played on Sunday but he didn't know the lyrics. He knew enough of the melody to strum a few chords before the song ended.

Since most of the crowd was with Pete, instead of going through their set like they planned, they played more of the songs that Pete knew. Although he didn't have a microphone in front of him, he sang every song and played along, and his friends sang with him, which got the rest of the crowd to join in.

Mark couldn't have been happier. The place was jumping and the beer and alcohol were flowing. People stayed longer and had more to eat, so his food sales were up, too. Sue and Brendan had been playing at O'Day's for a few months and they hadn't drawn as much of a crowd reaction as they were this day. Pete was enjoying himself and all of the attention he was receiving.

Pete was still learning how to play the guitar and he hadn't been much of a singer before, so this was all new to him. Although he'd been at it for over a year, he was still learning and he hadn't ever played with other people, especially people who played music for a living. It was good that people were singing along as that tended to drown out his voice and his guitar playing, but he was doing alright, or at least Sue and Brendan seemed to think so.

At the end of the last set, which was at 7:00, Mark came up to Sue and Brendan and asked if they could stay an extra hour. They readily agreed but Pete, who overheard the conversation, told them that he had to go. His back was beginning to ache. He had been up for over twelve hours, which was the longest period of time he'd been upright since the accident, and his body was telling him he had to lay down, and soon.

When Pete left, a number of his companions left with him, but the place was still alive. Mark couldn't have been happier and wanted to make sure that Pete would be back the following week. Pete assured him that he would. Sue and Brendan asked if he'd be joining them again on Sunday and he told them he was planning on it. The night had been a big success, for everyone.

"I think it's because I'm in a chair," Pete reasoned. "I'm not a threat to anyone and people seem to want to be nice to me. It's not because I'm such a great guitar player or anything," he told himself.

Whatever the reason, Pete was excited about all of the attention he was receiving, but when he got back to his van, his back was throbbing. He made it into his van and immediately got out of his chair and lay down on the foam mattress he had put in the back. There was a slight chill in the air and he pulled a blanket over him. He put a pillow under his head and was asleep within minutes. He had overdone it.

He awoke a few hours later when a noisy group of people who were parked next to his van, came stumbling by and one of them bumped up against his van, inches from his head. Pete felt well enough to get up and get home and he did. It was the first time he had driven by himself at night, which was a little different. He was glad he didn't have to get up and go to work the next day. He felt the effects of the three beers he had consumed, too, and he was much more careful than usual, but he made it home safely without any mishap.

When he awoke the following morning, he didn't immediately notice any undesired after-effects from the beer or the long day. He didn't have a throbbing headache, no sore throat, his back didn't ache, all of his body parts, those that were functioning, checked in and reported being ready for another day of duty. Most importantly, though, he had a smile on his face as he thought of the night before.

The whole evening had been like a whirl for him. He thought back on the disjointed conversations, the smiles from the girls, the laughs, the songs, the music…the whole event, and it made him feel good, and it made him feel like calling Abigail, but it was too early for that, it was only 6:00 in Montana. He'd have to wait. He picked up his guitar and started doing spider exercises and practicing making bar chords.

Hours later, before he had eaten any breakfast, it was noon. Time seemed to slip away when he played his guitar. He hadn't worn a watch before the accident, but in the hospital, his days were completely regulated by the clock. Now, on days that he didn't have to work, he let his body tell him what time it was, except today. Today he worried about what time it was in Montana.

"It's 9:00. She may be already at work, or maybe she's got Saturday classes, or maybe she stayed out late last night. He fretted over calling too early and almost talked himself out of calling at all, but he finally got up the courage to dial her number. A sleepy, somewhat groggy voice at the other end said,

"Hello."

"Hi, Ab. It's me, Pete. Did I call at a bad time?"

"What time is it?"

"Noon where I am. It should be 10:00 there, right?"

"I guess. I was out late last night and…"

"Want me to call back later?"

"No, that's alright. I'm up now," she whispered. "So what's goin' on? How are you, Pete?"

"I'm feelin' good today and I thought I'd give you a call."

"Thanks, I'm glad you did. I don't hear from you in a year and I get two calls in a week. So how am I so lucky?"

"I'm doing a whole lot better than I was, and you've been on my mind a lot lately."

"Well, I'm glad to hear from you, Pete. So what's goin' on that's making you feel better. What are you up to?"

"I'm havin' a lot of fun playin' guitar."

"Yeah? You mentioned that the other day when you called. You said something about singing and playing at a bar…"

"Yeah, it's no big deal, but it's been fun, just gettin' out and bein' around people, singin', laughin', havin' a good time. It reminded me of bein' with you."

"Yeah, we had good times together, but none of it involved playing music. We listened to a lot of music."

"Do you play anything, Ab?"

"I played piano as a child, but then I discovered canoeing, kayaking and rafting, and I haven't played in years but I've started playing the guitar, too."

"Really? That's a coincidence."

"After you got hurt, I had a whole lot more time on my hands and I just picked a used one up at the local music store one day and have been fooling around with it ever since."

"Maybe we could play some time together."

"I'm just learning," she responded.

"So am I."

"Yeah, I'd like that, Pete. What time you coming over?"

"Don't I wish. You're a long way away."

"What is it? 3000 miles?"

"Maybe a little less, but I'm in Florida, in the Southeastern part of the country and you're in the Pacific Northwest. We're about as far away as we could be, I guess, unless I lived in Miami or the Keys."

"Well, one of these days, maybe we will. So what have you been up to since we talked last week?"

Pete proceeded to tell her about the night before and his Sunday at Dock o' the Bay. She could tell that he was feeling good about himself. She also knew what he'd been through since she last saw him, although, in her mind, she still saw the same Pete. She hadn't seen him since their last night together, the night before the accident. She had never seen him in a wheelchair. She wasn't sure how she would handle that when she did. She listened as he went on and on about it, and when he finished, she asked,

"So tell me what other things you've been up to, besides work."

"I still like to be outside, especially when it's quiet, under the tree in our backyard. You'd be surprised how many types of birds there are here, even in a city. I see hawks, lots of hawks, osprey, even eagles, plus a whole lot of other things, and a lot of migratory birds…"

Again, Abigail let him talk and talk about the birds, bugs and insects. That was one of the things she loved about him. He loved being out in nature, and so did she. She'd never been east and had an idea what Florida was like from television, movies, pictures and other sources, but she let Pete prattle on about it, content with hearing him talk.

Pete then went on and on about watching the sun rise in the morning over the Atlantic. Now that he could drive himself, he'd go down to the beach most every weekend. He didn't today because of being so tired from the night before. Abigail had never seen the sun rise over the Ocean, or the sun set over the Pacific too many times. She was a mountain girl. She liked hearing Pete talk about it, though.

"And I still like to fish. My Dad and I were going fishing about every day there for a long while, but they're away on a camping trip still."

After half an hour, Abigail said,

"Pete, it's really good to hear from you, and I'm glad to hear you're doing so well, but I've got to meet some friends at 11:00 to go skiing."

"Where are you going?"

"Just here in Kalispell, nothing special."

"Sounds like fun. What's the weather like?"

"It's a beautiful, sunny day. Cold, but clear. We had some snow earlier in the week, so the conditions should be good."

"Are you seeing anybody, Ab?" Pete asked apprehensively.

Abigail wasn't really seeing anyone special, though she was dating. She hadn't been in a relationship since Pete left, at least not like the one she had with him, but she didn't want to tell him that. She knew why he was asking.

"I've been seeing a lot of people, Pete, this being my last year in college and all, but nobody real special. How about you?"

The question surprised Pete. He hadn't even thought about going out on a date or being with anyone, though he had noticed some of the pretty girls at the bars. He wasn't sure how to respond. He decided to just tell the truth.

"No. I've just started to get out of the house, to be honest, Ab. I've been laid up a while...a long while."

"Yeah, I know. I shouldn't have asked that question. I'm sorry."

"No, no, don't be!" Pete said. "You didn't know. I've only spoken to you twice in over a year. That's not your fault."

"Well, I'm glad to hear that you're getting out of the house now, and to hear about you and your guitar. I am going to have to start practicing more."

"I hope you do, Ab. I'd love to see you and play music together."

"That sounds good and we can talk about that later, but I gotta go. I really do. I'll be late if I don't get a move on right now. Take care, Pete, and have a good day."

"Yeah, you, too, Ab."

"I love you."

"I love you, too, Ab."

When he heard the dial tone, he held the phone in his hand and ran the entire conversation through his mind a few times. "What would I do if we did get together?" he thought to himself. "Why would she want to be with me?" He picked up his guitar and went outside to play some more and try not to think about it anymore.

22

A Setback

TUESDAY OF THE FOLLOWING week, two months after the lawsuit was filed, Pete got a call from Mr. Nickel late one night, after dinner, just before he was preparing to go to bed.

"I'm not calling too late am I, Pete? If so, I can call back tomorrow."

"No, that's okay, Mr. Nickel. It's 9:00 here. I don't usually go to bed for another hour or so. This is fine."

"I've got bad news, Pete."

"What's that?"

The Court granted their motion to dismiss your case."

"Why'd it do that?"

"Because of the release. The Court said that everyone knows that riding horses is dangerous and that the risk of falling off a horse was a foreseeable one, or one that you knew might occur."

"And I did. I knew that when I signed that release."

"But you didn't know that they'd put you on the wrong horse and that they'd commit an act of negligence when you signed that release, Pete."

"No, I didn't, but that's what horses do. They fight with each other and establish a pecking order. I knew that, too."

"And you didn't know that they'd put you right behind a horse that

227

a month before had knocked another rider off the same horse you were riding when the accident happened, did you?"

"No, I didn't know that."

"And that's why the release you signed is no good. It doesn't say that you released them from whatever they did. You accepted the risk that the horse you were riding might trip and fall, or something like that, but you didn't sign a release that said I release the Double-D Ranch even if its employees do something stupid and put me on the wrong horse."

"But the Court didn't agree with you?"

"No, it didn't. The judge who heard your case is an old cowboy himself. He's been around these parts his whole life. All of his people are cattle ranchers. He wasn't about to rule in your favor no matter what I said or did."

"You knew that before you even started talkin'?"

"I did."

"So why'd you bother to file suit in the first place?"

"Like I told you, I plan to appeal his decision to the Montana Supreme Court."

"Is that going to cost me money?"

"No, it won't. I told you that I'd pay all the costs and I will. If you win, though, then I get back the monies I paid as costs and then some, if we're lucky."

"So now you've got to file an appeal?"

"That's right."

"How long will that take?"

"Oh, at least six months, maybe more, depending upon how busy they are."

"And you're willing to do all that and not get paid a penny for over a year and maybe more?"

"Yes, Pete, I am. I knew that going in, but I think we have a chance to make some good law on this case and I'm willing to give it a go."

"Good law? What does that mean?"

"See, in cases like yours, and I'm talking about the legal issue of signing a release and waiving all your rights to sue, not your injury, the law is bad for the injured people like you, who are my clients. It's good for the insurance companies, but bad for me and my clients, so when I get a chance to make some 'good law' for me and my clients, I take it."

"Do you win very often when you do?"

"As a general rule, or I should say from a statistical point of view, the answer to your question would be no. It's my understanding that appeals are successful less than 10% of the time."

"Those aren't very good odds, are they?"

"No, they're not, but you've got to roll the dice, and besides that, it's important for me to show my fellow lawyers that I'm not afraid to take an appeal. If I win, it will help my business and it will make you and me some money. Now, I wouldn't do this if I didn't think you had a good case, Pete. If you just had a broken arm or even a broken leg, unless there were some serious complications, no matter how good the legal issue, I wouldn't touch it. The potential benefits wouldn't be worth the risk. I'd be spending more time and money on the case than the case was worth. See what I mean?"

"I understand. So, in my case, you're thinking that the amount of money you can get if we win is worth the time and money you're putting in the case. Is that it?"

"That's right, Pete, and as I told you from the very beginning, the fact that my nephew was with you, riding the horse that kicked your horse your horse, influenced my decision, too."

"I appreciate that, Mr. Nickel."

"Have you talked to him lately?"

"I called him and spoke to him after you and I talked the last time."

"He's a fine young man. I hope he comes to work with me after he gets a little experience. Don't misunderstand me, I'd take him straight from law school, but I couldn't get him the kind of courtroom work that he'll get with either the District Attorney's Office or the Public Defender."

"That's what he said he wanted to do, just like you told me last time."

"Well, it's his life and his career and I'll help him any way I can, and that includes helping you, his friend. So our next step is to appeal the decision of the trial court and the papers are being prepared as I speak. I'll send you a copy of the order entered by the Court here in

Bozeman and copies of the notice of appeal and things, if you'd like. Want to read them?"

"Sure, but it's hard for me to understand it all. You use words I've never even heard of before. I have to look them up in a dictionary half the time."

"That's called legalese. It's a language unto the law and lawyers."

"I can usually make sense out of it but it takes a while."

"I understand. I think you should read the briefs and all. It's important for you to understand what's going on. If there is anything you don't understand, just call me and ask. I'll explain it to you, but you understand what's going on so far, don't you?"

"Yeah. Basically, the issue is whether or not I can even file suit, because of the release I signed."

"That's right."

"But let me ask you this…if you win in the Supreme Court, does that mean we win?"

"Good question, and the answer is no, it doesn't, but if we don't win in the Supreme Court then we're done with. The game is over."

"So if we, or I should say you, win in the Supreme Court, then we have a chance to win something, is that about it?"

"That's a pretty good way of saying it, I'd say, but I'd go further than that. If we win, the chances that the insurance company is going to give you some money will go up dramatically."

"Really, why's that?"

"Insurance companies don't like to take chances. They make informed decisions based upon numbers and figures. They know that if they lose your case, a jury could award you millions of dollars and…"

"Millions of dollars?"

"Yes, Pete, millions of dollars. If we get that far, I'll hire an economic expert who will do calculations and tell a jury that your income-earning abilities were decreased significantly by your injury. I'll get a doctor to say that you're more likely to suffer injuries, like decubitis ulcers for the rest of your life and that your life…"

"I almost had one of those about a month or two ago…"

"You did? You didn't tell me about it."

"I didn't think it made much difference."

"It does. Tell me about it."

"I was laid up for a couple of weeks, but it was just a pressure sore, not an ulcer, thank God."

"But you couldn't work and it was painful, wasn't it?"

"It sure was and no, I couldn't work."

"And it was unpleasant."

"It was."

"I'll have a doctor tell a jury all about that, plus your life expectancy is less than it would have been before the accident, and…well, I could go on but you get the picture, right?"

"So that's gonna make the insurance company pay us money?"

"Yes, it will. The insurance company, and I know this one really well, doesn't want to run the risk of losing a big judgment. They'd rather pay you a small amount now than pay a large amount later."

"So why didn't they offer me something already?"

"Because they thought that this judge would rule in their favor and they were right. They hire defense lawyers who know the judge as well as I do, but they didn't know we'd appeal that decision. They're hoping we'll drop it right here, but I won't. If I was them, I might have thrown a little money at you, but not much. If the Supreme Court rules in our favor, that's a different thing altogether."

"Why's that?"

"Well, then they know that a jury is going to hear the case and no one can predict with certainty what a jury might do with this case. If they like you, Pete, a jury could award a whole lot of money."

"And if they didn't?"

"They might not give you anything at all. You never can tell, but I think a jury is going to like you. The important thing is that this insurance company isn't going to want to risk a big verdict."

"Why not, if they think they can win?"

"Because the insurance company doesn't have anything to gain in this whole deal. They will have to pay their lawyers a lot of money to defend the case and even if they win, all that happens is that they don't have to pay you or me. Now they could get a judgment against you for their costs, but they'd have a hard time collecting it, so they'd be betting a lot of money that they won't lose a whole lot of money. They have nothing to win. See what I mean?"

"So if you win before the Supreme Court, you expect them to offer us some money."

"Yes, I do, but not a whole lot of money. They'd call it 'nuisance value'."

"Nuisance value?"

"Yes, or 'cost of defense' is another term they like to use. It means that if it would cost them say, $50,000 to defend this case, and that includes costs, attorneys' fees and the fees for expert witnesses, depositions and all the rest, for them to go to trial and litigate this thing for months and months. I expect that they might offer to pay you say $40,000 before incurring all of the expense and risk losing more."

"That's a lot of money, Mr. Nickel."

"I'm just using that as an example, Pete."

"At $8.00 an hour, it would take me a couple of years to make that much money."

"Now that wouldn't take into consideration my fee of 40% and all the costs, so you'd probably end up with about $20,000 from a $40,000 settlement. You understand that, right?"

"Now I do."

"But keep in mind that if you were to go to trial and win, then you would have a chance to recover a whole lot more money."

"I know, but I could lose, too, and I'd have to pay their costs?"

"That's right, Pete. There are no guarantees. Insurance companies count on people like you being not willing to take a chance, so they offer just enough money to make you think about it."

"I guess that's good business on their part."

"That's why they own everything in the country, along with the oil companies, the banks, credit card companies, pharmaceutical companies and other big businesses, but the decision is yours, not mine. I can make recommendations and give you my advice, but in the end you make the decision on what to do, Pete. It's your case, not mine."

"We're way ahead of the game here, aren't we? You called to tell me we lost and here I am thinking about spending the money if we win."

"That's okay, Pete. It's good to be optimistic, and I am. I believe we are going to win. There are some good people on the Montana

Supreme Court. I'm confident in your case, or else I wouldn't be doing it. I'm not in this to do you a favor, Pete. No offense, Pete, but I'm using my knowledge of the law and my legal skills and trying my best to objectively analyze your case. I'm not doing this because you're my nephew's good friend. I'm telling you that I think we can win."

"Well, I'm glad to hear that, but today we lost, right?"

"That's right. Today we lost. And if and when we win before the Supreme Court, you can bet that I am going to do everything I can to convince you to take this case before a jury. We can win this case in front of a jury, Pete. I know we can."

"We'll cross that bridge when we come to it, Mr. Nickel. I appreciate all you've done for me so far and I thank you for explaining all that to me."

"You're welcome, Pete. I know how hard it must be for you and I really wish I had some good news for you, but I don't want you to be discouraged. This is a setback, but we'll get a chance to fight another day, and we will. As I told you, the paperwork is being prepared as we speak. Hell, it may be finished by now, as long as we've been talking. We're going to win this thing, Pete. Trust me."

"Thanks, Mr. Nickel. I do trust you and I'll read whatever you send me."

"Just call me anytime you'd like, Pete, and I'll do my best to explain it to you if you can't understand it. Take care, son, and keep the faith."

"Thanks, Mr. Nickel."

23

Just a City Boy, Lookin' for a Home

THE DAYS TURNED INTO weeks and the weeks turned into months. Pete's life had settled into a comfortable routine. Every week, from Monday to Friday, from 8:00 to 5:00, Pete was at work. The revised work schedule had helped a lot, although it meant an hour more at work per day. At nights, he practiced his guitar. Every Friday afternoon, he played music at O'Day's and every Sunday afternoon, he went to the Dock o' the Bay.

Sue and Brendan were happy to have him play with them and occasionally, maybe twice a month, they would get together on a Tuesday or a Wednesday and practice. Pete would go to their house. They lived down in American Beach, not far south from Fernandina on A1A.

Every Sunday afternoon, without fail, he'd call Abigail and they would talk. She had found a friend who was learning to play the guitar, too, and they had played a few 'open-mikes' at a local bar. It was still wintertime in Montana, but soon it would be spring. Though she liked the cold weather, and she liked being outside, skiing, snow-mobiling, and sledding down the hilly slopes around campus, the warm weather of Florida sounded good to Abigail.

"So why don't you come to visit? There's plenty of room here at the house and I know my Mom and Dad would love to meet you."

"I'm a poor, college kid. I don't have any money to do that. You know I'm paying my way through school, plus I'm trying to save up some money for graduate school. You should come out here."

Driving to Montana was not something Pete thought he was capable of doing.

"That's a long way, Abigail."

"You could fly, you know."

"I'd need a car once I got there, plus taking a plane isn't so easy for someone in my condition."

Abigail hadn't thought of that, and said,

"I thought you like it out here, Pete. Where is home to you? Here or there?"

Pete hadn't thought about that much. Every day was pretty much another day of survival. He was putting away a little money, but not too much. He had to pay his father for the van, and he was making double payments every month to pay it off as quickly as he could, plus he contributed some money for food and utilities. Despite his parents' protestations that it wasn't necessary for him to do so, he insisted. Playing guitar and singing were the biggest activities, outside of work, in his life, and he had grown accustomed to them being the biggest part of the new person that he was.

"That's a good question, Ab. I'm going to have to give that some thought, but in the meantime, you think about a visit to Florida, okay?"

"I will."

"We're going to have to figure that out some way to get together again, aren't we?"

"I guess so, or else we'll keep talking on the telephone."

"I enjoy talking to you but I'd like to see you, Ab."

"So do something about it," she responded. "Gotta go, Pete. Have a good day."

Pete thought long and hard about what Abigail had said to him. He was going to have to do something about it.

* * * * * * * * * *

At work, Pete was doing well, too well. One day, Randy took him aside and said,

"You gotta slow down, man! You're makin' the rest of us look bad!"

"I can't help it, Randy. It just comes easy to me. I've got it down. To be honest, I'm getting a little bored with it, because it is so easy for me."

"Well, you're either gonna take my job or else they gotta find another job for you, 'cause you're puttin' up numbers that the rest of us can't match!"

"I'm sorry. I really am. I'll try to slow down or somethin'. I don't know what to do."

"Man, I don't want to see you go, but you're good at this stuff. Maybe you should think about somethin' a little more challenging."

"Maybe I will, but I like it here."

"You think about it."

The next thing Pete knew, he had been working at Walgreen's for six months. Entering data in a computer didn't require much of an intellectual challenge for him, though it did require attention to detail and Pete had become good at that, too. Every now and then, he'd look through the classifieds to see what jobs were out there in the computer world. He needed to go back to school to get his degree to get some of the jobs, but he couldn't afford that. He had to work to pay bills and support himself, and the medicines he continued to take weren't cheap, even though he only had to make the co-pay.

His back was fully healed, and he no longer thought about it too much, as far as putting pressure on it. He had started lifting weights again, and didn't have much trouble doing curls with 30 pound bar bells, or bench pressing 175 pounds ten times. As Dr. Johnson had told him, a time would come when he wouldn't even think about wearing the clam shell anymore and he didn't. It would take a powerful traumatic event for him to re-injure his back.

Pete had lost the use of his legs, and that was never coming back. He knew that and he had accepted that as a fact, although he continued to pray for a miracle, a new discovery in the field of genetic engineering or something. Slowly, over time, he started to become more confident in his ability to take care of himself and venture out into the world some.

He started to go camping on his own. At first, he went with

his parents, in separate vehicles, to some of the campgrounds near Fernandina, like Fort Clinch, Talbot State Park and to Anastasia Park in St. Augustine. Then, when he was sure he could to do that, by sleeping in the back of his van and using the handicapped bathrooms at the parks, he began to go by himself to places like the Stephen F. Foster Park in White springs and to the Suwannee River State Park, just north of Live Oak.

He made sure to be back for music at the Dock o' the Bay on Sunday afternoons, but he'd leave the house on a Saturday morning, spend the night at a park, and then come back in time to meet with Brendan and Sue on Sunday afternoon. It reminded him of how much he loved doing the things he used to do, and how much he missed them. All he could do was take the concrete paths on the 'Nature Trails' offered by the park service, which was enjoyable, but pretty tame for a person like Pete, or what Pete used to be like.

One Sunday afternoon, about three months after Pete had started to play with Sue and Brendan, he received a frantic call from Sue.

"Brendan's come down sick as a dog from somethin' he ate," she explained. "We can't make it there today. Can you cover for us?"

"Me? I can't do that, Sue!"

"Yes, you can, Pete. You'll do just fine, I know you will. I'm here at the hospital with Brendan and there's no tellin' how long we'll be. He hasn't been seen by a doctor yet but I think they're going to have to pump out his stomach or something. I'm worried about him and can't leave him here like this. I can't."

"I'm not good enough to do that, I'm not."

"Please! Do it for us, Pete. I don't want to cancel with them. I'm afraid they might find someone else and we'll lose the gig altogether."

"But, Sue!"

"You can do it, Pete. For us, please?"

Reluctantly, Pete agreed. He showed up and explained to the manager what had happened. The manager had seen Pete there every week and didn't think too much about it. He came out a few times to see what was going on out in the patio area. People sat around, listening, ordering food and drinks, and seemed to be enjoying themselves.

When it was over, Pete was relieved. The manager came up and handed him $200 and thanked him. Pete had never been paid to play music before. There was over $50 in his tip jar, too. Sue called later that evening and told him that Brendan was fine. They were at home. They had pumped out his stomach at the hospital and Brendan was in bed, recuperating. She told him never to eat at the Mexican place on State Road 17. She was happy to learn that everything had gone well.

Pete called Abigail that night and told her all about it. She was impressed and Pete was proud of himself. "Maybe we can play some music together," she said. "What will we call ourselves?"

"Beauty and the beast," Pete replied.

She laughed and said, "We can do better than that."

"You think of something."

"I'll work on it," she said. "What do you like to play most? Rock 'n roll? Sixties? Seventies? What?"

"I guess I'm still doin' sixties and seventies, but I like some of the old Blues guys, too, like Mississippi John Hurt, Leadbelly, Robert Johnson, B.B. King…people like that."

"Ever heard of Keb-Mo?"

"Can't say that I have," Pete responded.

"Check him out. I like his music. He's got a few songs I like."

That night, Pete did a search for Keb-Mo and on lyrics.com and found some songs he liked, too. His favorite was one called 'City Boy', which he started to play. The lyrics were, "I'm just a city boy, lookin' for a home…I want to be…where the Buffalo roam…I'm just a city boy…lookin' for a home."

That became his new favorite song and he started to sing it every chance he got, plus some other ones, like 'Am I wrong'; 'Suitcase'; and 'Just like you'. He liked finding new artists, or artists he'd never heard of before. He liked Keb-Mo.

The more he thought about things, the more he realized that he had to find a way to get to Montana. There was nothing wrong with Florida, and he couldn't say he was unhappy, but things were missing from his life. This wasn't the life he had wanted for himself. He'd never, ever get that life back. He had lost a lot in the fall off the horse, but he still had a lot left, he told himself.

What he lacked was the money to get him to Montana. He'd need money to make the trip, plus money to get himself established. He'd need a place to stay, a job, plus a little cushion for a rainy day. Before he said anything to his parents about it, or to Abigail, he gave Reno a call. Reno was glad to hear from him.

"So how are things, Pete?"

"I'm doin' okay, hangin' in there."

"Glad to hear it. When are you coming back?"

"Funny you should ask, Reno. That's one of the reasons I called."

"Really? Well, what can I do for you?"

"You got any jobs open?"

"What are you talking about? I can't put you back in a raft, Pete, as much as I'd like to, can I?"

"No, not even close."

"Well, I didn't think that's what you meant, but I hope the day comes when I can use you on the river again, Pete. What do you have in mind?"

"I didn't mean as a guide. I was thinking of helping out in the store or helping you with your books, maybe set up an accounting system for you, whatever. I've gotten pretty good with computers since you saw me."

"Really? I could use some help with that for sure, and I could use you in the store, too. None of my guides ever want to work in the store. It's like I'm putting them in jail when they have to stay in and mind the store, or drive the buses."

"I'm not wanting to drive, either. You'd have to convert it and all and that would cost a lot of money."

"And you couldn't put any of the boats on top, either."

"I know, that's not what I was thinking. Just working in the store would be great."

"Well, sure, I can do that for you right now, and you're welcome to stay with us until you find a place."

"Thanks, Reno, I might take you up on that."

"And you know it would only be for the summer. I close up at the end of September and nobody has a job, not even me, although I stay busy with the brochures, the mail, the bookings and the rest. Come to think of it, you could help me with that, too."

"That's what I was thinking, Reno."

"That'd be great, Pete. It'll be great to have you back. We open up the middle of May, like always."

"I'll let you know. I'm just hatchin' this plan right now. I hear Abigail is working with you again this summer, right?"

"She said she was. I'm counting on her. She'll be my most experienced guide, next to Mark Stanley, but he just works whenever he wants to anymore, so she'll be my lead guide on most all of the trips I send her out on."

"Don't mention any of this to her, okay, Reno?"

"I won't say a word. Gonna surprise her are you?"

"I just don't want her to know anything about it yet. I'm not sure I can swing it financially, but I'll start workin' on it. I needed to know if I could have a job first. I'll need a place to stay, too, and all the rest, you know."

"Well, like I said. You're welcome with us. I guess I should say something to the Missus, but I'm sure she won't mind."

"I'll get back to you. Give me a couple of weeks to see about making all the arrangements."

"That's fine with me. You just show up and I'll put you to work, how's that? Whenever you get here, you've got a job. How's that?"

"That works for me. Thanks, Reno."

"I won't be able to pay you much, understand, but you'll get what I pay everybody else. I can't do any better than that, can I? How does that sound?"

"That'll be great, Reno. I wouldn't ask for anything more."

"It'll be great to have you back. Anything I can do to help, just let me know."

"Say, I'll tell you what, if you could keep your eyes open for a place for me to rent, or buy, maybe, that'd be great. It'll have to be handicapped accessible and all."

"I thought you said you don't have any money?"

Pete didn't know if Reno had heard about the lawsuit or not. He didn't want to mention it and he wasn't really thinking that he was going to win, but it was in the back of his mind that he might get some money out of it, maybe.

"I don't, so I'm looking to rent, but sometimes you can rent with an option to buy, or people will finance it for you and it's just like rent, right?"

"Sometimes, but not too often up this way, at least not that I know of."

"Well, just in case."

"I'll do it."

"Thanks, Reno."

"You're welcome. I hope to see you soon."

"I'll let you know once I know what I'm doin'. I'm just gettin' to the point where I can do this. I'm gettin' better, Reno."

"Glad to hear it, Pete. Glad to hear it. Stay in touch."

The seed had been planted and it was beginning to take root. The more he thought of it, the more he liked the idea, but he wasn't telling anybody about it who didn't have to know. Money was a problem. As soon as he got off the phone, he went on the internet and began looking for houses in the Glacier/Kalispell area that were handicapped accessible. There weren't many and they weren't cheap, but he had decided that he didn't want to be in a city. Glacier was his home.

24

The Montana Supreme Court

THE APPEAL FILED BY Mr. Nickel took a few months to reach the stage where it was to be heard by the Montana Supreme Court. Since there was no trial, the only matters contained in the record were the Complaint filed by Mr. Nickel on behalf of Pete, plus the Motion to Dismiss the Complaint filed by the attorney assigned by the insurance company to defend the Double-D Ranch, and memoranda of law submitted by both sides on the legal arguments involved. The main piece of evidence was the release, which was attached to the Complaint. The hearing had been recorded and a transcript of the hearing was included in the record on appeal.

The drive from Bozeman to Helena didn't take but a couple of hours. It was west on I-90 to Butte and then north on I-15. Mr. Nickel had been there many times before and had no problem finding his way around. Helena is a city of about 25,000 people and traffic wasn't much of a problem. He thought it was interesting that Helena, which had fewer people in it than Bozeman did, was both the capital and home to the Supreme Court. There were more than 27,000 people in Bozeman, but it was still only the fifth biggest city, behind Billings, Missoula, Butte and Great Falls.

Mr. Nickel hadn't been before the seven member court in several years and it had changed composition since he had last been there. There were two new members and it had a new Chief Justice. A woman named Carol Eastman had become the Chief Justice. He didn't know her, except from having been introduced to her at a reception honoring the Supreme Court that had been put on by the Montana Bar Association, but he had heard good things about her. He felt good about his chances of winning Pete's case, even though, statistically speaking, the odds were against him. Most appeals were denied.

Pete's case was the third one on the docket for the morning session, which started at 10:00. Mr. Nickel arrived early and he was in the audience when the bailiff entered the courtroom, at precisely 10:00 and said,

"Hear ye, hear ye, hear ye. All rise. The Supreme Court in and for the State of Montana is now in session. All those having business before it will be heard."

The hundred-plus people in the room stood as the seven members of the Court, each dressed in their long, black robes, walked from behind the paneled wall and took their seats. The Chief Justice took her seat in the middle of the seven maroon colored high-backed cushioned chairs. Behind her hung the great seal of the State of Montana with its picture of high, snow-covered mountains dominating the center of the seal. Once all seven Justices were seated, Chief Justice Eastman said,

"You may be seated."

Once everyone in the audience was seated and the clamor had died down, she continued,

"The first case to be heard today is the case of Palsgraf versus the Great Northern Railroad."

Six people stood and walked from the audience, through two wooden, waist-high swinging doors to the two large wooden tables which were positioned to their left and to their right. Two sat down at the table on the left and three at the table on the right. One person, a woman, walked straight ahead to a podium which was less than ten feet from the bench at which the seven Justices sat. Once she had reached the podium and placed a folder on the angled top, adjusted the microphone to the level of her mouth, she said,

"Good morning. My name is Shannon Frechette and I represent Mrs. Palsgraf, the Appellant in this Court and the Plaintiff in the Trial Court..."

Mr. Nickel listened with passing interest to the argument, which basically centered around the issue of whether or not the person who had slipped and fallen on water on the floor of the railway station had to prove how long the water had been on the floor or if the Railroad had the burden of proof. The Railroad, she argued, knew of the water being on the floor but did not clean it up or put up warning signs fast enough to prevent Mrs. Palsgraf from falling. Ms. Frechette argued that the Trial Court applied the wrong standard and that they shouldn't have been required to prove how long the water had been there, it should have been the other way around.

"The Railroad should be the ones required to present evidence as to how long the water had been there, not the Plaintiff/Appellant," she argued. Mrs. Palsgraf had lost her case in front of a jury in Great Falls and she was asking the Court to award her a new trial at which the Defendant, the Railroad Company, should have been made to prove that they weren't negligent once evidence was presented of water being on the floor. Her lawyer argued that Mrs. Palsgraf should only have been required to prove was that she was a business patron who had legitimate business at the Railroad Company's place of business, and that she fell on water that was on the floor. It was the Railroad Company's duty to keep the floor clean and they didn't. Mrs. Palsgraf didn't know how long the water had been there. How would she know? The employees who cleaned the place were in a better position to know that, she argued. The burden of proof in such matters should be on the Railroad, not the injured plaintiff. She was asking the Court to change the law and apply a new standard, as other courts around the country were beginning to do in such cases.

Once Mr. Nickel got a grasp of what the argument was about, he turned his attention to his case and he re-read the cases he was relying upon, jotting a few more scribbles on his legal pad, which was inside a leather-bound folder. He had been over his argument many, many times, but he wanted to make sure that he presented his argument in the best way possible. What he really hoped for was that the Justices had read his brief, understood his argument and agreed with his position before he stood up and walked to the podium. Since that was unlikely, his next best hope was that the Justices had read his brief and would pepper him with questions, which would reflect an interest in the issue he was presenting to them.

Thirty minutes later, when the lawyers for the two sides had consumed their allotted time, Chief Justice Eastman thanked them and called the second case on the docket.

"The next case to be heard today is the case of Wallace M. Beery versus the State of Montana," she said.

Four people stood up, two went left and two went to the table on the right. A tall, thin man with gray hair and a pony tail put his brief case down next to the table on the left and then walked up to the podium with just a legal pad, nothing else.

"Good morning, Madame Chief Justice and all Justices of this Venerable Court," he began. "My name is William C. Botts and I represent Mr. Beery, who was convicted of felony possession of marijuana with the intent to distribute..."

Mr. Nickel had a little more interest in this case than the first case as he had many such cases like that stemming from arrests made at Montana State University. He knew the law well and hoped that the lawyer, who was with the State's Public Defender's Office, would win. He thought that the law was unfair in that anyone who possessed more than a pound of marijuana was automatically charged with being a distributor. By State statute, a judge was to instruct a jury that it was to presume that anyone with more than a pound of marijuana was going to sell or distribute most of it.

Mr. Nickel felt that the instruction was unconstitutional in that it allowed for convictions of innocent people because of the presumption granted by the instruction. Montana was one of ten states in the United States which, together with the District of Columbia, allowed the use of marijuana for medicinal purposes and Montana was considered to be a fairly liberal state regarding the casual use of marijuana, except for this statute which allowed for a conviction of people if they possessed more than a pound of marijuana at any time. The burden then shifted to defendants who were required to prove they had no intent to distribute. He thought there should be no presumption of guilt without more evidence other than simple possession. He listened for a while and then went back to his notes.

Finally, at a few minutes after 11:00, his case was called. It surprised him how he continued to feel butterflies in his stomach when it happened. He had done this many times before, but he still felt the butterflies. "I guess when I stop feeling the butterflies, it will be time to stop practicing law," he thought to himself. "Appearing before the Supreme Court is an honor and a privilege and it excites me. That's all there is to it."

He strode confidently towards the podium. Two people, a man and a woman, walked before him and sat down at the table on the right. Mr. Nickel nodded to them, kept walking and when he reached the podium, he began,

" Good morning, Madame Chief Justice and good morning to all other Justices of this Court, I represent Peter Collins, a 23 year old man who..."

"Good morning, Mr. Nickel, "Justice King, the other female on the panel, interrupted. "We've read your brief and, although I can't speak for everyone on this panel, I think we are all sympathetic to his plight, but let me ask you...are you suggesting that he did not assume the risk that he might fall off the horse he was riding?"

"No, Justice King, I am not. Peter Collins was a river guide in Glacier. He knew that riding horses, like rafting, was dangerous. He liked dangerous activities. That isn't our argument. We are saying that he didn't assume the risk that the operators of the Double-D Ranch would be negligent."

"But that release he signed specifically says that he released ALL claims, demands, actions, liabilities AND Judgments that he may have or he may accrue as a result of that trail ride, doesn't it, Mr. Nickel?" Justice Liscomb asked.

"It does, your Honor, but that release does not include the word negligence. It does not say that he released any claims that he might have..."

"But it does say ALL claims, Mr. Nickel", Justice Miller interjected. "Excuse me from interrupting you, but I think you have to address that issue. We all have read the release and we all are fully aware of the fact that the word 'negligence' is nowhere to be found in that document. That is not the question being asked of you."

"Yes, Justice Miller. I understand. I'm aware of this Court's ruling that a pre-incident release is an effective bar to suit in that case coming out of the bar in Billings, but this Court has never addressed the issue, at least not as far as I could determine in my research, of whether or not it is necessary that the word 'negligence' be included in the release to make it a bar to suit."

"And I think that's what we need to address, Mr. Nickel," the Chief Justice added, "and that is if we are going to require that the word 'negligence' be included in a pre-incident release to make it effective."

"And I have included in my briefs cases from other states, your Honor…"

"I was the author of the opinion on that case out of Billings," Justice Beebe interjected, "and it didn't involve allegations of negligence against the owners of the bar. It was really a products liability case. The question there was whether or not the release was effective against the manufacturer of the 'Bucking Bronco Brahma Bull'. I'll never forget that name. It's hard to say three times in a row, isn't it? I, personally, don't think our decision in that case is particularly relevant to our analysis in this case."

"Well, I think that there are clearly some facts in that case which distinguish it from this case," Justice Varner responded, "and I wrote the dissenting opinion in that case. I voted then, as I anticipate that I might well vote here, that a pre-incident release, prepared by the entity which is enticing customers to utilize its services, cannot effectively bar a claim for negligence on the part of the employees, or any claim that the equipment utilized was defective under any circumstances. Especially so when it puts the exculpatory language in very small, very fine print on the back, just as an enthusiastic and eager patron is about to go on a ride or go rafting down a river. I think that this release, and all releases like it, should be banned as against public policy."

At that point, the Chief Justice interceded and said,

"Thank you for your comments, Justices Beebe and Varner, but I ask that you and all of your colleagues on this Court, including me, keep our comments directed to counsel. We can discuss this matter privately later. I was particularly interested in that case out of Florida you cited, Mr. Nickel. The <u>Witt</u> case, I believe. It involved riding with dolphins. In that case, the Florida Appellate Court, not the Florida Supreme Court, ruled that the release was ineffective to bar the suit, but as I read the opinion, it seemed to me that the Court was suggesting that it was a factual issue as to what was released and what was not released. As I understood the opinion, the case was remanded to the

Trial Court and a jury would have to determine, based upon the facts of the case, whether or not the specific act which caused the injury was an act which the plaintiff, Mr. Witt, assumed the risk of. Is that what you're suggesting we do in this case?"

"Actually, Madame Chief Justice, that is exactly what I am asking this Court to do. I seek a decision from this Court which will allow me to present this case to a jury and explore how and why Mr. Collins was injured. Our position is that it is a factual issue of whether or not he did, indeed, accept the risk that what happened to him was a foreseeable risk. Was it a risk he knowingly assumed? Our position is that a jury must decide that factual issue and that it is not a legal issue to be decided by a judge on a motion to dismiss. I would ask the Court to keep in mind that we're not here on a motion for summary judgment. We didn't get that far."

"That's true, Mr. Nickel, but Mr. Nickel," Justice Liscomb responded, "Your complaint lays out your theory of the case and the issue of whether or not you state a claim is squarely before us, in my opinion. As I said before, and I ask you again, was it not foreseeable that a rider might fall off a horse? I might also ask if it was foreseeable that the guide, who is a Defendant in this case, probably no older than Mr. Collins himself, would be negligent in some respect? And, more importantly, isn't that something that your client knowingly gave up when he signed that release? Is that not something that a reasonably prudent person could anticipate? I know I've been on trail-rides with my family before and God knows that I asked myself on several occasions if I really wanted to put my life in the hands of some of those kids who were leading the rides."

"But you did, didn't you, Justice Liscomb?" his colleague, Justice Varner asked, jokingly.

"I did and I assumed the risk of injury when I did. God help me, but I did," he responded, "But I remember thinking at the time whether or not I shouldn't have."

"Gentlemen, please." The Chief Justice chided them. "You may continue, Mr. Nickel. I believe Justice Liscomb makes a good point. Is that not a foreseeable risk? Is not negligence foreseeable?"

"Thank you, your Honor. I fully understand that the decision you make in this case could go either way. There are certainly compelling judicial reasons why you could collectively decide this case in favor of my client, Mr. Collins, but I understand that there are valid reasons why this case could go against us, too. I'm sure that this Court wants to make the decision that is the better rule of law for cases like this in the future, not just a decision on this case which can be justified or explained. I think Justice Varner made mention of one of the more telling issues to consider, and that is who drafted the release? I doubt that anyone would suggest that there was an equal bargaining position here."

Mr. Nickel's head was spinning. He felt like a pin-ball being bounced from one side of the room to the other. He felt as if he was being attacked from all sides. Only Justice Sullivan hadn't jumped into the fray yet, but as soon as that thought hit his brain, Justice Sullivan joined what had become a debate, not an argument, or at least not like any other oral argument he had been a part of. Clearly, the Court was quite interested in the issue.

"Mr. Nickel, I was particularly interested in that case you cited from the State of California, the case involving the Disney attraction which involved a trail ride, much like this case. There, the horses stampeded, apparently, someone fell off a horse and, like here, sustained an injury, but not one as grievous as the one sustained by Mr. Collins. In that case, the California court found that the release was invalid and ineffective because, it said, 'The plaintiffs did not knowingly assume the risk that the horses might stampede.' The plaintiffs in that case assumed, according to the opinion, that this would be a well-guided, well-controlled activity and it wasn't. Isn't that what we're talking about here? Isn't that a similar issue?"

"Absolutely. I completely agree with that analysis as well, Justice Sullivan," Mr. Nickel responded. "Our position is that Mr. Collins did not assume the risk that the trail guide would be negligent. At this juncture, I am asking in this appeal is that Mr. Collins' case not be dismissed by the Trial Court based solely upon the language in the release. As I said at the outset, our position is that my client did not knowingly assume the risk that the Defendant would be negligent."

"Now wait just a minute there, Mr. Nickel," Justice Miller interjected, before one of his colleagues could get the opportunity to speak, "I don't believe that what Justice Sullivan just said is what you apparently are interpreting him to have said, and I quote from the Restatement of Torts, Second, which reads: 'No agreement to assume risks not known to the plaintiff will be inferred unless clearly intended.' Now I agree with that statement, and I agree with what Justice Sullivan just said, but I'm not sure I agree with you, Mr. Nickel, because I think you would have us rule that ANY release that does not include the magic word 'negligence' is invalid as a bar against negligence. Am I right?"

"Yes, Justice Miller, you are correct. That is my position, although my argument applies only to the facts of this case and the specific release my client signed."

"That's what I thought," Justice Miller said smugly, as if he had concisely narrowed the issue for discussion. "So the question before us is squarely whether or not the word 'negligence' must be included in a pre-incident release for activities such as riding horses, white-water rafting, sky-diving and who knows what else, in order for it to be valid. Am I right?" he asked, as he raised his hands above his head and looked at his colleagues.

"I'm not so sure, Henderson," Justice King responded, before Mr. Nickel could speak. "I'm thinking that it needs to be analyzed in a case by case basis. What if the saddle strap broke? What if they put the bridle on wrong? What if they put on a saddle blanket that had a burr in it? Isn't that a different situation from one in which a horse trips on a rock or stumbles over the root of a tree? Are we going to lump all of these things together and say all of that is to be expected? I don't think that simply using the word negligence resolves the issue."

"Gentlemen, again, I ask you to direct your comments to counsel. We can talk amongst ourselves at our leisure," the Chief Justice reminded them.

"I'd like to read another part of that Restatement of Torts section that my colleague, Justice Sullivan just referred to. It reads: 'For an express assumption of risk to be valid, whether it arises from a contract or from voluntary participation in an activity such as a sport, it must be clear that the plaintiff understood that he was assuming the risk of the PARTICULAR conduct by the defendant which caused the injuries.' I think we need to examine exactly what is alleged in this case. I tend to agree with what Justice King just said. We need to look at it on a case by case basis, so let me ask you, Mr. Nickel, what is the specific conduct by the Double-D Ranch that caused the injury?"

"Mr. Justice Sullivan, as is alleged in our Complaint, an employee of the Double-D put my client on a horse, behind another horse, with knowledge that less than a month before that other horse, called Gentle Ben ironically…"

The Justices laughed when he said that, because it wasn't mentioned in the brief.

"No really," Mr. Nickel said, responding to the lighter moment, "That really was his name, and the name of the horse my client was on was 'Bucky'."

At that all of the Justices broke out laughing, as did the people in the audience. When order was restored, while some continued to chuckle, Mr. Nickel continued,

"With full knowledge that less than a month before Gentle Ben had kicked Bucky and a rider had fallen. Fortunately, in that case no one was injured, but the point is the conduct that caused the injury was the placement of the horses on the ride. With all due respect to all of you, I submit that there is no way that a reasonably prudent customer would have any way of knowing that would happen, or could happen, and that is an act of negligence which was not foreseeable."

At that, all of the Justices seemed to sit back in their chairs a little, as opposed to sitting forward in their chairs as they had been, with their mouths to their respective microphones, looking for an opportunity to be heard. As they did, Chief Justice Eastman looked to her left and then to her right, to see if any of the Justices had any further questions of Mr. Nickel, and then she said,

"Is there anything further you would like to add to your argument, Mr. Nickel?"

"I would like to suggest to this Court that I, personally, was persuaded by the reasoning in the cases coming out of Florida which involved racing cars around a track. Injuries and deaths are not infrequent in those situations and the Courts seemed to suggest that if the pre-incident releases included the magic word 'negligence' then they were upheld and if they didn't include the word 'negligence' then the releases weren't a bar to actions based on negligence. I cited several of those cases in my brief."

"Thank you, Mr. Nickel. We will now hear from the Defendant. Mr. Lemos, will you be making the argument today or will it be Ms. Fairman?"

"I will, your Honor." Mr. Lemos replied, but when he began to respond to the various issues raised in Mr. Nickel's argument and in his brief, the Justices became silent. They had apparently considered the matter to their satisfaction during Mr. Nickel's time before them. They had virtually no questions of Mr. Lemos, other than to confirm a few facts, and he spoke without interruption for a good ten minutes. When he was finished, the Chief Justice asked Mr. Nickel if he wished to respond to what Mr. Lemos had said. Mr. Nickel said that he didn't. He had said all that he had to say and nothing said by Mr. Lemos caused him to want to speak any further.

"Thank you both for your presentations. We expect to issue a ruling within a month. As you may know, I have made it my pledge when I became the Chief Justice to do so on all cases and I will do my best to see to it that we do so on your case."

When he got back to his office, Mr. Nickel called Pete and told him all about it. Pete still wasn't too optimistic. After all, he told himself, even if we win, all that does is give me the right to bring suit, or not have the suit dismissed. That didn't mean he'd be getting any money. Unless he did, though, he couldn't see how he could make it work. It made no sense to give up a good job, spend all that money getting out to Glacier, and then, at the end of summer, be out of work and out of money. As much as he wanted to go, he couldn't see how he could, without more money. This wasn't like the old days when if he had a dollar to his name he was good to go. He had to accept his limitations and he didn't like that.

25

Limitations and a Reality Check

IT WAS LATE MAY and in Fernandina Beach, although there were some cool nights and some days where the temperatures never reached the 80s, for the most part, summer had arrived. Spring in Florida, even in North Florida, is a short season. Pete discovered that his body didn't do as well in the heat as it did in the cold.

He awoke in the middle of a Tuesday night with a strong headache. He called out to his parents, who came into his room to see what was wrong. His mother felt his forehead and said that he was burning up. She gave him some Tylenol and put a wet hand-towel on his forehead.

Pete didn't know what was wrong, but he felt so badly that, when the headache didn't get any better half an hour later, he asked his parents to take him to the emergency room of the local hospital, which they did. An hour later, they were on their way back home. The doctors diagnosed the problem as a urinary tract infection, gave him some antibiotics and told him to see his primary treating physician as soon as possible.

Pete called in sick and made an appointment to see his doctor. She confirmed the diagnosis and gave him a prescription for two other anti-biotics. She explained to him that a urinary infection would take a while, maybe as long as a week, but probably only a few days, before the infection would resolve. Until then, he would just have to endure the pain and discomfort.

She went on to explain that he would be susceptible to urinary tract infections for the rest of his life, so he should expect to have more of them in the future. Since he had a catheter in him, the urine didn't drain completely out at times. When the urine collected and fermented, an infection would result. There was little he could do to avoid it or prevent it from happening. All he could do was to try his best to have good hygiene and be as careful as possible when cleaning the catheter and going to the bathroom.

He had used up all of his sick leave and vacation time with the first ulcer. As a new employee with less than a year with the company, he would not be paid at all for days missed. He was well aware of the fact that excessive absenteeism, even for good excuse, was grounds for dismissal.

Pete felt like a cold bucket of water had been thrown on his face. All of his hopes and dreams of going back to Glacier were being dashed. It was a reality check. He was a paraplegic and he had to fight for survival. He couldn't be going off on any wild excursions. What was he thinking? He wasn't the same person he was when he went to Alaska with barely enough money to get him there and none to get him back. Those days were gone.

He felt depressed and considered asking for some mood changing prescription drugs. He had been given plenty of them in the hospital, so much so that he had to fight to get off of them. The pain-killers were like candy, too. Even now, a single phone call could evoke a whole raft of prescriptions. He felt the need for some Percocet, or something stronger. Before he did, though, he decided to call Dr. Johnson. He hadn't talked to him in a while and he wanted to hear what he had to say.

"Pete! Good to hear from you. How are you? Still working at the same job, playing your music and doing the camping thing?"

"I was, up until this morning."

"What happened? Did you fall? Hurt yourself? What?"

"I got another one of these complications from my accident, Doc..."

"What is it? A decubitis ulcer?"

"No, it's a urinary infection this time."

"Those things are to be expected, and they can be trouble at times. Any other problems since we last spoke?"

"A few months ago, I had what I thought was a pressure sore."

"Where was it?"

"On my right butt, where I sit."

"Did you get moisture in there?"

"I had been out on a kayak a few days before, one of those sit-on-tops, you know?"

"I've seen them. How long were you out on the water?"

"Several hours. Me and my Dad went fishing on a lake just north of Lake City in a National Park up there."

"Well, that can do it. Moisture and heat are the two most common causes of a decubitis ulcer, that and the friction of being in a sling or something like that, like when we elevate a leg and the heel of the foot comes in contact with the canvas support. That has to be watched closely in a hospital. What's the temperature down there?"

"I haven't been outside today, but it's usually in the high 70s and low 80s this time of year."

"As I said, heat and moisture are two of the contributing causes of those ulcers. You're near the water and there's high humidity in Florida. It's something you have to be aware of, Pete. Those things can happen."

"Nothing I can do about it?"

"Not that I know of, except avoid the heat and the moisture and keeping your body too long in any one position. You really do need to change positions fairly often, but so do we all, don't we? It's not good for anyone to sit or stand for too long at a time. Unfortunately, in your case, you have no choice."

"So I'd be better off if I were in a colder climate, is that right?"

"I'd have to say that dryer is more important than colder, Pete, but cold and dry would be best. You like the cold, don't you? That accident you had took place up in the Glacier National Forest, didn't it?"

"That's right."

"Well, you do what's best for you, but you're right, you'd probably have fewer of those ulcers if you lived in a colder climate. Florida's even hotter than California, but it's not as bad as parts of Arizona, New

Mexico and Texas, I guess. At least you're on the water and get those off-shore breezes, right?"

"Yeah, we do. It's really beautiful in the early morning, before the sun comes up and starts to cook."

"My wife and I stayed at the Amelia Plantation several years ago. That's not far from where you are, is it, Pete?"

"No, not far at all. It's less than a half hour drive. It's in Nassau County, too. Fernandina is the biggest city in the county and it's at the far north and the Plantation is at the far south. They're both on Amelia Island."

"The St. Johns River goes through there, does it?"

"That's a little south of us. It goes through Jacksonville. It's right on the Atlantic, but there are rivers and streams running all through and around it."

"Sounds very nice, but it does get hot there in the summer from what I hear. We were there in November as I recall. It couldn't have been more pleasant."

"So what can I do about this infection, Doc?"

"Nothing, I'm afraid. You've got the medications to deal with it, for the pain and the discomfort, but basically you just have to ride it out. It sounds as if you're getting good medical care."

"I think so. So I have to just lay up, is that what you're saying?"

"Afraid so, Pete."

"The last bout I had took almost two weeks. My doctor here says this will take a week or so."

"That's the normal course. It's like a cold. If you take all the medications, eat chicken soup, drink liquids and follow your doctor's advice, it will take two weeks to get rid of a cold. If you don't, it will take fourteen days. Same thing here, I'm sorry to say."

"Thanks, Doc."

"Buck up, Pete. You've been through worse. You're a fighter. You'll make it."

"Thanks, Doc, but right now I'm feelin' a little depressed."

"It's completely understandable, Pete. You wouldn't be human if you didn't, but you've got to accept the fact that those ulcers are a known complication of your injury and your condition. It's part of your life. You can expect that it will happen, because it happens to most people in your situation at some time or another, but you can and you should do everything you can to avoid them. If it was a decubitis ulcer, you'd be down for a lot longer. You'll have to just ride out the storm on this one and be happy it wasn't worse. Keep your chin up. You'll make it."

"Thanks, Doc. I feel better hearing it from you. I didn't know that about the hot weather and the moisture, or if I did, I forgot about it. I've been thinkin' of moving back to Montana, at least during the summer months."

"And keep in mind that if you don't treat it properly, it can spread and become quite a problem. Be patient and let Mother Nature take her course. You can't hurry these things."

"I've learned that."

"It sounds like you've got a good doctor. Do what he tells you, Pete, and tell him to call me anytime he'd like, in case he'd like to discuss any aspect of your care, okay?"

"It's a she. I'll tell her.

"And please stay in touch. It's always good to hear from you, but as you will remember, I'm busy and have five people waiting on me right now. I've got to go. Take good care and good luck with that infection. Sometimes they're not as bad as others. Maybe this one will clear up a little sooner than expected."

Dr. Johnson's comments reinforced what Pete had been thinking. The more and more he thought about it, the more convinced he became that he should get back to Montana, at least for the summer. Even if he lost the lawsuit and didn't have any money, he could always come back home to his parents' house, if he had to, and he could always find another job. After all, Randy had told him how well he was doing. There were other jobs out there if he left Walgreens.

While he convalesced, he could use the computer and type, so he took the time to organize his music and put all of his sheet music into clear sheet protectors. He downloaded some of the songs he liked and looked for others he might want to play. He didn't want to tell Abigail or anyone else about this latest setback, but there was no way he could avoid telling Sue and Brendan. He was too sick to get together with them.

All he could hope for was that the infection would go away quickly and that he could return to his job and music quickly. He lay around the house all day, being as miserable as he could be, waiting for some improvement in the way he felt. It took a while for the medications to take effect. There wasn't anything he could do to make it go away any faster.

While he convalesced, he was able to make contact with some realtors in the Kalispell/Glacier area. He found a couple of nice, little houses, in town, which had the handicap ramps, wider entrance doors, handicapped accessible bathrooms and the rest. They were two bedroom units, with two bathrooms. Apparently they were built for a handicapped person and a caretaker. They were exactly what Pete wanted, and the extra bedroom and bathroom could come in handy if friends came to visit.

He was glad to learn that there were places available for him. He knew the street one of the houses was on. He had driven by it many times. He thought he knew the house, too, but he wasn't sure. He knew the neighborhood.

The cost of the house was surprisingly low. One was priced in the mid-sixties. He didn't have that kind of money, and he doubted that he would qualify for any loans, especially if all he had was income from a seasonal job with Reno. He could always fall back on SSI, but that wouldn't be much money, so he kept looking for a rental unit. There were several of them, but none sounded too attractive. He didn't want to be in a large rental complex with lots of other people. He remained depressed. His conversation with Dr. Johnson and all of the things he found out about housing in Montana gave him more information, but no solutions to his problems.

Listening to music and surfing the internet helped him pass the time. He thought about writing some songs, too, and looked up a few articles about how to do it. "Verse, chorus, verse, chorus and then a bridge. I can do that," he thought to himself. His mind played with rhymes and rhythm, and he made up a song about fishing.

However, in his current situation, he was feeling anything but capable and adventuresome. He was feeling his inadequacies and realizing how dependent he was upon others. The reality of his condition, and his limitations, weighed heavily on him.

26
Some Good News

O N THE FIFTH DAY of being out sick, as he lay there trying to decide whether to play Cribbage against the computer, listen to more music, or try to write another song, he received a phone call from Mr. Nickel.

"Are you sitting down, Pete?"

"Actually, I'm lying down. Why? What's up?"

"I've got some great news for you."

"I could use some. What's up?"

"The Supreme Court just issued its opinion. We won!"

Pete let the news sink in, knowing that it meant that he could go back to the judge in Bozeman who had kicked his case out of court in the first place, who was an old cowboy himself, and then said,

"That is great news. What does it say?"

"It was close. Four of the justices went with you and three went against you. Do you have a fax number? I can fax you a copy of the opinion. It's about ten pages long."

"Can you e-mail it to me?"

"I can't, but I've got a girl here who knows how to do it. I'll get her to do it for you when she gets in. A young college kid, you know, like you, knows all about that stuff."

"So now we can go back in front of the judge who ruled in their favor. What's he gonna think?"

"He's not going to be happy, because judges hate to be reversed, or over-ruled, but he'll have to do what they say, whether he likes it or not."

"So now I have the right to file the lawsuit, despite the release, right?"

"That's right, but they said a lot of things, things that are going to help us. It's an interesting opinion. Four of the justices wrote their own opinion."

"How does that work?"

"Well, they're called dissenting opinions, or concurring opinions, and basically each justice can write his or her own opinion on every case, if he or she wants to, but they have to agree on the outcome, which means that in your case four of the justices agreed that the Trial Judge should not have dismissed your case, but three of them did so for different reasons."

"Different reasons?"

"Yeah, like one said that releases like the one you signed are against public policy and should be outlawed. Another said that you, and others like you, would not have known and could not be expected to know that you were assuming the risk that they would put you on the wrong horse. A third said that the release was not specific enough and that because it failed to use the magic word, 'negligence', that it was ineffective. The fourth justice who ruled in your favor went along with that last justice and didn't write a separate opinion."

"And three went against us?"

"Yes. Basically, they said that you signed a document waiving your right to sue the Double-D Ranch and that you knowingly assumed the risks associated with riding a horse. One said that everyone knows that horses sometimes quarrel with each other and that was, therefore, a known risk. He said even if we prove that they shouldn't have put you on 'Bucky' and then put you right behind 'Gentle Ben' it was a risk you assumed when you signed that release. So we won, but it was close."

"Sounds like you're pretty happy about it, too."

"I am, and I'm happy for you, Pete, and remember, if you don't get any money, I don't get any money, so I'm happy for that reason as well. Winning a case in front of the Montana Supreme Court doesn't happen very often, Pete. It's special, and don't think that people won't hear about it."

"Really? Why's that?"

"It'll be in newspapers all across the State, that's why. It may even draw some national attention. It'll make all these outfitters, white-water rafting companies, hang-gliding companies and all the places like them go see their lawyers."

"No kidding. Will it include my name and all about me?"

"Absolutely. You're the first name they'll read. This might be front page stuff. I just got the opinion myself. It'll probably be in tomorrow morning's papers. I'll send you copies of the articles. I'll get copies of the papers from Butte, Helena, Great Falls, Helena and a few others. This is big news, Pete. It really is. I'm excited."

"I can tell. So where do we go from here?"

"Well, the opinion isn't final for ten days, and the other side could ask for a re-hearing or a clarification, but I doubt they'll do that, but when the order is final, the case is sent back to the court here in Bozeman and then we'll begin discovery. One of the first things they'll want to do is take your deposition."

"Will they come here to do that?"

"No, you'll have to come out here."

"Why's that? I can't afford to do that, Mr. Nickel."

"Pete, you'll have to. It's required under the rules that a person who files suit in the State has to make himself or herself available for a deposition in the State. If you don't, your case will be dismissed."

"I guess I'll have to do that then. When will that be?"

"It won't be right away, but it could be in the next few months, so you can start planning for it. We have a lot to do between now and then, and we will do what we need to do on our side. I'll be taking the depositions of witnesses, like that Sandra girl, the owners and the guide, of course."

"I've been thinking of moving back to Montana, but I really don't have the money to do that right now, plus I'm laid up and can't work."

"What's wrong, Pete?"

Pete proceeded to tell him about the urinary tract infection and what he'd been doing for the last week.

"Damn! Sorry to hear it, Pete. Well, I'm glad to be able to give you some good news."

"Thanks, Mr. Nickel. I appreciate it, and congratulations. It sounds as if you did a really good job for me."

"You're welcome, Pete. As I said, I think I may be even happier than you are about the whole thing."

"It sounds that way."

"And Pete, one more thing...I should tell you that this may cause the insurance company to offer you some money right now, or within the next few weeks."

"Why's that?"

"Well, now that they know that they're going to have to defend this case, and they know that they'll have to spend a lot of money to do that. They also know there's a chance that if you win you could get an extremely large verdict. I expect that they might want to buy it cheap, right now."

"How cheap?"

"I don't know, but Pete, so you'll know, I doubt that you'll want to take whatever it is they offer you, so don't get your hopes up."

"Without knowing how much it is?"

"I know insurance companies. They will offer you just enough money to make you think. Now that you're out of work, it will make it all the more enticing. They do this to people with low incomes, people who really need the money, especially to people who are out of a job, homeless...those who are desperate."

"I'm not homeless, and I'm not desperate, at least not right now. I expect to be back at work in a week."

"I don't know what they're going to offer, but I assure you that it will be a whole lot less than what the case is worth. This is a million dollar case, Pete! It's at least worth that! Don't sell yourself short, you hear?"

"They haven't offered anything yet, so let's wait and see what they do, but I'll think about what you said."

"And Pete, be happy. Today we achieved a great victory. There aren't too many times that you'll win a case like this in your lifetime, probably never again. Today, you should celebrate and be happy. We won!"

"Thanks again, Mr. Nickel. I might call you back after I read that opinion, but maybe not. You explained it all to me pretty well. I understand what's goin' on, I think, and I'll do my best to be happy today. This is really good news and I am happy about it. I really am. I just wish I could do something other than just lay here and wait for this thing to go away."

"You take care of yourself, Pete, and get better soon. Start making plans to be in Montana in the next few months. In fact, if you know when you can be here, let me know and I'll make the arrangements so that your deposition is taken during that time. How's that?"

"I'll give it some thought. First I've got to get well and see if I still have a job."

"You do that. I'll call you if and when I hear anything from the insurance companies. I'm ethically obligated to let you know about any offers they make, no matter how ridiculous they are, and I will do that."

"Thanks, Mr. Nickel."

After he hung up, Pete started playing with the numbers. If he could get enough money to buy himself a house in Kalispell and have some left over for the trip, emergencies and a little cushion, maybe he could get to Montana after all. He didn't want to get his hopes up, but it gave him something to think about.

27
The Breakthrough

WHEN HE RETURNED TO work the following week, Randy told him that the 'big boss' wanted to talk to him. He wheeled himself into her office, fearing the worst. She closed the door behind him after he did.

"Mr. Collins, I have a copy of your employment contract here and a copy of the Employee Manual you were given after you completed your probationary period. I want you to take these home with you tonight and read them. I, as the manager of this branch, have to answer to my superiors. I have to follow the rules, just like you do. The rules are clear...you cannot be absent an excessive number of times, regardless of the reason, and keep your job. It is as simple as that. Do you understand that?"

"I do, but..."

"There are no 'buts' about it. I know you've got significant problems to deal with, and I am sensitive to your needs and your situation. If you can find anything in your employment contract or in the Employee Manual which carves out an exception for you or anyone else who has medical, legal, financial, familial or any other kinds of problems, show it to me. I don't find one, except for the Family Medical Leave Act, and that doesn't apply here because it's mostly about having a baby. Will you do that for me?

"I don't need to read them. I know what you're saying is right. I understand."

"And Mr. Collins, don't get me wrong. Everyone here likes you and cares about you, as do I, and from all accounts you are doing an excellent job for us, when you are here. We are not unhappy with your performance, or your attitude, or any aspect of your work, but these are the rules."

"I understand."

"Now, having said that, you are not fired. I could fire you, or terminate your employment, but I'm not going to do that. If you miss any more days, or too many more days, I may have to do that. I don't want to do that. Please don't make me do that, okay?"

"I'll do my best. I really can't control when that thing will come back but…"

"I know you don't want to be sick. No one does. All I can ask is that you take good care of yourself and do your best to prevent it from coming back again, please. Will you do that for me?"

"I will."

"Once you complete a year with us, you will be entitled to more sick days, personal days and vacation days, but not until then. You understand that, correct?"

"I do."

"Thank you, Mr. Collins. I hate having these conversations with employees, but it's required of me. I hope you understand my position. That will be all for today."

When he went back to his cubicle, he buried his head in his work and didn't notice when Randy had walked into his office an hour later. He tapped Pete on the shoulder and said,

"Hey man, I want you to know that she came up to me this morning and asked me to tell you all that shit. I told her I didn't want to do it, so she agreed to do it herself."

"That could've cost you your job, Randy. I don't want to see that happen."

"Hey, that ain't right. Look at what you do with the problems you got. Ain't no way I'm gonna get on your case. Are you alright? Everything better?"

"Yeah, I feel fine now."

"Same thing as the last time?"

"This one was a little different, but I was just as laid up."

"You gonna be back playin' music on Friday?"

"I'm plannin' on it."

"It ain't the same with you not bein' there."

"Thanks, man."

The two shook hands.

As he was walking out of Pete's office, Randy said,

"The only good thing to come out of this is that you won't be takin' my job for at least another month or so, I'd say."

They laughed and Pete went back to work. He was tired by the end of the day and went straight home and was asleep early, but not before thinking about his life, Montana, Abigail, Reno, his lawsuit and other such things about a thousand times. That little 'pep talk' from his employer was another shot to his jaw and made him realize his limitations. From what he had learned, he was going to have to deal with infections, ulcers and other problems his whole life.

He hadn't talked to Abigail in two weeks. He didn't feel like talking to her while in a depressed state of mind, and he wasn't ready to tell her about his plans to move back to Glacier, or Kalispell. He told himself that it wasn't all about her anyway. He had other friends out there. He could go back to school and get a degree in computer science. He was tired of doing data entry anyway. So what if he lost his job, he'd get another one. He kept telling himself that he wasn't over-reacting, that he was being objective and rational, not delusional. At times, he wasn't sure.

Pete's accident and the aftermath had taken its toll on Anthony and Florence. While they would stand beside their son or any of their children, no matter what the circumstances, and Pete's presence in the home was always welcomed, this wasn't what they had planned for themselves. It was like being given a grand-child to raise, or becoming the permanent baby-sitter, as some of their friends had become. That wasn't what they had wanted for their retirement.

Having raised nine children, they needed some time off. They encouraged Pete to go back to Montana, if that's what he wanted to do. He could go back to school, work with Reno in the summer, and be closer to the mountains. He'd always told them that Glacier

National Park was the most beautiful part of the world he had ever seen, including the parts of Alaska he was in. If that was the place he loved the most, that's where he should be.

If necessary, his parents would help with the purchase of a home by acting as co-signers, but they really couldn't afford it. It would be best if he could pay the mortgage by himself. They suggested he think about applying for a student loan if he wanted to go back to school. It might include living expenses. They had heard that the government had special programs to help people with disabilities. They told him to give his friend Jorge a call, or John, or some of the other people in the hospital out in Seattle.

The forces in Pete's universe were coalescing around one common thought. He should go back to Montana. He'd miss Sue and Brendan and the friends he'd made at work. He had grown from being a beginner to being a performer and had proven himself as a capable employee. He enjoyed O'Day's and Dock o' the Bay and would miss those places. There were places like that in Kalispell where he could play, he told himself. He knew some of the owners and managers. They'd let him play. He went through the entire week, his mind numb, thinking all of those thoughts over and over, while mindlessly entering numbers onto his computer screen, trying hard to be careful not to make any mistakes.

His heart was a little heavier as he played at O'Day's that Friday and at Dock o' the Bay on Sunday. He knew that he might be leaving sometime soon and he viewed the whole occasions differently. It was fun, though, and he enjoyed himself, but it wasn't the same. Things had changed. Once the decision to leave had been made, it was only a matter of time before the end would come. Only his parents knew what he was thinking, though. He hadn't told anyone else, other than Reno, yet.

The breakthrough came two weeks later when Mr. Nickel called again.

"Okay, Pete, things happened pretty much as I expected."

"So that order is final?"

"Yeah, the order is final. The case is headed back to Bozeman, and the insurance company did just what I thought they would do."

"What's that?"

"They've made you an offer, but it's too low, way too low, just like I told you it would be."

"What is it?"

"They've offered you a hundred thousand."

"A hundred thousand dollars?"

"That's right."

"That's pretty good, isn't it?"

"Pete, your case is worth ten times that amount, probably more, much more. I'll hire an economic expert and he'll probably tell me that it's worth several million dollars. You don't want to take that offer, Pete. Trust me."

"How much of that will you get, Mr. Nickel?"

"Pete, don't even think about it."

"How much will you get? Just tell me."

"If you read the retainer, after costs are paid, I get 40%, since I had to file an appeal, but that was intended to apply only after trial, so I'd say you can figure 50%, and that's after you subtract costs."

"Do you take your 40% before or after you subtract costs?"

Pete had learned some things about finances and business accounting while working at Walgreens. He knew that could mean thousands of dollars out of his pocket.

"I get my fee off the top, before costs are deducted."

"And how much are the costs?"

"Pete, you don't want to take this offer."

"Just tell me how much the costs are, Mr. Nickel, please."

"I haven't added them up, but I'd say they might be $10,000, and that includes a $2500 retainer fee I'm prepared to give to our economic expert. I've used him before plenty of times and he does a great job in front of a jury. You'll be…"

"But you haven't sent him a check yet, right?"

"No, I haven't."

"So, if you take 40% of $100,000, that's $40,000, minus $10,000 in costs, so I'd get $50,000, right?"

"That's right, but…"

"But if you subtract the $10,000 from the $100,000 and then take your 40%, that would be $36,000 and I'd get $54,000, is that right?"

"Well, I haven't done the math, but that's not how I do it."

"That doesn't sound fair to me, Mr. Nickel. I think you should do it the other way."

"Pete, that's not how it's done, but listen, I'll tell you what, if it makes you happy, we'll do it your way, but I want you to tell me to reject this offer and let me work on getting you more money."

"How much do you think they'd pay?"

"You mean right now?"

"Yes, right now."

"I don't know, maybe $150,000...maybe. I don't know."

"And if we win, they could appeal, right?"

"Sure they could, and so could you."

"And that could take another year or two, right?"

"Yeah, it could, Pete. That's true. I can't deny that. The wheels of justice grind slowly at times."

Pete hesitated for a few moments, while he considered all that he had just heard, and then said,

"Here's what I want you to do...I want you to get back to them and tell them that I'll take $500,000 right now, or else we're going for the moon. Will you do that?"

"Pete, you're the client. I'm ethically obligated to do what you tell me, but I'm advising you not to do that. Your case is worth much, much more than that."

"I understand, Mr. Nickel, and I appreciate all you've done for me, but between you and me, if I can clear $100,000 after all the costs are paid and your fee is paid, I'll be happy."

"But Pete!"

"I understand, Mr. Nickel, but that's what I'm asking you to do for me. Will you do that?"

"Did you see all those newspaper articles I sent you?"

"I read every one."

"That means money! The insurance companies know that. Your case is worth millions, Pete! Don't do this!"

Mr. Nickel knew what Pete's case was potentially worth and he had Pete's best interests in mind, but he also knew that Pete's case represented a chance at a huge fee for him, too. A case like that didn't come along every day. The media would be following the case now that the Supreme Court had issued its ruling. This could not only mean a lot of money for him from Pete's case but also it would attract more clients for him. He didn't want to see this case go away. He wanted to do the best job possible for Pete but he also wanted to get all the publicity he could get and maybe, just maybe, get the biggest verdict ever in Bozeman. This was a great case, and he wanted a great result. He knew he could get more money than that, either from a jury or by way of an increased settlement offer. He didn't want this case to settle cheap.

"Mr. Nickel, you said that I'm the client and you are ethically obligated to do what I tell you, right?"

"That's right, Pete," Mr. Nickel replied glumly, sensing that his pleas and arguments were falling on deaf ears.

"Then please do what I've asked you to do."

"Alright, Pete, I will, but don't expect them to agree to pay you $250,000 just like that."

"But they might give us another offer, right?"

"They might."

"Please do the math. How much money do I have to get so that I will receive $100,000?"

While Mr. Nickel was doing his calculations, Pete was doing them, too.

"About $185,000, a little less, I think. So if you can get me anywhere close to that, which about half way between their number and ours, I'll take it."

"Pete, please…"

"Mr. Nickel…"

"Okay, Pete. Okay. We'll do it your way."

Going Home

A WEEK LATER, PETE RECEIVED a phone call from Mr. Nickel.
"Okay, Pete, they've agreed to pay you $175,000, not a penny more."

"Is that what they said, $175,000, when you demanded $500,000?"

"No, they came back at $125,000 and I went to $450,000, then they went to $150,000 and I went to $350,000 and they went to $175 and said that was it. They said they won't pay a penny more. I'll reduce my fee to make sure that you get a check for exactly $100,000, how's that?"

"That'll be great, Mr. Nickel."

"You know how disappointed I am, from a professional point of view, but if it makes you happy, then I'm happy for you."

"It does, and you got a lot of favorable publicity from winning that appeal. I read what they said about you in those articles."

"That's true, I did, but your case had so much potential…let's not go there. What's done is done and all that remains to be done is for them to send you a check and for you to sign a release. I'll send you the release by overnight mail. You should have it tomorrow. The check should be here within the next two weeks, I expect."

"That's for sure, is it?"

"You mean about when I'll have the money for you?"

"Yes."

"It's a done deal. They said they'd cut a check first chance, but a check that big has to be signed by one of the higher-ups, maybe two of them, I don't know, but I should have the check within two weeks. I can't guarantee that, but that's what they told me and that's what I expect. Why? Are you in a hurry?"

"Kind of. I'm planning on moving back to Montana."

"Really? What, have you had enough sunshine and blue skies, with temperatures in the 80s? Come on up here for a week and you might change your mind about that."

"I remember those cold winters, but I like it up there. It's the most beautiful place on earth, I think. It's the prettiest place I've seen."

"You mean up around Glacier? Yeah, it doesn't get much prettier than that and I've been around a bit, back when I was in the Navy and all."

"Yeah, I'll go back to Glacier for the summer and maybe start school in the Fall."

"At the University?"

"If I can get back in."

"Well, good luck, son. I'll call you when I have the check and you can tell me where to send it when I do. Just sign that release in front of a notary and put it back in the envelope. It's going UPS so you can just call the number on the cover and they'll come back and pick it up after it's signed."

"Will do, Mr. Nickel, and thanks."

"You're welcome, Pete."

"For everything."

"You're welcome."

"For taking my case, for convincing me to file suit, for winning that appeal and for everything."

"I'm glad to do it. This was one of my all-time favorite cases, Pete. I just wish you'd have let me take it further."

"I know, but this helps me get on down the road. You have no idea of all the things going on in my brain. This solves a lot of problems for me."

"Don't spend it all in one place, kid. If you need any financial advice, let me know and I can put you in touch with a good financial planner. That's a lot of money. Most people never see that kind of money all at one time."

"I just might do that."

"If you come this way, be sure to stop and say hello. I've seen some pictures of you that Dave gave me, but we've never met."

"No, we haven't and if I get to Bozeman, I will definitely stop and say hello."

"I'll look forward to meeting you, Pete. Take care."

The ball was in motion. Pete started to make all the arrangements. He called about the house and made an offer on it, sight unseen. It was tentative upon inspections anyway, and he would be out there soon enough. His offer was a little below the asking price, so he knew there would be some negotiations and he thought that it might be best not to pay the whole amount in cash, like he first thought. Maybe it would be best to finance it. He'd talk to a financial planner like Mr. Nickel suggested.

He called Reno to let him know he'd be coming. Reno had read the newspaper articles and knew all about the ruling of the Supreme Court. He was glad to hear of the settlement, too. The die was cast. There was no turning back now. He said his good-byes to the people at work and promised to write. Sue and Brendan were sad to see him go, but he knew that he'd see them again. They promised to visit if he could get them a 'gig' out there.

His parents had mixed emotions about him going. They weren't sure it was for the best. Florence didn't think he was ready. She knew how much support he needed because she had been providing it to him for years. Anthony wanted whatever was best for his son and if that was what his son wanted to do, he was behind him. He could always come home again.

When his bags were packed and he was ready to go, he called Abigail.

"So what are you doing this Saturday night?" he asked.

"I don't have any plans. Why do you ask?"

"Want to go to dinner and have a beer at the Moosehead?"

"Sure," she said. "You gonna be here?"

"Yep. I'm coming home."

THE END

Epilogue

This book is based upon a true story. It is not, however, a biography. Twelve years ago, a friend of mine, while working as a guide in Yosemite National Park, rode his horse down a mountain to check on some campers. On the way back, his horse slipped on the root of a tree, which was wet from the afternoon's rain. My friend fell off his horse, landed on his back on top of one of the roots and his horse landed on top of him, damaging his spinal cord at T-11. As an employee of a commercial enterprise he was eligible for benefits under a workmen's compensation policy of insurance, but not without a fight. The question wasn't whether or not he was entitled to any money; the question was how much money he was entitled to.

My friend's world changed that day, and although he was badly hurt as a result of the incident, he didn't die. He had to decide how to deal with his changed circumstances, just as many of us must deal with the shifting sands of health, happiness, prosperity and other such things in life. Over time, he regained his sense of adventure and, as Einstein put it, his 'rapt awe' of the world, and for that and other reasons he has my admiration. I recall the words of my mother when she told me on many countless occasions when I was feeling inept, insecure or otherwise inadequate…'count your blessings.' He did just that. He decided that he had more things to be thankful for, or appreciative of, and he chose to go on living the life he wanted to live, despite his injury and his limitations. He now lives in Sumter, Oregon, in a house he bought which looks out on the Elkhorn Mountains and fronts a large, clear lake. He plays music for drinks and tips, does woodworking and fishes regularly, among other things.

I choose to believe that there but for the grace of, as Einstein put it, an "incomprehensible God" go any of us. Why my friend fell off the horse and sustained the injury and not me or anyone else who rides horses up to the tops of mountains is another question altogether. When large numbers of people go off to war, ride motorcycles, jump out of airplanes or do any number of dangerous things, some return safely and others do not. Trying to make sense out of things like that is impossible. Why him? I find an answer in another of Einstein's quotes:

"The human mind is not capable of grasping the universe. We are like a little child entering a huge library. The walls are covered to the ceiling with books in many different tongues. The child knows that someone must have written these books. It does not know who or how. It does not understand the languages in which they are written, but the child notes a definite arrangement of the books…a mysterious order which it does not comprehend but only dimly suspects."

But that is not what this story was about. It is a story of what happened to my friend. It is also about a specific legal issue and it provides a warning of what to look out for when reading releases before signing them. It is also about what it is like to go from being a young, strong, virile male to life in a wheelchair. The moral of the story is that we know not the hour when the Master is going to return, or when our 'time' is going to come, so live every day as if it were your last. The message to take with you is that the glass is half full, not half empty, and to appreciate what you have, not to dwell on what you don't have. My friend does that.

In writing this book, I read <u>Spinal Cord Injury: Functional Rehabilitation</u>, Somers, Appleton & Lange Publishers (1992) to obtain the some of the medical information contained in this book. I thank Reno Baldwin of the Great Northern Rafting Company for allowing me to use his name and the name of his company. Several of the stories in here came from him while I was going down the Flathead River, together with my daughter, Caitlin, on a cold October day a few years ago. The rafting company was closed but he happened to be in the store when we arrived. He agreed to take us himself to accommodate us, since I was so anxious to go. His son, Bryce, is one of the most accomplished kayakers in the world and is one who goes over the sixty foot waterfalls as shown on ESPN or some outdoors special at times.

I only know of one person who refused to sign a release like the one depicted in this book. His twelve year old daughter was sorely disappointed when she couldn't go on a dangerous ride at an amusement park, and so was he, since he and his wife had driven an hour to get to the place, but he was a lawyer and he read the plain meaning of the words…'you waive your right to sue us EVEN IF WE ARE NEGLIGENT…'. He knew that it was wrong to sign a release with those words in it and he didn't.

Last, but not least, I hereby make a disclaimer. I do not know Montana law and such a release as the one used in this book may be unenforceable under the laws of the State of Montana as against public policy. I hope it is. I can tell you that the law as depicted in this book is 'good law,' at least as far as I know to be in the State of Florida. I handled a case in which that specific issue was raised and that is exactly what the Appellate Court ruled in that case, which involved swimming with dolphins. Personally, I believe they should be outlawed because they are 'contracts of adhesion,' or contracts in which there is absolutely no true negotiation of any of the terms. The larger point is that when you sign a document, not only must you read it; you must understand it and agree to the terms of it. If you don't agree with any of the terms, you should not sign it. That, and be careful when riding horses.

In conclusion, I thank you for taking the time to read *A Foreseeable Risk*. I hope you enjoyed it.

Pierce Kelley